D1482933

THE
CITY
OF
STARDUST

THE
CITY
OF
STARDUST

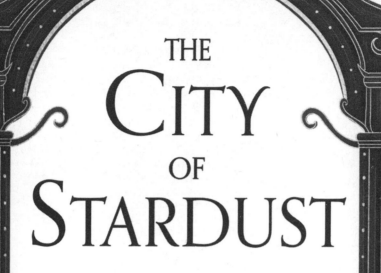

Georgia Summers

REDHOOK

This book is a work of fiction. Names, characters, places, and incidents are the product of the author's imagination or are used fictitiously. Any resemblance to actual events, locales, or persons, living or dead, is coincidental.

Copyright © 2024 by Georgia Summers

Cover design by Micaela Alcaino

Hachette Book Group supports the right to free expression and the value of copyright. The purpose of copyright is to encourage writers and artists to produce the creative works that enrich our culture.

The scanning, uploading, and distribution of this book without permission is a theft of the author's intellectual property. If you would like permission to use material from the book (other than for review purposes), please contact permissions@hbgusa.com. Thank you for your support of the author's rights.

Redhook Books/Orbit
Hachette Book Group
1290 Avenue of the Americas
New York, NY 10104
hachettebookgroup.com

First Edition: January 2024
Simultaneously published in Great Britain by Hodderscape, an imprint of
Hodder & Stoughton, a Hachette UK company

Redhook is an imprint of Orbit, a division of Hachette Book Group.
The Redhook name and logo are registered trademarks of Hachette Book Group, Inc.

The publisher is not responsible for websites (or their content)
that are not owned by the publisher.

The Hachette Speakers Bureau provides a wide range of authors for speaking events. To find out more, go to hachettespeakersbureau.com or email HachetteSpeakers@hbgusa.com.

Redhook books may be purchased in bulk for business, educational, or promotional use. For information, please contact your local bookseller or the Hachette Book Group Special Markets Department at special.markets@hbgusa.com.

Library of Congress Control Number: 2023939084

ISBNs: 9780316561488 (hardcover), 9780316561730 (ebook)

Printed in the United States of America

LSC-C

Printing 1, 2023

For my mum.

"She took a step forward, her brow pensive, her mouth a conspiracy of secretive emotion. Her foot lifted higher, higher —and then she was soaring, swallow-winged and beautiful, and altogether the most wondrous sight on that starry evening. For what was more natural than flight to these creatures of such peculiar whimsies? And it was our greatest regret that we plain mortals could not join her."

—Hyacinth Watson, *The Fairy Knight's Daughter & Other Stories*

Non est ad astra mollis e terris via.
There is no easy way to the stars from earth.

—Seneca the Younger, *Hercules Furens*

THE
CITY
OF
STARDUST

Prologue

I

N PARIS, A child goes missing.

A baby, to be more precise. One minute he is in his pram, making chubby fists while his mother wheels him around a grocery shop. For a moment—*just a moment*, she will insist afterwards—she glances away to examine her shopping list, certain she's forgotten something, but unable to recollect what. The next, he is gone, whisked away by sure, confident hands. By the time his mother looks back at the soft place where her baby used to be, the perpetrator has vanished. In the heart-stopping seconds between her realisation and the scream that wrenches its way past her throat, she catches an unusual vanilla scent in the air.

In Vienna, the child is two and visiting an art gallery for the first time. She is lulled by a song that sounds like a memory from the womb, like a melody she has never heard, and yet has been hearing all her life. While her parents pause to admire a painting, she slips through a crowd of tourists to waiting arms and vanishes forever. There are phone calls to the police, then accusations and a lawsuit. The detectives dutifully check the security camera footage, only to find that it's irretrievably corrupted. Someone mentions a woman who smelled like vanilla, but the detail goes ignored and the child remains lost.

In Prague, it's a boy with eyes the colour of grey sea glass. He mumbles in his sleep, one amongst so many in this orphanage. A woman wearing a vanilla scent approaches him with her calculating gaze and her sure hands, her conscience untroubled by the crime she is about to commit. She can already see his life without this intervention: unremarkable, unloved, possibly traumatic. A life where there are no heroes or last-minute rescuers. No fairy-tale parents to whisk him back home, a prince mistaken for a pauper. In Prague, he will live and die a nobody.

But where *she* is going, he will be more than anyone will ever know.

She leans over his bed and whispers, "I hear you singing, little dreamer. And I come to answer the call."

Marianne Everly is walking into a thunderstorm.

It's a night that promises only disaster: lashing rain that rattles against the windowpanes as though the house itself has committed a crime; bruised clouds flashing with white fury; ominous puddles hiding their treacherous depths. It would be better, Marianne reflects, if she could have waited until the morning, with the sun and goodwill chasing at her back. But she can't ignore the song thrumming through her bones, or the whisper that the time has come to say goodbye to her rambling house and its occupants.

Her brothers' silhouettes frame the doorway, their expressions unreadable. Guilt, grief, anger—they have already run the gamut, and all that remains is the steady certainty that there is no turning back now.

Aside from the house, she's leaving behind so little. A silk-bound book of fairy tales, the edges fuzzy with wear. A pair of bracelets that glitter with unusual lustre. An ancient and useless sword with a dulled edge, passed down from one fusty ancestor to another.

A daughter, too, if she wishes to be thorough.

Against the shadow of the house, her daughter's light is on, though she was fast asleep when Marianne pressed a farewell kiss to her forehead.

For a moment, Marianne pauses, her gaze trained on the bright window. Maybe she hesitates because despite everything that has led to this moment, the call of her child is almost stronger than the call of elsewhere.

Then again, maybe not. Perhaps she's throwing off the mantle of motherhood with relief, shedding a load she never wanted to bear.

Watching her in the rain, it's hard to say.

The darkness closing in on her, Marianne Everly takes a worn key from around her neck, turns it in the air—and vanishes.

A curse can be many things. A wish left out to spoil in the sun, putrid and soft, leaving behind only calcified desire and oxidised envy. Or a poisoned chalice, a mistake tattooed across an entire family tree, with every generation promising, *vowing* to never sip until they do. Sometimes, it's a deal and bad luck conspiring like old grifters closing in on an easy mark.

For the Everlys, it begins with stardust.

PART ONE

CHAPTER

One

YEARS FROM NOW, this is what Ambrose Everly will remember.

Not the rain sheeting down the windows, squeezing through every neglected gap, filling the Everly house with soft plinks as water drips into various bowl-shaped objects. Nor the white flash of lightning, which promptly short-circuits the electricity and sends him rummaging through the cupboards for candles and a book of matches. But the unbearable stillness, as though the house is holding its breath, waiting.

So Ambrose is almost relieved when someone bangs on the door like a thunderclap, though it's short-lived. It can't be anything but mere coincidence, but his gut still tightens as he pads down the long, dark hallway, past the ancestral portraits who eye him with glum indifference. So few people know that the house is even here, let alone feel welcome enough to knock. He opens the door, uneasy.

At first all he can see is the gloom, rain guttering from the roof's overhang. Then the world is briefly illuminated by a flash of lightning. A man in a leather jacket stands on the doorstep, soaking wet. His gaze is hidden behind tinted sunglasses, even though it's pitch-black outside. Behind him, a violently orange sports car sits in the driveway, sleek and predatory.

"You changed the locks," the man says.

"Gabriel?" Ambrose says, and then again because he can't quite believe that the man standing in front of him isn't an apparition.

"We need to talk, little brother," Gabriel says grimly.

Ambrose doesn't move. He sucks in a deep breath, trying to make sense of the scene in front of him. This should be impossible. It *feels* impossible. But here's his older brother, gracing the driveway as though he's never been away, even though it's been over two years. Only the car is different, but it still carries all the hallmarks of his brother's taste: ostentatious, loud, ugly beyond belief. A flashy middle finger to the world.

"What are you doing here?" Ambrose says.

Gabriel pushes his hair from his forehead, and glances behind him at the open driveway, as though expecting something—or someone —to appear. "We should talk inside."

Sudden alarm flashes through Ambrose. "You think you've been followed?"

"No, I was careful. But still."

"Then should you even be here?" It isn't supposed to come out as an accusation, but Ambrose hears the bite in his tone and winces.

"It's important," Gabriel says.

There aren't many reasons why he would risk coming home, and all of them are alarming. The terrible anxiety in Ambrose's gut surfaces again.

"Okay," he relents.

As Gabriel steps over the threshold, the house sighs in greeting—a stray Everly, returned at last. Ambrose leads him down the hallway, past the numerous leaks, the faded wallpaper, the inches of dust covering unused furniture. To Ambrose, the house looks exactly as it did in their childhood, if a little shabbier, a little in need of love. But now that Gabriel's critical gaze sweeps across the rooms, he's suddenly ashamed of his failure as a caretaker, with all those repairs he's never quite found time to finish. Then annoyance flashes through him; who cares what the house looks like? It's not as if his brother has been around to lend a hand.

In the dark, Gabriel trips over something and swears. Ambrose picks it up—one of their niece's dolls, outfitted with tinfoil armour and a sword made from cocktail sticks. He smiles fondly. There's an entire set scattered around the house, and although Violet declares she's too old for them, he still finds them propped up in unusual set pieces. Fairies in armour, knights bearing roses, a princess lifting her sword in triumph.

"That belong to the kid?" Gabriel says.

Ambrose straightens out the crinkled armour. "It belongs to Violet, yes."

Gabriel gives it a long, hard look. But he doesn't say anything.

The only place with the lights still working is the library, with its original oil lamps installed in brackets along the wall. Gabriel toys with the notepad on the desk as Ambrose lights them with the last of his matches. A warm glow illuminates the room, glinting off the foiled bands ridging the book spines.

Ambrose leans against the old wardrobe at the back of the library, trying to contain all his questions. They've never been the hugging kind of siblings, so he hangs back, his hands digging into his pockets. It's been two long years since Gabriel walked out of the house, and although they agreed that this was for the best—although it had never really been a question which brother would stay and which would leave—he can't help but feel a pang of resentment, too. Two years of making tinfoil armour, but also learning how to be a parent at the very worst possible moment, arguing furiously over bedtimes and meals, wrestling a semblance of education into their niece while his own studies languished—and Gabriel has borne none of it. But Gabriel had the lucrative job that would keep the house afloat, not a half-finished degree and vague aspirations to academia. And only one of them needed to stay.

Gabriel catches him watching. "The kid, Violet. Where is she?"

"Asleep," Ambrose says, though truthfully he has no idea where their niece is. She probably thinks he hasn't noticed her sneaking out of bed at night, but the house sings a symphony of creaks whenever she does. "What do you want, Gabriel?"

Silence. Gabriel stares out through the dark windows before closing the curtains, the rotten fabric fraying at the edges. Again, the feeling that something is tilting horribly sideways returns. Ambrose starts to pace, trying to shake the coil of uneasy energy from his limbs.

"Look, I've done everything I can," he says. "She's happy, she's fed, she's safe—"

"Actually, little brother, you're wrong there."

Ambrose stops pacing. "What do you mean?"

"Violet is no longer a secret. Whatever Marianne has done— whoever she's talked to—she's not been careful enough."

Their sister's name sits like a stone between them. Ambrose's heartbeat rushes in his ears. Dread curls in his stomach.

"Are you sure?" he whispers, and Gabriel nods. "Fuck."

Fuck.

What else is there to say? For years, he's worried about the worst possible outcome, and now it's here. *Violet is no longer a secret.* In his mind's eye, a shadow descends over his fierce little niece, and he suddenly feels sick with fear.

"Are you sure this isn't your doing?" Ambrose says, suspicious. "You must have slipped something in your travels, doing God knows what—"

Gabriel cuts him off. "If you think for one second I'd risk the kid's safety—"

"If you cared, you would have stopped this charade with the scholars years ago!"

Thunder rumbles overhead as they size each other up. Ambrose runs an agitated hand through his hair, his chest heaving with unspent anger. He tries to take several deep breaths, but all he can feel is the panic fizzing through his thoughts. What the hell are they going to do now?

"She's my niece, too. I care," Gabriel says, hard. "Besides, it's not just about the money. How do you think I heard the rumours about Marianne? About Violet?" He raises an eyebrow. "I'm not too proud to do what must be done. Are you?"

Ambrose takes another deep breath, and this time it's a little easier. For Violet's sake, he has to get it together. Slowly, he begins to sift through the possibilities with a methodical logic, forcing the panic into the recesses of his mind.

"We could send her away," he says, thinking aloud. "Somewhere out of sight. You have contacts—you could take her." Even though he hates to imagine it.

"It's far too late for that," Gabriel says darkly. "Tell me: who would you trust with Violet? Which of my 'contacts' would risk their lives for us?" He raises a wry eyebrow. "Hell, would you trust me?"

Ambrose falls silent. There's no good answer to that question.

"We would buy months at best, little brother. And we need more than that."

Again with the *little brother*. It's been a long time since Ambrose has felt young enough, naïve enough to be condescended to.

"Violet deserves a *life*," he says. "Marianne would have wanted—"

"Marianne fucked off and left her child here," Gabriel snaps. "I really don't care what she wanted."

"She didn't have a choice. She went *for* Violet. You know this."

"Do I?" He glowers. "When someone looks like they're running, that's because they're running. And leaving us to clear up her goddamn mess. As usual."

Ambrose bites back a retort. Where Gabriel is concerned, Marianne is like a bruise, searing with pain at the slightest pressure.

"So that means..." He can't bring himself to say *her* name, as though by saying it, he'll summon the force from which he's protected Violet for so long. "When will she get here?"

Gabriel shakes his head, his mouth a hard, thin line. "Sooner rather than later, I think."

Ambrose thinks it over. There must be a solution he's not grasping clearly. But his thoughts, usually organised like clockwork, fail him. His head swims with thoughts of Violet, of the long, dark shadow stretched over the Everlys. He needs more time to think. He just needs—*time*.

"We'll invite her," he says suddenly. "We'll make a deal. You said we needed more time. So...we buy more time. For next steps, a plan. Anything."

For Marianne, he adds silently.

He waits for Gabriel to shoot him down. But instead Gabriel rubs the back of his wrist, nodding slowly as he comes to grips with the idea.

"She'll ask about Marianne," he warns.

"I know."

Gabriel adjusts his leather jacket, fiddling with something inside the pockets. "And I can't stay—I'm already late for a meeting with the Vernes. You'll have to do the talking for both of us."

"I know that, too."

After Gabriel leaves, Ambrose slumps on to the desk, his heart sinking at the sudden enormity of what he has to do. Never mind what the hell he's supposed to tell his inquisitive niece. She's forever asking questions, but it's been a long time since he's had any easy answers.

He stays up into the small hours of the morning writing letters, scrubbing down the dusty kitchen countertops, washing all the sheets he's suddenly found time for—anything to take his mind from what will happen next.

Inside the old wardrobe at the back of the library, Violet Everly clutches her book tightly, her mouth pressed against her jumper to hide the sound of her startled breathing.

CHAPTER

Two

V IOLET EVERLY IS twelve years old, and dreaming of other worlds.

This usually involves climbing into the old wardrobe at the back of the library, and shutting the door in a whirl of cedar and dust. There she sits, with a thin torch between her teeth and a fat book spread across her lap, its thick and creamy pages layered in old-fashioned type and rich with glossy sentences. Every one of them whispering adventure.

The worlds spring up behind her eyelids: cities of gold and silver filigree buildings; lands of intertwining waterways with bright boats sculling through the water; a forest of witches, their skin shades of eggshell blue all the way to deepest twilight, constellations twinkling across their shoulders. All of this a siren song that she can't quite shake.

It's because of her desire to escape into a good book that she finds herself hidden inside the wardrobe, as Ambrose converses with a stranger in his midst. Then he says, "What do you want, Gabriel?"

Gabriel. Her other uncle is so rarely here, but whenever he visits, the rooms seem brighter, warmer, as though the house itself recognises the return of its wayward inhabitant. He never comes empty-handed, either, bringing gifts that are as magical as they are beautiful. Clockwork statues of princes and knights, fairies and queens, with intricate workings and gossamer wings stretched taut along thin wire. Or, once for her sixth birthday, a set of nesting dolls that never revealed the same object in its innermost hold. On his last visit, he gave her a dim light to read by, which never went out and yet never seemed to need batteries, either.

From eavesdropping on late-night phone calls, she gathers Gabriel does something vaguely illegal, but Ambrose is tight-lipped about the details. More than half of the travel books in the library belong to Gabriel. He must have been all over the world.

Adventure, Violet thinks, and a thrill ripples through her.

Then he mentions her mother, and she almost falls out of the wardrobe. Marianne Everly.

Her mother has long dissolved from her life, like so much salt in the sea. That is, she's nowhere to be found, and yet she's everywhere: her lingering perfume on moth-eaten coats; a slim gold watch abandoned on her vanity; the chair no one uses. Mostly, Violet imagines her in the blank spaces between paragraphs, or the invisible inhale before a sentence. Whereas her father is an entirely missing book— one that her mother holds the key to, if she holds anything at all. It's a parent-shaped hole that Ambrose has tried to fill, in his own way.

After that, it's impossible to concentrate on anything else. Besides, most of the conversation is frustratingly beyond her. A good half of it is muffled by the wardrobe, Ambrose's footsteps on the creaky floorboards—and the sound of her own heart, pumping furiously in her ears as she tries to put it all together.

Only three days after her uncle's mysterious visit, they receive another visitor. Instead of his usual rumpled jumper and jeans, Ambrose wears an ironed shirt and smart trousers to greet them, his shoes polished to a high shine. His hands twist around themselves nervously.

"Come, Violet," he says. "There's someone who wants to meet you."

The woman is sitting in the living room, perched elegantly in Ambrose's favourite armchair. Her hair is a pale flax gold hewn in a soft bob curling at her ears, and her hands are perfectly smooth, unadorned by rings or callouses. Her clothes are nondescript, but they have a tailor's expert fit and the material looks silky and expensive. The woman smiles pleasantly, offering her hand in greeting. The barest hint of vanilla drifts in the air.

Violet shivers and draws away.

"Hello, little dreamer," the woman says, her voice as soft and unassuming as her appearance. "It's a pleasure to finally meet you."

She offers her slender hand again, but Violet stays where she is. Behind her, Ambrose puts a reassuring hand on her shoulder.

"She's a bit shy. It's been a long time since we've had any visitors," he says with his usual mild warmth.

He gives her a small nudge, and she reluctantly crosses the living room to shake the woman's hand. But instead of shaking, she clasps Violet's hand in both of hers, her thumbs pressed into Violet's palm. After a moment, she releases Violet and claps her hands, delighted.

"Well, you are your mother's daughter," she says, then turns to Ambrose. "She's the spitting image of Marianne at that age. And just as talented, no doubt. What a fortuitous discovery. To think you have been holding out on me for so long. All those birthday cards I never got to send."

Ambrose's forehead knits, but before he can say anything, a small figure sidles past him to stand behind the woman. A boy, slightly older than Violet, with dark curly hair brushing the nape of his neck. His eyes are the colour of grey sea glass, almost translucent. He holds himself stiffly in old-fashioned clothes: a faded red woollen waistcoat, threads unravelling at the hem, over a shirt gone fuzzy at the collar with age.

"Ah, my assistant." The woman gestures to the child behind her. "This is Aleksander."

The boy watches Violet suspiciously, as though *she's* the one standing in *his* living room. She glares back.

Ambrose diverts her attention. "Vi, why don't you give Aleksander a tour of the house? Wouldn't that be nice? Penelope and I have a lot to catch up on."

The woman smiles at him with perfectly straight teeth. "We certainly do. Aleksander?"

As quietly as he came in, the boy detaches himself from Penelope, with the heavy air of an older child forced to babysit. It's the absolute last thing Violet wants to do, not when she knows that she's the topic at hand. Not when she could creep up to the second floor, remove the two loose floorboards Ambrose is forever threatening to fix, and drop into the tiny crevice above this ceiling, where the conversation would float up to her in perfect clarity.

Violet flashes a dark look at Ambrose.

He leans down and whispers, "Go on, Vi. Please."

It looks like answers will have to wait. With a long-suffering sigh, Violet leads the boy out of the room, closing the door behind them.

Ambrose is not an old man—far from it. In fact, for years it seems as though he's slipped into a kind of physical stasis, even as he drifted past his thirtieth birthday and is now slowly creeping towards his fortieth. But today he feels weary with responsibility, and underneath it all, a terrible panic at the mess he's found himself in.

Such carefully laid plans, undone in an instant.

"It's been a long time," Penelope says, as Ambrose sits across from her in the living room. "I was beginning to think you were hiding from me."

"This is the Everly house," Ambrose says with a shrug that sits on the knife-edge between bravado and stupidity. "Where else would we be?"

No need to tell her that the house was an abandoned wreck twelve years ago, buried deep in English countryside. That none of them had wanted to stay in a childhood home when the childhood was so bitter. As the youngest, Ambrose had been the last to leave, and the first to vow that he'd never return—yet here he is, anyway. There's something terribly ironic about returning to raise Violet, climbing back on to that wheel of destiny he'd been so desperate to escape.

Between their absence and its dilapidated condition, it's been practically wiped from the map. Certainly removed from any correspondence, archives or detritus the Everly brothers could get their hands on. As long as Ambrose kept quiet—as long as Gabriel conducted his business elsewhere, as long as Violet didn't leave the house—who would suspect they were hiding a child here? Penelope couldn't seek what she didn't know existed.

Until now.

He can just about claim a desire for peace and quiet if she pushes —but they both know how much solitude can look like secrecy.

Penelope taps her fingers on the edge of the armchair. "You owe a debt, if you'd care to remember."

"So you say," he says carefully. "But I don't recall asking any favours."

He's on thin ice speaking to her this way, but he can't let go without a fight. Maybe it's because this is the first time he's seen a glimmer of peace, a faint reward for having to while away time in this house. Maybe he just doesn't think his family deserves to be served up to a monster.

"I'm not negotiating, Ambrose," Penelope says with infuriating calm.

"The Everly name owes a debt. Not me," he says.

"And aren't you an Everly?" she asks.

"Don't pretend that this is the same, that—"

"Ambrose."

She doesn't have to say his surname for him to hear it echoing close behind, the way it has his entire life. Stubborn like an Everly, brave like an Everly, doomed like an Everly. But an Everly nonetheless. If only he could reach into his ribcage and pluck the Everly out, tender and intangible as dreamstuff. If only he could erase that part of himself for good—which is to say, all of him.

He would do it without hesitation, if he thought it would save them.

"Fine," he spits out, "but that doesn't mean—"

"Then you are indebted, as is your niece. I could simply take the girl now, if you'd prefer," she continues. "Violet is quite as good as her mother, I assure you."

His stomach lurches at the thought.

"We can find Marianne," he says quickly. "Gabriel is looking for her as we speak."

He is just buying time, he tells himself. As much of it as he dares. And if that puts Marianne at risk, if they find themselves at these crossroads months from now, with mother and daughter weighed up on the scales and no way out—

He's not a gambling man, but here he is, putting every last coin on his sister to be smarter than their clumsy machinations. *Forgive me*, he thinks desperately.

"You're very confident in him. Are you sure he isn't hiding her?" Penelope asks softly.

"Yes," Ambrose says. Then he adds, "We don't even know why Marianne left."

Which, of course, is a lie. But he practised this in front of the mirror, saying it until the words felt like meaningless syllables. Until they became their own kind of truth.

"Violet's just a child," he continues, stretching out the lie. "She's worth nothing to you."

Penelope's smile widens, and Ambrose feels the ground shift underneath his feet, the tilt of the knife-edge sliding them all towards disaster. Yet neither of them say the word strung between them: Violet is worth nothing—*yet*.

Penelope stretches out the pretence of civility by taking a sip from her cup of tea, and every second is agonising. "Very well. I will make a deal with you, Ambrose Everly. I'll leave Violet alone if you find Marianne. But I won't wait forever." Her eyes narrow. "Ten years is a sufficient amount of time, don't you think?"

"Ten years," he echoes. "And you won't harm Violet in the interim?"

"I see no reason to," Penelope says.

"That is..." He swallows. "Generous of you."

Ambrose notes, the way he always does, how ageless she seems, like a rose stretched to fullest bloom and then frozen in unnatural beauty. Like a glass just before it shatters.

"We have a deal," he says, forcing the words out.

She holds out her hand and he takes it quickly. He's made enough devil's bargains in his lifetime, and he has no desire to linger over this one. But her fingers tighten on his. Pain lances through his wrist, racing up his arm. The lights gutter, then vanish, as shadows gather at his feet.

He sinks to one knee, then the other, the breath punched from his lungs. But Penelope's hand remains a vice. Someone—perhaps him—gasps a shameful, *"Please."* His mind short-circuits, every thought tuned to red, roiling agony.

Then Penelope lets go, and he collapses to the ground. The chill of the wooden floor is merciful against his throbbing skin. He drags in lungfuls of breath, unable to do anything else. His face is damp with tears. When he finally musters the strength to lift his head, Penelope is watching him coolly, no longer smiling.

"You should have told me about the girl, Ambrose."

After a beat, he climbs unsteadily to his feet. The lights are still on; outside is the same gloomy grey day. But the ghost of a burning ache flickers through his veins.

"Ten years," she says. "I trust you won't forget."

Ten years to find Marianne Everly. It sounds like all the time in the world, and none at all.

Three

 IOLET AND ALEKSANDER walk in painful silence down the long corridor, through the great hall with its cavernous fireplace, and towards the kitchen. It takes them past the wall of stuffy portraits and chipped busts depicting generations of Everlys, and Violet catches Aleksander eyeing the unique décor with a measure of derision, which she does her best to ignore. She used to make a game of matching the portraits' features to hers: a defiant, pointed chin from *this* ancestor; hazel eyes from *that* one; an upturned nose from a particularly snobbish grandfather. And then there is the curse, imprinted on her in invisible yet permanent ink, like every Everly before her.

She believes in curses like she believes in stories. For a curse is just another kind of story, dark and toothy and razor-edged. It's the unspoken tale singing its way through her family history: once a generation, an Everly walks into the dark, compelled by the shadow beside them.

Her ancestors stare down at Violet in grim disapproval. And she doesn't blame them. If she was braver, stronger, she would have already ditched the boy to eavesdrop on the conversation between Ambrose and the blonde woman. Instead, she leads him into the kitchen where he drops sullenly into an empty chair.

"Um, I hope you had a good journey. It's, uh, raining today," she says, in a valiant attempt at conversation.

When the response is stony silence, she tries a different tack. "Is that your mother? Penelope?"

The boy snorts, as if the question is too stupid to be asked. "No."

"Where are your parents, then?"

"I don't have them," he says stiffly.

"That's ridiculous. Everyone has parents."

"Fine," he shoots back, "where are yours?"

"My mother's on an adventure," she says proudly. "And one day I'll join her."

To the effervescent sea under the sun. To the northern witches in their deep forest homelands. Her skin tingles at the thought.

Aleksander looks dubious. "Adventures are for fairy tales."

"Well, *she* went on one. When I was ten—but she'll be back."

She knows it. Sometimes her belief is so strong, she's surprised the force itself doesn't whisk her mother back to their doorstep. The thought makes her pause, as she listens out for the click in the lock, the sound of her mother's voice ringing through the house again. She says she's too old for fairy tales, but if she just believes hard enough, wishes *enough*—

Aleksander snickers. "Yeah, right."

Violet snaps back to the present. "I'm not lying!"

They glare at each other, fury working its way under her skin. What does he know, anyway? If she wasn't on her best behaviour, she'd settle this the way they do in her favourite novels: hand-to-hand combat. No mercy—nothing but the firm hand of justice. But as it is, she ignores the boy and makes herself a cup of tea, slamming the cupboard doors with as much anger as she can muster.

"You're awfully loud for someone so small," he remarks coolly.

"Well, you're just as rude as I'd expect from someone with no parents," she snaps.

As soon as she says it, she knows she's gone too far. She expects him to retort with something equally cruel, but he's silent. When she glances away from her tea-making, he's staring at the wall, his jaw set, his eyes bright with a telltale liquid glimmer.

Begrudgingly, she asks him if he wants a cup of tea, too. He nods.

They sit at opposite ends of the table, watching each other over their mugs. Rain tap-taps on the skylights above. Violet picks at a whorl on the wooden table, guiltily avoiding his eyes.

"Want to see a trick?" the boy says suddenly.

She glances up. He fiddles with a small, iridescent black marble in his hands, rolling it between his thumb and forefinger. He places it flat on the table, then rolls it over to her, where it catches in the whorl. When she picks it up, it's strangely warm and incredibly beautiful, layers upon layers of sparkling dust within.

"Solid, right?"

She rolls it back to him. "Yeah."

He gives her a quick, shy smile. "Watch this."

His concentration slides from her to the marble, and suddenly the air crackles. He takes the marble, puts it flat in his hand and squashes. Then, he pinches it and *pulls*.

The marble expands in his hands to a fist-sized sphere, with the translucency of a soap bubble. An entire solar system spins on the surface. The black fades to a deep purple, and glittery light shines outwards, projecting constellations on to the walls. Violet can count them all: Orion's Belt, the Plough, Cassiopeia, the North Star.

It's utterly impossible.

It's magic.

The frown across his forehead deepens as the sphere expands, lighting up the dim room. Violet sucks in a breath when she sees that it no longer sits in Aleksander's hands, but hovers above them. He flicks his wrist, and the constellations suddenly shift into unfamiliar stars, with unfamiliar planets, moons lazily rotating around them. Violet reaches out to touch the thin membrane.

"Aleksander."

The sphere shatters into dust, glittering on the table.

Aleksander startles, guilt written all over his face. His hands are covered in black grit, fine as sand.

Penelope stands in the doorway, and for a second she looks furious, a thunderstorm of anger. But the second passes, and she's back to the calm, impassive woman from the living room. Behind her, Ambrose strides in, then stops at the mess.

"What—"

"Aleksander and I must depart," Penelope says, sounding sincerely regretful, even though Violet knows it's a lie. "It's been so lovely to visit, though—and far too long, Ambrose. We will have to come again."

She smiles, close-lipped. But when Aleksander gets up, his hands are clenched into white-knuckled fists.

"Say goodbye to Violet," she says. "I'm sure we'll see each other again."

Aleksander looks up at her, and his brittle, disinterested expression returns. "Goodbye, Violet."

"Thanks for coming," she says. And when Penelope turns to go, she mimes holding the sphere, then gives him a thumbs up.

Aleksander smiles faintly at her as he's pushed out the door.

That evening, Violet doesn't go to the library. Instead she cuddles up against Ambrose in one of the smaller living rooms, the low ceiling making the room feel comfortably snug. She can't stop thinking about the marble shattering, the boy suddenly so terrified.

"It's like she was wearing a mask," Violet says. "Like the person we saw wasn't her at all. Who is she?"

Ambrose stares into the fire, one hand clasped around a glass of whiskey. His brow is furrowed, as though he's forgotten something.

"Penelope . . . has known the family for a very long time." He looks down at her sharply. "What did her assistant show you?"

Violet purses her lips. "Nothing."

Ambrose laughs softly. "I remember when that was nothing, too." His hands shake as he sets down his glass. "Vi, what you saw in the kitchen stays between you and that boy, understand? He should never have shown you in the first place, but it's too late for that now."

"I swear I won't tell anyone," she says, her eyes big and serious.

Ambrose sighs. "Oh Vi, if only it was that easy."

It's the middle of the night, but Violet is wide awake. Night settles around her in a hush of anticipation—the witching hour, luminous with possibility. She sits cross-legged on her bed and sets her hands in the same position as Aleksander's had been. A marble, plucked from the dusty games drawer, rests in her palm. She frowns, trying to concentrate. She mimics his movements: the precise way he'd lifted with his fingertips, how he had pinched and pulled. She holds her breath, so full of wanting.

And for a second, she thinks she catches that same charge in the air.

For a second, her thoughts whisper *magic*.

But the marble stubbornly remains a marble. No galaxies, no otherworldly stars. Just her and the shadows in her room, closing in.

Four

A WHISPER IS CHASING across the world.

A woman in Italy hears it, and that night, she locks up her house. She bundles her children into the car, along with as many belongings as she can pack. When they ask where they're going, she only accelerates down the twisting countryside roads, grim determination reflecting back at her frightened children in the rear-view mirror.

The whisper reaches a jeweller in Seattle, who promptly faints after scanning the letter. He keeps trading—what else can he do?—but buys a gun, storing it carefully underneath the till point. Six months later, he's discovered dead in his back office, slumped over his desk with the gun still in his hand. The police assume suicide and close the case, even though his wife insists they were being watched by a woman who could vanish into thin air.

In Osaka, Gabriel Everly overhears the whisper as he sits alone in a café, dusk falling across the horizon. He closes his eyes, holding on to it for a painful moment, before releasing it back into the world. The next evening, he's in a different city, in a different country, and only then does he feel the tension in his shoulders give way.

The whisper gathers pace like a boulder careening downhill. It passes through telephones and hidden letters burned after reading, encrypted emails and clandestine meetings by candlelight. And somewhere in between, it crosses to a different world, carried on a breeze to a city of snow and starlight, where it has already been circling for quite some time.

Where is Marianne Everly?

CHAPTER

Five

MUCH AGAINST HER wishes, Violet grows up, rocketing from a short, half-feral child to a taller, half-feral teenager. She reads every book in the library twice over. She explores the length of the attic, traversing the narrow beams with an overconfidence that leads her to one day plunge a foot through the ceiling. She ventures outside to their overgrown garden, where she builds—and later on, tears down—a complicated fort of frayed ribbon and twigs. But she never leaves the confines of the Everly house. Not to go to school—"Why bother when I'm such a good teacher?" Ambrose says with an unconvincing smile—not to see friends, family, or the world that seems forever pressed up against the border of their garden wall.

Instead, every year, first with furious hope and then simply with fury, Violet waits for her mother to walk through the door. A letter, a phone call, semaphore flags on the roof—something to let her know that she hasn't been left behind to gather dust with the rest of the house.

On her fifteenth birthday, Ambrose finds her outside shredding the leaves of their enormous wild mint bush, her jaw set and her face red with the effort of not crying. Her hands are stained green, her eyes shimmering with unspent tears.

"I'm making tea," she says stubbornly, even though with the amount she's plucked, they'll be drinking it for weeks.

Gently, Ambrose pulls her away from the plant. "Violet—"

"She's not coming back, is she?" She tears out another handful of leaves. "And you won't tell me where she is, or even *why* she left. This is the curse, isn't it?"

Violet's not so young anymore that she fully believes in the curse the way she once did. Once she thought it was literal, and spent weeks waiting for her own shadow to rise up and claim its place next to her. Now she knows the spectre for what it really is: death. The afflicted Everlys are forever youthful in their portraits. But whatever the curse truly is, it takes one Everly per generation. And her uncles are still here; Marianne Everly is not.

Ambrose blinks, startled. "Violet, why would you say that?"

"Is it?" she asks insistently.

He sighs and rubs his forehead, a sign that Violet recognises as him working up to a lie. "I don't know where she is. Truly. Or why she left"—and there's the lie, right there—"but she'll come back, I promise."

Somehow, this promise feels worse than the lie. And he does not, she notices, refute the curse.

Every so often, Gabriel drops in on the house, and though he never stays for long, his visits are always memorable. He teaches her how to punch—"Thumb *over* fist, kiddo!"—how to move like a shadow, how to play darts like a pro. One birthday, the lesson is accompanied by a set of lock picks, despite Ambrose's protests.

Violet's not sure these qualify as gifts, exactly, but there's a kind of thrill from prying open her first lock, or walking down creaking floorboards without making a sound. Yet there are also times when her uncles hole themselves up in the library, leaving Violet to amuse herself. Days when she's certain she hears her name muffled behind its closed doors—or that of her mother. She suspects Ambrose is afraid that if he answers her questions, she'll disappear like Marianne —on a black, starless night with rain sheeting down the windows, never to return.

Sometimes, she thinks he's right to worry. Because adventure, it turns out, is a dangerously seductive word. It reaches underneath Violet's ribcage and pulls, like a cosmic string attuned to a compass point elsewhere. She spends hours cloistered in the library, poring over a map in its appropriately sized atlas folio splendour, until her vision bleeds faint blue latitude and longitude lines. She collects city names like other people collect spare change, letting the words linger in unfamiliar satisfaction.

She imagines, too, what it would be like to be that person heaving the bag over her shoulder, her diary stuffed with tales of the delights and dangers on the road. The stories she would bring back, wonder itself captured in her scrawled handwriting. A dozen languages on her lips, a hundred histories at her fingertips, every sight unforgettable.

See? Seduction.

Ambrose tells her it'll fade as she gets older. But that peculiar time when magic fades and cynicism sets in never happens, so there's always a part of her waiting for *something*.

Two weeks after her seventeenth birthday, she's curled up in a threadbare library armchair, idly toying with her bracelets, when she hears a pummel of footsteps. To her shock, Gabriel strides past the doorway—which is impossible, because as far as she's aware, he's supposed to be in some far-flung country, oceans away from the Everly house. She hasn't seen him in almost a year, and the last time for only an afternoon, at that. It never occurred to her that he might be dropping into the house to see Ambrose, avoiding her entirely.

Quietly, she unfurls from the chair and steals after him.

She almost loses track of him twice as he makes his way through the labyrinthine corridors. He's wearing a three-piece suit, his jacket slung over his shoulder. Then he pauses in the hallway, and she has to cover her mouth to stifle a gasp. He would look like he's on his way to a dinner, were it not for the black eye and split lip. Blood stains his crisp white collar in a vivid red spatter.

Violet knows then that she was never supposed to see this.

She quickens her pace. Gabriel might tell her where he's going if she can catch him on his way out. Might tell her why he's covered in blood, or why he's here at all.

Her footsteps are barely a whisper on the floorboards. But a whisper is still noise, and Gabriel is the one who taught her that trick. So when he vanishes between one room and the next, she's disappointed but not surprised he's managed to elude her.

She's about to head back when a gleam of light catches her eye. At the end of the long, dark hallway, a door stands slightly ajar. A chilly blue glow spills from it, casting shadows across the floorboards. It's supposed to lead to an unused guest room, and on every other day, it does.

But not tonight.

In the sliver between the door and the frame, a city sprawls below, as though Violet's suddenly standing on the edge of a vast cliff. Snow falls in heady fat flakes, clustering at the edge of the doorway. Rooftops sparkle white, illuminated by honey-coloured lamplight. Stars, brighter and more numerous than any she's ever seen, in constellations Violet has no name for. And the sonorous song of the mountainside rolls across the clifftops, a hum accompanied by the pop and judder of shifting ice.

It can't be real. Yet ice rimes the floorboards, creeping into the house. A breeze sends snowflakes skittering towards her, with a cold that snatches the air from her lungs.

Violet, the wind murmurs.

She takes one step, then another—

The door slams shut, as if someone's tugged it closed from the other side.

Violet freezes, precious seconds ticking past. Then she reaches for the doorknob and yanks it open. The dark, dusty guest room stares at her. When she steps back, the snow has already melted, soaking into the floorboards.

She thinks of the boy and his marble, wandering galaxies dancing in the air, a woman who wore her smile like a weapon. Her mother, and the mystery wrapped in every syllable of her name.

A voice whispers *adventure*.

Aleksander, too, receives a gift of sorts on each of his birthdays.

For his thirteenth birthday, it's punishment for showing the Everly girl the trick with the reveurite marble. Twenty lashes with a birch whip.

Reveurite is the metal of the gods, Penelope says softly, as he's led away to a cold, dark room. Not to be toyed with, and *never* to be manipulated in front of the ignorant. Really, the punishment should be more severe. But he isn't just anyone's assistant, and so Penelope is merciful. This is what she says, and he believes her, even as the first lash descends and he bites down hard on his lip to stop himself from crying out.

On his fifteenth birthday, Penelope takes him to Paris. She drops him in the city with no money, no way of contacting her and no map —just the name of a café. Seven hours later, he arrives, exhausted, hungry and wet from the constant drizzle. Penelope glances at her watch.

"You must do better, Aleksander," she says.

Over the following days, there are new cities and new destinations, until the cityscape feels like a second skin. He memorises street maps, tracks the flow of pedestrians into city centres, learns to pickpocket phones and ask for directions in over a dozen languages. On his twentieth drop-off, he finds Penelope within an hour, and she smiles approvingly, a gift all on its own.

He is almost seventeen when he falls into a heady romance with another boy. There is awkward fumbling and later, hasty undressing in the depths of the archives when they should be studying. For a month Aleksander is unfocused, distracted by the shape of the boy's mouth, the feeling of another's hands on his skin.

It's during one of these secret trysts that Penelope herself comes to fetch Aleksander, five minutes late to a forgotten meeting. There is punishment, of course, for his missed attendance. But Aleksander discovers that he's not absent of learning, for here is the new lesson: shame.

Two weeks later, the boy is caught stealing a scholar's key to *else-where*. A crime beyond crimes, sacrilege, treason. The keys are the only door to the outside, the only way Fidelis can bring in vital resources that they simply cannot recreate in the city. Aleksander listens with the dead weight of horror, imagining—as the other scholars must surely also be doing—Fidelis without its precious link, its crucial imports.

A city in ruins, which is no city at all.

The boy protests his innocence, but the charge is clear. Aleksander bows his head quietly as the boy is escorted from the scholars' tower, expelled forever. The next time they pass each other on the street— Aleksander in his scholar's robe, the boy in agriculturalist overalls— they walk past, with no acknowledgement of the other, were it not for the studious way they avoid each other's eyes.

Aleksander throws himself back into his studies. There are no more distractions. Which is a good thing, he tells himself, given how much there is to learn.

He studies the history of Fidelis until he can recite it by rote. He memorises long-dead languages, piecing together fragments from fragile manuscripts. In a dim classroom amongst a dozen other assistants, he moulds reveurite with his hands into self-perpetuating cogs and pulleys for the engineers, or fine strands to weave through airship rope, giving it preternatural strength. Then there is mathematics, chemistry, astronomy. On his own, with Penelope as his uncompromising tutor, he learns the languages and cultures of *elsewhere*, building on the foundations of his excursions with her. Other days, he spends hours with her identifying fellow dreamers on wet *elsewhere* streets, trying to ascertain the telltale golden glow of talent that surrounds every scholar of Fidelis.

Three days before he turns nineteen, Aleksander wakes in his narrow cell of a room, one of many on the mid-level floors of the scholars' tower. The comforting noises of home echo around him: the gurgle of hot water pipes; the energetic snoring of a fellow novice next door; mountain birds calling sweetly to one another above the early morning mist. A melody he's heard all his life, but one he never tires of.

He's always awake by dawn, waiting for a note to be slipped under his door. Written in Penelope's elegant script, this one says: *Pack your things. We leave within the hour.*

Hastily, he pulls on a clean shirt and trousers, patched at the knees. The cuffs have been let out, and then let out again, but they still skim his ankles, giving him the peculiar yet accurate look of someone who has shot up very quickly, and perhaps may grow forever. Unlike the other scholars, he has let his hair grow to his shoulders, tying it back with spare bookbinding ribbon.

He makes his way through candlelit hallways and up the impressive staircase that seems to extend infinitely in either direction. Even beyond the archives' prodigious memory, there has always been the scholars' tower, casting its long shadow over the rest of the city. A pillar of knowledge for those blessed with the combination of wit, talent and perseverance to study in its halls. To Aleksander—especially in this golden hour—even standing here feels like an act of reverence.

His feet slip easily into the worn indents on the stone, where thousands of other scholars have stepped before, treading the staircase smooth. Penelope's rooms are the highest in the masters' wing, a privilege of her position. Though the air is cold, Aleksander is sweating by the time he reaches her study.

Penelope is waiting for him inside. "I expected you sooner."

He hears the cut of disappointment in her voice. "I'm sorry, Mistress."

He considers asking where they're going, but immediately thinks better of it. Instead, he follows her through her study, towards a door at the back. There might once have been a room beyond, but now Aleksander stands in front of an open archway, the city of Fidelis spilling outwards below him. It's far from the first time he's been privy to this view, but it takes his breath away every time. Dawn skims the mountainside, casting a rose-gold glow over snow-topped roofs and precarious stairways, bridges swaying in the breeze. From here he can see the forges blazing like stars to the west, where the craftsmen wrestle with reveurite on their anvils. And to the east, up on the peaks, jagged ruins with sawtoothed silhouettes.

Fidelis: home of the scholars; of myth and wonder; of all that he loves. The cradle to other worlds. He's lived most of his life here, and he'll never understand how anywhere could even begin to compare.

Penelope offers him her hand. "Shall we?"

He takes it, making sure to look straight ahead and not to the sheer drop below. They step up to the rim of the archway, toes curled over the edge. The wind tears at Aleksander's clothes, pulling his balance out of joint. But Penelope looks serene, as always. Her key is already out, the air glittering with an otherworldly light.

Courage, he tells himself—

They step into the open sky.

In the library, there is a locked drawer that Violet has not yet discovered. Late at night, when he's certain his niece is elsewhere, Ambrose unlocks it and pulls out a battered notebook with intense, looping handwriting, and *Marianne Everly* scribbled over the first page. Inside, rows of names line the notebook, most of them in Marianne's scrawl, and only the last few in his own. Some of them are underlined, or pinned in place with a question mark, but many more—too many— have been crossed off as dead ends. It's taken years to unravel Marianne's cypher, and longer still to work through the names on her list. True, Ambrose can't chase Marianne to the ends of the earth from this house—not when he's responsible for Violet. But if his elder brother is the arrow, then Ambrose is the bowstring, gathering energy, directing Gabriel's efforts.

"She's still out there," Gabriel had told him quietly, on his last visit.

Ambrose has tried to send so many messages to her over the years, in the hope that they would reach her. Three years ago, one of them did. The response was a letter with no return address, not even a signature. Just two words, in handwriting Ambrose would recognise anywhere: *I'm close.*

If there is anyone who can break a curse, it's her.

If anyone can escape their fate, a treacherous voice whispers, *it's her.*

Ambrose runs his hand through his hair. There are strands of premature silver woven into sandy blond, and when he looks into the mirror, his father's face leaps out at him before his reflection settles as his own. And he's not the only one who's changed. Violet is growing up, too, the years passing between blinks. Every birthday, he feels a renewed terror for her, and Penelope's face looms under his eyelids.

Ten years to find Marianne Everly, then five, then two. His sister has left ghostly imprints of herself all over the world, but still she refuses to appear.

They are running out of time.

Once a year, Penelope descends into the underworld to visit a monster.

No assistant to look after, precious little light to see by. The underworld smells like hatred and pain, like suffering stretched taut across centuries.

For a while, she and the monster study one another's faces in the gloom.

We await your question, star-daughter.

"Tell me," she says softly. "What do you know of curses?"

Six

VIOLET EVERLY IS twenty-one years old, and dreaming of other worlds.

Mostly, she dreams of a world where coffee orders are simple—black, white, latte, cappuccino—and not "two shots, hold the froth, soya but only *this* brand of soya, small but in a big cup" when the queue threatens to stretch out of the door. A world without customers complaining their panini is overpriced, or the rose biscuits taste more like lavender, or that the sugar is too sweet. A world which, dare she dream it, might not involve her working in this godforsaken café at all.

Her co-worker, Matt, squeezes past her with two coffees and a teetering plate. "Look alive, Biscuit!"

He alone had been absolutely tickled by her name matching one of their signature floral biscuits. By the time she'd cottoned on, the staff and even some of the regulars were calling her Biscuit, and she was too tired to argue it. *Because you're sweet,* he explained. *Would you rather be Burnt Coffee Grounds?*

Maybe!, she wishes she'd said. At least *Burnt Coffee Grounds* sounds like she's seen something more than the inside of this café.

As a teenager, she'd envisioned herself as a historian in some grand library, holed up with mountains of books in barely legible handwriting. Then she'd toyed with archaeology when the library hadn't felt big enough to hold her ambitions. Anthropologist, travel writer, journalist, diplomat, translator—it didn't matter that she hadn't quite settled on a choice yet. For a wild, thrilling moment in her life, it seemed the future was opening up to her, and everything had felt possible.

How easily it's been taken from her.

It would be different, she reflects, if she knew that there would be more than this. That she could still go off and become any one of those people. But it had all come crashing down when she was seventeen, a few months after she'd seen Gabriel in his bloodied suit. When she learnt the magnitude of what Ambrose had sacrificed on her behalf when he'd decided to keep her at home. So she'd received an education, yes. But no qualifications. No exam results. Not even half a chance to pursue a degree.

"Why?" she'd begged.

Ambrose had given her a long, meandering and utterly unconvincing explanation. But even if she'd believed him, the damage was already done. So she's tried to let it go. She has.

But she's never forgotten the door leading to the city, the snow, the song of the mountainside. A secret that she's held even from her uncles, for fear of its unravelling. And she finds herself lingering in the same dark hallway, her chest brimming with the unplaceable feeling that something vital's slipped through her fingers.

Matt snaps his fingers next to her ear and she jumps, slopping milk over her hands.

"Christ on a *bicycle*," she swears.

"I'm told we share a resemblance." He jerks his head towards one of her tables. "Pay attention, Biscuit. You're up."

She's halfway across the linoleum, menu in hand, when she notes the man sitting at her table. He sits with his head bowed, focused on his hands clasped in front of him. Golden afternoon sunlight kisses his skin, the line of a tattoo barely visible above his collarbones. His profile is all sharp lines, bladed from the bridge of his nose all the way through to his jaw—the bone structure of a Grecian statue. His dark curly hair is pulled into a bun at the nape of his neck. *Unfairly pretty*, she thinks.

Suddenly, she's conscious that she's been working all day, sweat wicking through her shirt, that she smells like stale coffee, and that there's an unidentifiable stain—probably jam—just underneath her collar.

The world is desperately cruel sometimes.

Reluctantly, Violet approaches, praying for invisibility—and at least in this, the gods oblige. The man doesn't even look up as she sets the menu down, and she turns to leave. But despite herself, she steals another glance over his shoulder to see what he's so focused on. With surprise, she realises that his hands aren't clasped together, but holding some kind of metal object. Then he does something she remembers so clearly it runs like a lightning bolt through her head.

He pinches it, and *pulls*.

The galaxy over her kitchen table. The boy with his dark curly hair and fuzzy collar.

She sucks in a sharp breath—just in time to meet his curious gaze. Sea-glass grey.

"It's you," she says.

She takes a step back, colliding with another co-worker bearing an armful of empty plates. When she gets to her feet, the man is already halfway out of the door. She darts forward, heedless of the other customers watching her.

There have been so many *near misses* and *almosts*. She refuses to let one more opportunity slip away from her. It was him. It was *him*.

"Biscuit," Matt calls after her.

"Back in a sec!" she shouts.

Violet glances up and down the road, and catches the edge of a figure disappearing into the alleyway next to the café. Heart pounding, she takes after him, wind snapping at her apron.

The alleyway is empty. The man's gone.

Her stomach sinks at the knowledge that once again, she's just missed another glimpse of the extraordinary. To come so close, and then no further.

Her hands wring her apron helplessly. It'll always be like this. The café, the customers, the empty Everly house, and these fleeting echoes of the other life she might have had. But no more than that. And it'll never be enough.

Then she spies movement out of the corner of her eye—and what she'd originally mistaken for a shadow coalesces into the silhouette of a man, sitting on the low wall. Her heart restarts in her chest, cautious joy racing through her veins.

As she approaches, she waits for him to leap up and sprint away. But he doesn't run, and this time he meets her gaze with a frank inquisitiveness that leaves the back of her neck burning.

"May I?" she asks, and he inclines his head.

She sits down next to him on the wall, partly to see the object in his hands better and partly in the hope that his body will block out the brutally cold wind. A glint of silver flashes between his fingers.

"It *is* you, isn't it? Aleksander?" When he startles at the sound of his name, she continues, "We met once, a long time ago. But you probably don't remember."

Why would he? He must have seen a thousand more interesting things than an angry twelve-year-old girl and her uncle. A fierce wind blows over them and she hugs herself.

"You're shivering," he says.

Gallantly, he offers her his jacket, and she accepts. It smells strongly of soap, but also unexpectedly, the faint sweetness of charcoal.

"And I do remember you, Violet Everly." A smile pulls his mouth upwards. "How could I forget? And now here you are. Out of all the cafés in the world."

Like fate, reaching for her hand. And how nearly it had slipped from her grasp. A quiet thrill goes through her.

"I didn't mean to take off like that," he adds. "You just surprised me, that's all. It was going to be hard to explain the bird."

Violet tilts her head to the side, confused, and carefully, he opens his cupped hands. The crude shape of a bird appears on his palm, its wings half moulded as though struggling to escape its metal confines. He passes it to her and she tilts it in the light. Its feathers glitter dimly, like it was forged by moonlight and not Aleksander's slender fingers.

"It's beautiful," she says. "And you made that? With magic?"

He coughs, masking what Violet suspects is laughter. "It's reveurite. Star-metal, or god-metal if you want to be theological about it. Not magic."

"It looks so real," she says, handing the bird back.

But he shakes his head. "Keep it. This is nothing," he says, although he sounds pleased. "You should see the forge masters in Fidelis."

"Fidelis?"

She's certain she's heard that name before. It rings against a deeper memory, one she can't quite place. She opens her mouth to pursue the question, but another frigid breeze rolls over them and he rubs his hands together. Possibly he's already regretting his act of gallantry, she thinks.

"Biscuit!" someone yells, and Violet flinches.

Aleksander's eyebrows raise. "Biscuit?"

"My, um, co-workers have this—well, it's not really a *joke*, but—" She tries to gather herself. "Do you want to come back in?"

He beams at her, and she feels an unexpected glow of pleasure. "Lead the way."

When she returns inside, Aleksander in tow, Matt gives her a pointed look of intrigue that she ignores. She settles Aleksander on to her favourite table by the window and reluctantly hands back his jacket.

"I finish in half an hour," she says. "If you can wait?"

He smiles at her. "I can wait."

The next thirty minutes move at a crawl, and with every one of them, Violet is torn between the desire to check Aleksander's still there, and the fear that if she does look, he'll be watching right back. She busies herself as best as she can, wiping down counters and pouring away the dregs of coffee. As soon as Matt flips over the sign to *Closed* and locks the door, Violet sets two cups and matching slices of cake on Aleksander's table, pulling a chair towards him.

"So tell me," she says, desperate to keep him here, to hold on to the moment for as long as possible. "What do you get up to when you're not hanging out at cafés?"

Over the table, Aleksander tells her about his travels. He names cities, countries as though he simply steps between them, and every anecdote is filled with the kind of marvels that she's only ever read about. If she feels a stab of envy, it's only at how much he's seen, and how little she has to offer him in return.

"And...I'm training to be a scholar," he confesses, like it's a secret she's not meant to have.

She starts to ask what it means, a question shaping her lips. But he's already racing ahead with his own, and it falls into the back of her mind. At his insistence, she tells him about herself, the eccentric and sometimes irritable customers at the café. She even tells him about the Everly curse, for want of a story that feels equally fantastical to his own—though they both share a wry smile at the fairy-tale-esque details. They have both, she's noticed, avoided using the word magic again, but it's impossible not to feel it shaped between them, in every question she's asked, and all the ones she hasn't.

"And your mother?" he asks. "Is she still on her adventure?"

The air in her lungs freezes. "It's complicated."

"Complicated how?"

Her hands go to her bracelets, one of Marianne's few possessions Violet's claimed in her absence. How could she possibly begin to explain? Marianne seems to haunt every one of her uncles' hushed conversations, and yet Violet still has no idea where she went or why, if she's even alive—

She forces a smile. "Just...complicated."

For the first time, she catches something in his expression like unease. But it's gone in the next second, and she wonders whether it was just a trick of the light.

He drains the last of his coffee and sets the empty cup down. "I'd better go. It was lovely to meet you properly, Violet Everly."

Violet has the sudden panic that if she waves him goodbye, she'll never see him again. And the soap-bubble dream of today will burst, leaving her with nothing in her hands but those tantalising echoes. She knows there's more—so much more—to ask.

"You should come again," she blurts out. "To the café."

God forbid Aleksander show up at the Everly house. If Ambrose and Gabriel are entitled to their secrets, she's more than earned her right to keep this one.

He smiles at her, his eyes crinkling at the corners. "I'd like that."

"Here, then." She hands him a small card—ten illustrated coffee cups, with the first two already stamped over in blue ink. "If you keep coming, you'll get a free coffee."

He looks at it and smiles. "Then I guess I'll have to come back, Violet."

That evening, Violet coaxes her rusty bike across countryside lanes as she makes the familiar, meandering journey home. She turns into the driveway, and as always, something knots in her stomach at the sight of her home, with its Gothic turrets and overgrown rose bushes climbing the gate. Not for the first time, she wishes it could be enough.

Ambrose, as usual, is at the kitchen table, trying to read a sheaf of handwritten documents and patch an old jumper at the same time. As soon as Violet enters, he shuffles the papers underneath the jumper, out of sight. Irritation prickles over her skin.

"Good day?" he asks. "Anything exciting happen?"

She shrugs, feeling the half-guilty thrill of a lie. "Not really."

Leaving Ambrose in the kitchen, she heads to the library. It's still her favourite place in the house, a treasure trove of books and curios gathered over generations of Everlys. A rusty sword hangs precariously along one wall, framed by a dozen family photos and scraps of artwork from some obscure Victorian artist. She used to spend hours imagining the knight that bore it, and the places he must have seen.

Now Violet pulls down atlas after atlas, flipping through the pages she used to pore through as a child. Something that Aleksander had said is still worrying at the recesses of an old memory, wreathed in dust and the crinkle of old paper. Nothing jumps out at her—and yet she knows she's heard that name before. *Fidelis.* When she whispers it to herself, it tastes like spun sugar, like snowmelt and starlight.

Eventually, she comes to her favourite book of fairy tales, bound in green silk, with foil decorations stamped in burnished gold. It was the last gift she received from her mother, and it's the most precious, her mother's dedication scrawled in her handwriting.

For Violet—may the stars sing for you one day.

Half of the foil has rubbed off and the deckled edges are soft with age, but Violet loves it all the more for its worn beauty. Every story is set in a different imaginary city, with hand-painted maps and beautifully precise details. Suspiciously precise, now that she's re-examining it.

She flips through until she finds the one that she's after. It's more illustration than map, showing a city perched high on a mountainside. She's always loved it for the way the streets seem to twist around themselves, with fanciful names like *Tullis Gate-Arch* or *Etallantia Sky Way*. Her hands touch the top of the page, where the name of the city is hand-lettered in delicate serifs.

Fidelis.

CHAPTER

Seven

I N THE ALLEYWAY next to the café, Aleksander checks to make sure no one's watching before he pulls out a reveurite key from under his shirt. He holds it out in the air, feeling for the slight resistance that marks the boundary between worlds. It's easier with a door and a keyhole, but Aleksander is well-practised now, and the thin membrane parts easily for him. A flash of blue light, a whirl of metallic noise, and then he's standing inside Penelope's quarters, half a step from the open archway and the view of Fidelis. Outside, snow is falling in fat, heavy flakes, visible against the honeyed lights of the city below.

From a hook next to the archway, he retrieves his assistant's robes and pulls them on over his *elsewhere* clothes. Better if they were full scholar regalia—dense silver embroidery on navy silk, with a thicker fur lining of his choosing, and whatever vestments he wants underneath—but it's only his position that keeps him from being forced to wear the simpler novice robes, which he is nearly too old for, anyway.

As he reaches for the door, he hears the sound of one of Penelope's gatherings in full swing. His stomach tightens; he'd hoped to catch Penelope on her own. Dread winding through him, he opens the door. The conversation dies as he steps in, and five scholars turn to stare at him in accusatory silence.

"Aleksander," Penelope says brightly. "We were just discussing the resourcing for this winter. Please, join us."

Yet another task tacked on to a scholar's remit: procuring suitable resources and lines of business across both worlds, to accommodate the limitations of this one.

Aleksander swallows nervously as he takes an empty seat by the window, observing the group that has graced Penelope's study this evening. There's the stern Verne matriarch Adelia; Katherine Hadley and her wardrobe-sized bodyguard, Magnus; the Matsuda twins, identical in floral suits. Even Roy Quintrell is here, sporting his ridiculous velvet jacket, which by all rights should have been decommissioned into a less offensive cushion cover years ago. He senses their eyes on him, sweeping over his rumpled hair, the awkward hunch to his shoulders. Judgement flashes across their faces, even though none of them have the authority to directly challenge Penelope's invitation.

Stupidity, though—definitely.

"But this is rather important," Roy says peevishly. "Surely your assistant should make himself scarce? If *I* had an assistant—"

Penelope's smile is still in place, but her eyes sparkle dangerously. "What would you have me do with him, then?"

There's a gleam of panic in Roy's face as he tries to backtrack. "I wouldn't dare presume—no, of course not—"

"Then be quiet and take notes," Adelia says.

The conversation turns to the harvest shortfall—a little worse than the year before, despite the new ingenuities the greenhouse workers have come up with—and what foodstuffs will need to be replenished midwinter by the *elsewhere* lines of supply. Likewise, the ageing water pipes, which will need to be replaced before next year, and the quantities of copper required. Then the intake of new scholars: who amongst the families' new generations proves the most adept. Rumours of a scholar auctioning stolen artefacts *elsewhere* to the highest bidder.

Penelope listens to them all carefully before dispensing her commands. But Aleksander can't help note the scholars' occasional disapproving glances towards him. As if he can't be trusted with the specifics of Fidelis' resourcing. Even though these scholars no longer live in Fidelis, and barely travel back from their comfortable *elsewhere* lives. Scholars in little but name—except that the name is, of course, everything.

And Penelope was supposed to be on their side. She was supposed to pick one of the families' heirs—in this case, Adelia's insufferable grandson, Caspian—on whom to impart glory, wealth, and most importantly, the secret of longevity that some scholar lines are so blessed with. And no doubt they have all envisioned taking Penelope's place as head of this room—as if such a thing could even be possible.

Anyone else would be ushered in with welcoming arms, but not Aleksander. *Other assistants aren't hand-picked by Penelope. Other assistants aren't outsiders chosen by one of the most powerful people across both worlds. Other assistants didn't fuck up Adelia Verne's plans.*

The sun has long vanished from the sky when the scholars finally say their goodbyes to Penelope and exit through the archway. Aleksander allows himself to raise one satisfied eyebrow at Roy, who shoots him a dirty look as he leaves.

Then it's just Aleksander. Not awkwardly lingering to ask Penelope's favour, or to beg advice, or to simply catch a few wayward sparks of glory. But here because he belongs. Which is more than any of those people can say, no matter how much the other scholars dislike him.

Penelope gestures to her cupboards, and Aleksander hastily pulls down a bottle of wine and two glasses. He fills hers first and sets it on the table next to her. He waits until she's had her first sip before pouring for himself.

Penelope leans back in her chair. "How was she, Aleksander?"

He doesn't need the name to know who Penelope's asking about: Violet Everly. In as much detail as possible, he outlines their meeting. How he'd purposely walked into the café, looking for all the world like it was nothing but coincidence that had led him there.

"She seems…normal," he says.

It had been risky to use reveurite in public, with so many observers. But he had to make sure that Violet would recognise him. And, truth be told, he wasn't entirely prepared for her response, or the way she'd said his name, like she'd been waiting for him to walk in.

It's you.

He thought it would take more prompting on his behalf, too, to know the girl from the Everly house. But even before he'd felt her gaze on him, even as she handed him the menu, he could tell it was her. The same burning curiosity, the same wonder when he'd shown her the reveurite bird.

"I'm not sure she knows anything of the scholars or even Fidelis," he continues cautiously. "She wouldn't tell me about Marianne."

"Well, that's to be expected. It's only your first time. There'll be plenty of opportunities to build trust."

"And Fidelis?"

Penelope shrugs. "Tell her whatever you wish. You said she liked the idea of magic? Use that. Anything it takes to get her to talk about Marianne."

Aleksander sets his glass down on the table, his heart in his throat. "Mistress, I've done everything you've asked of me. I'm not—I'm very grateful, always, but—" His hands touch the spot on his arm where his scholar's tattoo should be.

Will be, one day. Whatever the other scholars may think.

"You wish to know what the point of all this is." Penelope taps the arm of her chair. "Aleksander, they may be the best scholars of their families, but they're human, too. They fear what we all fear: change, old age, irrelevance. Their family names vanishing into obscurity, their wealth and talent diminished. You remind them that, as much as they wish, the world moves on—and they may be left behind."

Aleksander is pretty sure none of those fears are quite as acute as the thought of failing to gain the scholar's tattoo, but he says nothing.

"You are an unknown quantity. Not from a family of note—or any family at all, for that matter. Just one more abandoned child, destined to some miserable existence, with nothing to suggest your capability for greatness—except your talent. It's why I chose you, when I could have had any number of mediocre yet tolerated assistants," Penelope continues, and Aleksander feels just a hint of smugness at Caspian being described as *mediocre*. "They will come round to you eventually, given enough time. They just need a little persuasion."

"Persuasion," he echoes.

Persuasion means casual threats. Or an offer of something of extraordinary value that coin can't buy. But Aleksander is no threat to anyone, and if he had anything of value to offer them, he wouldn't be in this position in the first place.

"Put it out of your mind for now. Was there anything else that Violet mentioned?" Penelope prompts.

"We talked, and I asked as much as I could. But..." He frowns. "I don't understand, Mistress. If the Everlys are a scholar family—"

Penelope cuts him off. "The Everlys aren't scholars, and never will be. Befriend Violet Everly by all means, and learn as much as you're able, but remember that she has no place in our world. Am I clear, Alcksander?"

"Yes, Mistress," he says.

Later that night, as he settles onto his uncomfortable mattress, he keeps returning to Violet Everly. The echo of his name in her mouth replays in his mind. *Aleksander.* Bright and heedless, like a clean spring sky, with no regard for who he might be: an assistant no one wants, threat and disappointment rolled into one.

In another life, they might have been friends. In this one, she's a means to an end. Nothing more.

He promises himself that he'll remember this, the next time they meet.

Eight

I T'S A COLD, forbidding day in Moscow, as Penelope steps out from underneath the doorway to a dour apartment complex. She deftly avoids the icy slush collecting in the gutter, and the litter that rustles over the street like leaves. Despite the near-zero temperature, Penelope only wears a light dove-grey coat for warmth, her throat exposed to the bitter wind. Cars stream past her in a constant blur, and pedestrians hurry onwards; no one is keen to take in the sights in this weather.

Winter presses its grey fingers upon everything: the skies, the buildings, the people. Crumbling façades and fading pastel edifices raise the ghosts of a grandeur long vanished, of fur-trimmed coats and jewelled horse-drawn carriages like enormous Fabergé eggs. Then a car thunders past, and the vision melts into the snow.

The dilapidated building in front of her is an all-too-familiar picture of what might have been. Cracked plaster flowers and an elaborate iron gate suggest it might have once belonged to a wealthy merchant, or some minor noble—a townhouse to pair with a rambling dacha in the countryside. Now it hosts a block of flats, each a fraction of the original living space.

Without bothering to ring the bell, Penelope enters and climbs the narrow staircase all the way up to the top floor, then down a damp corridor to the last flat. She knocks twice on the door. Frost rimes the inside of the hallway window, and her breath clouds the air.

After a moment, the door unlocks and a man appears, looking haggard and weary. But when he sees Penelope, his expression drops. Panic flashes across his face.

"Penelope? I—"

"Strasvuitye, Yury," she says pleasantly, in fluent Russian. "It's been a while."

"I wasn't expecting—" He gathers himself. "Please, come inside."

The entire flat—just one room—could fit into the Everlys' front hallway. Portable radiators blaze warmth, so that condensation drips down the windowpane. And every inch is covered in keys: hung on the wall, layered thick on the floor, or spilling out of enormous boxes stacked on top of one another. There are diagrams and illustrations, too, furled tightly into scrolls and propped in a corner, or draped across furniture. Despite the heat, Yury wears several thick jumpers and a heavy overcoat. His lips are chapped and blue at the edges, and he stays as close as he can to the radiators. He fumbles with a kettle, his hands visibly shaking. Penelope notes with interest that underneath his fingerless gloves, his skin is black and withered.

"Where is your faithful assistant?" he asks.

"Aleksander? Oh, I have him on another errand at the moment," Penelope says. "But he sends his regards."

The last time Aleksander had come here, he'd blanched at the state of the apartment and Yury's own condition, both of which had deteriorated from their prior visit. She'd asked him about it, curious at his reaction, but all he'd said was, *It looks like it must hurt.* Although she has managed to train Aleksander into a competent assistant, he is so easily wounded by the thought of others in pain. A weakness she must temper from him, she reminds herself.

"I did what you said," Yury says, pouring hot tea into chipped mugs. "I spent just about every rouble I had on those blasted keys. And then some."

He waits for a response, but Penelope isn't forthcoming. He clears his throat, and offers her a cup. While she drinks, she studies him carefully. Yury is not even thirty, but his face is prematurely lined, and he holds himself with arthritic pain. His eyes are unusually tinted: a lustrous onyx that seems to shift colour in the light.

"I was not expecting you so early," he says.

"Neither was I," she says truthfully. "But I've had to expedite my plans."

She examines the keys, picking up each one. Most of them are antiques: plain copper, steel, bastard metals rife with impurities. But there are also keys pressed in gold and inlaid with jewels, carved in thick mahogany, or blown from delicate glass, light shining through. None of them are made of reveurite, however, and therefore they are all useless.

As she browses, Yury watches her anxiously. Absently, he presses his hands on the boiling kettle, and the stench of burning flesh rises in the cramped flat.

"There is still so much to be done—I haven't even gone through everything yet—and did you bring the—" He accidentally knocks his mug and it shatters on the ground, tea soaking into the rug under-foot. "Ah, fuck. Fuck!"

Penelope ignores him. Her search becomes more frenzied, less methodical, as she turns her attention to the illustrations. Paper tears, and ink smudges under her warm fingertips. She casts each useless image on the floor, where they quickly become sodden and unreadable.

Finally, she looks up. "Where is the rest of the research I asked for?"

"Gone. The day after, there was a fire. Whole shop, gutted. They say it was so hot"—he licks his lips, his eyes suddenly distant—"the lead roof melted."

Set a man on fire, so he'll be warm for the rest of his life. But Penelope knows that Yury hasn't been warm for three years. His fingers are blistered with burns, his arms twisted with scars; yet he shivers in this sweltering room. A digital alarm goes off on the watch loose around his wrist, and he quickly silences it. With one shaking hand, he retrieves an opaque packet from his coat pocket and tips its contents into his mouth. The sound is like crunching rock.

It's not the results she'd hoped for when they started this particular experiment, but Yury has fared better than the other scholars thus far. He is alive, for one.

"So Marianne Everly has beaten me yet again," she murmurs.

Yury looks at her desperately. "Did you bring it? Please tell me you brought it."

"I cannot bring what I do not yet have," she says.

"You *promised*. You said you had a cure, you *said* if I drank it, if the experiment didn't work—"

"Have I ever broken my word?" she says sharply. When he doesn't answer, she continues, "I will make sure you receive the cure for your...side effect. But in the meantime, you still have your end of the deal to fulfil. I don't care how you get hold of it. If you have to pry that key out of cold, dead Everly hands, so be it."

Yury waves his frostbitten hands at her in acknowledgement. "Fine, fine. But for the love of God, bring the cure before my xuj falls off. Three of my toes are already gone, and my hands..." He swallows. "I can't live like this, Penelope. No one can."

"Then find me that key," she says, "and live a little longer."

Nine

IOLET CAN'T BELIEVE it when Aleksander turns up the next week, half an hour before closing. Or the week after. On the fourth week, Matt digs his elbows into her ribs as Aleksander walks into the café yet again, a book tucked under his arm.

It takes her that many weeks to build up to the question she's been desperate to ask. Not just for fear of being laughed at or dismissed, but for the sheer finality of the question itself. The metal magic—the *reveurite manipulation*, she has to remind herself—is irrefutably real. But there is another, larger truth that she suspects. That maybe she's always known, and now there's nothing else standing in her way to confirm it but this one question.

That afternoon, Aleksander is later than usual to arrive, and Violet spends most of it pacing up and down the aisle behind the counter, anxiously twisting her mother's bracelets around her wrist. When he finally shows up, she has to hold back a sigh of relief. Today his hair is loose and curling around his shoulders, softening the angular lines of his face.

She eyes the sunburn bright across his cheekbones and he smiles ruefully. "I'm sorry I was late. I was in Bogotá on an errand this morning."

The way he says it, so casually. Like everyone travels halfway around the world for *errands*.

"How did you make it back so quickly?" she asks.

He taps his chest, and at first she thinks he means it's a secret, but then he pulls out a long silver chain from underneath his shirt. On the end is a key, glittering with the same strange metal as the bird. Reveurite.

"This is the way home," he says quietly, his eyes on Matt busying himself at the till point. "When you're a scholar, you get your own and you can travel at will." He slips it back into his shirt. "Mine is on loan."

"A key to anywhere in the world." Now *this* is magic she can believe in.

He gently corrects her. "A key to anywhere you've been before. As long as it's made of reveurite, one is all you'll ever need."

A memory rises from the depths of her consciousness. Her mother sitting at the library desk on another late night, her silhouette haloed by lamplight. Marianne Everly turns a key over in her hands, a frown puckering her forehead—

Violet takes a deep breath. "It's not just our world, is it? Because there's also your world. Fidelis."

She says it as casually as possible, but her heart thuds in her chest.

Aleksander leans towards her, holding her gaze, close enough to see that the beautiful grey of his eyes is shot through with dark speckles. His fingers graze her knuckles, and she realises that her hands are clenched into fists, pressed hard against the table.

"Yes," he says.

All this time she's wondered, but now she *knows*.

The way Gabriel could arrive in the middle of pouring rain with perfectly dry clothing, or with snow clinging to his shoes even though outside was the picture of summer. The constant whisper in her head that something extraordinary was happening in the Everly house, if only she could peel back the veil of secrecy her uncles had erected. That longing for adventure, lodged like a wishbone in her throat.

"Explain it to me," she says. "Please."

Aleksander pulls a napkin towards him and holds it up. "Think of it like this. You see this side? This is here, now. And the other," he says, flipping it over, "is Fidelis."

That word again. A thrill ripples through her.

Aleksander takes his butter knife and stabs it through the napkin. "*This* is the scholars. But not everyone can be the knife. Not everyone can cross the border."

That evening, Violet makes dinner alongside Ambrose, the house in its usual companionable silence.

"Ambrose," she says.

He doesn't look up, half focused on chopping vegetables. "Mmm?"

"Have you ever heard of a place called Fidelis?"

The knife stops. Ambrose looks at her sharply, all easy humour gone. "Where did you hear that word?"

Violet shrugs, keeping her eyes on the sudsy water in front of her. "I don't remember. Maybe Gabriel."

Gabriel hasn't been home in almost a year, so he's not here to call her out on the lie.

"Do you know where it is?" she asks. "I thought you might have—"

Ambrose cuts her off with a strained smile. "No, I've never heard of it."

Violet thinks about the back of the wardrobe, imagines it unfurling into a set of stairs, then a doorway, easing open the way she'd dreamed about as a child. A sliver of a snowy city down a long, dark hallway.

Marianne Everly, vanishing into a thunderstorm.

From then on, every week, she asks Aleksander a question about Fidelis.

What's the most beautiful road in the city?

What does a scholar learn?

What does a day feel like?

He answers, as best as he can. He tells her how to bind a book, to chart the night sky, to take apart a language that's not her own. It's as though someone has pulled away a brick in the dam of her curiosity, and now it's all spilling out, unstoppable.

One day he brings a bead of reveurite with him, and working stealthily, he creates another, smaller bird in front of her to match the one she now keeps on her windowsill, plucking wings, a beak, an inquisitive eye out of the metal. He hands it over and she marvels at the tiny golden sparkles that glitter at the edge of her vision.

"Could I do this?" she asks.

To her surprise, he glances away from her. "Well...it's unlikely. For lots of reasons. To be honest, I'm not really supposed to be showing you." Gently, he catches her wrist and tilts it towards the light. "But look, your bracelets are made from reveurite."

Marianne's bracelets. Violet stares at them, her delight vanishing in an instant. She shouldn't be surprised by the depths of her uncles' secrets, not now; yet every time she thinks she's come to a resignation, if not acceptance—

"Surely your mother told you?" Aleksander says, frowning. "Where did you say she's gone again?"

"I—I didn't know," she says, her gaze still on the bracelets.

Aleksander looks at her intently. "Where she went, you mean?"

"I don't..." Violet's brain catches up to the rest of the conversation. "No. She didn't say. To me, at least."

It's hard to articulate why, exactly, she's so keen not to discuss Marianne with Aleksander. She's held him so carefully at bay from her home, her uncles, and any mentions of her mother, even though with every question answered, it's clearer than ever how intertwined Marianne and the scholars are. For the first time, she has an inkling of how Aleksander might have ended up in the Everly house, all those years ago. And yet her mother feels like an uncrossable line.

"Is this what the scholars do all day?" she asks instead, teasing. "Crossing worlds to have coffee?"

Aleksander grins and flicks a napkin at her. "We search for *talent*, Violet Everly." When he sees her blank expression, he adds, "People who can manipulate reveurite. This coffee business is just the reward."

"For what, though? Why—" She cuts off and turns away to hide her creeping blush, aware that she's asking too many questions.

When she sneaks another glance at him, his smile softens. "Talent —and reveurite—runs Fidelis. And we have other roles besides.

Historian, chronicler, alchemist, archaeologist, explorer—they all come under the heading of scholar. It's a huge responsibility, but it's the greatest privilege I've known."

"So which will you be?" she asks, no longer teasing.

To her surprise, he shrugs, indifferent. "I'll go wherever Penelope sends me. That's the role of an assistant."

"But what would you *like* to be?" she persists.

For a while, he's silent, and Violet waits patiently, watching emotion ripple over his face like clouds.

"I like history, I suppose," he says, pensive, "and the archives. So I would be a historian—no, something like an archaeologist, which is what you would call it. On the other hand, though, I'd miss the travel, so maybe—" He cuts himself off. "But it doesn't matter."

He looks down at his hands, and Violet follows. On his left ring finger is the tattooed outline of a gibbous moon.

"I owe Penelope my life," he says quietly. "I owe the scholars everything."

Violet doesn't reply, but she recalls the blonde woman standing in the doorway of her kitchen, and the way her fingers had dug into Aleksander's shoulder as she steered him out of the Everly house.

After work, they walk alongside the river, the last of the day's sunlight draped across their shoulders. Though the temperature has pitched downwards in recent weeks, Violet feels a glow of warmth with Aleksander beside her.

"Why did Penelope call me a dreamer?" she asks, still musing over that long-ago visit.

Aleksander tilts his head up to the sky. "She says that we were once nothing more than the dreams of stars. Then the stars moulded us from clay, and gave us shards of themselves so we might create in their honour. And we were happy, for a time. But, even though we have our feet on the earth, every time we close our eyes, we dream of being stars again."

At night, Violet touches the bracelets around her wrists, admiring the golden sparkles that shimmer across the metal like an oily patina.

She closes her eyes and imagines herself as stardust, winging her way through the night sky.

Winter in Fidelis is marked with a series of snowstorms, thunder booming across the mountainside. Aleksander wakes to find a thin crust of ice on the inside of his windowpane. Shivering, he grabs his towel and descends to the hot springs. It's never quiet in the communal baths, and this morning is no exception. Loud shrieks from small children echo in the vast subterranean room as they leap into icy plunge pools, while adults converse under hazy steam, scrubbing themselves as they talk. Faded mosaics depict ancient battles and forgotten myths, while noisy pipes shunt water upstairs to the masters' rooms.

Afterwards, dressed and wringing the damp from his hair, he makes his way from the lower floors to the entrance, up the long, twisting scholars' staircase.

As he walks along the cobbled streets from the scholars' tower, past the sky-docks and airships laden with goods, he has to admire, as he always does, how contained his world is, compared to Violet's vast *elsewhere*. Fidelis perches high on a ring of mountains, cupping a valley dotted sparsely with farming lands. But the mountains that protect them also keep the city isolated—no airship can ascend over the peaks; no tunnel can bore through the impenetrable rock. Sometimes, on sleepless nights when the stars burn through the sky, he wonders what the other side of the mountains might look like.

But mostly, he thinks about how much Violet would love to see it all.

In his head, he hears Penelope telling him not to get too involved, to befriend her but not trust her. He can tempt her with Fidelis, but that is all.

"It's of utmost priority we find Marianne Everly," Penelope had said. "*That* is the goal."

How many times now has he opened his mouth to ask why, and then shut it again?

When he was very young and still unable to contain himself, Penelope told him the story of a reveurite blade that sung questions to its owner in a never-ending loop of melody. At the end of the story, the owner threw the blade off a cliff, driven to madness by its endless singing.

"You are my blade of knowledge, little dreamer," she'd said and ruffled his hair. "But to be a blade, you need to be controlled, unbreakable, unquestioning. Or I might just have to throw you off a cliff, too."

She'd said it with laughter, but even so, he's never been entirely certain how metaphorical the cliff edge is. So he tries his best to be her blade, and he bites back the questions that he'd otherwise ask.

It makes answering Violet's questions all the sweeter, even if he's constantly worried about giving too much away. Only the other day, she'd asked what the scholars do, in a more specific sense, and he'd had to recalibrate his answer with his mouth already half open, ready to spill every secret he knows.

He's grown used to the routine of these past few months, so he's a little taken aback to be summoned to Penelope outside of their regular meetings. Even though he's halfway through the delicate task of repairing a fragile document from the archives, he abandons everything and climbs the scholars' staircase to her quarters.

As he waits outside her door, three master agriculturalists barge past, their hair still stiff with melting icicles. Aleksander watches them stomp downstairs in their tough outdoor gear, their faces wind-bitten and prematurely lined, and a knot forms in his stomach. He already knows they've struggled to maintain their harvest quotas this year, but there are rumours they're low on apprentices, too. Every year it seems like the city is squeezed a little tighter by winter, transferring the same pressure to the scholars as they rush to solve the problem, or at least stymie it until a solution can be found.

Still thinking of the agriculturalists, he knocks on the door to Penelope's quarters, and enters.

"So, my assistant," she says.

Aleksander freezes in the doorway, his pulse ratcheting. Penelope's back is turned to him, but her tone is silky. Dangerous. Frantically, he runs through all the things he might have fucked up in the last week. His mind comes up a terrifying blank.

"Mistress?" he says nervously.

"How many weeks has it been now, Aleksander? Eight, nine?"

It takes him a fraction too long to realise what she's getting at. "Since—"

"Since I charged you to extract information about Marianne Everly from her daughter." Penelope turns, her mouth thin with anger. "And have I not been patient? I've listened to your useless tidbits about her café friends and her likes and dislikes. Do you know what I haven't heard yet, Aleksander?"

Aleksander bows his head, shame creeping over him. "I just need a few more weeks, I swear. I've been working on it, but she's very reluctant to talk about Marianne—"

The blow is not unexpected, yet it catches Aleksander's jaw with shocking ferocity. Fire blooms across his face, pain briefly eclipsing his thoughts. He glances up, eyes watering, to Penelope's impassive expression, her hand still raised.

"I dragged you out of the gutter to give you the chance of a decent life. To fulfil the potential I thought you possessed."

Aleksander's head is still reeling, but he tries to pull himself together. He resists the urge to touch his face and probe the damage. He has to say something to fix this. But all he can think about is the starburst of pain, the metallic taste of blood in his mouth.

"You are not a Verne, a Hadley, a Persaud or any of the other families of note. *Their* failures might be tolerated, even indulged, but then their places are secured." Penelope's tone finally softens. "I cannot advocate for you if you do not advocate for yourself."

"Yes, Mistress," he whispers.

"I am running out of patience, Aleksander," she says. "I will give you a few more weeks. But that is all."

Aleksander exits, trying to ignore the hot throb in his jaw. When he glances at his reflection in a window, the red outline of a handprint is streaked across his face. Already a bruise is forming.

He's trying to do his best by Penelope, to be her blade. But he is failing. As usual.

On his next trip to the café, he stands outside for what feels like forever, despite the frigid weather. Through the fogged windows, Violet moves between tables with ballet-like precision. The café is quiet today, and he watches as she meanders back to the countertop, where two of her colleagues are clearly bickering over something. The window gives Aleksander a perfect view of the area behind the till point—and the book Violet has cunningly stashed there. She tucks a curling wisp of hair behind her ear, drawing his gaze from the soft curve of her neck to the way she bites her lip, clearly engrossed by her contraband. It's only when he catches his own reflection in the window that he realises he's smiling like an idiot. Smiling at her.

Aleksander debates for a minute, but there is no one watching him. He allows his eyes to refocus, greying out the surroundings. His mind falls still, seeking out the presence of another dreamer.

Only those with talent can use the keys. Only those with talent can become scholars. And the Everlys are not a scholar family, even though they possess so many of the hallmarks that Aleksander still wonders what they did to make themselves outcasts.

Even if by some miracle Violet did possess talent, it would only be a whisper of gold that would never see her admitted as a scholar, nor anything else that Fidelis might need. So she'll never know the mountainside song Aleksander loves so much, never see the year's first snowfall, never stand at the edge of the city with him, in a world he has only just begun to dream of sharing.

He's spent long enough indulging the foolish whims of an imagined friendship; there's simply too much at stake. But he has to *know*.

His breathing slows, stops—

The world explodes in a shower of golden light. Violet at the epicentre. She's not just another dreamer, not just another anything.

It's impossible, he thinks. And yet.

Ten

THE YEAR IS turning; a visit is owed.

Midnight breaks across a village deep within the French mountainside. Stars cluster against the night sky in their brilliance, and the roads are all but silent. Then a flash of blue light intrudes on the darkness, and Penelope ducks through a doorway into an alley. She holds a small package, which occasionally wriggles in her grasp.

A man with sunken cheekbones and a haunted expression steps out of the shadows to meet her. Penelope dumps the package in his waiting arms.

"I almost thought you weren't going to come," he says nervously.

She observes him levelly. "I always keep my promises, François."

Penelope leads the man through the one main road in the village and then to the wild countryside beyond. The road turns to rock and dust underneath their feet, and the trees grow larger, midnight black. François' eyes dart to the bundle in his hands, but he says nothing.

Finally, down a track hidden by overgrown bushes, they reach a dilapidated house with weeds shooting up through the gravel pathway. Penelope treads carefully over the entrance. She guides François to the kitchen, where she reveals a trapdoor beneath a rucked-up carpet. Underneath it, something keens, the sound sending the glassware juddering in the cupboards.

François opens the trapdoor then hesitates.

"I would say he doesn't bite, but..." Penelope's smile widens as François flinches.

Gathering up her dress in one hand, she slides off her shoes and descends the ladder in bare feet. A faint smell of rot and something sweeter emanates from the hole, growing stronger as she descends. At the bottom, it's almost pitch-black, and there's only a dim outline of a figure hunched against the back wall.

"Tamriel."

The creature moans softly. But a voice reverberates through her head, sounding like broken wind chimes.

Star-daughter, you return to us.

"Once a year, as always. I have not forgotten the terms of our contract."

A pact from another lifetime, another world. Penelope and Tamriel survey each other in the darkness, weighing up the changes another year has marked on them. Time has not been kind to Penelope in many senses, but it has been abjectly cruel to the creature before her.

As is only fitting.

Penelope taps on the ladder twice, the sound ringing up to the top. A minute later, François descends, cradling her package. He shakes so badly, he almost drops it as he waits to hand it over.

"Your offering," Penelope says. "As promised."

The creature lifts its head, sniffing.

We smell blood, the taste of life at its most sweet. We must eat O WE MUST EAT.

"Then you shall feast," Penelope says.

With a sudden push, she thrusts François forward, into the creature's path. There is movement, razor-quick. A sharp tearing sound. Screams.

The room is suddenly filled with the copper tang of blood. For a while, there's nothing but the sound of snapping bones and slurping, tearing and gobbling. Penelope leans against the wall, waiting.

The creature sighs in a gust of blood and death. The smell of rot is overpowering.

They tasted of sunlight and heart-life, sky and morning dew and fear, O yes. We are still ravenous, but the hunger does not pierce us so deeply. Our gratitude is bestowed upon you.

"I didn't come here for gratitude," she says.

The creature sounds disappointed, even petulant. *Very well. We await your question, star-daughter.*

"Tell me what Marianne Everly is looking for. Tell me where she is."

There is a rumble of laughter. *A star-cursed woman plagued by a mortal problem. O how history repeats itself.*

"I will not be goaded by you, Tamriel."

It is the truth. She seeks the city of stardust. The beginning of the end.

"Elandriel," she breathes. "Still?"

The name is older than the dirt beneath their feet, like a snatch of melody with missing lyrics. It's been a long time since it's fallen from her lips, but she relishes the taste.

We tire of this game, star-daughter. The stars do not change their mind, no matter how many times we ask on your behalf. If the answer did not satisfy you then, it will not do so now.

Penelope raises an eyebrow. "Did the stars not change their mind when they cast you out? You, whose jewel was supposed to hang eternal in the night sky? Who swore to never tarnish the glory with which you were charged?" She smiles wryly. "The stars can be fickle, too."

And yet we will be here until time runs backwards, until we no longer recall our brethren, our crime, our selfsame personhood. We are astral, and our fates are not so mutable as the mortals with which you toy.

Penelope takes a step forward. "Marianne is close, then."

She is as close as the stars to the earth, the wind to the ocean depths. She is closer than you, O star-daughter. Tamriel laughs, a cavernous sound that scrapes the inside of the room.

Penelope's fists clench, and she takes another step forward. "Don't play riddles with me. I will have Marianne's whereabouts, one way or another."

O star-daughter, you presume too much of us.

Quick as lightning, the creature lashes out at her ankles. But Penelope is already back against the far wall, one hand on the ladder.

You have already exchanged for your truth, and we owe you no more than that, the creature says, amused. *You think we do not see you as you are, Astriade, daughter of Nemetor? We may wear different skins, but O, we are the same. We carry the same hunger, the same malice within our hearts. To ignore the call is to ignore the truth of ourselves.*

"Then you cannot answer my question. How disappointing."

Penelope starts to climb the ladder. But halfway to the top, Tamriel cries out in harsh, screeching laughter.

There will be others who go down this dark road to visit us, to sate our hunger and bring us offerings of the flesh. And they will ask of you. And we will answer.

Penelope pauses on the ladder. "The daughter?"

We have already told you before, she cannot seek what she does not know.

Penelope nods to herself. Then she smiles.

"It is distasteful sometimes to be reminded that we are kin, but you are right, dearest cousin. So when you fell, I opened my arms to you: I offered you a lifetime of protection in exchange for those questions. Have I not brought flesh to you, at great risk to myself? Have I not found you shelter?" She gestures to the dank basement around her. "And do not try to convince me you would prefer the alternative, *cousin.* I know as well as you where that road lies."

Tamriel hisses between his teeth, and in that hint of voice is the man Penelope might recall, if she cares to delve far enough into her memory. He jangles his chains softly, the strongest act of defiance he can muster for all his predatory speed. He would be stronger with more flesh, and there was a time when Penelope had weighed up what it would take to restore him to his former might, when such a thing still held possibility. Perhaps the astral would have proven a less reluctant ally.

Perhaps the monster would have outgrown his chains.

Star-daughter, we ... cannot deny your generosity. We are grateful, cousin, kin, that you remember us as your own.

"But if the skies are so immutable, as you claim, then your answers are of no use to me. Perhaps it is time we part ways, Tamriel." She shrugs, and if it weren't for the malice in her eyes, her smile would look genuinely apologetic.

You would not dare.

"You have killed your keeper," she says, "and there's no one to take his place. There will be no more feeding, no more visits. You may rattle your chains until the stars themselves are dead—or you may simply succumb to your hunger. But rest assured, you will never be given the opportunity to breathe a word of me to another." Her lips curl, savouring the moment. "Goodbye, Tamriel."

With that, Penelope leaves, slamming the trapdoor behind her.

Eleven

A FTER WHAT FEELS like the world's longest shift—two sets of screaming toddlers at an impromptu birthday party, whimsical sugar art that felt decidedly less so when she was cleaning it up, Matt off sick with some hideous cold— Violet cycles into the Everly driveway to see every light blazing against the darkness. Which can only mean one thing.

But before she can go hunting for Gabriel, Ambrose greets her in the doorway, his tired smile not quite meeting his eyes. He glances down the hall.

"Gabe's home," he says.

"I see that."

"He won't be here for long"—*of course*, Violet thinks—"but we've been invited to a soirée of sorts. Tonight." He pauses. "All of us."

Violet takes a couple of seconds to process this. "You want me to go to a party."

Ambrose, who wouldn't let her go to school, who barely even tolerates her working at the café, wants her to go to a *party*. She can believe in other worlds and magical keys, and even in Aleksander's miraculous weekly appearances, but this somehow feels like a stretch too far.

"It's from Gabriel's . . . how do I say this? Colleagues."

"You mean his criminal enterprise," she says.

It's an old joke between them, one that Violet's recently grown tired of. As a child, it was the only answer she could come up with for

Gabriel's extended travels, given her uncles' reluctance to tell her the truth. And Ambrose probably thought it was better for Violet to believe her uncle some mafioso wannabe. That Gabriel's long absences are to do with smuggling or drug-trafficking, forged identities and chests filled with stolen money. That they are illegal activities, but perfectly mundane.

Better to believe that, than an extraordinary truth.

"Gabe will tell you more, but before he gets hold of you, I wanted to talk." Ambrose lowers his voice. "These guests tonight... They're an odd bunch. Be careful, okay?"

Violet tilts her head to the side, puzzled. It could be Ambrose's usual fussy overprotectiveness, but she's rarely heard him sound so nervous, or so serious.

"Why, are you planning to ransom me off?" she says lightly. "Tell them I won't take less than two million. I'm worth that much, at least."

To her relief, Ambrose only sighs and rolls his eyes, morphing back into his familiar self. "Gabriel's in the kitchen."

Sure enough, Violet finds him at the kitchen table, already in a three-piece suit and looking every inch the mobster as he flicks through a hefty-looking folder, sunglasses propped on the bridge of his nose. He flips the folder shut as soon as he sees her.

"Ambrose tells me you're planning to ransom me to your criminal friends," Violet says conversationally, as she puts on the kettle.

Gabriel looks at her over his sunglasses. "No way, kiddo. Couldn't give you away even if I wanted to."

"What a relief," she says.

"He's right, though," Gabriel continues. "These people, they're not like you and me. Well," he amends, "maybe they're a bit like me. But they're wolves. And if I gave them even an inch, they would eat me up and carry you off."

"Then why invite me at all?" she says, frowning.

"One of my criminal friends would like to meet you. And Adelia Verne does not take no for an answer." He shrugs. "Sometimes when the wolves are at the door, you have to invite them in for canapés."

Violet tries to picture the "wolves" that Gabriel is so eager to entertain, but they remain a stubborn blank in her mind. If Ambrose had his way, they would be a sea of mobsters, with gold teeth and violin cases, eager to haggle over whatever illicit contraband Gabriel's smuggled back to the house. In a fanciful moment, she even imagines the guests as real wolves, unnaturally upright on their hind legs, licking blood from their dense fur. *Oh, what big teeth you have.*

Violet eyes his suit. "How fancy is this party?"

"Check your wardrobe," he says.

For a second after she leaves the kitchen, she stands in the corridor, waiting for her unease to fade. She hasn't forgotten the evening, all those years ago, when Gabriel was here, wearing the very same suit, his shirt spattered in blood. Her uncles have spent her entire life treating her like something to be kept away from the world. Why invite her to a party now?

Upstairs in her room, a dress in deep burgundy velvet with gold clasps at the shoulders and a thin satin sash across the waist is waiting for her. It's beautiful and regal, pulled straight from a fairy tale. Violet looks at it apprehensively. Is this what her uncles want to do—dress her up as a doll and parade her around a group of strangers?

She almost doesn't put it on. But then her hands trail over the soft fabric, admiring the gorgeous stitching, tiny gold threads shivering in the light. She bites her lip, wavering. She's never had a reason to wear something so luxurious, and she'll never have a chance to do so again. For all her wanting of elsewhere, Violet will forever be tethered to this house. Forever tethered to the sliver of possibility that her mother will still walk through the door one day—and the terror of missing it.

Maybe, just this once, she'll take the fairy tale.

When she tries it on and looks in the mirror, her hair falling around her shoulders in soft brown curls, her mother looks back at her. There are fragments of Violet's features that are decidedly non-Everly—dimpled cheeks, faint freckles across pale skin, a tint of gold in her hair—but for the most part, she's Everly through and through. *We*

Everlys have to stick together, Ambrose is forever saying. But not, apparently, tell each other the truth.

Whether her uncles like it or not, maybe there are answers tonight for her, too.

By the time they reach the ostentatious estate house, Ambrose and Gabriel bickering the whole way there, the eponymous *they* have already preceded them, one flashy car after another walling in the driveway. The guests move in a swathe of rich fabrics: silky white shirts, luxurious sequin-dusted coats, frothy dresses the colour of sea foam. As Violet steps over the threshold, she feels a stab of apprehension, a sense of just how many miles there are between her and these elegant, otherworldly creatures. They smile at each other with bright, shining teeth.

Wolves.

When she enters the house, straight into a cloud of perfume and cologne, she's not quite sure where to look first. Lilting music fills the ground floor, as an unassuming man in a tuxedo plays the grand piano. Drinks are poured and crystal glasses manoeuvred around the guests by a team of eerily efficient staff bearing silver platters. People crowd the ground floor, marble tile clicking underneath their stilettos and wingtip shoes. They all seem to know each other, circulating with smiles and nudges, like beautiful sharks. But with Gabriel and Ambrose flanking her like bodyguards, no one even attempts to make introductions.

Wisps of incomprehensible gossip float past her:

...expect to see a new intake of scholars any day now...

...and I told Adelia, no one simply vanishes from a convent in Moscow and reappears in Seoul two days later...

...I heard she's coming tonight with that assistant of hers, but I'm not holding my breath for...

...warmer at this time of year, how nice...

There's something oddly similar about the partygoers, but it takes her a moment to register it, between all the silk and sequins. She's stealthily filching a shrimp canapé when she catches a faintly ridged pattern on one of the guest's pristine shirts and it all comes together. Keys: dusting cuffs in silver thread, or strung from gold chains to rest in hollow throats—and tattooed on forearms, in black ink that seems to sparkle in the light. Keys like the one Aleksander showed her.

Her mind races back to the conversations she'd walked past moments ago. This isn't just any party—this is a party for *scholars*.

She turns to Ambrose, unable to disguise her shock. "You told me you'd never heard of Fidelis."

Gabriel stares at her. "How the hell do you know about that?"

"Apparently *you* told her, Gabe—" Ambrose mutters.

But Gabriel cuts him off. "She sure as shit didn't hear that from me."

"Then who—"

"The Everly brothers fighting at my party? Surely not."

An elderly woman comes up to them in a floor-length gown the colour of storm clouds. Diamonds the size of raindrops pour from a chain at her throat. Violet notices the thin black line of a key tattoo underneath translucent sleeves. Another scholar, she guesses.

"Adelia, this is Violet," Gabriel says impatiently. "Just like you asked. And in exchange?"

Adelia waves him away. "Oh yes, she's here somewhere, with that assistant of hers, no doubt." She turns to Violet. "Let me take a good look at you."

Violet has the distinct sense that she should be angry about being discussed like an object, but suddenly all of Adelia's attention is focused on her, and every thought vanishes from her head. Adelia's gaze roves over her with a clinical interest.

"Very talented," she says, apparently satisfied. "I wouldn't expect anything less from an Everly. Why don't we take a walk together, just the two of us?"

"I don't think that's a good idea," Ambrose begins.

"Oh, come now," Adelia says. "Surely you can spare her for a moment. Besides—"

The conversation ripples with interest, as a tall, pale woman sweeps into the room. Her flax-blonde hair is twisted expertly into a bun, secured by a gold clasp studded with emeralds, and her chiffon dress is the colour of sunlight, winking with clusters of seed pearls. But instead of reaching for a glass of champagne or greeting the other guests, she smiles at Violet. The other guests scatter, giving them a wide berth.

She looks naggingly familiar, but Violet can't quite place where. Like something out of a dream, too perfect to be real.

"It's been too long, little dreamer," she says with a beatific smile.

The shock of recognition hits her like a gut punch. Penelope. And behind her, looking surprised to see Violet here, of all places, is Aleksander. She catches a glimpse of his puzzled wave to her, before Penelope obscures her view.

"Those Everly eyes, just like your mother's." Penelope cocks her head to one side. "Gosh, don't you look like her."

"That she does," Gabriel says, with more than a hint of menace.

"Gabriel, Ambrose. I didn't expect to see you here." Her gaze slides from the brothers to Violet and Adelia. "I hope I'm not interrupting something."

Ambrose doesn't return the smile. "We need to talk. In private."

"Oh, how thrilling," Penelope says, sounding amused. "Well, whatever it is, I'm sure I'll be delighted to discuss it."

"Perfect," Adelia says, taking Violet's arm. "Then we shall leave you to it."

Ambrose looks like he wants to argue further, but Adelia is already steering Violet out of the brightly lit room. She catches Aleksander's gaze for just a second. Then they turn the corner, and the party vanishes from sight.

Twelve

A DELIA LEADS VIOLET down a series of long corridors, further away from the party. Violet knows she's supposed to make conversation, to try and ease the silence between them. But she's still reeling from the conversation with Ambrose and Gabriel. She should be thrilled to be here: a chance to learn more about the scholars, and the world that her uncles have been so desperate to hide from her. But not like this, with the sneaking suspicion that they've literally just *bargained* her away.

Adelia must sense her unease because she pats her on the arm. "I'm not going to spirit you off somewhere. For one, I'm much too old to fight your uncles."

Despite herself, Violet smiles. The thought of her uncles facing off against diminutive, elderly Adelia is an absurd image. But even as she pictures it, she glances at Adelia, with her steel grip and the quick intelligence behind her eyes, and her uncertainty returns.

"They asked for this invitation, you know. For themselves, that is," Adelia says conversationally. "And I thought, what better chance than now to meet you? After all, I've heard so much about you."

Violet frowns. "Really?"

"Of course. Marianne is a dear friend of mine."

Marianne. Violet freezes in a rictus smile to stop herself from reacting to her mother's name. Adelia says it with pure delight, as though she's talking about a long-lost family jewel. Violet can't recall Ambrose and Gabriel ever using that tone when discussing her mother.

"I—I wasn't aware," she says.

"No, I wouldn't think so. Your uncles made it very clear that they didn't want you involved. But you must forgive an old woman her curiosity."

They turn into a small reading room, with moonlight falling through a high window on the armchairs below. On any other occasion, Violet would appreciate her surroundings—the perfect hideaway for a book lover—but she can't stop replaying the conversation in her mind. Her uncles didn't want her involved. In what?

"How do you know my mother?" Violet asks carefully.

Adelia taps the tattoo on her forearm and smiles. "I was one of her teachers in Fidelis. And after she passed her exams, we were scholars together."

Violet's not sure she heard right. "Scholars?"

She guessed her mother would be a part of that world, from the bracelets and everything she's ever witnessed in the Everly house. But a scholar, like Aleksander—

"Just so," Adelia says.

A growing suspicion washes over Violet. "Have you seen her recently?"

Adelia's gaze turns sharp. "That's not for me to say." Then she brightens. "But enough of that. I also wished to introduce you to my grandson, Caspian."

A tall man unfolds from an armchair and stands up. "Caspian Verne." He holds out his hand. "It's a pleasure to meet you, Violet."

Violet takes his hand, dazed. "You know my name?"

A flicker of confusion crosses his face. "You're Marianne Everly's daughter. Everyone knows who you are."

Even though Violet knows no one—*is* no one. And…she'd thought Marianne was the same. She glances back at Adelia desperately; there are too many questions to ask, but the conversation is slipping from her grasp.

Adelia looks over them, and nods to herself. "Well, I will make my excuses and leave you. It's so hard for young people to make friends these days."

"Wait, I—" Violet begins.

But Adelia simply leans in for a hug. As she does so, she whispers, "Perhaps it's time you asked your uncles. Before it's too late to ask anything at all."

With that, she clasps Violet's hand once, and leaves.

The silence in Adelia's wake is thunderous. Violet desperately wishes she could follow her out, but Caspian smiles at her expectantly, and she has no idea how to extract herself from his company. She starts to put on her café face—an armour of charm against the most difficult customers—but it keeps slipping every time she returns to what Adelia said.

The implications of her words hover threateningly over Violet's head. Has Marianne been around all this time, and it's simply that she never wanted to return home? No, that can't be right. Her uncles have been willing to evade her questions for years, but they wouldn't lie to her about something as important as this.

They wouldn't.

Just as she's about to make her excuses and find her uncles, a crowd of people crash through the reading-room doors. They barely pause to take in Caspian before their gazes snap to Violet. She tries not to flinch as a woman in a deep blue backless dress strides towards her.

The woman does an affected double-take. "Marianne? It can't be—" She gathers herself. "But of course. You must be her daughter, Violet."

A man in a lavish velvet jacket pushes Caspian aside to join them. He places a heavy hand on Violet's shoulder that she tries and fails to surreptitiously shrug off.

"I wish I'd seen her in action." Despite his hand on Violet's shoulder, his attention is focused on the woman. "She used to run rings around the other scholars, I heard."

Another man wearing a cape sidles up to them. "No one could craft like her. Remember those exquisite timepieces she used to make for the engineers? And she'd do it easy as breathing."

"I was so envious," the woman says. "She was everyone's darling."

"What a waste. To throw it all away."

Mr. Velvet Jacket looks down at Violet, as though he's just noticed her there. "I can see great talents in your future, though. And we certainly won't squander those, hmm?"

Violet's heart starts to beat rabbit-quick. The guests have her pinned into a corner, and the man's hand weighs down heavily on her shoulder.

Suddenly, the weight lifts, and Mr. Velvet Jacket's arm is wrenched into the air by Caspian's tight grip.

He smiles pleasantly. "Roy, you know how much our grandmother hates it when you bother the guests."

Mr. Velvet Jacket shoots him a poisonous glare. "As if I need your permission—"

"Grandmother needs you upstairs." The smile becomes steely. "Or I could let her know you're too busy?"

Mr. Velvet Jacket—Roy—looks like he's about to argue again, but with an audible huff, he stomps out of the room, towards the stairs. Caspian looks pointedly at the other guests; one by one they mutter their excuses and leave.

"I apologise profusely for my cousin," he says. "Let's just say he doesn't get out much." He peers at her. "Are you okay?"

She tries to take a deep breath, but it feels like the oxygen has been sucked from the air around her. She needs to sit down. She needs to leave.

"A glass of water," she says. "Please."

Caspian's smile returns. "Of course—I'll be back momentarily. And don't worry about the others." He lowers his voice to a whisper. "I think she'll scare them off."

As he leaves, he gestures to a blonde woman admiring the bookshelf nearest the doorway, and Violet realises it's Penelope. Her dress sparkles underneath the warm lamps of the reading room.

Violet waits a few minutes—long enough for Caspian's footsteps to fade down the hallway—before she approaches the doorway. She has no intention of waiting around for Caspian to return, so she can be reminded over and over again how little she knows.

But Penelope stands in the middle, blocking her way. "You know, you really do look like your mother."

Normally Violet enjoys the comparison, but she's heard that one too many times tonight to find it flattering. She waits for her to move out of the way, but Penelope tilts her head to the side, with an expression that's not quite curiosity. Even though the room was bright moments ago, the lights seem to dim, and shadows throw spidery tendrils across the floor.

"I suppose you wouldn't know where Marianne's gone, after all these years."

Violet knows better than to say glibly, *Oh, she's on an adventure.* But there is something in Penelope's gaze that makes her hesitate to say anything at all.

"Not even an inkling. How curious."

"Whatever you've entangled my uncles in, that's between you and them," Violet says.

She won't give this woman—this stranger—the satisfaction of knowing that she's pressed a sore spot. Yet her mind wanders back to that stormy evening, the warm cedar scent of the wardrobe, Gabriel saying, *Violet is no longer a secret.*

Penelope smiles, as though she knows exactly what Violet's thinking. "I wonder if that's what Marianne thought. You should ask your uncles, Violet Everly."

The second time she's been told that tonight. But there's an anticipatory hunger about the way Penelope says it. Her eyes burn cold, and for a second, the shadows darken across the floorboards, fanning around her feet like wings.

Despite herself, Violet shivers. "About Marianne?"

Penelope's smile widens; a flash of teeth. "All of it."

Thirteen

VIOLET PACES DOWN the hallway of a house she doesn't know, surrounded by people she doesn't recognise, from a world that she barely understands. She was upset before, when the scholars had talked about her mother with the kind of familiarity that she'd only ever dreamed about. But the hard, tight knot of anger in the pit of her stomach is growing with every step, pushing out any other feeling.

Ask your uncles. As though she hasn't been asking them for years. All the secrets they've been so desperate to keep from her.

Violet finds them arguing quietly in a dark hallway, far from the revels in the main part of the house. Gabriel's expression is thunderous, but it's the shadows on Ambrose's face that unnerve her the most. A second later, she catches it for what it is: *fear*.

"So that's it, then," Gabriel is saying.

"I told you this was a bad idea," Ambrose says. "We should never have asked Violet to come."

"Then Adelia wouldn't have invited us, and by the time we saw Penelope again, it would be too late."

Ambrose pinches the bridge of his nose. "She was never going to give us more time, Gabe. We were lucky enough to get what we did."

"We had to at least try—unless you have a better idea, little brother?"

"There must be something else we can offer her. If you would just give me a minute to think—"

"You've had more than a goddamn minute. You've had *nine years*. And what the hell do we have to show for it?" Gabriel's expression darkens further. "If we had talked to Violet sooner—"

"But you didn't talk to me."

Violet steps forward, unable to contain herself any longer. The fury that's simmered in her all night roils in her veins. At every step, they have lied to her. But she had no idea how far it went.

If she'd never met Aleksander, if she'd never known about the scholars—would she have remained in the dark forever?

"You asked me to come, knowing that they would talk about Marianne. I was *bait*, and you didn't even tell me why." Her voice breaks, and she's all the more furious for it. "Marianne knew these scholars. So she went to Fidelis? Is that it? Is that why you lied to me —because you didn't think I could handle the truth?"

Ambrose glances uneasily down the hallway. "Why don't we talk about this at home. We can—"

Violet cuts him off. "Now. Or I'll find someone else here to ask."

Ambrose exchanges another desperate look with Gabriel.

"We were going to have to tell her eventually, little brother," Gabriel says.

"Do you really want to know?" Ambrose asks quietly.

She swallows. "I do."

They turn to her, so familiar she'd known them by their silhouettes alone in this dark corridor. But tonight, they seem like strangers.

"What does this have to do with Penelope?" she asks, a little more nervously than she intended.

Ambrose sighs and runs his hands through his hair. "As long as there have been Everlys, there has been Penelope," he begins slowly. "But it's more complicated than that. Our family are bound to her. We owe a debt."

"Our blood," Gabriel says, holding out his hand like an offering.

Violet has the brief but dizzying sensation of submerging into a dream. Of pinching herself and feeling the pain dissolve because there is no pain in sleep. But she remembers the way Penelope had looked at her, with such terrible hunger in her smile.

"Every generation, she takes the one of us with the most talent. The one who can manipulate the scholars' star-metal," Ambrose adds, seeing her confusion. "It doesn't work for all of us. I haven't got a drop of it in me—I wouldn't be able to walk between worlds."

"I can," Gabriel says unexpectedly. "But Marianne was the gifted one of us—and too powerful for the scholars to ignore. Not when so much of their city relies on their damn talent." He shrugs. "So Penelope trained her. *She* is supposed to be the next of us."

"Penelope is older and more dangerous than any of us can fathom. There's a lot we don't know," Ambrose admits. "But we made a pact. We promised each other—myself, Gabriel, and your mother—that the Everly line would end with us. The suffering would stop. Penelope would stop."

"Then Marianne met your father, whoever the hell he was. Didn't speak to us for two years, until she turned up on our doorstep with you," Gabriel snarls. "She was always selfish, even when we were kids. Whatever she wanted, she took. And—"

"We've all done things we're not proud of, Gabe," Ambrose says, a warning note in his tone. "None of our hands are clean."

Gabriel falls silent.

Ambrose clears his throat. "Anyway, Marianne was secretly looking for a way to undo the curse. She dug deep in the scholars' archives, and found . . . something. Written in a cypher, which was maybe why it had been overlooked in the first place. But when you were born, she had to flee Fidelis, taking the research with her. Penelope had no idea you existed, you see. It was a chance to keep you safe."

Violet tries to imagine her mother slipping between worlds, a baby cradled in her arms. With a dull shock, she realises the implications of his words. She was born in Fidelis. Another city—another *world*.

"It took her years to understand the documents she'd taken, but eventually she cracked the cypher. And it was big, Vi. Game-changing. A key to . . . another world. Not here, or Fidelis, but somewhere else. A place that could help us remove the curse. She wouldn't tell us more than that," he says.

"As if her own brothers couldn't be trusted," Gabriel says scornfully.

Violet stands there in silence, trying to comprehend everything she's learnt. It all sounds like make-believe, and yet so many conversations are slotting into place. *I've been so stupid.*

"Nine years," she says in disbelief, recalling Gabriel's earlier outburst. "You waited nine years to tell me this."

She turns to leave, but Ambrose follows suit. "You were a child when she left, Violet. What else was I supposed to do? It was all just another story to you. If you'd had any notion—no, it would have been too cruel. And," he adds reluctantly, "we thought Marianne would be back by now."

A terrible silence falls over them.

"So where is she?" she asks. "Is she in Fidelis?"

Ambrose and Gabriel look at each other.

"We really don't know. That's the truth," Ambrose says. "We haven't heard directly from her in years."

"Penelope is still looking for her," Gabriel adds. "And that means she doesn't know where Marianne is, either."

"So wherever she is, she's still safe from Penelope," Ambrose says.

A cold, sinking feeling hits the pit of Violet's stomach. "If she's gone, why are you still tiptoeing around this...this Penelope? What did you mean, *more time*? If Marianne isn't coming back, I don't understand why—"

"She still needs an Everly," Gabriel says, and it's with such a gentle tone that goosebumps prickle Violet's arms. "There's time left, but not much of it. That's why we need to find Marianne. To break Penelope's hold over us."

Those Everly portraits on the walls. Young men and women, forever.

"No." Violet's hands are shaking. "That's not true. That can't be true."

She thinks about the way Aleksander flipped the napkin between his hands, showing her the way to Fidelis. Two sides. Magical and mundane. Light and shadow.

Fairy tales...and the curses that come with them.

"Vi, listen to me," Ambrose says urgently. "The scholars are dangerous. Why do you think we kept you at home for so long? We wouldn't have brought you here unless we had no choice. You can't tell anyone about this, understand? If you did—"

"I don't owe you anything!" Her gaze sweeps across them both, disgusted. "You lied to me. About all of this."

She's spent half the evening trying to get back to her uncles, but now she can't bear to spend even a second more with them. She pushes past them, back towards the party. Let them argue over the best way to keep her in the dark. Fuck them both.

"Violet!" Ambrose says.

Gabriel shakes his head. "Let her be."

A curse is just a story, just a fairy tale to frighten children into good behaviour, to mistake coincidence for causality, to explain why a mother would leave her child without so much as a backwards glance.

So much she doesn't know, and may never understand. And the box in her head that she can't bear to even look at—the one that has her mother's eyes, her warm laughter—rips open, spilling hurt like blood.

She stumbles back into the party, and into the sea of strangers. But after the dim hallways, the room is too bright, the guests' laughter sharp and high-pitched. They eye her with bright hunger, and she hears a name on their lips. *Marianne. Marianne Everly. Her daughter.*

Everywhere she looks, there are people she doesn't recognise. And yet they all know her name. A molten anger slides around her gut, and suddenly her skin feels too tight, pins and needles shooting through her fingers. Caspian Verne makes towards her, holding a glass of water as promised, but she can't bear the thought of more "conversation."

Spotting a break in the flow of people, Violet bolts for the wide back doors and through them, outside. Lanterns light up the patio, casting a honey glow across the flagstones, but the rest of the garden is swathed in velvety darkness, the moon soft and hazy against the clouds. From here she can see straight through the house's enormous arched windows, framing the party like a painting come to life.

Dropped-waist dresses and frothy tulle skirts—wolves with expensive taste, clearly.

Wolves who know Marianne Everly.

Her hands grip the skirt of her dress tightly, crushing the fabric.

A figure slips out from the back doors to join her, and she tenses before realising who it is. It seems impossible that Aleksander should exist out of his weekly appearances at the café, that they should be meeting like this. Out of everyone tonight, even her uncles, only he looks the same as he always does, even if he's swapped out his casual clothes for a slightly ill-fitting suit and smart shoes.

"I thought I'd never find you," he says, then he glances at her face and his smile fades. "What's wrong?"

She opens her mouth to tell him everything—and stops. He's Penelope's assistant. Even if she's still furious with her uncles, a faint alarm bell sounds in her head.

"Did you know?" she says.

He stares at her. "Know what?"

"About Penelope, my uncles—all of it. Did you *know*?"

But he looks at her blankly. "I have no idea what you mean. Violet, what happened?"

Her shoulders slump. Of course he doesn't know. She can't decide if it's a relief or a disappointment.

"Take me to Fidelis," she says suddenly, taking his hand.

He blinks. "What?"

"Don't tell me you've never thought about it," she says. "Because I have, every single day you've walked into the café."

"I—I can't." Gently, he pulls his hand away from hers. "I would love to, but..."

"Then why all of this?"

He blinks. "What do you mean?"

"Why visit the café? Why tell me what Fidelis looks like, how the keys work?"

Why tell her everything and then keep the door shut?

Ambrose, Gabriel, and now Aleksander. Everywhere she turns, no one will give her answers.

Something flashes across Aleksander's face, too quick for her to identify it. Then he spreads his hands out. She notes several tiny scars across his knuckles, silvery puncture wounds like constellations.

"You asked," he says simply. "Violet, you asked me and I told you. If I could take you across, I would." He laughs to himself, without humour. "But only scholars get to make that call."

"And aren't you a scholar?" she demands. "What about you is so different to the other people at this party, right now?"

She knows she's pushing him. All the times she's ever heard him talk with such reverence about wanting to be a scholar. The way he's looking at her now, as though she is slowly twisting a knife through him. But she doesn't care. There's no one left to ask.

Tears burn at the back of her throat. "Marianne is *gone*. If it was Penelope missing, if it was your whole world, wouldn't you do anything to get her back?"

For a moment, Aleksander is silent, and she worries she's gone too far.

"What do you mean, Marianne is missing?" he says quietly.

Violet shrugs miserably. "Exactly that. No one will tell me, but... I think she's in Fidelis. So that's where I need to go."

Ambrose and Gabriel have spent nearly a decade looking for her. And Violet thinks of all the clues she left behind: the book of fairy tales, the reveurite bracelets. Where else would she be?

Aleksander touches the side of her face, the warmth startling in the cold night. She finds his other hand, and laces her fingers through it.

"And you would do anything to find her?" he asks.

"Anything," she whispers.

"Okay," he says.

She glances up, startled. "Okay?"

"Not tonight," he says, glancing back at the brightly lit windows. "But yes, I'll do it. I'll take you to Fidelis."

Fourteen

T HERE IS ONE week every year when Fidelis shakes off the cold and becomes something ancient and daring. An enigmatic smile of a city. People don starry crowns and paper wings, pluck multi-stringed instruments, steal a kiss from their beloved or beg an extra pinch of luck for the forthcoming year.

Illios's Blessing. The week novices are made into scholars.

The week that Aleksander normally dreads. He can hardly bear to watch another cohort of scholars go through with their newly inked tattoos and shared, secretive smiles. The way their expressions change when they see him, knowing how complete his failure is. But tonight it's different.

Tonight, he is going to steal Penelope's key.

He would never dare to ask her for it outside of her pre-approved outings—and he can't, not after she's been so adamant about keeping the Everlys and Fidelis separate. *You can tempt her with Fidelis, but that is all,* she'd said. But after months of visiting the café, Aleksander finally has a lead on Marianne Everly. If he can get Violet to trust him, if he can just pull this off correctly, he'll fulfil Penelope's request. She'll see that he hasn't outgrown his usefulness.

And if he feels a little guilty about using Violet's trust like this—well, it's something he can live with, if it means he'll be a scholar. Surely there's nothing so terribly wrong if they both get what they want?

Tonight, the mountain's song is drowned out by preparations for Illios's Blesssing. Instead of their usual chores, novice and assistant scholars clear away the snow in the square so that the mosaic tiles gleam. Forge bearers string up tiny beads of reveurite that glow like stars, while the masters build the enormous effigy of a winged creature in the centre, muttering to themselves secretively over the hidden fireworks display within. Coffee houses open late, stalls are erected, and fortune tellers pull out their cards, still glittering with reveurite dust from the previous year.

It's an unspoken rule that Aleksander has the week off, as long as he doesn't ask questions. In all the years he's known her, Penelope's never attended, despite the importance of the ritual. Instead she simply vanishes into the city. He doesn't know where she goes, but she's not in her chambers, the archives, or anywhere else he's surreptitiously searched. Yet she's in Fidelis somewhere; twice he's had to fetch something from her rooms—a forgotten notebook, a misplaced scarf—and seen her key hanging from its hook.

When he was eleven, and only two months into his overwhelming new role, he'd asked her where she went. He felt it before he saw it: fire blooming across his cheek, her hand raised to strike again. And when he looked up, he saw the wrath of a goddess, elemental fury. Penelope's eyes were the flat blue of a glacier.

"Do not make me regret you," she said.

So, no questions. But tonight offers him the perfect chance to steal her key: any number of distractions to keep the other scholars occupied; Penelope away to wherever she goes; and best of all, the kind of night Violet will love. Even though he's bringing her for a mission, rather than revelry. Normally, he'd be nervous of discovery.

Not that it'll matter, though, he thinks, trying to smooth away his worries. Because he won't get caught.

For most of the day Aleksander clears away snow from the streets, his back aching with the effort. Then, as afternoon draws to a close, he joins the other revellers to work on their costumes. These are thin strands of copper wire twisted into loops for wings, with feathers cunningly pieced together out of scrap paper, silk and fraying linen. With a few clever tricks, the resulting creations are surprisingly convincing, fluttering in the breeze.

The novices cluster around one another, adjusting wire crowns and pulling stray threads from fabric feathers. The crowns are always elaborate affairs: golden circlets ringed with tiny stars, diadems of leaves dipped in silver, bands speckled with painted constellations. Aleksander puts hasty touches on a simple band for himself. No one comes over to adjust his wings or remark on his handiwork, but he's used to that, and tonight he's banking on it.

On any other year, he would put more effort in; it's rare he gets a night away from Penelope, and rarer still that it isn't filled with another chore. But his mind keeps returning to the highest floors of the scholars' tower, and the bend in the corridor that snakes towards Penelope's chambers.

In the evening, he peels away from the crowd and makes his way against the tide of people surging towards the lower tiers of the city, past the greenhouses and the airship docks. Another load of visitors from the valley's farmland disembark the aerial lifts, half of them complaining about the cold.

The scholars' staircase is unusually empty, though there are still scholars milling about, finishing up work or descending to the festival, already tipsy. His hands are sweaty with nerves, and he hastily wipes them on his cloak. There's no reason to be concerned about their sidelong stares; in fact, he'd be worried if one of them smiled at him. Still, it's as if every scholar can see straight through his head, as he turns the corner to the uppermost corridor, where only a single set of rooms live.

Penelope's quarters feel empty without her presence, as though she takes a piece of furniture with her every time she leaves. Without her, it's just another series of rooms, stark in their ordinariness. Although she must have travelled to countless cities, there are no souvenirs, no knick-knacks or maps. He'd asked about this, too, when he was younger, right before Penelope had told him the story of the singing blade.

"That world is full of pretty things, isn't it?" she agreed. "But it's an impure, poisoned beauty. They have forgotten the stars above, the gods." She ruffled his hair with unexpected affection. "Better that we remember who we are—where we really belong. That world is not for us, little dreamer."

If that world isn't for Aleksander, then why has he spent so long trying to prove that he belongs in this one?

He can't spend the rest of his life in the shadow of all the things he's not, all the deficiencies the scholars have impressed upon him. Not from the right family—or any family at all, for that matter—not grateful enough, too eager to please, too quick to ask the wrong questions.

That damning voice inside his head whispering, *they are right*.

This will change everything. It has to.

Penelope's key hangs in a cupboard in the antechamber before the travelling room. Aleksander wipes his hands on his cloak again, and then opens it. Every key is unique, handcrafted by a forge master at the height of their talent and skill, twisted into being from reveurite. Most are embellished with fanciful whorls and tiny etchings, veined with gold or silver and strung on a necklace with precious gems. Some are even imprinted with quotes from long-dead poets, or the names of the stars that were once said to walk amongst mortals. But Penelope's is stark and straight, a harsh line glittering onyx under the light.

Heart in his throat, he reaches for it.

There is a jagged crevasse on the fringe of the mountain range that rings Fidelis, unsoftened even by snow. To come here is strictly forbidden; the ruins are dangerous, and more than one life has been lost to the icy abyss, as crumbling paths give way. What remains clusters on precipitous cliffsides that sheer off to a steep drop wreathed in fog. Every so often, a building falls into the crevasse, succumbing to time at last. Beyond—nothing except the horizon. It's as though the ancient city remains were cleaved in two, leaving absence where land should exist.

Penelope stands on the remnants of a bridge, staring at the edge where it crumbles into oblivion. Underneath her feet, the stone has been worn smooth by time. The wind howls around her, glittering with the porous haze between one world and another.

The city is on the precipice of change. She feels it like pressure in the atmosphere, squeezing down on them. The people of Fidelis have grown complacent in their little refuge, replacing history with legend and then fairy tale. There is nothing left to remind them who they once were: travellers, warriors, worshippers of the gods that walked amongst them. Nothing to remind them of their true home, so close and yet so far from this pale imitation. If she closes her eyes and outstretches her palm, she can almost imagine the whole of the half: the city that it should be, and not the fragment that it is.

Then there is Marianne Everly.

Marianne, who stole decades' worth of research, and vanished like a thief in the night, taking the last possible answers to a centuries-old problem with her.

A key. Such a small thing, and yet how Penelope's life has unravelled because of it.

But Penelope has spent generations watching the Everlys fight and die for one another. She knows what would drive a mother to leave her child, and what would compel her home. And if the Everly brothers still remain in the dark on her innermost secrets—well, that is no terrible thing.

Let Violet be the bait that brings her mother out of hiding, along with her research. Let Penelope devour them both.

Marianne Everly may have turned her back on Fidelis, and the promises she made.

But she cannot outrun a god forever.

In the alleyway behind the café, Violet waits for Aleksander. He's supposed to be here by now. Maybe he's running a little late. She runs her hands nervously across the brick wall, thinking of her fairytale book with the street names she's worked so hard to memorise. Every time she closes her eyes, her mind conjures up a city before her, leaning on everything she's gleaned from her conversations with Aleksander.

She deliberately doesn't think about Ambrose and Gabriel. She's ignored Ambrose's half-hearted attempts to apologise when they both know very well he isn't sorry at all. Gabriel has already left, either too cowardly to face her, or too indifferent to stay.

The sky shifts from a glorious winter blue to pastel orange and pink as the last of the day's sunlight washes away. The moon rises slowly, stark against the darkness. Violet paces up and down to stave off the cold.

Pink to violet to indigo. Violet starts to shiver, but she keeps waiting. Even at midnight, as she reluctantly starts to wheel her bicycle out of the alleyway, she keeps an eye out for a tall silhouette— Aleksander rushing from whatever has kept him so occupied.

But he never arrives.

Fifteen

T HE NEXT DAY, Violet waits for Aleksander to meet her at the café, but he doesn't appear. Or the day after. She starts to worry that maybe she said something—or that she's somehow misconstrued their friendship. He isn't beholden to her, after all. He might easily have changed his mind again.

And there's so little she knows, *really* knows about him.

On her lunch break, she sits at the table she's come to think of as theirs—with the excellent view of the river—and morosely pours sugar into her coffee. Outside, it's pouring with rain and the window is foggy with condensation.

A shadow falls over her table, as a tall, slim woman sits down opposite her.

"Hello, little dreamer," Penelope says. "My, haven't you been busy."

Penelope might not be wearing a chiffon dress winking with jewels, but Violet recognises her immediately. She glances around to make sure no one else is listening. But the café is bustling as ever, and no one even thinks to look their way. Her muscles coil with tension.

"Where's Aleksander?" she asks immediately.

Penelope doesn't answer. Instead, she surveys the scene around them, toying with a milk stirrer. Not for the first time, it occurs to Violet that Penelope looks exactly as she did the day she walked into the Everly house. Immutable.

"I see why he liked to come here," Penelope says. "It has a certain charm, I suppose, in its ordinariness. It must be an easy place to discuss all sorts of things. After all, what's one singular secret amongst so much gossip?"

Worry flutters in Violet's stomach. "Where is he?"

"He won't be returning, I'm afraid."

"Then why—"

"Why am I here?" Penelope looks straight at her, and Violet has the sudden, dizzying sensation of staring into an abyss. "He told me everything."

Horror envelopes her. "No. He—he wouldn't."

"Oh, but he did."

Violet has spent the past few months wondering why Aleksander kept coming back to the café, why he'd been so willing to share his easy, open-hearted smile and Fidelis' magic. She thought it was friendship.

She should have known better.

Penelope's eyes narrow. "I am only going to ask this question once. Where is your mother?"

A feeling like icy water runs down Violet's spine.

"I don't know," she says.

"Odd, isn't it? You don't know where she is. Your uncles don't know where she is. And yet you Everlys are like bees, always working to the same purpose. Always trying to escape justice."

Panicked, Violet tries to catch Matt's eye, but when she sees him, she reels back in shock. The entire café is suspended in motion: Matt, midway through bringing coffee to a table; her manager with his mouth wide open, berating someone on his phone; a woman with two toddlers, their arms frozen in a wide arc. Penelope's shadow elongates behind her, bleeding across the linoleum. Violet's skin feels tight, itchy with panic.

"Your family is cursed, Violet Everly." Penelope's mouth curls. "Cursed to walk into the dark, a devil beside them. Or I suppose that's the story your uncles told you. But tilted on its side, a curse is a fitting punishment for a terrible crime, is it not?"

Violet has to get out of here. She slides back in her chair—or tries to. Penelope snatches her hands, pinning them to the table.

"The curse isn't real," Violet says. "And you're crazy if you believe that."

A flash of annoyance crosses Penelope's face. But then she smiles softly. "Do you really believe the curse isn't real? That the divine never touches you? That the wheeling cosmos is but an abstract of chemicals? Do you not hear the stars sing, little dreamer?"

Violet tries to pull away, but Penelope's grip on her hands is too tight. Her mouth is dry with sudden fear. Her bones crack under the weight of Penelope's hands.

"Your family owe a debt. Blood. It should have been Marianne, of course, but now...there is *you*." She smiles at her, teeth bared like fangs. "Would you like to know what happens?"

Penelope presses down harder, and searing pain races across Violet's knuckles. Something gives way and she cries out involuntarily.

"You will be taken to Fidelis, like you so desperately wish. You will be escorted to a tower, where no one will hear you scream, or weep, or beg for mercy, as so many of your pathetic kin have done. And you will be drained of your blood, week by week, until only a corpse remains."

"No," Violet whispers.

But she has always known, deep down inside. Since before her uncles told her the truth, before she ever even caught a glimpse of the extraordinary world alongside her own. The Everlys go into the dark with death beside them—and they do not return.

She will not return.

"No?" Penelope says softly.

Abruptly, she releases Violet, leaving long red fingerprints streaked across her skin. She stands up and makes her way through the frozen customers. For one hopeful moment, Violet thinks she might be leaving. But instead, she stops at Matt, his eyes fixed ahead, unseeing.

"His name is Matt, isn't it?" Penelope strokes the side of his face, brushes sandy hair out of his eyes. "Your closest friend here. Maybe your only friend. Aleksander told me all about him."

Violet's breath catches in her throat. "He has nothing to do with this."

"Oh, I know," Penelope says. "But as they say, seeing is believing. Observe."

She slashes her hand across Matt's throat. There is an awful, wet, meaty sound, before she pulls back, her arm slick and red. Blood sprays in a violent arc across the floor. Violet tries to scream, but she can't seem to get enough air in her lungs.

"Your uncles can squirrel you away in that mansion of yours," Penelope says. "They can dress you up and parade you around as normal. For the rest of your life, you can even pretend to be one of them. But you cannot ignore the call of the stars. And as you hear their song, so too must you answer to them."

She snaps her fingers, and the motionless café rouses in a burst of sound. There is a split second of normality—a second in which Violet thinks the damage will reverse, that the world will continue on uninterrupted—before Matt collapses, coffee cups shattering around him. Chaos erupts: someone calls for an ambulance; someone else faints; one of the customers is noisily sick, as another leaps out of their chair to assist him. But Violet can barely hear anything above the sound of her own pulse, hammering with terror.

From the doorway, Penelope surveys the scene calmly, her arm gloved in bloody red. No one else looks at her.

"There is a year on your contract, Violet Everly. And if Marianne isn't found, then it will be you walking through the dark with me."

CHAPTER

Sixteen

P ENELOPE'S SHADOW WEIGHS heavily on the Everly house tonight, as what remains of the family reconvene in a desperate attempt to scrape together a plan. There is talking, arguing when talking fails, and subsequently silence, as each Everly considers how best to persuade the others of *their* plan.

Then, one by one, the Everlys depart.

Gabriel Everly is the first. He parks his ugly, expensive car in the garage and pulls a key from the chain underneath his shirt. Like most of his valuable possessions, the key once belonged to someone else, though it's been some time since the owner cared about its whereabouts. He glances behind him, noting the dark outlines of his brother and niece at the window, then turns the key in the side door of the garage. It shouldn't make any sound at all—the lock has been broken for years—and yet it clicks. Blue light unfurls at the edges, and a chilly winter wind wraps around Gabriel's legs from the gap underneath the door.

He takes one last look at the house. Then he opens the door, and vanishes.

Ambrose Everly packs two bags, ready to go into the trunk of a much less remarkable—and indeed, less ugly—car. One for himself, and one for Violet. Their destination is on no map he knows of and eventually they'll have to abandon the car to trek the rest of the way on foot, but it's safe, which is all that really counts. For a time, anyway.

As Ambrose packs upstairs, Violet Everly sneaks down to the library. Carefully, the way Gabriel taught her, she picks a lock on

Ambrose's desk drawer and steals a notebook. He thinks she hasn't noticed the way he locks himself in here for hours at a time, or how protective he's been over this one particular drawer.

Moonlight shimmers against the windowpane as she flicks through it. Names, places, contact numbers. Half of them are crossed out in firm red pen, but there are several with promising question marks next to them, and a handful of Ambrose's notes.

Saw M last.

Bought map from him? G says stole—unsure.

Won't answer phone. New line? Threatened?

Where is she???

Back in her bedroom, Violet pushes open her window and shimmies through it into the pouring rain. She hasn't done this since she was a teenager—hasn't needed to—but something tells her that her uncles won't just let her walk out the front door. And she can't forgive them for keeping the truth from her. If they'd told her, maybe Matt would still be alive. Maybe she would have been able to do something besides *sit there*, useless and terrified.

She readjusts the backpack on her shoulders, weighed down with everything she can carry. Her lock picks, her clothes, the stolen notebook—and her green silk-bound book of fairy tales, to give her courage. She slides down the drain pipe, hands in a death grip, until her feet land in the flower bed. Rain falls in fat droplets, and her hair is quickly plastered to the back of her neck.

No one puts up a fight like an Everly. And if a year is all she has, then she'll damn well do something with it. No more waiting in this empty, grey house, eavesdropping on her uncles, hoping for a miracle that'll never arrive. No more *sitting around*.

Marianne is out there. And when Violet finds her, they'll triumph. It's inevitable.

Curses, after all, are made to be broken.

Deep in the bowels of the scholars' tower, there is a place which does not belong to the scholars. It has lain in slumber for centuries, unheeding of the stone dungeons above it, the sewer systems, the kitchens and baths, the novice dormitories and the assistants' quarters—the hidden foundation to a many-tiered organism. It may have once appeared on an architectural diagram or in the very earliest records tucked in the archives. But one by one, these articles have been recorded as lost, misplaced or otherwise destroyed, so that there are truly no records left. Even the night attendants, who stitch their own mouths closed in servitude to the scholars' tower and whose skin is blurred with tattoos of devoted scripture, have no knowledge of this room.

Light does not penetrate here. And the smell is of stale air, threaded with decay. The ground is deep mountain stone, slick and marbled with grey-green lichen. Yet the walls suggest that this room used to be known. Figures dance along the room in red paint, or blood, cradled in the bowl of what could be a sun, its rays shooting spindles outwards.

In the darkest part of this already dark room, there is a door, or what remains of it. Hammered reveurite, thick as stone in some places, has worn away to paper thin in others. An inscription flows over the door, barely more than gentle ridging, and almost incomprehensible, even to those who speak the centuries-dead language. Curiously, although it is obviously a door, there is no keyhole—only two iron hands outstretched, as though waiting for an offering.

For a long time, Penelope sits on the stone floor, her forehead pressed to the cool metal of the door. She runs her hands over the inscription, long memorised by her fingers even if the language is no longer one she speaks aloud. That language, and the world to which it belongs, lies through a doorway beyond this door. There are no other ways home; if there is a crueller punishment, she can't conceive of it.

In the beginning, she used to believe she could hear singing beyond it, the familiar hum of her brethren that made her weep with want. Then it faded to a thrum that rattled her bones. Now, she hears nothing.

But she remembers the sound like it was five minutes ago, like it's still escaping the edges of the doorway.

There's a lot from those days that she still recalls.

One day, this door will open. And she will be the first to step through it.

Not Marianne Everly.

PART TWO

An Old Story

I F THERE IS a god they worshipped, it was her.

They say she was born of the stars. That she was so beautiful it hurt to look at her, and prolonged exposure could permanently blind you. That she was powerful and true, wielding retribution and mercy like dual swords of divine justice.

From the stars she brought reveurite, element of the gods. She taught a gifted few to work it, manipulating it on their anvils with tools of palladium and cobalt. Around their forges, a city sprang up. They carved reveurite doors across worlds, and invited others with the talent of wielding god-metal to join them. Whitewashed buildings appeared overnight as travellers set down their bags to stay, building on top of ancient foundations so that from a distance, the city looked like a tiered wedding cake. The forges blossomed, and at night, their fires burned like stars.

The dream catcher looked on in satisfaction, her plan at work just as it should be: a city of dreamers—pruned and nurtured, and occasionally weeded of threats, but one that thrived under her careful touch.

And then, something happened that was *not* part of her plan.

She fell in love.

He holds no name, no face, blinding or otherwise. Some say he was mortal; others insist he, too, was kin to stars. Most agree he had a way with his hands, a craftsman's care that drew her to him. Although he didn't know it, he held her heart on a string, and she found herself attuned to every tug that dragged him away, every slackening that meant he was near.

Eventually, she visited him at his forge. For a while she watched him work, with no more than an indifferent gaze. But as time went on, she showed him the deeper secrets of reveurite crafting, which had passed amongst her kind and no further until now. How to create galaxies in glass bottles, or jewelled music boxes that would play the siren call of the stars. How to forge blades of reveurite that never dulled or broke, no matter the strain. How to unlock the doors to other worlds, with elaborate keys that glittered on their chains. And all the while, his heart felt hers, an insistent pull.

They say his hands were still covered in reveurite when he could resist no longer and grasped her waist, her thighs, so there were imprints of his fingers forever tattooed on her skin. They say he pulled her into the forge with him, and they made love amongst the flames like ethereal creatures of old. Or—if he is mortal in this version—they say he led her towards his bed, with its hand-stitched sheets and soft pillows, and made her feel human as she'd never felt before, and never would again. That he smiled at her with his eyes crinkled around the edges, a lifetime of wear and tear she would never know.

In the forge, or in his bed, she whispered, *This will be our knowledge alone to bear.*

As time passed, they married in secret, dipping their hands in reveurite dust to place the delicate tattoos of fidelity and love on the soft curve of their shoulders. And for a year and a day, they lived like this. Hot and dizzy with passion at the moon's apex, leaving them scorched and smouldering during the day. Their marriage bore a child, with clever hands and curious eyes, and the song of the stars thrumming in their heart.

But nothing lasts forever.

There is a day, an argument, a reckoning. Maybe he grew older, and saw how she could not. Or maybe the dream catcher, with her fatal foresight, saw the end of everything, and wished to preserve him as he was. Maybe he wished for a child who wouldn't carry the legacy of a god. Maybe there was infidelity on her side, on his. Maybe a curse from the stars themselves.

Maybe many things.

But a year and a day after their secret marriage, a fury grew within the dream catcher until it could be contained no longer. And she ripped their world apart. Streets buckled, houses reduced to ruins. Lives obliterated in an instant, as the city rent in two.

Those who could escape through the doors did so, their gifts scattered like ash over thousands of worlds. And they forgot their skills, or failed to pass them on, generations of history lost in a moment.

Dream catcher. Star swallower. City destroyer.

Some say she lost her mind, in the end—that in her despair, she returned to the stars, her tears the constellations. Others say she is still trapped in the city, her voice vanished from a millennia of screaming. But most believe she roams countless worlds, immortal and invulnerable, a solitary wraith with vengeance for a heart.

Yet another version of the story suggests that the man, too, wanders the earth, made immortal through her wrath, if he was ever mortal to begin with. And it is he whom she searches for, her heart still attached to his. Whether to ease the pull of the thread, or to sever it altogether, no one can say.

Seventeen

RMED WITH A stolen notebook and stubborn hope, Violet Everly is on a quest.

It helps to think of it that way. After all, a quest is a kind of adventure, isn't it? And a quest always ends in the *finding*: the grail, the sword, the key. The woman who vanished into thin air over a decade ago, leaving a target on her daughter's back.

This is what she tells herself in dingy train stations, on dark streets, under bus shelters dripping with rain. With the battered notebook to guide her, she moves from country to country like her passport's burning a hole in her pocket, eating away at generational Everly wealth with every ticket stub. In Rome, she learns that her mother was reserved and travel-worn. In Accra, the contact, an old friend of Gabriel's, recognises her bracelets. In Mumbai, a teenager steals out of his house in the middle of the night to hand her a new list of names and addresses to try. *You look just like her*, she's told, over and over again. But other times, she arrives to empty houses, shuttered apartments, or people who refuse to let her in.

"No bloody Everlys here, thanks!" a man in Melbourne shouts through his letterbox. "Tell Marianne to go fuck herself."

Sometimes, she pauses on a quiet road or in the middle of a crowd, caught by certain details. A familiar laugh. A dark-haired man framed in a shop window, the glass warping her vision. Or it's the sound of a key turning in a lock, and a person disappearing from the crowd.

Every time she tells herself it's not worth looking, that it was *him* who abandoned *her*, at a monster's behest. There are days where she resists and spends hours afterwards wondering if she shouldn't have; there are days where she caves and turns around, only to feel foolish when she locks eyes with a stranger. But still, she senses it: a prickle between her shoulder blades, a mirrored step in time with her own. The unsettling sensation of being watched.

A year quickly trickles away. To six months, then three.

Ambrose leaves her long, panicked voicemails, begging her to come home, to go with his original plan and vanish into some safe house. She ignores them, the way she ignores Gabriel's curt text messages telling her that she's a bloody fool. If she's ever swayed to consider replying, all she has to do is remember the way they'd looked at her when she'd asked about Fidelis, the lies stacked upon lies until it was a wonder that she'd ever believed any of it.

But she had, fully and terribly. And she can never forgive them for it.

Then, inevitably, there are the scholars. She learns the family names, their endless squabbles and shifting alliances. That to talk to a Matsuda about the Persauds is to court a fist fight, that the Hadleys employ bodyguards for good reason, while the Quintrells are disdained by just about everyone, including their own extended family. That Marianne wove between the families with a politician's slippery touch and a spy's predilection for betrayal.

No one knows if her mother found what she was looking for, or where she went next. It's as though Marianne Everly stepped through the space between worlds—and vanished, taking every trace of her journey with her.

And always, Violet feels time breathing against her ear, pressing a knife into the small of her back. Now it's just six weeks—time she could tick off on her fingers, that she could fritter away or count out wisely like hard-won savings, but that she spends anyway because she has no choice. A small voice suggests that perhaps now, while there is still a chance to live, to see the world, she should let Marianne go, and trust that her mother will find the solution.

Or ... because this is all that's left. And even if she can't experience the mountain song of Fidelis, she should still see *something*, before the deadline swallows her whole.

Time, she has discovered, wears Penelope's smile.

Eighteen

UNDERNEATH THE NIGHT-STREAKED sky of New York City, Violet is crashing a party. Strictly speaking, it's infiltration via a stolen invitation and a borrowed dress that's definitely meant for a taller, bustier woman. Occasionally, she glances towards the brightly lit street to make sure no one is watching her as she adjusts her horribly itchy wig: black to cover up her true hair colour. But this is the beauty of New York—anonymity is a right.

There are other things she loves about the city: the dazzling theatres, the sheer volume of tiny restaurants and takeaways, and even the way the high-rises seem to keep the sky aloft, like architectural Atlases. She admires the grit beneath her fingernails, the way people's gazes slide over her as one more faceless person in the crowd. If she had a couple of months here, she could spend every day doing something different and never get bored. Museums! Galleries! Endless walks through Central Park.

If only she had a couple of months to spare.

In more respectable hours, this building is a thriving bookshop, brimming with tourists posing against the bright memorabilia, or couples writing love notes to one another on the chalkboard wall. The photos online are full of comments about the eclectic yet perfect array of books, the delicious hot chocolates served at the connecting café, the hand-painted stars on the ceiling with made-up constellations. A real highlight for book lovers everywhere, she'd read on various travel blogs. *Unmissable!*

She'd visited it the day before, trying not to look too conspicuous amongst the other browsing people. It had lived up to its online ratings, and in any other circumstances, Violet could have lingered for hours. It seemed so beautifully ordinary in the way it catered to the camera-clutching tourists. And it *is* a lovely bookshop.

Tonight, the shop is closed for a private event. There are no specifications on what kind of private event, but Violet has it on good authority that this is another scholars' soirée, like the one Adelia Verne held. Except this time the host is one Yulan Liu, who isn't a scholar herself, but one of the many people orbiting them—in this case, an antiquarian books dealer, with an eye for the rare and illegally acquired. A dealer who, if Violet has pieced this together correctly, has a particular map in her possession—to an object that can answer any question. Allegedly.

The woman in Accra—the one who'd recognised Violet's bracelets—had told her that this was what Marianne had gone after, the last time she'd seen her, only a few months before. Once Violet had stopped kicking herself for not arriving earlier, missing Marianne by such a slender span of time, she'd turned her attention to the map. It sounds like wishful thinking, but she's learnt that very little is wishful where the scholars are concerned.

So she squares her shoulders, smooths out the invitation in her hand, and puts on an expression that says *I absolutely belong to this party*. A bouncer at the door is checking guests in.

"Juliet Green?" he says, glancing at her invitation.

Violet gives him her most winning smile, and prays the wig is a sufficient disguise. "That's the one."

One of the many hard lessons she's learnt over the last year is just how many scholars Marianne's made enemies of. Several of them will be here tonight—hence the disguise as Juliet Green, some minor scholar of middling talent and no family connections whatsoever, who should be perfectly invisible.

The bouncer ushers her through. The lights are dimmed, and a purple carpet ribbons between the tables of stacked books, towards the back. Other people are already mingling, a mixture of tattooed guests with key cufflinks and earrings, and the unadorned, who look distinctly more uncomfortable. There's a familiar metaphor here somewhere about wolves and sheep, Violet muses. After the year she's had, she wonders which group she belongs to now.

Violet follows the winding carpet past silent till points and up two flights of stairs, where photographs of famous dead authors hang haphazardly on the walls. On the third-floor landing, two glass double doors are guarded by more intimidating security. Thick burgundy curtains shield the room beyond from prying eyes. Although there's nothing to worry about, Violet's palms are sweaty.

She hands over her invitation, and this time, the security guards scrutinise it more closely. Violet's palm sweatiness intensifies.

"Juliet Green," she announces, as if she can bridge the gap between lie and truth simply by stating the name as her own.

But after a further agonising second, the guards let her through, parting the velvet curtains.

"Enjoy your evening," the taller of the two says after her.

The hall in front of her is a far cry from the shop downstairs, which was all tourist knick-knacks, glossy hardback bestsellers and cheap second-hand paperbacks, their spines cracked. It reminds her of the library in the Everly house, only with twice, three times the space and ceiling height. Rare books, pamphlets and scrolls are encased safely and spotlit behind glass for guests to admire. Whoever decorated must possess a lust for the bloodthirsty, because what isn't bookshelf space is devoted to wickedly sharp-looking weapons arranged like threats on the walls, or portraits of surly men doing the threatening to hapless animals. A string quartet serenades guests underneath a statue of a scantily clad man hoisting a dead goat over his shoulder.

Violet hovers near the edge of the party with her drink, studying the guests. Men and women, mostly older than her, converse in tight clusters, all clearly familiar with one another. She spies one or two from other parties she's attended—a scholar and her bodyguard, built like a shed; her brain tries and fails to cough up a surname— and makes a note to avoid them. Blonde hair glints in the light and

Violet's heart stops for a split second, but then the woman turns, and her nose is longer, her eyes a washed-out green.

Not Penelope, then. Not that Violet had expected her to show up.

But she also can't help scanning the crowd for another face she might recognise. A sharp jawline, dark curls falling over unreadable eyes. It's certainly not the person she's supposed to be looking for, but a quick sweep over the party confirms that Aleksander isn't here, either. Even though there's nothing to be disappointed about, it sticks in the back of her throat.

You are not here to think about him, she tells herself sternly. She looked up Yulan's photograph online, but there's no one here who looks remotely like her. There's nothing for it except to keep searching, then.

As Violet passes one room, she catches the sounds of an auction taking place, the auctioneer calling out such an absurd amount of money that she double takes. The book in his hands is a slim, tired-looking paperback whose plain front cover is sheering off the spine, but the quiet intensity of the room suggests this is not merely valuable, but *in*valuable. And everyone attempting to buy knows it.

She's gleaned enough about the scholars by now to understand that this is their natural habitat: illicit goods, champagne in crystal glasses, secretive smiles and furtive whispers. Opulence spurred by absurd wealth, thanks to bartering between their connections here and in Fidelis; Violet can imagine all too easily what someone would be willing to give in exchange for a glimpse of true "magic." She catches wisps of conversation around her:

. . . starting at two million dollars for this bust of Nemetor with craftsman mark intact, said to come from the old scholar-city itself . . .

. . . Goro Matsuda said the booze was spiked, but I'm pretty sure that's just edible glitter . . .

. . . they brought an asteria over for us, did you see? Up the staircase, the top floor . . .

The last one makes her pause. It's not the first time she's heard of asteros cards, or the asteria who read them.

Intrigued, Violet follows the directions, taking the winding staircase at the far end of the hall. Inside her head, she hears the *ka-ching* of time being paid out. But she can't find Yulan anywhere, and anyway, there's no harm in a little detour. It's been so long since she's given into her curiosity, and the guilty pleasure of five stolen minutes to herself sends goosebumps pinpricking up her arms.

The top floor turns out to be a large glass dome, like a greenhouse without much greenery. Naked bulbs are carefully suspended from wire strung overhead, so that the view of the night sky is eclipsed by hundreds of tiny lights swaying on an invisible breeze, burning like meteors. It's much quieter here, and the hum of conversation below is almost completely cut off.

At the back of the room, surrounded by large ferns, a tent has been erected. It's the only point of darkness. At first, Violet thinks no one's there, but then a voice calls out from its depths.

"Please, stay for a reading." A man's voice.

Despite her curiosity, she hesitates, but then she ducks underneath the tent. After the bright lights of the glass dome, it's almost impossible to see anything. She catches the outline of a man, the sharp edges of a table—and a pack of cards. The asteria and his asteros.

"Sit," he commands, and she does.

The man spreads out the asteros cards in front of her. There's a lustre to them that seems oddly familiar, twinkling with golden sparkles. The artwork reminds her of an art nouveau mural she'd seen at the Met, all fluid lines and silky curves.

"You can pick three of the asteros," he says. "Whoever you choose will clarify your present and assist you in your future."

Violet flips the first card over. A woman in a long cloak that pools at her feet holds up a lantern, the only bright point in a sea of dark-hued paint. At her feet, dim silver lines fan outwards.

"Erriel, astral of the lost," the asteria says.

Astrals instead of arcana. Violet knows very little about them, but from what she's gathered, they seem like the scholars' version of gods or saints.

"You are seeking something important to you, I think, but perhaps have taken a misstep. Erriel will illuminate your destination, but she cannot guarantee that you will be pleased with it."

The next card is of two naked men entwined with one another, as thorns climb up their bodies. Each one carries a knife in one of their fists, hidden from the other's eyeline. Their mouths are parted, only a millimetre between them. Even though they're just paintings, there's something about their sensual longing that makes Violet blush.

"Interesting," the asteria says, a smile playing over his lips. "Tullis and Berias, astrals of lovers and betrayers. You are stifled by conflict that can be resolved in several ways. But a sacrifice must be made. You have a lot to lose. Perhaps too much."

If Marianne isn't found, then it will be you walking through the dark with me. Violet swallows.

The last card is of a tall, regal woman, her blonde hair curled around her like a halo, and wings outstretched behind her in stylised brushstrokes. Her hands are clutched around the hilt of a sword buried in her heart. For a moment, neither Violet nor the asteria say anything. The longer Violet stares, the more the woman's face looks like a skull, her eyes hollow pits.

"Ah," the asteria says.

Violet picks up the card and flips it over; she can't bear to look at the woman anymore. "What does it mean?"

"Not what," he says, "but who. Astriade, astral of devastation." He takes out a velvet drawstring bag and shakes it, but it's empty. "I don't usually put her in the deck; she must have joined the cards herself."

"Astral of devastation," Violet echoes. "That sounds...unhelpful."

Against her better judgement, she picks up the Astriade card again and tilts it in the light. There's something in her sorrowful expression, her hands grasping the sword's hilt, that makes her look like devastation made manifest.

The asteria looks at her solemnly. "She is a curse."

Nineteen

IOLET STUMBLES DOWNSTAIRS into the light of the party. Her head reels from the reading, even though the asteria told her nothing she doesn't already know. Devastation, curses, betrayal…and sacrifice. Seeing it all laid out on the table was dizzying. A bad idea, in retrospect.

She knows she has six weeks left. She knows she has no idea what she's doing. She knows that her mother, to all intents and purposes, is still a ghost. She doesn't need a pack of cards to tell her that.

Violet has no idea how long she was with the asteria—it felt like five minutes, and also an hour—but the party has degenerated somewhat in her absence. Empty champagne flutes line the bookshelves, and more than one guest totters unsteadily towards the ravaged canapé table, now mostly crumbs and empty wrappers. The auction she passed earlier is still going, but the mood has soured considerably and the betting is more calculated, the losses more bitter. The string quartet has been replaced with generic jazz music floating down from overhead speakers. She scans the crowd for Yulan again, but there are too many people now, too much noise for her to concentrate.

A man in a black silk shirt and velvet suit jacket comes to stand next to her, leaning on the bookshelves with a sloppy grace that she envies. But there's a whisper of relief, too, underneath the envy; finally, a familiar face at this party, even if it's one she doesn't entirely trust.

"Juliet," he says, eyebrow arched.

"Caspian," she counters.

It's impossible not to spend a year chasing scholars, and not rub up against some of the same elbows. Caspian Verne, all-round English scoundrel and thief, is one such elbow. She'd run into him several months ago at a similar event in Novosibirsk, then again in Melbourne. And of course he'd recognised her from that fateful evening at Adelia Verne's house. He'd been the one to mention this party to her.

"I see you're making the fullest use of my invitation." He taps his fingers lightly on the edge of the bookshelf. "What I can't figure out is why you didn't come here under your own name. You'd get more attention."

"Not the kind I'm interested in. Anyway," she adds, raising an eyebrow at him, "I thought this was a scholars-only invite?"

"Ouch," he says, not sounding particularly offended. "I'm a Verne. It would be a scandal if I *didn't* show up."

That's the other curious thing about Caspian. Heir to the most influential scholar family, beloved grandson of a formidable master scholar—yet not a scholar himself. His position usurped by some upstart nobody, or so she's heard. Stuck between worlds, like her.

"How's the search going for your mother?" he asks quietly.

She gives him a sideways glance, suddenly wary. If he weren't so close to the scholars, she might consider him a friend. Might press him for more information than she has already. But Marianne's whereabouts, she's come to discover, are an illicit subject, for all the gossip the scholars have indulged in. Penelope's interference, no doubt. *Exiled*, someone had told her, *for betraying our secrets*. And a warning, should anyone have any ideas about helping her daughter.

So she can push, but not too hard. And she's already pushing pretty damn hard just by showing up to this party.

"It's going," she says eventually. "How's your grandmother?"

"Oh, the usual. Furious at the scholar council over some nonsense. Desperate to marry me off and produce a gaggle of talented monsters." He pulls a face. "Keeps suggesting Kat Hadley, though I don't know how she hasn't realised that particular ship's sailed. She asks after your uncles, too. Especially Gabriel."

"I don't think she likes him very much," she says.

She can't tell if Caspian is trying to pry about her relationship with her uncles, but she's not taking her chances. As far as she can tell, they haven't told anyone they're no longer on speaking terms.

He catches her eye. "Well, I like you, *Juliet*, so I'm going to offer you another invitation. Free of charge," he adds, seeing her expression. "Should you ever return to Europe..."

He hands her what looks like a business card, along with a silver coin. There's an address on the business card, somewhere in Prague, and a date, mere weeks from now.

"Don't spend the coin," he advises.

She lets herself linger on the card. "What is this?"

"A third option." He shrugs. "We're not scholars, so why play by their rules?"

"You mean the keys and the tattoos?" Violet suggests archly.

His smile widens. "Come and find out."

It's a sincere offer, and if she was anyone else, she would take it. She's heard whispers of Caspian's legendary parties and those lucky enough to grace them: otherworldly creatures with voices like nightingales; magical duels conducted by bitterest rivals amidst candlelight; once, a spectacular orgy involving lawn games and an aphrodisiacal fruit punch—though Violet suspects Caspian was the originator of *that* particular rumour. And...doors. Always doors and the siren call of elsewhere. But the event is simply spare time she can't afford. And yet she pockets the card and coin with a guilty pang. Just in case, she tells herself.

"I'm not looking for trouble," she says.

His eyes glint with sudden recognition, and he pulls away from the bookshelves. "Looks like trouble's come to find you, anyway."

Violet looks at him, puzzled, but he only winks at her before sauntering away towards the auction room, his eyes alighting on someone he knows: "Goro, what a *pleasure*. How's the yacht working out for you?"

Well, Caspian can be as mysterious as he pleases.

A woman joins Violet to watch the sea of people. Silver feathers climb across the deep navy of her tea dress in elegant stitches, and her glossy black hair is swept into a pristine bun. Violet tucks her hands behind her back to hide the fraying fabric on her cuffs.

A man and a woman stumble past, almost knocking Violet over. The woman sighs. "This is supposed to be a meeting of the great minds of Fidelis. A chance to showcase our talents to our more illustrious colleagues. What lofty ambitions I had."

"It's a very impressive party," Violet admits.

"Well, I have certainly tried my best. Tell me, what did you make of my asteria, Violet Everly?"

"I think—"

She freezes. No one is supposed to know who she is.

The woman very carefully sets down her glass on a sideboard. "You'd better come with me."

Violet hesitates. It would be so easy to be spirited away down one of these labyrinthine halls, never to be seen again. An interloper, quietly disposed of.

The woman tilts her head in the direction of two men in hefty suits. "I assure you that Hector and Eli are very good at their jobs, and they can remove you rather swiftly. But not, I fear, before making quite the scene." She raises one careful eyebrow. "And how *interested* our guests would be to know that an Everly is here amongst them."

Violet's gaze turns steely-eyed. "If you know my name, then you know what I'm looking for. You're Yulan Liu, aren't you?" she says, and the woman bows her head in acknowledgement. "I was told you could help me, so—"

A group of people enter from the auction room, noisy in their victories or losses. Several of them recognise Yulan and start towards her.

"This is a conversation best had elsewhere," Yulan says. "Of course, it is entirely your choice as to how we get there."

Violet glances at the bouncers again. That's not a fight she's going to win. So she allows Yulan to lead her to a small office in the back, through a door that Violet had passed earlier and mistaken for a cupboard. Inside, Yulan props herself on the edge of the desk and folds her arms.

"I commend you for your intrigue, but I can't imagine what made you think it was a good idea to gatecrash my evening," she says.

"I contacted you about a map last week," Violet says. "I'd like to buy it."

She tries not to sound too interested, like it's something as small as a lost earring, rather than a very literal lifeline. But her tone slips at the last minute, betraying her. Inwardly, she curses.

"I've heard a lot about you. The daughter of Marianne Everly," Yulan says curiously. "The resemblance is...remarkable."

For a second, her gaze slides over Violet and she has the uncomfortable sensation of being studied. It isn't the first time, but Violet always wonders what they must see, what parts of her mother have been reassembled into this secondary version.

"Well, I'm sorry to disappoint," Yulan says, "but the map isn't available."

Violet's prepared for this, too. She pulls out a chequebook from an inner pocket. Another of Gabriel's teachings: *cash is easily stolen; a cheque suggests there is more money to come.* It worked well enough in Novosibirsk, when she'd had to buy her way into the gathering of scholars there. And look what it had brought her: Caspian's allyship. Sometimes good old-fashioned bribery is all it takes.

"Ah, you misunderstand me." Yulan gestures to the closed door, where the sound of the party drifts through. "I don't need more money."

"If it's information you're after—"

"I sold the map yesterday. There was another interested party." She shrugs. "They simply moved faster than you."

Violet's stomach plummets. Of course they did.

"As I understood it, no one was supposed to know about the map," she says carefully.

She'd been sure of it. It was a closed deal, and the map would have gone on auction tonight as a finale of sorts. To the scholars, it's just one more trinket, one more expensive artefact to put on display.

"News travels," Yulan says. "They made me an offer I couldn't refuse."

Violet's hands tighten on her wallet. "I couldn't persuade you to reveal the buyer, could I?"

"And risk the scholars finding out?" Yulan arches an eyebrow. "I have a good reputation for a reason. Besides, you'll find the Everly name carries a high price. Too high for either of us, I'm afraid."

"But—"

"I must return to my guests. You'll find an exit through the back door. I suggest you use it." Yulan smooths down her dress. "And Violet?"

Violet turns around. "Yes?"

"Don't come here again."

The door leads out next to the same dumpster she'd stashed her backpack behind. Violet stares at it helplessly. Back where she started.

She pulls out the faded notebook with Marianne's handwriting scrawled across the front and flips to the last page. There are so very few names left.

She closes her eyes, willing herself not to cry or scream or do any of the things that might draw attention to her. She clenches her fists, nails digging into her skin until the pain drowns out her thoughts. When she opens her hands, pinpricks of blood dot her palms.

So *close* again.

Even from her lowly vantage point, she can hear the noise of the auction carrying on. The people in there have been scholars their entire lives, already proficient at this game of seduction and persuasion. Caspian might not be a scholar by name, but he's still one of them. And he's right; no one would dare refuse a Verne—or a Matsuda, or a Hadley, or any of the other names that mark out the scholar families. Whereas even after a year, Violet is still running to catch up.

If she wasn't an Everly, then perhaps Yulan would have kept the map for her, or at least revealed the buyer's identity. Then again, if she wasn't an Everly, there would be no curse on her shoulders, no promise of blood and cruelty awaiting her at the end of this too short road. If she wasn't an Everly, she wouldn't be here at all, trying not to cry next to a dumpster, of all places.

She thinks about the woman with the sword in her chest, devastation already in motion, and a sick, panicky feeling rises within her. Not for the first time, she pulls out her phone. No missed calls from Ambrose or Gabriel this time. No texts, either.

Maybe they've given up on her.

Frustrated, she tears the wig off her head, a dozen bobby pins scattering across the ground. Then she tugs off her painful heels and flings them over the side of the dumpster. But as she picks up her backpack, something crinkles in the front pocket—a distinctly unfamiliar sound. She rummages in the pocket and pulls out a crumpled note in choppy handwriting.

I have your map. Come find me, Everly.

An address at the bottom, in German.

Someone else recognised her at the party. Someone else knows her name, or at least recognised her well enough by her features to guess at her origins.

She glances back at the shop, sudden tension crackling through her bones. It could be yet another dead end, but she doesn't think so. She has questions.

And somewhere out there, someone has the answer.

The New York party is over by dawn, and guests stagger out of the bookshop into the streets. Inside, weary staff start the arduous process of cleaning up the night's excesses. Upstairs, in the room with the glass ceiling, the asteria is packing away his canopy when a blonde woman appears. He glances up, halfway through shuffling his cards back into their velvet bag. His hands glitter with reveurite dust.

"I'm sorry, readings are done for the night," he says.

The woman doesn't leave. "Surely you can spare one minute for me."

"I said—"

"A reading." The woman's voice is steel. "If you please."

The asteria mutters something under his breath that might, to keen ears, sound like *bloody scholars think they can demand bloody anything they damn like*. Nevertheless, he unfolds the table again and takes out his cards.

He gestures to the table, the deck spread out. "Choose a—"

"Oh, I know how it goes."

She plucks three cards from the deck quickly and turns them over one by one. A man in shackles, his head bowed into his manacled hands as bloodied golden feathers circle the floor. Then another, proud and stern with his hands wrapped gracefully around a lance of pure sunlight. A woman, with a sword buried in her heart.

How much that sword must hurt.

Penelope looks up and smiles at the asteria, who flinches. "Tell me, what did you say to Violet Everly?"

The asteria blinks. "Who? I didn't—"

With one sure motion, she reaches out and wraps a hand around his neck. He chokes, his fingers scrabbling against her hold. Beneath her feet, shadows pool and writhe.

The asteria gasps and struggles, bloodshot eyes bulging as, one by one, his veins rupture. He squeaks out a word that might be *help* or *stop*, but nothing that proves useful to her. So she waits patiently as his motion stills, his swollen tongue parting his mouth. His head lolls to one side.

"I made it clear that the Everlys were not to be helped," she says. "And I don't tolerate failure."

She picks up the velvet bag of asteros cards and places them into the asteria's hands. His body slumps at her feet.

A warning.

Twenty

 WEEK LATER, VIOLET stands near the entrance of the MuseumsQuartier in Vienna. On either side, impressive buildings rise gracefully behind vast pavements. Signs in several different languages point tourists in various directions. Although it's drizzling and the sky is a leaden grey, the weather does little to dim the spectacle.

Violet clutches the address tightly in one hand, her umbrella in the other. When she'd searched for it online, she assumed it would be for a house, or a flat. Not a room in one of the most renowned museums in the world. The Kunsthistorisches Museum sprawls in front of her, grand and thronging with crowds. A ripple of excitement shivers through her.

Come find me, Everly. Well, here she is.

She ducks into the queue, pays for the eye-wateringly expensive ticket and makes her way through the gilded atrium. A statue of Theseus beating a centaur takes pride of place on the staircase, Theseus' club poised at the height of the killing blow. It looks so smooth, too clean for such a bloody act.

The museum is so large Violet loses her way more than once. Painted eyes watch her from beautiful landscapes and haughty portraits, as she moves from room to room. Twice, she whips around, certain that someone is watching her. But the tourists amble past with no concern for her, their gaze sliding from one artwork to the next.

It's just nerves, she tells herself.

After nearly an hour of searching, she finds the room listed on the scrap of paper. It's one of the smaller ones, filled with biblical depictions and pastoral scenes with lush greenery. There are fewer visitors, and no one lingers.

She examines every painting, then wanders the room in slow, looping circles, feeling increasingly foolish. Maybe the note wasn't really meant for her, but for another Everly, no relation. Maybe she's got the wrong room, or the writer has already given up on waiting for her.

Maybe she's walked into a trap, and she just doesn't know it yet.

On her fifth turn around the room, she hears footsteps. Behind her, a staff door opens and a curator steps out: a middle-aged man in professorial tweed, with wire-rimmed glasses and a grey beard. He sees her and his eyes light up.

"Marianne Everly, you took your time—" Then he stops and looks at her properly. "You're not Marianne."

"No," Violet agrees.

The man frowns at her. "You have the look of an Everly."

"I'm her daughter," she says, then holds up the piece of paper. "You left this behind?"

"Scheisse." He sighs and rubs his beard. "Oh hell, I suppose I should have known better than to expect Marianne to attend a party. It's just, I heard the name Everly, and you were a woman, and I thought...Marianne's daughter." He says this as if trying out a phrase in a foreign language. "Huh."

For some reason, this rubs Violet the wrong way, though it shouldn't, given the amount of times she's been mistaken for her mother despite the obvious age gap. Marianne's daughter, her obedient shadow. The abridged edition.

"It's Violet, actually," she says instead, sticking out her hand.

The man shakes it firmly, his hands surprisingly calloused underneath her palm. "Johannes Braun. I think you would like an answer, yes? To my note." He glances at several passing tourists. "But not here."

With a hasty glance at the cameras, Johannes leads her through a door marked STAFF ONLY, swiping his key card. She follows him quickly through a maze of narrow corridors, squeezing past other staff members. Snatches of chatter drift in and out of her hearing.

Eventually, Johannes draws them into a small office, stacked high with books and files. Grainy CCTV images of various galleries flicker on an ancient TV balanced precariously at the top of a bookshelf. Between all the clutter, there's just enough room for a desk and two faded armchairs, precariously worn. He gestures for Violet to sit; she does so gingerly, springs *gloinging* underneath her, and leans her damp umbrella against the desk. Instead of joining her, however, he rummages through his cupboards, coughing occasionally as clouds of dust whirl upwards.

"Ah, here it is," he says triumphantly.

He sets a photograph down on the desk in front of Violet. The quality is poor; a lens flare obscures most of the image. But there's her mother. Young and defiant, her head tilted away from the camera. Next to her is a young man who might bear a passing resemblance to Johannes, his arm slung around her shoulders possessively.

"We were very good friends once," Johannes says. "We were novices together, then assistants to the same master scholar. But I'm afraid we drifted apart afterwards."

Violet deflates slightly. "You haven't seen her, then."

"Not in many years," he acknowledges. "We had a bit of an argument and... Well, she was never much concerned with being liked. But you know that, of course." He smiles to himself, his gaze suddenly distant. "She was so exceptionally talented. She had a mind like a knife. The other assistants used to complain endlessly—she would eviscerate them with a sentence, you see. But she was so clever, no teacher would discipline her." He sighs. "We'll never see a gift like hers again."

Violet stares at the photograph. It refuses to match up with the person she has in her head—fragments of soft hugs, laughter. Kindness. Not someone who would get into arguments, who could be cruel.

"What are you doing here, in Vienna?" she asks, diverting the conversation.

He gestures around him. "This is my work now."

"So you're retired?" Violet asks curiously.

Johannes shakes his head. "Scholars don't retire. Or quit, for that matter. It's not a job." His hand absentmindedly goes to his forearm. "But I'm done."

"Why?" Violet asks.

He takes off his glasses to clean them and sighs. He's quiet for so long Violet thinks he won't answer at all. Then he replaces his glasses and looks up at her.

"Your bracelets are very beautiful," he says. "Reveurite?"

She pushes her sleeves up so he can see. "Yes."

He tilts her hand gently to the side, examining the bracelets. "Marianne made these; I can tell. Talent like that is rare." Seeing her expression, he adds, "It is everything. Life itself, bottled like lightning into rock. Proof that the gods once walked amongst us. Yet so few of us can use it to its fullest, and every generation, more children are born entirely without it."

"I'm not sure I understand," Violet says.

"There is a cost to our hidden knowledge. A bloody, terrible cost. They tell you some of it, before you sit in the tattooist's chair. They parcel it out like poison, and by the time you realise what they've done—what *you've* done—you've already swallowed the bottle."

Violet waits for him to elaborate, but he doesn't. And when she opens her mouth to ask, he shakes his head, eyebrows creased in obvious pain. She thinks of her uncle's warning. *Wolves.* Then what does that make Johannes Braun? Suddenly she wishes she'd not been so eager to leave the safety of the public hallways to meet with him.

"Anyway," he says. "I presume you're not just here to listen to my regrets."

Violet unfolds the crumpled piece of paper with the address on it, and smooths it out on his desk.

"Why did you take the map?" She inches forward, her heart thumping.

"Marianne Everly stole something from me," he says simply. "I would like it back."

Violet turns it over in her mind. "Yet you didn't try to expose her at the party." She narrows her eyes. "What do you need from her?"

Johannes barks a surprised laugh. "You even sound like Marianne. Straight to the point. Suffice to say, she hasn't appeared, so I don't yet have it. We both remain frustrated in our efforts, I'm sure."

A long-winded way of saying, *I'm not going to tell you*. Well, she knew this wasn't going to be straightforward.

"Do you know why she stole from you?" she asks carefully.

She already has an inkling of the *what*. Marianne's forays have left a trail of furious scholars across the world. A missing ledger here, a stolen book there; such-and-such precious illustration won in a card game. All to do with keys. But how much can she give away? How much does Johannes really know? Underneath the desk, she clenches the edge of her cardigan, her knuckles white.

"Oh, I'm sure she had her reasons," he says lightly. "As do I."

He eases back into his chair. For a moment they observe each other, Johannes' cornflower eyes on hers. A scholar who isn't a scholar, and yet seems to take a keen interest in their activities. Who was willing to travel all the way to New York on a rumour, but wouldn't approach her to verify the truth. They've tiptoed around this long enough.

"You know what she's looking for. The key," Violet says.

The one thing that can undo the curse.

Johannes' hands tighten on the edge of the desk. "We are a people on borrowed time, Violet Everly. I told you that we scholars are few and far between. But once we were innumerable, before calamity fell on our city, fracturing it forever." He pauses. "That city is not Fidelis."

Violet frowns. "What?"

Johannes laughs humourlessly. "You think we are the only two worlds in existence? The arrogance. There are as many worlds as stars in the sky, and once we could traverse them all. Yet we are exiles from our true homeland. Fidelis is but a fragment, and I mean that quite literally. The mythology calls it a calamity; we call it a rift in the very fabric of existence." He sighs. "There may be other such city-islands cut adrift, but they all belong to one true homeworld."

"So Marianne is looking for this 'homeworld'?" she says, her fingers curled into air quotes.

"We are *all* looking for this world. It's what the scholars were made for," Johannes says. "She seeks Elandriel."

Elandriel. Violet rolls the unfamiliar name on her tongue.

"To be the first person to rediscover it…what a thing that would be. Our ancestral home, untouched for a thousand years. They said the very walls used to be lined with doors leading elsewhere, that scholars from countless worlds came to study in our hallowed halls. Imagine the knowledge we could regain. Imagine the *possibilities*. The rebirth of an entire world."

And Violet does imagine, with a kind of longing that stuns her with its ferocity. Her mind is already conjuring a city full of potential libraries crammed wall-to-wall with books, adventure only a step through a doorway. Even though it's something she's supposed to have outgrown, she can't help the thrill that runs through her.

To the effervescent sea under the sun. To the witches in their forests. To mysteries beyond comprehension.

"Marianne was obsessed," he says. "She read every origin myth she could get her hands on, every scrap of detritus that even hinted at Elandriel. She kept talking about doorways no man could open, magics we couldn't comprehend. Fairy-tale stuff. Of course I asked her why. But she was always so secretive."

"I need that map," Violet says quietly. "If the object is real, if I can ask any question—"

"Do you realise what you ask of me? For you, Elandriel is a bartering tool. Just an interesting bit of history, to be stolen and thrown away. But do you know how many scholars would kill to possess the key? Or what it would mean for the person who found it—but you don't understand." Johannes slams his hands down on his desk, startling her. "You will never understand."

Instead of backing down, she stands up. "Do you know what happens to the Everlys?" She can't quite bring herself to say Penelope's name, but she notes Johannes' sudden stillness. "There isn't a lot of time left. And if I don't find Marianne—"

"I'm sorry for your predicament," Johannes says. "Truly. However, that's not my problem."

"I thought you wanted to help. I'm Marianne's daughter. You were friends," she says, almost but not quite pleading.

"*Were.*"

She tries a different tack. "You said this was important to the scholars. That I could never understand. But if you tell me—"

"Don't!" he says sharply, and for the first time, she catches a glimpse of fear underneath the easy professorial guise. "No, I'm sorry, but I can't help you. Now, I think it's best if you leave."

"But I—"

He looks pointedly at the CCTV footage. "You can explain to someone else, if you'd prefer?"

Johannes' gaze possesses a coolness that seems miles away from the placid curator he'd presented himself as only moments ago. He draws himself up to his full height, all sharp edges and promised cruelty.

Angrily, she snatches her bag. "You were desperate enough to ask my mother here. And you were desperate enough to talk to me even when she didn't come. I need those answers. If the object is the only way to get them—"

"Object?" He appraises her once more, a curious look in his eye. "So she really didn't tell you anything, then."

The comment hits like a dagger in her chest. Violet sucks in a breath, trying to school her expression back into something that doesn't resemble shock. After so many years, she should be inured to her mother's inherent unknowability, to the lack of information that's carved so many holes through her life. But it *is* a shock, to hear it put so bluntly.

And by a stranger, who so obviously was told *something* by Marianne Everly, once upon a time.

She tilts her chin up, jaw defiant. "I'm not going to stop."

Johannes steers her towards the door, and the hallway beyond. They pause outside the staff door.

"Then you have my pity, Violet Everly. But not, I'm afraid, my assistance."

Outside, the drizzle has turned to a full-blown torrent. All around her, people fumble for umbrellas, but as Violet reaches for her own, she realises it's still in Johannes' office. Swearing under her breath, she draws her sodden cardigan around her.

She'll come up with a new plan. Find another way to persuade Johannes to hand over the map. She doesn't need his *pity*—she needs him to answer her goddamn questions—

But she can barely think beyond her misery. Rain plasters her hair to her forehead, and she pushes it back irritably. Wind chases leaves across the street, and she shivers in her wet clothes.

Only one other person is getting soaked in the rain with her. A tall, angular man looks up at the museum with a thoughtful expression. The collar of his overcoat hides most of his face, but she catches a glimpse of sharp lines, a constellation of three dots inked around the curve of his ear. Violet blinks rain out of her eyes. *Unfairly pretty*, her brain says automatically. But it can't be him. It's never him. She starts to walk away, her thoughts already back in Johannes Braun's office.

Then the man shifts, his face coming into the light. She stops in the middle of the pavement, her heart in her throat. She knows that walk, that particular tilt of the head. Those liquid grey eyes, bright and dangerous with promise.

It can't be.

"Aleksander?"

CHAPTER

Twenty-One

THERE'S AN INFINITE pause before the man turns around. And in that infinity, Violet recalls all the times she thought she'd caught glimpses of him: the curve of his smile in a crowd; a flash of sea glass-grey eyes across a busy shop; a laugh that sounded just like his, sharp and unexpected.

His eyes meet hers, and surprise washes over his face. "Violet?"

It *is* him.

A million thoughts fly through her head. *What is he doing here? What happened to him?* And the one that sends a jolt of fear through her: *he is still Penelope's assistant.*

"Wow," Aleksander says. "Violet Everly. Hi. Hello." He rubs the back of his neck. "I don't even know what to say."

Neither does Violet. Her breath catches in her throat.

She's thought about this moment for so long. Every scenario she's constructed in her head has been a delicate ballet of conversation. An argument, or accusations, or an apology more than a year in the making. He could have come back for her. He could have at least tried to explain before he vanished from her life altogether. It would be better if she was furious with him, if she knew exactly what ground she stood on. He told Penelope everything, she reminds herself. Yet her anger is falling through her fingers like water.

Has he spent the last year searching for her in crowds? Does he remember the night of the Verne party the way she does, his hand skimming her face, his fingers laced in hers?

But nothing seems enough in the wake of sheer bloody coincidence, while she's still reeling from her conversation with Johannes. If it *is* coincidence.

They look at each other, breaths held.

"I almost didn't recognise you," Aleksander says. "You look... different."

"So do you," she says truthfully.

There's a tiny scar above his eyebrow, the glimmer of a new tattoo snaking underneath his collar. And his hair—his stupid, curly man bun that she'd grudgingly liked—has been shorn down to his scalp, leaving a soft scruff that looks like velvet. The man from the party had worn a certain fragility, but this new Aleksander looks a little more lived in, as though the world fits more comfortably around him.

And what does she look like? What changes has a year wrought on her?

"On another errand for Penelope?" she asks, too casually.

He shakes his head, raindrops gliding down his face. "No. I'm not— I— Look, can we go somewhere and talk? I know I owe you an explanation."

His hands twist around each other nervously, before he buries them in his coat pockets. She would so dearly love to say yes. But the spectre of Penelope looms over them both like a shadow.

"What are you doing here?" she asks again.

"Messenger," he says, grimacing as thunder rumbles overhead. "Letters. Some people have family across both sides of the, er—well, you know."

"And Penelope?" she asks.

She doesn't care if she's being too obvious. If Aleksander knows the truth of her mission—if he's always known—then it's already too late. Her eyes flicker over his shoulder, searching for blonde hair, blue eyes, a smile to carve her to pieces. If he registers her worry, then he shows no sign of it.

"It's just me," he says.

Violet clenches her teeth against the cold. She could claim she's busy. She could say she has an urgent errand, a meeting she can't miss, a train to catch. He would respect that.

And then he would walk out of her life, again.

She has already let so much go.

"It's really good to see you," she says at last.

Aleksander runs a hand over his hair, slick with rain. "How about a drink? I know a place near here."

One drink couldn't hurt. She knows to be careful.

"Sure," she says, breaking into a smile. "I'd love to."

Aleksander leads her to a tiny restaurant away from the tourist hotspots, cosy and intimate. He orders a bottle of wine in perfect German and they sit at a table close to the window, rain gathering on the windowpane. Violet studies him surreptitiously as she sips from her glass. He seems totally at ease here, with no sign of stumbling unfamiliarity. Confidence suits him, she thinks.

In the early evening light, she searches for other changes. Like his visibly rough hands, which had been so soft and smooth before. The graze of stubble over his throat. She knows she shouldn't stare, but she can't stop looking at him, waiting for the dissonance between her memories and the man in front of her to slide into one cohesive whole.

"I can't believe you cut your hair," she says mournfully.

A strange expression flashes over his face, but it's gone before she can decipher it. He fixes his gaze on her. "So what are *you* doing here?"

"Backpacking," she says, which isn't totally a lie. "Seeing the world. I've never been to Vienna before."

"Vienna is a beautiful city." He leans back in his chair. "Did you go into the Kunsthistorisches Museum?"

"Not today," she says. "Maybe tomorrow."

They lapse into an uncomfortable silence. In the café, there was barely time for them to draw breath, never mind watch the seconds tick past. But that was before she really understood what it meant for him to work for the scholars—and Penelope.

Aleksander looks at her as though he can hear her thoughts, clear as glass. His smile fades, and for the first time, it occurs to Violet how sharp he looks without his soft, elegant curls. He closes his eyes briefly, his long dark eyelashes stark against pale skin, then glances away.

"You should know," he says, more to the window than to her, "that I'm no longer Penelope's assistant."

Violet blinks. "Really?"

He looks down at his hands. "It happens."

But if Aleksander only wanted one thing, it was to work with Penelope. Can a year really have changed him that much?

She glances at his forearms, covered by a shabby jumper, where the scholar's tattoo would be. "But I thought—does this means you're a scholar now?"

His entire face tightens. "No."

"Then why—"

"Why do you think, Violet? I got caught stealing the key," he snaps.

Violet flinches. Horror, spiked with guilt, washes over her. She knew there was a chance it might have gone wrong, that something would hamper Aleksander's effort. But Penelope had made it sound as though it had never been his intention to steal the key for her in the first place. And even though there was every reason to doubt, she'd believed her.

She'd known that there would be consequences, yet she'd pushed anyway. For her mother. For herself.

"I should never have asked you," she says abruptly. "It was too much."

His expression finally softens. "At that point, I would have taken you anywhere you wished."

She doesn't know what to say to that, so she takes another sip from her glass. But a flush crawls up the back of her neck.

"Anyway," he continues, slightly calmer, "when I went back to the café, they said you'd quit. So I never really had the chance to catch up again."

Violet tries to imagine what her ex-colleagues would have said to him about the way she'd left. In the early hours of the morning, she'd posted her apron and keys through the front door, along with her resignation. Her phone had buzzed incessantly that day, until she'd blocked the number. She'd felt bad about leaving them like that, but in that moment, time had felt like sand running through her fists; two weeks' notice seemed absurdly wasteful.

"I hope you got your free coffee, at least," she says.

To her surprise, he gives her a quick smile. "You know what? I completely forgot." He pulls out the stamp card and flashes it at her. "I still have it."

They lapse into silence again, listening to the rain patter outside.

"Can we start over?" Aleksander says suddenly. "I promise I didn't come here to behave badly. Did you ever find your mother? You were looking for her, right?"

Violet hesitates. She knows how precious this information is, how many people would turn against her if they knew the extent of her search, or why. But Aleksander has asked for a fresh start; she owes it to him to try.

And how easy it would be to spill everything. How much she wants to. It's been so long since she's let someone else shoulder her burdens with her.

"Not yet," she says eventually. "That's why I was here. I tried to meet with one of the museum curators."

"Johannes?"

She frowns. "How did you...?"

"I ferry messages, remember?" He touches the chain on his neck, the outline of a key just visible through his shirt. "I know most of the scholars around this area. How was he? I've heard he's a practically a recluse."

Scholars don't retire. Or quit, for that matter. Even if Johannes has set aside the scholars, they clearly haven't forgotten about him.

Quickly, Violet outlines the gist of the conversation, leaving out any references to the curse. She tries to keep the details sparse: just the mention of the map and her frustrated efforts to retrieve it. Aleksander may no longer be under Penelope's influence, but she knows how quickly information travels.

Aleksander leans back in his chair thoughtfully. "And you've been doing this for a whole year?"

"Just about." She sighs, fiddling with her napkin. "But maybe..."

He tilts his head to the side. "Maybe what?"

"Sometimes I think I should just give up," she admits. "Marianne clearly doesn't want to be found." She looks down at her napkin, now in tatters. "But that's not really an option."

Aleksander draws forward, as though reaching for her hands. But at the last moment he stops.

"Sorry, it's just—never mind." He pulls back. "That's tough. The Everly curse strikes again."

She looks up at him, startled; she'd forgotten she told him about the ancestral portraits—all those Everlys walking into the dark, never to return. The way he says it makes her only more certain that he has no idea who Penelope really is, or what she's capable of.

"Well, if she's out there, I'll find her." She shakes her head, trying to clear her thoughts. "So anyway, tell me: what have you been up to in Vienna?"

They talk for hours, Aleksander peppering the conversation with questions, almost too quickly for her to get in her own. Eventually the restaurant starts closing down. Aleksander pays for the bill—"I insist," he says—and when Violet stands up, the room lurches with her. She grabs on to the back of her chair for support. Her hands are too warm, her face flushed. In the bathroom, she wets her hands and presses them against her neck and the high pink spots on her cheeks.

Then Aleksander is linking his arm through hers and propelling her out of the restaurant. She smiles at him gratefully as they stumble into the cool night air.

"Where are you headed?" he asks. "I'll walk you."

She gives him the address of the hostel, and they walk together, arm in arm, through the streets of Vienna. Through the rosy wine-glow, she observes that there is something lovely about this moment, like stepping through a sepia photograph.

They pause by the Naschtmarkt, where golden light spills across people queuing at the stalls. Soft chatter and the clatter of footsteps compete with the sound of traffic. To any passers-by, Violet and Aleksander simply look like two old friends, walking in the evening. And maybe that's what they would be, in another life. In another world.

Even though he tightens his arm around hers, she notices the way his gaze turns distant, towards the glimmering horizon. She gives his shoulder a little nudge, and is rewarded again by the upturn of his lips.

By the time they reach the hostel, Violet's head is beginning to throb. Aleksander gently unlinks himself from her and she feels the loss of his warmth keenly.

"We should meet up again," he says. "If you can."

She bites her lip, hesitating. She'd intended to spend the evening plotting a new way to crack Johannes Braun, but somehow time has escaped her. And the next couple of days will be crucial in persuading Johannes to spill his secrets.

It's been so long, though, since she's let herself think about something other than her mother. Since she's been able to walk side by side with someone.

And...it's Aleksander.

"I'm only in the city for a few days," he adds. "At least let me give you my phone number. In case you change your mind. We could grab a coffee."

She pretends to hold out for another second. But in truth, she'd given in the moment he'd asked.

"I suppose that's only fair," she says, handing her phone over. "It would be a shame to let your stamp card go to waste."

He laughs. God, how she's missed that laugh.

"I'll hold you to that promise, Violet Everly," he says.

She watches as he walks into the city, swallowed by the night.

Twenty-Two

I N MOSCOW, A man is weeping silently in his flat.

Yury is thin and getting thinner; his throat is agony from drinking boiling water, and now he almost can't bear to eat anything at all. Blisters ooze on his hands, necrosis creeping up his arms in scaly black. Every dial on his heaters is turned up as high as they'll go. The air shimmers with heat.

But he is still cold, so cold.

With trembling hands, he opens his fridge and stares at the contents: a packet of beef that expired three weeks ago, a mostly empty bottle of milk furred with mould—and a single vial of golden liquid. The liquid within seems to swirl of its own accord, emitting a light that dances against the white walls of the fridge.

For a long time, Yury stares at the precious vial, shivering, his mouth parted with want. Then he presses down on his forearm, right on the remnants of a key tattoo, and he screams. Agony yanks through him, sharp enough to edge past the cold. A clear-headed kind of pain. He slams the fridge shut, breathing hard.

It was not always like this, pain and willpower and cold.

Once, Yury was a gifted scholar, specialising in the history of the lost scholar-city, and the origins of the reveurite keys. Such a limited method of travel to him, even then. He had dreamed of *more*.

But that was before the experiments, the weeks of sitting in a frigid room—or was it warm, and he was already beginning to feel the effects, even then?—as he choked down raw reveurite. Before he injected its white-hot liquid counterpart into his veins, screaming then blacking out.

This is how Illios made his Hands, the first true scholars to set foot upon other worlds, he was told again and again. *Glory and reveurite, and yes, blood, too.*

You want to see Elandriel, don't you, Yury? To walk across worlds unfettered by keys, to reignite the hearts of those who would doubt our brilliance. First of your kind, first after a millennia of nothing.

Then you must embrace pain.

Even in the midst of his screaming, what a seductive voice that was.

The cold crept in the way pneumonia starts, with a slight cough, a touch of dizziness. At first it was just his fingers, so he carried around a pair of gloves. Then it was a few extra layers, even though outside was warm sunshine. A shiver he couldn't shake off, or him shuffling closer and closer to the fire, ready for the blazing glow against his face and feeling nothing.

More injections, more pain, even as others died around him, imperfect vessels for godhood. Waiting for the miracle of reveurite to burst through his skin and remake him into someone more powerful.

All at *her* command.

And when it didn't work—exile.

"I need you out here. If you cannot be a Hand of Illios, then you must find me the key to Elandriel," Penelope said. "Whatever it takes."

By this time his fingers were turning black; not the lustrous velvet of reveurite, but a necrotic, poisonous black that exposed flesh and yellow fat, then grey bone. Scholars were beginning to whisper. Six months later, the first fingertip would go, leaving him with a permanent phantom itch on the tip of his left ring finger.

Now, his pain has crystallised into a glacier that erodes mountains in his mind. There are days when he wakes and he cannot remember his own name.

The vials are supposed to be a stopgap, a way to slow the process of losing his body, piece by piece. Only blood of the gods can save him now. Blood of an astral. And for as long as an hour, he may feel the faint flickers of warmth again.

There is only one vial left. Only one more respite before the pain continues to saw away at his mind.

Astrals may no longer walk this world freely, but there is another where they retain godhood, where their veins run with the liquid miracle that will cure him. Elandriel.

Whatever it takes, Penelope had said.

He opens the fridge again, snatches up the vial, and drinks.

Johannes Braun is a man of many regrets. Regret for the way he's conducted himself in life, for all the times he was complicit in someone else's devastation. Regret, too, for all those missed opportunities, for every no that should have been a yes. He should have returned to Fidelis to teach, even if it was beneath him, and built a devoted group of young scholars to wield. He should have picked fewer fights with the Hadleys, or at least made the effort to befriend a more powerful family—though it had never occurred to him to see the other scholars as anything but competition. He should have watched his back just a little more carefully. At every crossroad in his life, he seems to have picked the wrong path.

Marianne Everly is one such crossroad. In his office, rain pitching down the windows in fat droplets, he considers the last time he saw her. They'd both still borne the arrogance of supple youth, he only a few years older than her. And perhaps because of that youthful arrogance, he'd laughed in her face when she'd suggested they be allies. They were both ambitious, she'd said. They both knew the current system of scholars would fail sooner rather than later. They both believed in the presence of doorways beyond the reveurite keys—and what it would mean for Fidelis to be whole again, to have unfettered access to the resources it lacked. Why not?

He'd sat at a desk much like this one, his arm freshly pink underneath his new key tattoo, as he refused her. Already tasting that first sip of poisonous knowledge, already craving more. Why not, indeed. If only he'd been a little older, a little wiser. But with supreme—misguided—confidence, he'd thought, why bother when the wheels of his own success were already in motion?

On the other side, Marianne Everly stood in front of his desk, her arms folded over her chest.

"You're a weak, snivelling excuse for a man, Johannes," she said, every word carefully drawn out to a vicious point. "I thought better of you. Let me know when you find your spine."

A week later, he opened his drawer to find all of his research—a lifetime of work on Illios and his Hands—gone. He shouldn't have been surprised; he'd known Marianne was looking for a way to cross between worlds without the reveurite keys at all, if such a thing was possible. Yet there it was, her knife dipping into his chest before he'd even seen the blade.

And today? Today was like seeing his choices summed up in a vicious haunting: Marianne Everly, returned through her daughter. A chance to right a historical wrong. Instead, he did what he's done for over twenty years: hide in his office and proclaim ignorance.

Marianne was right. He is weak. Though the key tattoo has faded, it still stands out in dark reveurite ink, shimmering under the light. Even in his self-imposed exile, he is tied to the scholars. There are debts to be paid.

For a long time, he sits with his head in his hands. Then, wiping his face, he dials Violet's number.

In a secluded street, Aleksander picks up his phone.

The voice at the other end is calm, assured. "What did you learn?"

Aleksander tells Penelope everything.

Twenty-Three

I N THE MIDDLE of the night, Violet's phone goes off. Half the room's occupants groan; the others continue to snore furiously. She staggers out of bed and pads into the hallway, still wreathed in the fog of sleep. The number is unfamiliar; not one of her uncles, then, she thinks with an unexpected pang.

"Hello?" she says sleepily.

Johannes Braun's voice is urgent on the other end. "Violet, I'll give you the map. But there's more to the story—I must explain—"

All at once, she's wide awake.

"It's complicated," Johannes continues. "You don't know the whole— It's better if I explain in person."

"Now?" Outside is inky and still, an inhuman hour.

"If you can."

"Wait, what address?"

"I'll send it to you," he says. "Just—come. Please."

She closes her eyes, fighting off the wave of exhaustion. She knows her face is pale and drawn from too many sleepless nights. But this is *it*.

"I'll be there," she says.

In Johannes Braun's dusty house, the door sighs open so softly it could be an errant breeze. A floorboard creaks, a piece of paper ruffles.

Johannes pushes his glasses up the bridge of his nose, sweaty with exertion, and surveys his bedroom. He has only just finished packing the last of his suitcases, each one stuffed to the brim with documentation, clothes, mementos he can't bear to part with. Hidden in the lining of his briefcase are five passports under different identities, his photograph plastered in each. His car sits idling in the garage, ready to go.

First he'll drive down the coastline of Italy, he thinks. It's been so long since he's seen the ocean. Blue waters, and a hundred different villages to disappear into. He'll get fat on rich pasta and wine. Maybe a few months to lay low, then another country, and another, until he's too much effort to chase. There are so many wayward scholars—one more will surely go unnoticed.

In the kitchen, something topples over.

Slowly, Johannes reaches for his bedside table drawer, and the gun hidden beneath the false bottom. His hands tremble as he fumbles with the safety.

"You should have cleared out by now, Johannes."

A man blocks the doorway. It's not someone he recognises. *But it wouldn't be, would it, Johannes?* an awful voice whispers in his head. It's been so long since he's visited the scholars' tower, or attended the soirées. His own key rusts in a box, packed deep in one of his suitcases.

When was the last time you heard the stars sing, Johannes?

"I—I haven't done anything wrong," he says, levelling the gun at the intruder. "Who the hell are you?"

The man doesn't answer. Instead he reaches into his pocket.

Johannes takes aim and fires.

Nothing happens. He fires again, but the chambers are all empty. Impossible. He's certain he left it loaded.

"Penelope said you would be here," the man says, half to himself. "That you'd talked to an Everly. You know the rules. The consequences."

The intruder takes something from his pocket—a packet of glittering rocks and a lighter, tucked between his gloved fingers. Visibly shaking, he tips the packet into his mouth and *crunches*. Johannes has a flash of relief that it isn't a gun after all, before he locks eyes with the man and recognition strikes him.

"I do know you," he says, his eyes wide. "Yury Morozov."

Yury flicks the lighter on, off, on again. It *is* him, though the passing years haven't done him any favours. His clothes hang on him like a starved man, and a painful-looking scab crawls across the underside of his jaw. His eyes shine black under the lighter's flame.

Ingesting reveurite will do that to a man.

Yury mumbles something under his breath that could be a prayer, or a curse. Then he pulls out his own gun, sleek and shining.

"You shouldn't have talked to her," he says.

Johannes' stomach drops.

"Wait, wait, I can give you what you want! You want the Everly woman, don't you? I can give her to you—the map, whatever you want—whatever she's asked—"

"Where did she go?"

"God help me, I didn't want any of this. I didn't have anything to do with Marianne, I swear! I just need a little more time," he says, pleading. "Please."

"You cannot give me what you do not have," Yury says. "I'm sorry, Johannes."

Wet warmth creeps down Johannes' trouser leg as terror overtakes him. He lunges for a cane—at the same time that Yury raises his hand and fires.

The bullet takes Johannes between his ribs. White pain engulfs his chest, and he slumps against his bed. His hands scrabble against his wound, and they come away stained red. He sucks in a ragged breath and the pain is like a red-hot iron laid bare through his chest. Briefly, he blacks out.

When he wakes, Yury is gone. Thick, acrid smoke roils in the room; flames crackle in his doorway hungrily. He tries to stand, but his legs don't seem to be connected to the rest of his body. Every breath burns, the heat from the flames kissing his cheeks.

Poor Johannes Braun, they'll say. A lonely, peculiar man. House like a tinderbox.

In the doorway curtained by flames, he sees Marianne Everly, her arms folded, her expression scathing. *You are a weak man, Johannes.* He tries to talk to her, to tell her he's sorry, but his mouth is dry with ash. If only he could undo it all.

The fire reaches in tenderly, and engulfs him.

Twenty-Four

 PREDAWN HUSH HOLDS over the city as Violet makes her way through the streets, her heart thumping in her ears. It's utterly silent, and golden light streams from the lampposts. Twice she feels a prickle between her shoulder blades and whirls around, certain that someone's watching her. But it's only the wind, rustling through the trees.

The address is on the edge of the city, in an otherwise unremarkable suburban street. As she gets closer, she pictures a neat, two-storey home with trimmed hedges and prim rows of flowers bordering the garden fence, like every other house around it.

But even before she reaches the address, she knows something's wrong. The loud wail of sirens cuts through the quiet morning, and two fire engines race past her. The air is acrid with smoke.

She breaks into a run.

Breathless, she halts outside of Johannes' house. Her heart stops in her chest. An inferno churns in front of her—right where his house should be.

A dozen firefighters struggle to contain the blaze, as neighbours pace up and down anxiously in their pyjamas. Even on the other side of the street, Violet can feel the heat of the flames against her face. The noise is a crackling roar, as windows explode and furniture shatters inside.

She watches for more than an hour as the fire slowly recedes and extinguishes. The police arrive and start cordoning off the street. He'll come out, she thinks desperately. He'll be okay.

Then she sees it. A gurney. A sheet.

The body.

One of the police officers sees her and shouts something in German, but she barely notices. This can't be coincidence. Whoever did this...it was because of her. *She* sought out Johannes. *She* wasn't careful enough. She might not have killed him, but this is her responsibility, her fault.

Johannes is dead because of her.

Violet turns away and throws up, retching until there's nothing left.

The next moments are a blur. But when Violet's thoughts finally return to her, she's streets away from the fire. Exhaustion fogging her thoughts, she checks her phone. A missed call pops up, hours old, and for an awful, hopeful second she thinks it's from Ambrose. *Come home*, he would say.

But to her surprise, the voicemail is from Johannes.

"I've changed my mind; it's too dangerous. I'm leaving—now," he says, his voice tinny in the recording. "I...I'm not a good man, Violet. None of the scholars are, whatever they tell you. But if Marianne thinks she's found a way to Elandriel...I believe her." He laughs to himself. "I was an idiot."

These are the words of a ghost, a dead man, Violet realises. Maybe the very last.

The voicemail is long, punctured with the rustling sounds of packing. But at the very end, Johannes gives her an address. And a warning.

"Violet, this object—you must be careful. If you knew what you were really searching for, you would not go," he says. "Most scholars who went looking did not come back. It's—" Johannes pauses, his breathing heavy on the other end of the line, as though listening for something. "I've got to go."

The voicemail ends.

Violet listens twice more, taking down the address. A building in a French village, hours by train from here.

For another second, she thinks longingly of her home, of Ambrose mending jumpers in his favourite armchair, Gabriel teaching her how to throw a punch again. *Thumb over fist, kiddo!* Of them together, safe in the shelter of the Everly house.

What she wouldn't give to be there right now, to set aside her anger and simply write off the last year as a bad dream.

Then she forces the thought aside, and sets off towards the train station.

Aleksander stands outside the scholars' tower in the cold, watching movement flicker from the crack in the doorway. As always, it's alive with activity, humming with messengers and errand runners, scholars and their assistants. He watches them for as long as he can bear, then longer. From his vantage point outside, he can just about smell the ink, the warm bread baking in the kitchens below.

How easy it would be to cross that threshold. And how impossible.

Before anyone can notice his presence, he flips his hood over his head, sinking into shameless anonymity. He walks around the side, to the edge of the terrace, where the cliffside falls away into a deathly nothingness. From here he can see the lower settlements in the valley, lights twinkling defiantly against the persistent fog.

Penelope is standing on the very edge, watching with interest as an airship docks below. She barely glances at him as he comes to stand beside her. He waits, in agonising silence, to be acknowledged.

"How is she?" she asks.

He swallows, thinking of all the things he could say. That seeing Violet had been like a punch to the stomach. Older, and yet unchanged, still half feral and recklessly beautiful. Still compelling in the way that fire captivates from a distance. He hadn't even realised he was already halfway to burning himself on her. Then everything that followed came flooding back, wave upon wave of shame.

She has no idea what she's cost him.

"Look at me," Penelope says.

He raises his head, afraid to think of all that he's revealing to her in his face alone. As his eyes meet hers, he tenses, bracing himself for her fury.

It's his fault. It's all his fault.

"I have granted you one last chance to prove yourself worthy," she says. "If you fail me again, there's no going back, do you understand?" Then her sternness falls away, and she becomes the Penelope from his childhood once more. "Aleksander, I was loath to give you up. But you broke our most sacred rule. And I can't bring you back now, untested. The council won't allow it."

She takes his face gently in her hands, her touch like ice. His throat aches with unshed tears. What he wouldn't give to go back in time, to undo everything.

"You are capable of so much more than this." She turns away from him. "But you must prove yourself worthy again. Find out what Violet knows. Everything. Do this for me, and make yourself the scholar I know you to be."

Twenty-Five

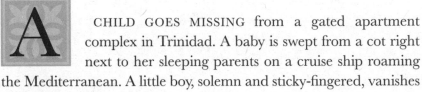CHILD GOES MISSING from a gated apartment complex in Trinidad. A baby is swept from a cot right next to her sleeping parents on a cruise ship roaming the Mediterranean. A little boy, solemn and sticky-fingered, vanishes from a state fair in Illinois.

Not all of them disappear with the wreath of vanilla scent in their midst, or a wisp of blonde hair, or such dainty, sure hands. Others are lured away with songs and tricks and promises, or under lesser competencies, drugged, their bottles and drinks laced with an achingly sweet sedative.

When they wake, in an unfamiliar room, in an unfamiliar city, they are greeted by a gentle scholar, who tells them that they are one of the few who possess talent. They are *special*. A reveurite bead, crafted for this specific purpose, is placed into their tiny palms. When it lights up, the scholars nod at each other, pleased. Had they been born into the families of Fidelis, they might have grown up to be forge bearers, agriculturalists, engineers, doctors—perhaps even a scholar if they're strong and gifted.

Instead, the children are brought up to a small high room in one of the adjoining towers, their chubby fists wrapped around someone's finger. *It will be so quick, like falling asleep*, a voice says in soothing tones. The scholars look at one another, acknowledging the needful but terrible act they have already committed to.

There is the flash of sharp fangs, the hot red of blood glimpsed between bites. A goddess, lowering her mouth once more to this sacrifice.

And then, the goddess gives back to her scholars. A drop of blood the colour of golden sunlight, and the taste of power, placed on lips like a kiss: an extra moment of life; a prolonging of youth. The reward for those who have borne the child—who have risen above their fellow academics. Every senior scholar, every master has touched this room, knowing it's a price that must be paid.

Later, there may be time for regret, to anguish over the road that has led to this point of no return. But there is only now, the coppery tang of time itself, jewelled ruby-red; a slurp that belies *such* hunger, restrained for so long. Each drop a second, a minute—another moment of a lifeline stretching forward endlessly into the future.

Astriade, bringer of devastation, licks her lips and smiles.

Twenty-Six

THE FRENCH VILLAGE comes into view just as the sun sets, casting shadows everywhere. Above, snow-capped mountains scrape the sky with their jagged peaks, like fairy-tale giants fallen deep in slumber. In between, a forest of dark pine trees skims the cliffs, miles of sultry green dotted by tiny Alpine homesteads. The trees sway with a casual rise and fall, like the world itself is breathing.

The taxi driver slows to a halt at the edge of the village. "We're here."

Violet adjusts her backpack and clambers out of the car. Her clothes still smell like smoke, the colours dull with ash.

It takes her a few tries in broken French to ask for directions before she finds someone willing to tell her the way. The address is hidden at the end of a dirt path partially obscured by undergrowth, far beyond the village. Hidden behind sprawling, shaggy trees sits a large, tumbledown house, with obvious signs of neglect. Paint crumbles off the walls, and the windows are cloudy with grime. The front door yawns open, swollen from damp. Turgid mushrooms creep across the bottom in dangerous shades of pustule yellow and orange.

Violet stands at the gate for what feels like an age, trying to psych herself up to go in. It looks like the kind of house where something unspeakably terrible has happened, so dreadful it left a tangible stain.

The darkness behind the door looms. The wind picks up, and she shivers, pulling her cardigan around herself.

Everly. We know you.

Unconsciously, she finds her hand pushing the gate open, her feet walking her towards the door. As if in a dream, she nudges it open, dust scattering. The ground beneath her feet feels soft and spongey, and the air is stale and wet in her lungs.

Violet's halfway down the hallway before the strange compulsion snaps. Suddenly, her heart rate soars and she scrabbles blindly for her phone. White light illuminates the darkness, leaping off dusty photo frames and revealing the weed-strewn floorboards.

How has she come in so far? She hadn't meant to even enter... or had she?

Behind her, something creaks and she whips around. But it's only the wind, pushing the door back and forth.

The rest of the house feels just as abandoned. When she puts her first foot on the staircase, it bends alarmingly underneath her and she pulls back. If there are answers upstairs, she won't be able to reach them without breaking her neck. Likewise, the ground-floor rooms are half-empty, broken furniture pushed out to the edges. It's been a long time since anyone's lived in this house.

She rests her hands on her hips and sighs. The map is obviously a false lead. And it took forever to get here—

Everly.

Violet freezes. She heard that: a voice that isn't hers, whispering against her thoughts. Slowly, she withdraws her penknife from her pocket, gripping it tightly in her fist.

"Hello?" she calls out.

A breeze ripples through the air, and the rustle of decaying furniture sounds like laughter. Every hair on the back of her neck lifts.

She backs away into the kitchen, and trips over the mouldy rug, sprawling on the floor. Wincing, she eases herself up—and notices a trapdoor, scored deep into the floorboards. The sensible part of her is urging her to get out of the house as fast as possible. She *should* leave. She's obviously not going to find anything useful here.

But she's certain she's not alone. She holds her breath—and another, almost invisible breath whispers through the entire house.

So she tugs on the large ring pull, dragging the trapdoor open. A gust of something dry and rotten wafts upwards, and she nearly gags. A ladder snakes downwards into the darkness. Casting her phone's light, she sees packed earth, not more floorboards.

Something groans within, sounding terribly human. Someone trapped?

"I'm coming down," she says.

The only response is another groan, more concrete this time. She swings herself over the edge, testing her weight on the ladder. But it's iron, and seems to hold. Carefully, she pockets her penknife and descends, feeling her way down until her feet hit the ground. The smell down here is worse, the unmistakeable reek of an unwashed body, and she takes shallow sips of air through her mouth.

"I'm here—the door was open—let me help."

She sweeps her light over the room, and the figure screams, a harsh cry that resonates through her skull. Violet screams, too, and backs up against the wall. She drops her phone and briefly, the entire room is aglow in white light, revealing the source of her sudden terror.

The creature is chained to the other side of the wall, naked and cringing away from the light. His enormous black wings lie on either side of him, torn and scarred, in a gruesome masquerade of a puppet with strings cut loose. Black ichor oozes from wounds. Dark strands of hair are plastered over a face that might once have been beautiful, godly, even—but is so sunken that it's impossible to tell. Silver eyes glimmer wetly in the light, and his mouth is open in an "oh" of pain, sharp teeth glinting like spearheads. The rest of him, though, looks human enough. Like a man, if every bone was broken and reset anew, if muscles and sinew withered away to the skeleton underneath.

He screams again. It's a language that Violet's never heard, like shards of glass shattering over and over, but words form inside her head, breeching her thoughts.

It hurts us! We cannot bear it!

Trembling, Violet picks up her phone and covers the light with her hand, so that it no longer blazes across the room. The creature sighs, his breath coppery with blood.

Ahhhh ... he breathes.

Violet knows the world is wilder and more extraordinary than she could ever conceive. But the scholars are human, whereas this—this *creature*—is emphatically not. Johannes' warning echoes in her head.

This is too much. She needs to leave.

She inches towards the ladder, hoping he won't notice her movement. Praying his chains are stronger than they look. Then the creature speaks again, a jangling melody that runs unbidden through her mind like music.

We have been waiting for you, O star-child. We saw this day when we were but a chemical dance of light, when the world was dark and infinite and O so ripe for taking.

"What are you?" she chokes out.

What are we? The tone is amused, in a self-deprecating way. *Once we were inconceivable, immortal, invulnerable. Once we called the stars kin, the sky home. We are astral.*

Astral. A god of Fidelis. It's impossible. And yet here he is, so obviously a creature of elsewhere. She thinks back to the cards the asteria flashed at her: astrals of lovers and betrayers, of the lost. Devastation. But he looks like none of the cards she'd flipped over.

The map led here. Not to an object, but a *god*.

Then her thoughts catch up to his earlier words. "You knew I was coming."

Like mother, like daughter. History calls to itself yet again.

"My mother was here?"

O yes. She was clever with her offering. The astral's eyes lock on her shrewdly. *We sense no gift from you.*

Johannes didn't mention anything about a gift. And everything in her backpack is worthless to anyone else.

"I have nothing to give," she says helplessly.

You have brought yourself. We would take but a morsel, he croons. *A finger, a thumb.* His chains groan under his weight as he inches forward. *A hand would be a most excellent gift.*

She recoils, shaking her head.

But at the same time, her thoughts whisper, *just one finger.* Nothing big—a pinkie, or perhaps her littlest toe. As if in a dream, she bends down to untie her shoes, her fingers methodically working through the laces. What, after all, would she not give for the knowledge of a thousand lifetimes?

Something flickers distantly in her mind, but it can't be important. She slips off her socks, her bare feet digging into the soil. Her penknife tucks into her fist like it's meant to be there. Dimly, she's aware that the astral is drooling, spit stringing from his mouth.

It's just one toe. Just one foot, and then all the worlds' secrets will be hers.

She raises the penknife.

We are so hungry. We have not tasted flesh for seasons innumerate. Our heart grows weary, O star-child. Our faculties diminish, our body betrays. We, who are supposed to live forever! O give us one digit, a knucklebone to savour so we may taste all the world, dewdrop sky, the green of grass, the honeyed sunshine. Our stomach roars WE MUST EAT O WE MUST DEVOUR—

His chains strain again, and the rattling sound breaks the compulsion.

Violet suddenly becomes aware of her bare feet, cold against the packed earth floor, the knife gripped in her hands like a saw. The desire to cut off her toes one by one vanishes in an instant. She scrabbles backwards, horrified.

She would have done it. She would have cut off her own feet to satiate this monster. And she would have done it with a smile.

Violet grabs the ladder to get out. She has no business being here, talking to something bent on eating her. She feels sick with horror at what could have happened. Her mouth is dry with fear, adrenaline fizzing through her veins.

You will not find what you seek without us, the astral says slyly.

The voice is oddly compelling, but she ignores him, focusing on one hand in front of the other.

Do not leave us yet, O star-child, the astral says desperately. *We will not meddle again.*

One hand in front of the other, she tells herself firmly.

Violet Everly, the astral says again, his voice pleading. *Star-child whether she knows it or not, traveller of a thousand worlds to come, daughter of Marianne Everly. Seeker of the bright, ruinous, ruined city.*

Violet stops climbing. She roots around in her mind, doubting, but she's certain she's still herself.

"I'm looking for a key," she says.

And where do keys lead? Marianne Everly came to us, when we were still a warrior in our chains. She visited us often, took pleasure in what company we bestowed. On her last visit, she offered us a gift. Not of flesh, that warm, red life-ocean, life-light, tasting of everything we have lost, we still crave— The astral sighs. *Flesh, memory, light. We once dealt in many currencies, O star-child.*

And in exchange, we gave her what she asked.

"Which was?" Violet says.

It is not in our nature to give without taking. We require an exchange.

"I'm not giving you my fingers—or my feet," she says.

The astral seems to be considering. *We will take a memory, Violet Everly. A song for a song. We still remember the exchanges of the old days, between star-kindred.*

A thousand thoughts flash through Violet's mind at once, all conflicting. She could find another way to reach her mother. And it would be madness to trust a *thing* with so much power over her mind.

But if the astral is telling the truth, her mother once came down here, in the dark, and left alive. With information.

"Swear you won't hurt me," she says. "Swear you won't take anything . . . extra."

We swear it on our mother's battle helm, our father's sun-spear. We swear on our name, that we still hold close to us when all else is dust.

It will have to be enough.

It takes every ounce of her courage to climb back down the ladder, back into the dark. She watches him watch her, mouth parted, as she puts her shoe back on. Then she stands as far away as possible, uncertain of what to do next.

You must come closer.

She takes two steps forward, and then another. His breath washes over her, reeking.

Closer.

Violet is so close that even in the dark, she can see the scars across the astral's torso, the open wounds still weeping across his ruined body. It's easy to see how he might have been something close to a man once. Sudden pity washes over her.

Touch our flesh, O star-child, and see what you will.

Ignoring the squeamish feeling in her gut, Violet presses her palm against his chest. Something pulses, violently rippling across the room, and she goes flying backwards. Her head cracks against the wall. *You lied*, she tries to say, but the words feel like slurry in her mouth, and her jaw stubbornly refuses to move.

Then she notices the woman standing in front of her. At first she thinks she's having an out-of-body experience, watching herself relive the last moment of her life. But then Violet notes how long the woman's hair is, the slightly different posture, the unfamiliar clothes.

It's her mother.

Twenty-Seven

MARIANNE EVERLY STANDS in front of the astral, utterly fearless, as though the time to worry about losing limbs has long passed. Violet stares at her, transfixed. It's been almost twelve years since she last saw her mother. She's spent so long trying to conjure her and yet here she is, right here. Violet reaches out her hand, desperate to touch her at last—

She catches a glimpse of her mother's face and her hand falls back. Marianne Everly now would be older, her face wearing a decade and change. Yet this version looks even younger than Violet, her face soft and round, hazel eyes bright with determination. Her bracelets glint on her wrists. With a shock, she sees her mother's stomach, taut and so very pregnant.

This is a memory. Only a memory.

"I seek an audience, Tamriel," she says, and Violet's heart aches for a voice she hasn't heard in years. "Will you listen?"

Over Marianne's shoulder, Violet can see the astral—but not as he looks in her present. Not a creature at all, but a naked man, golden-skinned and beautiful. Eyes the silver of starlight, black tattoos banded across his chest in an unfamiliar script. His shredded wings are still feathered, white down stained gold with his blood. But his legs hang at the same awkward angle, the bone smashed to pieces.

"Marianne Everly," he says, his voice unexpectedly soft. "We hear your name on the wind. Will you free our bonds?"

"I can't, and I wouldn't. I've heard of you, too, Tamriel. I know what you did to end up here." She straightens her shoulders. "By my birthright, I claim the law of exchange. A truth for a truth."

Tamriel narrows his eyes. "We could refuse." Then he sighs, and the expression on his face is so human that Violet is ashamed of her fear. "But as you are kindred, we will not. We await your question, star-child."

She hesitates, and for a second she looks every inch as young and uncertain as she is. "How do I break the Everly curse?"

Even as she says it, the vision starts to bubble, Marianne's words muddying in the air.

"Wait—" Violet says.

The memory changes, twists like a knife. Violet blinks and her mother is still in front of her, opposite Tamriel. But this is no youthful portrait, or distant memory. There are lines etched on her face, grey shot through her hair. She looks older than Violet recalls, with a bitter weariness that settles heavily over her features. And Tamriel looks as he is now, blood and sinew, almost unrecognisable as a man.

Violet bites back a gasp. This is no decades-old memory. This is recent, mere months.

"I need an audience with the last Hand of Illios. The last worlds-walker. How do I get it?"

You ask much of us, Marianne Everly. We might suspect you are mocking us, if you were so foolish as to do such a thing. He looks at her shrewdly. *Why?*

"Is this your exchange?"

He smiles and Violet shivers, seeing nothing human in it. *Yes. It is a great truth we offer you at our own cost, and so you must offer one in exchange.*

It's Marianne's turn to smile, and Violet's shocked to see the same viciousness etched on her face. "My great truth is that I will find what Astriade wants most in the world. And I will take it from her."

Astriade. Violet thinks of the card she was dealt, warning of calamity, the blonde-haired astral who clutched at the sword in her chest. It can't be who she thinks it is, and yet—

Tamriel bursts into whispered laughter, his entire body shaking. His wounds weep fresh blood, his chains rattling like music instead of manacles. And although it must be agony to move, his laughter is slow to subside.

We look forward to that day. He shakes his head in amusement. *Very well, Marianne Everly, we will grant you your boon.*

A blur of cityscape shimmers in the air, turrets and waterways. The astrological clock of Prague, St. Vitus Cathedral and its spires blur past, wreathed in rain. Then the vision closes in on a church, tucked into a corner of an otherwise unremarkable street. An archway, shimmering with golden light. The outline of a woman on a rock wall, light seeping through the cracks, hands pressed on either side.

There is still a price that must be paid.

Marianne nods wearily. "I know." She stares down at her hands. "A curse is just a contract, really."

The scene holds for another second with a lustrous fragility. Then it dissolves, and Violet's back in the dark room, her palm still pressed against Tamriel's chest. Not collapsed on the ground. Her mother is gone, whisked away by time. The creature's chest heaves, his breathing heavy with effort.

We have shown you. And now we will take.

"I—hold on a minute—"

An immense pressure descends across her head, and images flash through her mind. A viridian field; her mother tucking her into bed, looking so sad. A story falling from her lips in her soft, easy voice. The faint trace of perfume as she bends down to kiss Violet's forehead. This is the last day she saw her mother, she realises. *Not that one!* she tries to say. There are others—Marianne arguing with Violet over something misplaced; Marianne half cooking, half reading in the kitchen; Marianne pushing Violet towards her uncles because *I have work to do*, always—and he can have them. But not this one. Not the last.

Then the pressure abruptly disappears. She reels back, trying to hold on to…what was it? But already the images have drained away like water. Her face is wet, tears streaking down her face, though she has no idea why. She wipes them away furiously.

"What did you take?" she demands.

We took what is fair. The exchange is complete.

"I don't understand," she says. "A price? What do you mean, Hand? Will they have the key? Prague is a big city! How am I supposed to find them?"

That is not our concern. We will never see beyond this darkness again.

There's something about the way the astral says it that makes her pause and look at him again. After Marianne's memories, it's impossible not to see so clearly the remnants of a god. Astral. Her gaze drifts to his reveurite chains.

"What was it like?" she asks softly. "Elandriel?"

Tamriel watches her with his silver-rimmed eyes, his unfathomable expression.

It was without peer. Elandriel, the doorway to untold worlds. A dream, thousands of years in the making. Our brethren had such plans for this world of worlds, this treasure of ours.

Yet heavy dreams make for heavy burdens. And look how it weighs upon us. He tilts his head to the side, curiosity evident in his gaze. *Why do you ask us of this?*

"I—" She opens her mouth to tell him about her mother, the Everly curse, her own internal clock ticking downwards.

But it would be a lie to say those were the first things she thought of. She thinks of the talent that runs through her veins, that might still let her walk through worlds one day.

"I just...wanted to know," she says.

He leans close enough to her that his chains jangle with the strain. *You remind us much of another. We see your mother, she who wanders, but there is something else...*

The astral suddenly looks up at the ceiling, as if sensing something there. *The time for a reckoning is almost at hand. Leave us, O star-child.*

"But I—"

LEAVE! he screams, and the command is so heavy that she has no choice but to obey. She's halfway up the ladder before she even realises he has compelled her again. But whether she wants to or not, she keeps going. She has so many questions, waiting to explode off her tongue. Elandriel, birthright, her mother, what will happen to Tamriel—

She emerges from the basement covered in dust, feeling as if she's spent a lifetime down there. The sun has descended, leaving the kitchen swathed in darkness. Something creaks in the house and she freezes.

A reckoning comes. But for who?

Penelope emerges from the shadows, watching Violet leave the house. It's always curious how fast children grow up, she observes. What they take with them into adulthood; what they leave behind. And Violet takes after the Everly line, with little trace of her worthless father—whoever he might have been.

But then again, Everly blood is stronger than most. Stubborner than most.

Penelope descends the ladder to the basement, where Violet's footprints are still embedded in the dirt. Tamriel looks up and laughs softly.

"Tamriel," she says. "You lied to me."

O star-daughter, you return. As we knew you would.

"You told me she wouldn't come looking for lost things," Penelope says, every word dagger-sharp. "You said I would be safe. How dare you."

He laughs again. *What joy it will bring us to see you undone.*

She steps forward, into the dark. "You're mistaken if you think you will live to witness anything past today."

We foresaw this day, as we do all things. And your time is coming, Astriade. We will relish it, whether we are ashes in the wind or motes in sunlight.

Penelope steps up to Tamriel, close enough to kiss. She strokes his ruined face.

"Oh, Tamriel. It's been a long time since you were in conversation with anything but your poor, deluded self. I've read the skies; my future—my *eternal* future—is assured." She smiles, baring her teeth. "The heavens change their minds, too, you know."

She places one hand on his grey, scarred chest, right above his heart. He blinks slowly at her, just once. Knowing what she's about to do.

We see a thousand dying lights, he hisses suddenly. *We see a prison against the skies, streets buckling, a city aflame. We see a mortal man, loved and hated and O so precious to you, Astriade—*

Her nails sink into his flesh. He gasps, shuddering as life itself leeches from him. His mouth opens and closes uselessly, and his hands claw at the air. Slowly, his skin turns dark grey, the texture of dry paper. His eyelids sag closed. He breathes in once, a harsh, inhuman sound—then stops.

His chest stills. He slumps forward, his chains clinking with the effort of supporting his body.

Penelope groans softly. Her fingertips are dripping with blood. But she is sated, for now. Delicately, she licks her fingers clean, as though it's the end of a meal. In a way, she supposes, it is. She's taken his lifeblood, his talent. The remnants of his vigour.

Finished, she surveys Tamriel's corpse, his stinking mortality.

"Always eager to get the last word in, Tamriel," she says. "You thought you were so clever, so invulnerable. A lifetime of protection, dear cousin. That's what I offered, and I have kept my promise."

She stays with his corpse long enough to watch the first flies settle in the blood on his chest. Then, grace itself, she rises, renewed strength flowing through her. Another parcel of time, bought and paid for.

But even as she climbs out of the hatch into the cresting sunrise, a thought worries at the edge of her mind. Violet was never supposed to come here. And whatever she learnt in the dark with Tamriel, she's one step closer on the path to Marianne Everly. Mother or daughter, it doesn't matter—they cannot be allowed to find Elandriel first.

Violet Everly is becoming a problem.

Twenty-Eight

N AN ABANDONED house on the outskirts of some Austrian village, Yury falls into a deep slumber. He sleeps so little these days, but when the urge takes him, the compulsion is so strong, he can do nothing else except give into it. When he does sleep, the vials give him incredibly vivid dreams, and he often wakes up unable to tell the waking truth from his sleeping one.

Lately, he has been dreaming of hard reveurite scales protruding from his skin. The agony is as real as if it was truly happening. His necrotic skin sloughs off to reveal exquisite, tender flesh underneath. Then rock bursting through his veins, glittering plates overlapping like fledgling armour: pauldron, cuirass, breastplate enfolding him in a stony carapace.

The reveurite is transforming him into a miracle. Into someone *more than.*

God, his thoughts murmur. *Astral.*

"Yury."

He wakes to a man standing over him. He can't see much beyond an outline, but he recognises his voice. The ingestion of reveurite is slowly crystallising his eyesight, his pupils clouded by cataracts.

"Aleksander," he says, with intense relief. "You are here. I have run out—the last vial is—"

"You were supposed to *talk* to Johannes." Aleksander looks away, and Yury hears the horror in his voice. "You weren't supposed to kill him."

"I... did not mean to—the fire—"

Heat against his face. Warmth unending.

"Because of you, the scholars are asking questions. Questions Penelope cannot answer without complications."

"I just need—the vials—"

"You promised you had yourself under control!" Aleksander says. "Now Johannes is dead. You killed a man—a *scholar!*"

Yury swallows, aware of the burn in his lungs. "Aleksander, I—"

He can still feel the echo of the breastplate on his chest. He just needs more *time.* He is so close.

"It's over, Yury." Aleksander pauses. "I'm going to Prague alone. I'm sorry."

After he leaves, Yury becomes aware of a keening sound, like an animal caught in a trap. Sometime later, he realises it's him.

For an indeterminate period, he drifts on an ocean of white-hot needles. No vials means no reprieve from the pain. He is so cold, he is no longer sure where the agony stops and his flesh begins. Time stretches and twists.

But somewhere within the agonising current, a plan emerges. His mind has not so fully betrayed him yet.

To become a god, one must present a gift to them. A sacrifice, if you will.

And there is a young woman Penelope is *very* interested in.

Forget Aleksander and his cringing deference. Yury will be astral. He will be light itself made manifest. He will shuck mortality for eternal glory, like shedding a skin.

It will be glorious.

Piece by piece, Yury claws what remains of himself upright and begins the long journey to Prague.

PART THREE

A Fairy Tale

WOULD YOU LIKE to hear a story?" Ambrose asks.

Violet is just past ten years old, brooding and resentful, her mother two weeks into her "adventure." Ambrose can't really blame her. In his mid-twenties, he, as the long-suffering, pliable youngest—and also not Gabriel—has been dragged away from his postgraduate degree in literature to mind his niece. When Marianne comes back, he'll resume his studies, of course. There is a reason why he was so reluctant to return, even when Marianne showed up with a baby, and the Everly siblings were forced to regroup. Back to the house with its long stretch of memory and baleful portraits, where the Everly name supersedes all. But the truth is, he'll never be able to go back to his degree, and by the time he realises this, his niece's bright inquisitiveness and tenacious heart will have already won him over.

Tonight, though, they are still strangers, and Violet is on the edge of tears and angry about it. Angry at the world. Still, she perks up when she hears the word *story*. Reluctantly, she nods.

"It's a good one, I promise," Ambrose says, settling in with her on the couch. "And it's your legacy. Because it starts with an Everly. He wasn't the first, and he certainly wouldn't be the last, but he was perhaps the most extraordinary of us all." He clears his throat, and begins the same way Marianne had explained the origins of the Everly fate—with a fairy tale. "Once upon a time, in a magical city on a distant shore, lived Ever Everly."

"That's a stupid name," Violet mutters.

Ambrose hides his smile. "Ah, but you see, he was a clever man."

He was a craftsman, Ambrose says, and an amazing one at that. With a blow of his hammer, or the twist of a screw, he could make magical toys beyond compare. And people loved them. But Ever Everly had a secret, and it was that no one had ever loved *him*.

He hadn't minded, at first. If that was the way of the world, then let it be so. Yet as he grew older, and watched couples filter in together in the shy throes of new love, then pregnant, and then perhaps with two children at their side, he yearned for how neatly they fitted into one another, like puzzle pieces. And if he was a puzzle piece, he was the one missing from the box, unable to be part of the picture.

Then, one day, a woman came into his shop.

To say she was beautiful would be to call the moon a rock. She was so beautiful, people would weep at the sight of her, and said she looked like a star upon the earth. So beautiful, and yet missing something, too. For just as Ever Everly had never been loved, she had never *loved*. Magic, however, she had in spades. She took one look at him, and she knew he longed to be the half of a whole.

For Ever Everly, she decided, she could learn what love is. So she offered him a deal: she would love him for a year and a day, and then she would give him a choice: either she would eat his soul, or the soul of everyone in the city. He was a good man, and she knew he would choose the former. A soul fat on love was a very powerful thing indeed, and she had no desire to taste the souls of the city, most of whom were mealy and unripe.

The woman thought this was a fair exchange, and so, in his own way, did Ever Everly. Apart from love, he had lived a good life, and he would be ready to give himself to her when the time came. A year and a day of love, he reasoned, was generous for a lifetime. They married underneath the swords of their ancestors, and it wasn't long before they bore a child.

What the woman hadn't counted on, however, was what love did to *her*. Love gave her strength. Love made her weak. Love made her want him more than she'd ever wanted anything else. She loved the care he took over what he made, the way he asked after every customer's family. The way he said her name, like a jewel in his mouth.

But she had entered a binding contract. At the end of the year and a day, she would be forced to either eat his soul, or the souls of the city. Unbeknownst to Ever Everly, she was making her choice.

Six months went past. Then nine. A year.

On the last evening, Ever Everly got his affairs in order. He tidied his workshop, gave away his toys, and closed up his shop for the final time. Then he turned to the woman and told her he was ready to be eaten. She wouldn't have him, however. He was too precious to her. She would rather take the city.

Ever Everly tried to stop her. But love had made her impervious to his pleading, and she swept him aside. The city had thousands of souls, and she would eat them all just to be with him. He looked on in despair, thinking of the children, the couples he had watched from afar. What could he do?

And because he was a clever man, the answer came to him. In his consuming love, he had forgotten that he was not half of a whole at all. He was a person in himself. And there was still a choice to be made. She could not protect a soul that did not exist.

So he took his ancestors' sword from the wall and he plunged it through his heart. The magic that had made him such a brilliant creator exploded from him, and froze the woman in a statue as unbreakable as their contract. He had stripped her of her magic, so she could eat no more souls. The city would be safe.

"And then," Ambrose says, "with the stars in his eyes, he heaved a great sigh, and he died."

In the ensuing silence, he wonders if he should have picked a story that didn't end in death and gore. But when he risks a look at Violet, her eyes are wide with wonder.

"Wow," she whispers.

He smiles down at her. "I know. And deep down, inside her crystal cage, the woman still yearns to consume his soul because it's the only way she knows how to love."

Which, of course, isn't really love at all.

"I wish he hadn't died," Violet says later, on their way up to bed.

Ambrose tucks her in—the first time she's let him do so. He ponders the thought for a moment. Marianne would say something about heroes and sacrifices, but he can't bring himself to lie that an Everly went willingly to their death. *We do not go gentle*, he thinks sadly.

"I think Ever probably wished that, too. Who knows what he might have done with the rest of his life? But he died saving their city. He died saving what matters." Ambrose kisses the top of her head. "He died, but he won them the world."

CHAPTER

Twenty-Nine

P RAGUE. AND ONLY a few weeks left until Penelope's terrible deadline.

But after a year of searching, Violet is *so* close. She has barely been able to sleep, much less forget Tamriel and his words ringing through her head. Perhaps this is what the asteria meant by sacrifice—and already the choices he laid out for her are in the past. She's always considered her mind her own, but what Tamriel had almost made her do—what he'd made her see—

A stab of unbidden anger goes through her at the thought of her mother, surprising her with its intensity. Anger doesn't bring Marianne back, or stop Penelope's curse. But if Marianne had told her what she was doing, or where she might go, then maybe Violet wouldn't be standing in the middle of an unfamiliar city with no idea what to look for next.

Maybe Violet wouldn't have had to venture into that cold, black basement to deal with a monster.

With no real idea of where to find the vision church, she meanders across the city until she reaches the Charles Bridge. For a while, she simply leans on the wall and watches other people cross, the breeze teasing out her hair from its hasty pony-tail. She'd once seen an illustration of the bridge in an old book, from before she could even read, really. With the book on her lap, she'd sit in her wardrobe and tell herself stories about each of the statues. Saints were a mystery to her, then; no, these statues were obviously of magicians, with their long robes and solemn demeanours.

This city is a feast, and for the first time, she feels hollow at the thought of not having anyone to share it with. She tolerated it in New York, Accra, Melbourne, but now that she knows what it's like to walk arm in arm with someone else, she aches for companionship.

Before she can change her mind, she snaps a photograph of the bridge and her beloved magicians, and sends it to Aleksander. A moment later, her phone beeps. *I hear the coffee in Prague is beyond compare.*

A smile steals across her face. *Come and see for yourself.*

She closes her eyes, and when she opens them again, he's there.

"Violet Everly," he says, his sea-glass eyes sparkling. "What a coincidence."

His hair is still dusted in snow, and she brushes it off, his skin cold against her hands. Absentmindedly, she reaches to touch the scar above his eyebrow, but he steps back, leaving her hand hanging in the air. She quickly tucks it behind her back, her face colouring.

"I know I said coffee," Aleksander says, "but I was thinking of something a bit more substantial?"

On cue, Violet's stomach rumbles.

"Guess that means yes," she says, trying to shake off her embarrassment.

Aleksander leads them to a tiny restaurant off a busy street, and they sit at a table overlooking the river sparkling in the sunlight. Once again, Aleksander orders fluently, his Czech accent flawless. The waiter says something and when he responds, the waiter bursts into laughter before sweeping away with their menus.

"Have you been to Prague before?" she asks.

He shakes his head. "I like languages. And Penelope was keen for me to have a comprehensive education."

Violet looks out the window to hide her displeasure at hearing Penelope's name; it's always like being doused in icy water, no matter how many times the topic comes up. She hasn't seen her since that day in the coffee shop, and sometimes even that feels like a hazy dream. Only one woman, and yet she's shaped Violet's entire life. It would be nice to have a moment that she hasn't touched, just once.

She's still staring out of the window when she realises Aleksander has asked her a question. "Sorry?" she says.

"Did you get hold of the map in the end?" he asks.

It takes her a second to process what he's asked her. And then it hits her: he doesn't know about Johannes. It had been one thing to tell Aleksander about the conversation in the museum, when that's all it was—a talk, nothing more. But she's not sure she can even begin to explain Johannes' awful death, never mind the horrors of Tamriel's basement and the vision he'd showed her. Her stomach churns with unease.

"It's a long story," she says.

Aleksander leans in closer to her, his hands grazing hers. "I have time."

Violet bites her lip, just before she relents. "I'm looking for the Hand of Illios. Or 'a' Hand, possibly. I'm not sure."

Aleksander blinks. "Excuse me?"

She lowers her voice. "Illios. Something about keys and doorways and—well, I don't know what it means, but my mother did. It's supposed to be here, in Prague."

She waits for Aleksander to explain, to unlock the answers for her. But he only stares at her.

"I didn't know you were aware of the astrals," he says quietly.

"I've learnt a lot in the last year, Aleksander." She tries to say it playfully, but even to her, it sounds like a jibe.

He frowns. "Are you sure?"

"Positive," she says.

Violet waits for him to say more, but then the food arrives and all conversation ceases. Afterwards, they linger at the table. Violet is full and content for what feels like the first time in ages. Aleksander, though, is deep in thought, his brow furrowed.

"Everything okay?" she asks.

When he turns to her, his frown has disappeared. "Of course. Come on, let's go exploring."

They meander down the mosaic pavement, along the river. Out of the corner of her eye, she glances at Aleksander. He seems completely at ease now, with no signs of his earlier agitation. And yet she can't shake the feeling that there's something off.

As they walk, she keeps an eye out for the church in Tamriel's vision. But there are churches *everywhere*. Her heart sinks. There's already so little time left.

Then she stops.

"What is it?" Aleksander asks.

She's been so focused on the hunt for her mother and the key that she'd totally forgotten about Caspian's invitation. And yet here she is, in Prague, just in time for it. The scholars and their parties, she thinks, smiling despite herself. But who better to ask than Caspian Verne, with all his contacts and goodwill?

She thinks of that long-ago feeling when she'd first run into Aleksander, of fate stretching out a hand. If she hadn't taken the opportunity then, would she have seen as much of the world? Would she be here now, as close to victory as she's ever come?

Maybe this is that hand again, reaching out. Besides, it's been so long since she's had a little fun.

"Hey, what are your plans in the next week?" she asks.

He blinks, startled. "Not much. Why?"

"Can I take you somewhere?"

CHAPTER

Thirty

TWO DAYS LATER, Violet meets Aleksander in an alleyway just as dusk settles over the city. They cross the Charles Bridge, past the magician-saints and the sketch artists packing up for the evening. But instead of heading up the hill towards the castle, Violet veers left, along the river, then down a series of increasingly narrow alleyways. Shadows chase at their heels.

"Do you know where we're going?" she asks.

He frowns at her. "Well, since *you're* the one who invited me, not really. Unless I'm supposed to?"

She's surprised to hear the pang of anxiety in his voice. She waves it away, her smile widening.

"No, this is my surprise," she says.

Aleksander has taught her so much that it feels like a victory to find something he might not actually know about.

She memorised the directions earlier for no real reason other than to give Aleksander a bit of a show, but she still holds her breath as she knocks once, then twice, then once again on an unremarkable door. Seconds tick past, and now it's Violet's turn to be uncertain. Either she's about to be confronted by one angry stranger, or—

The door eases open and a woman holds out her hand. "Token, please."

Dutifully, Violet hands over the coin Caspian gave her in New York.

"And a plus-one," she adds, gesturing to Aleksander.

The woman gives Aleksander a once-over just long enough to make Violet nervous, then she nods.

"You'll vouch for him." It's not a question.

The door leads directly to a stairway bracketed by candles dripping wax across the floor. The stairs lead down, where the sound of thumping bass judders upwards. Something hangs from the ceiling and it takes Violet's eyes a moment to adjust before she realises what it is: keys, hundreds of them, in all shapes and sizes. Feathers, too, dipped in gold paint and strung up so that they twist gently above.

Aleksander takes in a quick breath.

Feeling bold, Violet takes his hand. "Come on."

She's been brushing up on her reading, and there's an entire city underneath Prague, like a second skin. Old cellars bricked up and then rediscovered; eerie dungeons engraved with illegible graffiti; whole streets buried underneath the new buildings. Officially, no one's allowed in except via carefully guided tours. Unofficially, there are hundreds of entrances, and no one to police them.

She suspects that if she ever sees Elandriel, it'll look something like this.

As they reach the bottom of the stairs, Aleksander gives her hand a quick squeeze. But he doesn't let go. Violet smiles to herself in the dark.

The stairway opens out to an enormous cellar with a low barrel-vault ceiling. Candlelight competes with strobe lights, bouncing off the brick walls. Bass pulses underneath their feet from an enthusiastic DJ. Someone has laid down carpets to muffle the sound, and people kick off their shoes to lounge on them. It's a chilly evening, and others have brought down heaters, plugged into "borrowed" electricity, or drape themselves in blankets. Violet spies a grubby pack of asteros cards, spread out for a small but captive audience.

It's as different from a scholar party as she can imagine. And yet just as thrilling to be here.

She spies a couple of scholar keys, ringed around fingers or twined around forearms, alongside plain black bands, or glittering tattoos of lace next to bold slashes of colour. But there are far more people wholly unadorned by tattoos, keys or otherwise.

People like her.

Next to her, Aleksander raises his eyebrows. "Who did you say you heard about this place from?"

"I can have more than one friend, you know," she says, teasing.

But he only looks more apprehensive. "I'm not sure we should really be here. These people aren't..."

"Scholars?" she suggests.

That's a bit rich coming from you, she wants to say, but can't. If she hadn't asked him to steal the key for her, he would probably be one of them by now. She thinks about how isolated she'd felt at Yulan's private gathering, and her heart pangs sympathetically. It can't be easy, she muses, being amongst so many scholars.

Here, though, he doesn't need to be a scholar. And neither does she.

There's almost too much to look at, dozens of nooks with a different surprise hidden in each one. A couple of enterprising spirits have set up stalls, selling just about everything: hot drinks to combat the subterranean chill; fragile books and scrolls, in dozens of languages; antique glass bottles that glimmer oddly in the candlelight. There's even a stand trading stolen scholar's keys—but Violet decides to steer Aleksander clear of that one.

Instead, they meander towards a nook decked out in bright fairy lights. There's a table speckled with chips of glittering rock, and at first that's all they seem. Then she catches a faint golden glimmer and her heart thrills.

Aleksander picks up a piece and immediately puts it down. "There's not enough reveurite in there to power a light bulb."

The last space at the end of the vast hallway is so shrouded in shadow that Violet does a double-take when she realises someone has set up another deck of asteros cards. No one else seems to have noticed; this stretch of the underground hallway is empty.

"You." The woman points at Aleksander. "Stay for a reading."

Aleksander glances at Violet and she shrugs. She's already seen her fate in a pack of cards, and she'd rather not show it to Aleksander.

"Free of charge," the woman adds.

Aleksander rubs the back of his neck and Violet can see that he's wavering. She gives him a nudge towards the table and smiles.

"I can look after myself for a bit," she says.

He touches the side of her face, just once. Violet's cheeks warm, and she's suddenly grateful for the dark.

"I'll only be a moment," he promises.

She watches him go, her own smile lingering.

A man in a black silk shirt comes to stand next to her. "They say if you see an asteria naked, you'll be cursed for three generations."

Caspian Verne has swapped out his formal wear for a dark leather jacket and darker jeans. It's a casual look, and yet on him it's still infuriatingly suave.

"So you're extremely cursed, then," she says.

His mouth twitches. "Indisputably. I'm glad to see you made it, Violet." Then he peers at Aleksander's retreating figure. "And what interesting company you've brought with you."

"Aleksander?" she says, surprised. "We're just—I mean—"

"It's okay, we all have our sins."

She brushes aside the comment. "I actually came here on a mission. I want to talk to you about something."

"Funnily enough, so do I." Caspian gestures to the labyrinth of underground rooms. "Take a walk with me, Everly. Unless you can't bear to be parted with your white knight."

Violet rolls her eyes. "He's not my knight."

But she glances at Aleksander all the same. He'll be fine without her; it's only five minutes. Besides, while she and Caspian have made casual chit-chat over the various gatherings and run-ins over the last year, they've never spoken properly. Not until now.

"Tell me, then," she says. "What wisdom can the great Caspian Verne impart?"

Caspian's smile glitters in the darkness.

Aleksander approaches the asteria with a healthy amount of scepticism. Normally, they're around during Fidelis' various fairs, plying fortunes and favours, quibbling over the best decks and competing for the most elaborate costume. Most use masks to disguise their day-to-day appearance, but Aleksander's seen enough of them to know that behind the disguise is usually the butcher, or one of the agriculturists. Ordinary people, pretending they have a hotline to the gods.

This woman wears no mask. Instead, her face is painted in simple gold lines, slashing across the contours of her cheekbones and extending into her hairline. The rest of her outfit is simply a black slip that belies how cold it really is down here. Her eyes meet his and every single hair on the back of his neck lifts.

Wordlessly, she starts to spread the cards.

The asteros deck is as simple as her outfit, with matte black backs, like someone painted over the original illustration in a hurry. But they have the telltale glitter of reveurite dust that marks them out as genuine.

It's been a long time since Aleksander's visited an asteria, even for fun. He touches each of the cards, wondering which astral holds his fate in their hands. Will it be Nemetor, carrying his staff of infallible wisdom? Or Etallantia herself, gentle patron to the scholars and their assistants? At this point, he'd even settle for the trickster twins Mirael and Finrael.

He makes to turn over three cards, but the asteria holds up one hand. Instead, she keeps laying them out.

"There are only supposed to be three—" he starts.

The asteria cuts him off with a single look, and continues until there are seven cards in front of him, spread in a semicircle. Seven astrals. She spreads out her hands in a clear gesture: *now you may see your guides.*

The first card is Fillea, a decidedly uninspired card. The astral of choices stands with her back to him, her arms outstretched to indicate the forked path before her. He doesn't need an asteros card to tell him that there are choices to be made.

He turns over the next card, already regretting this endeavour—and stops. It's undeniably Berias and Tullis, twined in their classic pose of love and betrayal. But Berias wears a woman's body and Tullis, his unseen knife angled high—

It's Violet and Aleksander.

The likeness is undeniable: Tullis' tattoos match his, down to the three dots curving around his ear; and Berias possesses Violet's teasing smile, her curling hair. Aleksander glances at the asteria, but she only tilts her head to the next card.

He swallows, and keeps going.

The third card is Etallantia, bearing her book of wisdom and cup of knowledge bestowed only to the scholars. But once again, the astral wears Aleksander's face. Then Illios the First Scholar, who bridged the gap between mortal and astral, surrounded by his Hands. Aleksander's painted expression is screwed up as he drinks golden liquid from the goblet that will elevate him to godhood.

The fifth card is Tamriel the Desecrator. An astral in the raw breastplate and skirt of a warrior, his hands uplifted to the sky as blood runs red in the city below. Aleksander's smile of ecstasy. Aleksander's hands stained red.

Unable to stop himself, Aleksander turns over the next card. He doesn't recognise this one, and yet he is in it again, the wings of an astral erupting behind him, golden tears tracking down his face. A body hangs limp in his arms, the face hidden in the crook of his elbow. But the soft brown hair, the graceful curve of the neck, the dangling wrist with one half of a pair of bracelets he knows so well—

He stumbles backwards, knocking over a stray candle. Its glass cup breaks, scattering shards across the floor. Wax pools on the floor.

There is just one card left, but Aleksander can't bring himself to touch it. He doesn't want to know what it will reveal.

"I can't," he whispers.

Dispassionately, the asteria flips over the final card: Erriel, astral of the lost. Her face, illuminated by a single lantern, is solemn. The rest of the card is streaked black. Nothing.

The asteria surveys him, her face unreadable underneath the face paint. Her gaze meets his, and he reels back. Her eyes are so terribly ancient. How had he not noticed before?

"We see the shadow behind you," the asteria says. "We see the shadow ahead. From nothing, to nothing."

Aleksander takes a step back, then another. It is all deception and trickery, he tries to remind himself. This is someone's idea of a joke. The cards are just cards.

Tullis and Berias. Aleksander, entwined with Violet, his lips against hers—

In the last glance before he flees, he notes that the cards placed together look like an archway. A door.

Thirty-One

V IOLET WALKS WITH Caspian along the endless underground hallway, away from the asteria's shadowy nook. Caspian is no less at ease here than he was at Yulan's party. He seems to know everyone by name, and those few he doesn't, he greets with effortless charm. It's not lost on Violet that he's using this same charm on her, which means he wants something. But it's still awfully hard not to fall for it.

"I suppose I can't ask why you're here in Prague," he says eventually. "With Aleksander of all people."

Violet glances sideways at him. "You could."

He steeples his fingers thoughtfully. "Ah, but then you would tell me an untruth, and then I would have to pretend I believe you. Let's not make liars of us both," he says—then adds with a sly smile, "Besides, I would be disappointed if it wasn't as exciting as the rumours."

"What are the rumours?" she asks curiously.

"That you're chasing a lover across the world," he says, ticking down his fingers. "That you're a spy. That you are already walking between worlds." Caspian halts mid-step. "That you're looking for a doorway to the lost scholar-city, Elandriel."

Violet gives him a sharp glance. He's not looking at her, but she has the sense that he's listening very carefully to every intake of breath. He runs his hand across the crooked nub of an exposed brick.

"What do you think?" she asks, as breezily as she can manage.

He just smiles at her, but she has the feeling she's already said too much.

They pause by a nook with dozens of maps for sale pinned to the walls. Violet recognises the outline of Fidelis from her fairy-tale book, but it's still odd to see it so obviously displayed, and not squirrelled away like a secret. The other maps are all squiggles and vague instructions, with little enough detail that they could be anywhere. Violet's seen a few of these before, all claiming to lead to fairy realms, or other worlds entirely. *Drink this potion at midnight on a blood moon and walk three steps backwards into a stone circle under moonlight,* et cetera.

There is a part of her that knows these aren't real instructions, or even real places. But there is another part of her that imagines all too easily the stone circle, moonlight pouring downwards, the steps backwards into the unknown. To the witches in their forests, to the stairs inside the wardrobe. A word that still rattles around the inside of her skull, clutching the edges of her dreams. *Adventure.*

"I've seen it, you know," Caspian says quietly. "The gateway to another world."

The reverie vanishes; Violet nods. "I know. The keys."

But he shakes his head. "The keys are a crude tool, wielded by the uncurious or unskilled. They can only take you to where you've already been."

"A key is still better than nothing," she reminds him.

"And be even more beholden to the scholars than I already am? I won't be part of that," he says.

"Why not?" she asks.

It's not as though his reputation imbues him with some misplaced purity.

"Do you know how one makes a scholar?" he asks.

"Talent," she says.

"Talent is innate; the scholars are a construct. And you're not a scholar, yet you have a lot of talent. Did you know that?"

Violet looks away to hide her irritation. "I do, in fact."

Not that she's been able to do anything with it. She's no closer to possessing a key than she was in the café last year, and every clue of

Marianne's whereabouts has pointed away from Fidelis. Even if she did manage to get her hands on reveurite, it's just metal to her. Malleable metal—but nothing else. Maybe if she was a scholar, it would be different. Maybe her talent would mean something.

"You should ask yourself who the scholars place power in when they choose to go down that path. What they sacrifice in return. They might call themselves colleagues, and pretend they share the same goals, but they're all dragons at heart, guarding their hoards of knowledge. And they'll never fulfil their true potential because of it." He shrugs. "Revolutions aren't built on the backs of an individual."

Not dragons, Violet thinks. *Wolves.*

"Speaking of—I might not be a scholar, but I've heard a great deal about Aleksander," he continues. "Not all of it pleasant. Are you sure you know what kind of man he is?"

Violet almost laughs at his concern. "He's my friend. Do you think I would have brought him here if I didn't trust him? Anyway, he's not a scholar. He's not like them."

If it wasn't for Aleksander, she wouldn't be standing here now.

"If you're sure," he says, but he still sounds uncertain—a rare tone for Caspian.

"I'm sure."

But even as she says it, she thinks back to those odd moments between them. The way he'd snapped at her in Vienna, all those probing questions—

"I have a confession," Caspian says suddenly. "But I'm not sure you'll like it."

Ah, *finally*, the reason Caspian asked her to walk with him. Possibly the reason why he'd invited her to this gathering in the first place. She'll give him this much: he knows exactly how to persuade people to bend around him.

"About two years ago, your mother asked to meet with my grandmother. She was looking for a way through worlds that didn't require a key: a doorway. And of course, we Vernes were the best people to ask. Yours truly being a particular expert, if I say so myself."

Doorways. Elandriel. Violet's heart clenches.

"Marianne had been running for a long time. And she was ready to stop. I don't know what she was running from." He looks at her. "But you do."

"Why didn't you tell me this earlier?" she demands.

Caspian's tone remains light, but there's a new steel underneath it. "I must admit, I didn't think much of it when your name started to pop up," he says. "Violet Everly, daughter of Marianne Everly, asking questions here and there. It happens. People drop in and out of our world all the time, often not by their own hand. But you were extraordinarily persistent, even though you held nothing of value. No secret information, no exceptional object to barter with."

Violet guesses where this is going. "And you got curious."

"Outsiders who want something that badly are usually dead or one of us within a year. And you're not a scholar." He levels his gaze at her. "I am giving you a gift now. Understand?"

Slightly chastened, Violet nods.

"I don't think you're going to find your mother." He pauses. "She asked my grandmother to destroy her research. She said she didn't want to be followed."

"That's impossible," she says. "Marianne wouldn't do that."

Not without undoing the curse first. Not without coming back for Violet.

"They were good friends, you know. God knows how—even I wouldn't call my grandmother a warm person. But she took a real shine to Marianne. And she wouldn't lie to me about this," Caspian says.

"But that's why I'm here," she persists. "I'm looking for a church. There's supposed to be something there—a 'Hand of Illios,' whatever that means—I'm not really sure—"

"You mean the Blessing of Illios?" he says, surprised. "You *have* been busy."

"Yes, exactly," she says with relief.

His eyebrows raise. "I wasn't aware you were planning to be a scholar." Then he sees her frown, and his troubled expression clears. "Ah. The Blessing of Illios is their yearly ritual. A week of blood oaths, ass-kissing, masochistic tattoos, and so on, then hey presto, you're officially a scholar. It's not such a big song and dance here, but the scholars in Prague like to gather at Our Lady Victorious to celebrate."

Violet takes a mental note of the name. "That's where my mother was headed. It must have been. Maybe she destroyed her research, but—she left *something* for me to find. She wouldn't have just… gone."

Violet's stomach lurches at the thought. There are so few days left. Marianne wouldn't simply pack it in and leave. *The way she left her brothers? The way she left you?*

"I'll ask my grandmother. She might know more." Caspian hesitates. "I really hope you find her, Violet."

"Thank you," she says, and means it. "For everything."

"Well, it's quite fun to thwart the scholars' plans every now and then. And you're the most exciting thing to happen to them in years." Then he smiles warmly at her. It's a genuine smile that reaches the corners of his eyes, and maybe the first one he's ever given Violet. "Besides, it would be an awful pity if the scholars remade you in their image."

She smiles back, oddly touched by his concern. If Penelope wasn't forever at the forefront of her mind, or Elandriel, or her mother, or any number of more pressing concerns—then maybe he would have a right to worry. But until then—

"Ah, your knight reappears," he says, glancing behind them both. "I will leave you, then. But remember, we don't have to be anything but what we are. We're not scholars—but we're not *nothing*, either. Keep the third option in mind."

He gives her a stupid flourish of a bow—all politician, all charm again—then disappears into the crowd. Violet stares at him as he walks away, trying to burn the conversation into her brain so she can pick it apart later. He can't be right about Marianne. Everlys stick together; she'll come back.

Aleksander reappears, his face flushed. "There you are," he says. "I've been looking everywhere for you and— Is that Caspian Verne? What the hell were you doing with him?"

She snaps back to the present. "He just wanted to talk."

"Talk. Right." Aleksander folds his arms. "Do you know who he is? Who his family are?"

"Does it matter?"

"The Vernes are assholes," he says with surprising vehemence.

"Caspian's the one who invited us. And I don't *trust* him, exactly, but...there aren't a lot of options, you know."

Violet can feel herself getting exasperated, and tries to shrug it off. Every scholar has at least one skeleton in their closet, and it usually belongs to another family. And Aleksander, of all people, has no right to judge who she speaks to.

He glances away from her. "Why did you bring me here?"

His tone is so sharp that she finally takes him in properly. Aleksander's eyes are shadowed, and his entire body is one knife-like line. The man in front of her is a stranger, dark and angry. Miles away from the person she left in the hands of the asteria only moments ago.

"I thought you'd be pleased," she says, bewildered. "I thought—"

"You thought you'd take me down into some dark cellar"—something in Aleksander's voice squeezes painfully—"to muck about with amateurs who have no interest in—no *respect* for—the scholars. If you knew me at all, you'd know I'd hate this."

Violet takes a step back.

"I guess I don't know you at all, then," she says quietly.

Aleksander runs a hand through his hair in agitation. "You don't understand. You asked so much of me. Too much."

"If this is about Caspian—"

"This has nothing to do with him. This is about *you*," he snaps.

"Then you should never have given me your phone number!" she says furiously. "You could have walked away. You could have pretended you didn't recognise me. *You didn't have to stay.*"

His expression shifts, his eyebrows knotted in confusion. As though it never occurred to him that it was ever a possibility to turn away. He rubs the back of his neck, and she catches a glimpse of shame.

He says, "I—I couldn't. I didn't—" He swallows. "How could I let you go?"

He says it like a confession, like it's something to feel guilty for.

She looks at him helplessly. "Then what do you want from me, Aleksander?"

He makes an agonised noise, his mouth pressed together in indecision. Somehow in the course of their argument, they've ended up inches from one another. Close enough for her to see the silvery glimmer of the scar above his eyebrow. Close enough for her to feel the huff of his breath against her forehead.

"I want..." he murmurs, in a husky tone that sends shivers across her whole body.

His hands glide over her shoulders, his thumb sliding achingly over her collarbone. His eyes flick to hers, and she catches the question in them. She touches the side of his face, just once.

Violet is still furious with him—she can feel it simmering underneath her skin—but there's something else alongside it, not entirely unfamiliar. The same feeling she had every time she caught herself looking for him, every time a flash of grey eyes or dark curly hair caught her attention. The bitter disappointment afterwards because it was never him. No matter what she wished.

But here he is. Right in front of her.

And how much she wants him.

She lets herself lean into the solid warmth of his body. Lets her fingers wander across the top of his waistband, and feels his sharp intake of breath as they find the gap between his shirt and trousers.

Then he presses his mouth to hers, harsh and urgent and full of want. She tastes mint, salt. Blood. Her teeth graze his lower lip and he groans, an exquisite torture. His hands tangle in her hair, tracing little agonies across the nape of her neck. She kisses back fiercely and he groans again. She could lose herself in him.

This is a bad idea. Not while she's upset. Not when she has no idea where she stands with him. What this means to him.

With great difficulty, she pulls away. She can feel her mussed hair, the lingering sting on her lips. He looks no better; his shirt rucks up tantalisingly, and the top button has somehow come undone. It would be so easy to fall back into his arms again. To let temptation consume her. She takes in a deep, shuddering breath.

"Aleksander," she whispers. "We can't."

His hands fall away from her immediately. He steps back, but not before she catches something in his eyes. Hurt, perhaps.

"You take too much from me, Violet," he says, and this time it sounds like an accusation. Then he shakes his head. "You're right. This was a mistake."

Before she can say anything else—before her anger resurfaces—he tucks his shirt back into his waistband, and it's like nothing ever happened. His expression is a mask of harsh disapproval.

Violet wants to make him stop—to grab his arm, to push him back, to kiss him again. *I give up*, she wants to scream. *Let me have two more weeks, and then nothing at all.*

Instead, she lets him walk away, her heart hammering in her chest. Frustrated tears sear her vision.

Elandriel. Marianne. Penelope. The scholars. And now Aleksander. She is holding on to too many threads, and they're all fraying in her fists.

Just as she thinks she might be about to break down and sob in public, someone in a shimmery gold dress hands Violet a bouquet of gold-dipped feathers. They startle her out of her anguish by pressing a kiss to her cheek. Their crown is a simple gold band that twines around their hair, black as ink.

"Erriel sends her regards," they whisper.

Even through all of her upset, the name rings a dim bell in her head.

"Wait," she says.

But the person is already gone, vanished into the shadows. Violet touches her cheek and comes away with dark red lipstick on her fingertips. In the dim light, it looks like blood.

CHAPTER

Thirty-Two

N A SMALL, high room, sharp fangs flash in the darkness. A breathy gurgle. A shuddering swallow. And then—silence.

Four scholars kneel at the altar, their hands lifted, trembling with adrenaline. Their robes indicate positions of power: an archivist, a notary, and two master scholars—all well versed in this particular ritual.

Because of Penelope, they will lead longer lives, fulfil their obligations to the tower and restore lost knowledge. Her fledgling city trying its hardest, even if no one remembers the grand empire it once was.

She drinks deeply, coppery blood staining her mouth as strength flows back into her bones. But not as much as she needs. A thousand years ago, it was a drop of blood. Three hundred years ago, it was an offering from the wrist. Fifty years ago, it was a sacrifice. Now it is a steady stream of children with light singing through their veins—or the occasional incompetent scholar, if needs must.

None of it as sweet, as bitter, as potent as Everly blood.

She's meted out their bloodline for centuries, holding back for as long as she can. Now though, she feels the gap between generations, the time stretched too thin. Despite every effort, her body is failing on her. If she had Marianne, and the key to Elandriel—

If she had them, she would not be here at all, languishing amongst ruins.

How deeply she regrets this savagery. But ten years is ten years. And Penelope always keeps her promises.

Another child stumbles up the tower, gripping a scholar's hand tightly. Already sedated, the child looks up at her and smiles. Hopefully. Foolishly.

"Close your eyes," Penelope whispers, soft as a kiss.

A storm is coming.

The Everly brothers are together for the first time in nearly a year. Sitting side by side, heads bent over a purloined volume on the astrals, their shared resemblance is, for once, impossible to ignore. Twin aquiline noses, twin mouths with deep philtrums, both pulled downwards in worry. They exchange looks of apprehension at the page before them.

The night before Yulan Liu is supposed to get on a plane to Prague, she lies twined in bed with a scholar, tracing the soft curve of her breasts. They are still supposed to be pretending that this is a fling, that either of them could walk away unharmed. Then the scholar touches Yulan's face and says, "Don't go to Prague." With Illios' Blessing at hand, there are plenty of opportunities for Yulan—new customers, new books to acquire, new avenues to work—but the scholar's expression is serious. After a beat, Yulan curls into her warm body and kisses the divot of her collarbone. "I won't," she whispers, and so she doesn't.

In an underground city built on the ashes of the dead, Caspian Verne thinks of his shadow-self, Aleksander: the man who he could so nearly have become. Very rarely does he let himself consider the path taken from him—what point is there ruminating on a past he had no hand in, when the future is all to play for? Yet tonight, it takes all his effort to drag his thoughts away.

Carelessly, he tosses a coin in the air. Heads, he stays to see how it all pans out. Tails, he leaves. It lands in his palm and he claps his other hand over it. Silver sword or golden feather? Later, he will curse himself for cowardice; later still, he will thank every god he knows for the slip of luck that makes him leave.

Yury Morozov wakes from the purest dream yet; his armour is nearly complete. He eases his trousers past his skeletal hipbones to probe the necrosis that has at last made its way to his groin. There, right at the seam between his pelvis and his left thigh, a shiny reveur-ite scale protrudes from his skin. The promise of a miracle on his flesh, come too late.

Deep within the mountain caves, where the ground is still soft and loamy from centuries of ice melt, Penelope offers the last rites to a child, in a graveyard known only to the master scholars. There are well over a hundred graves, all unnamed and unmarked—and yet Penelope recalls every one. So much potential lost to a greater cause. But she cannot stop, not now.

Aleksander presses his fingers to his mouth and closes his eyes. *What do you want from me, Aleksander?* Nothing he's allowed to have.

In the dim corner of a hostel, Violet cradles her phone in her hands, the light illuminating the remnants of her tears. Carefully, she reads over an unsent message to Ambrose. For a long time, her thumb wavers, ready to press send. Finally, she wipes her face and deletes it, word by word.

And then . . .

In a long dead world, amidst the pin-drop silence of books no one will ever read and doorways no one will ever pass through, along passageways furred with dust and alleyways untravelled for thousands of years—

Something stirs.

CHAPTER

Thirty-Three

S EVERAL DAYS LATER, Violet waits underneath a streetlamp, smoothing out the last few creases in her new outfit. Her dress is powder blue, with a high collar and long sleeves to conceal her lack of tattoos. After so long wearing the same comfortable, travel-worn clothes, she's grown used to soft fabric and forgiving elastic. Her new shoes pinch her toes; the stitching along her ribs itches. She adjusts her cuffs, pulling them down as far as they'll go.

Violet checks the time again, trying not to worry at a cut on her lip. Aleksander is running late. She hadn't planned to ask him to come with her, but she isn't a scholar, and she doesn't have the tattoos to give the illusion that she belongs. Caspian had unexpectedly refused her, citing an unmissable family meeting. So she'd had no choice but to ask Aleksander.

You take too much from me.

They've barely spoken since the argument. Since the kiss. Her mouth still feels bruised from that night, like a wound she can't stop touching, even though it hurts. Too much, and not enough, all at once.

It doesn't matter. After tonight, they'll go their separate ways. Caspian is right, much as she hates to admit it. There are the scholars and Aleksander, and then there are people like Violet. Even if she wasn't on a deadline, even if she wasn't trying to find her mother, and stop Penelope, and just live her goddamn life—

She will always wonder about him. But Violet is tired of pretending that they could still slide back into their friendship as easily as puzzle pieces. He's changed. So has she.

As the minutes tick past, she starts to worry that he won't show up at all. Then he appears, jogging down the road with a glittering object in his hands.

"Sorry, sorry," he says breathlessly. "I had to pick this up first. Otherwise you won't look the part."

He hands her a gold mask, trimmed with lace and sequins. She places it over her eyes, the ribbons trailing down her collar.

"Here, let me help."

Aleksander's hands reach around to pull the ribbons behind her head. Gently, he ties the mask securely, his fingers brushing the tips of her ears. His breath is warm on the nape of her neck.

His own mask is made of steel-blue silk stretched taut against a wire frame that curls upwards into spiky silver horns. And no ill-fitting suit for him this time; his jacket sits snugly across his chest and his cuffs are the correct length, with silver cufflinks to match his mask.

"How do I look?" she asks, tugging nervously on her own cuffs again.

It will have to be enough. It has to work.

Aleksander tilts his head to the side. "You look beautiful," he says quietly. "As always."

And Violet would blush with pleasure were it not for the hint of resentment in his voice. She takes a step back, towards the light.

"And they won't see your lack of tattoos," he adds, then holds out his arm. "Shall we?"

Violet hesitates before taking his arm. But she can't let herself be distracted by anything else, no matter how tempting it is to try and unpack their fight. Tonight, she'll find Marianne, find the key, find out how to stop Penelope.

Tonight, it finally, *finally* ends.

With the same uncanny precision he'd shown in Vienna, Aleksander leads her around a series of winding streets. He barely glances at the signs, instead pulling her down alleyways no tourist would ever think to walk through.

"I thought you said you hadn't been to Prague before," she says.

He shrugs. "I'm good with cities."

She pauses to look at him again, brow furrowed. There's an unhappy tension stretched between his shoulder blades, as though his whole body is braced for something unpleasant. Then he stops on the street.

"Do you really think you'll find what you're looking for?" he asks.

"Yes," she says, no hesitation.

Everything has led her to this moment: her uncles' notes, Tamriel's vision, her mother's own footsteps. Even Caspian and his suggestion of other worlds.

Do you really believe the curse isn't real? That the divine never touches you? That the wheeling cosmos is but an abstract of chemicals? Do you not hear the stars sing, little dreamer?

Once upon a time in that café, she'd believed, even if she hadn't yet understood what that belief meant. What it meant to embrace the monstrous and the divine.

She believes she'll find her mother. So she will.

"I admire that about you, Violet," Aleksander says unexpectedly. "You know what you want, what it costs to go after it." He looks down at his hands. "What you'll do once you have it."

An errant streetlamp paints his shoulders gold, and Violet recalls the asteros card of the woman with the sword through her chest, her head bowed as Aleksander's is bowed now. He wears the elegant, sombre face of a Renaissance angel, and she wonders, not for the first time, what happened in the last year to make him like this. Distant and unknowable as a star.

"I will find her," she says again.

He looks at her. "I believe you."

They keep walking.

"You do look nice, by the way," he says, after a pause.

She glances at him. "So do you."

As they turn the corner, the street is awash in light from the church. Several people mingle outside smoking thin cigarettes in holders, their heads bowed together. A man monitors the entrance.

Violet's stomach churns as they approach the doorway. But the man only has to see the tattoos on Aleksander before he nods and lets them through. Gold keys glint on his cufflinks, and his hair is tied back in silver ribbon.

"See?" Aleksander whispers. "Easy."

He'd said, after all, that he could gain them entrance, even though she hadn't really believed him. She glances at the tattoo visible on his hand: seven thin black lines disappearing, she knows, up to the inside of his forearm where they twist into abstract branches, or roots. She's spent so long with the scholars, but there's still so much she doesn't know. What draws a person into their circle; what shuts them out forever.

Apart from a few other revellers, the church is quiet and the faint scent of incense still lingers. Saints gesture mournfully at one another in stained-glass windows, artificial light throwing faint rainbows on the floor.

Another man—this one in a midnight-blue tuxedo and matching mask—leads them down the nave, before turning left to the north transept, and towards a door. As they descend the spiral staircase, a strange hum intensifies, echoing off the stone walls. And there's a heavy pressure in Violet's head, as though they're underwater. She glances at Aleksander, but he looks just as puzzled as she feels, his forehead puckered in a frown. The stone seems to glitter, even in the darkness.

Then, with an audible pop, the air pressure releases. The stairs finish.

And Violet steps out under an open sky.

She blinks and then blinks again, but it's real. Clouds scud across the moonlight, and the chilly breeze makes her grateful for her long sleeves. Mountains curl inwards on them, imposing and unbreachable. The floor is worn stone, but Violet catches glimmers of silky silver and gold veins running through it. It's too smooth, too perfect to be the product of natural erosion. Around the edge, tall pillars wend their way upwards, and even though half of them are broken or smashed, it's still a spectacular sight. A courtyard, made by human hands.

Violet recalls Caspian's words. *A door to another world.*

Her skin prickles with excitement.

The party surges up to meet them, larger than any she's been to before. Scholars, dozens of them from across the world. They all wear masks in stunning displays that put Violet's and Aleksander's to shame. At a glance through the crowd, Violet spots wrought-iron cages and veils of silk, masks made of gold leaf and delicate stained glass, or bracketed by pearls dripping from fine silver chains. A string quartet plays amidst them, in sombre black masks.

Now that they're actually here, Aleksander is all nervous energy, twisting his hands over themselves. She doesn't blame him; so many scholars together makes her jittery, too.

Then she sees it: a heavy archway with a pointed roof, supported by twin columns carved to look like wings flaring outwards, and yet crumbling with age. This was what had struck her in Tamriel's vision, that she'd never seen anything quite like it in all her travels, or her books. That it had instantly felt otherworldly.

She's about to walk over when she notices someone staring at her. She recognises him instantly: Mr. Velvet Jacket, who had so unsettled her in Adelia Verne's home. His eyes catch Violet's, and narrow.

"Come on," she says, tugging Aleksander away.

A sudden spike of fear thrums through her. Who else has decided to attend this party? What if Penelope is here somewhere, circulating amongst the guests? In their masks, it's hard to tell, but any one of them could be her—smiling, drinking, devouring. Violet shivers.

Aleksander takes off his suit jacket and swings it over her shoulders. "It's cold out."

"What about you?" she asks.

He shrugs. "I'll be fine."

Violet looks at him—really looks. The man she once knew and the stranger, overlapping in the way he smiles at her. Again and again they seem to be walking this thin line of friendship, moving through the same dance-like motions and yet circling back to the beginning. She told herself she wouldn't be distracted tonight, but how can she not ask?

"Aleksander—"

He cuts her off. "We must be in another part of Fidelis."

She blinks at him. "We didn't have a key."

"No, but..." He tilts his head up to the night sky dotted with stars. "I recognise the constellations. Tullis and Berias, see? And that's Etallantia."

All Johannes' talk about the fractured remnants of Elandriel had made no sense in the moment. But here, standing under these stars, she knows with sudden clarity where she is. An island, broken off a greater whole.

She glances back at the doorway they came through. From here, it's another entrance nestled within the mountain, a curious wooden door that seems incongruous against the heft of its rocky pillars. But it's halfway open, and she can see the staircase winding its way up from the church basement. The two images wrestle side by side, headache-inducing.

"The Blessing is this way," Aleksander says, nudging her to the archway. "That's what you came for, right?"

A man in a gold mask stands underneath the archway, a knife in his hands. Violet glances anxiously at the other scholars. Without the tattoos, she feels naked, dangerously exposed. One quick glance at her unadorned skin could see her thrown out—or worse. But she has to find a way to get close, so she swallows her apprehension and approaches.

The archway reveals a snug hollow with just enough room for the man in the gold mask, one or two scholars and what at first glance looks to be a lectern. Up close, Violet notes that it's more like a church font, with a convex basin instead of concave. A knife flashes in the darkness, as one by one, scholars slice open their palms and wipe blood on the convex mound.

"You must make an offering," the man in the gold mask says.

The blade has already been wiped clean, and it gleams on the table. Violet hesitates, but only for a second. Then she slices the pad of her ring finger, and sharp pain blooms just long enough for her to squeeze out a drop of blood over the raised stone. Though it should sink into the porous rock, it rolls over the smooth surface and into the shallow channel, away to some subterranean destination.

Violet is unceremoniously ushered out, as the next scholar presents their hand to the gold-masked man. She has no choice but to mill around until most of the scholars are back at the party, their act of ritual already forgotten. The musicians start up a waltz, the tune echoing off the mountainside. Briefly, she laments the scholars' fundamental lack of interest in their surroundings. Maybe this place is already well traversed for the scholars, a marvel dismissed as ordinary, but she can't stop admiring the way the starlight glints off the floor, or the carved marble ivy twining up the pillars, as though stretching towards the sky.

Another world—and she'd crossed the threshold without a key, with barely a thought. How many other doors exist like this one, jealously guarded by the scholars? Or else abandoned, forgotten? She could take half a step and vanish to somewhere else entirely, out of Penelope's grasping reach.

It's a tempting thought.

With one careful eye on the crowd—the man in the gold mask is talking to a woman halfway across the courtyard—Violet slips back underneath the archway. She glances overhead, and the dappled pattern of feathers is the same as in Tamriel's vision.

There, at the back of the cave, is the image of a woman carved into a wall, a light held proudly above her. Violet recognises her from the asteros cards: Erriel of the lost.

This has to be it.

Just as the vision had showed her, she places her hands on the wall, breath held. The rock grinds underneath her fingers. A narrow staircase unfolds, slippery with moisture, leading into darkness. *Doors within doors,* she thinks wondrously. She checks to make sure no one's watching before she takes off her shoes; the last thing she wants to do is fall and break her leg.

Aleksander follows her. "I'm not sure we should be here."

"I just need a moment," she says.

Tamriel's vision hasn't been wrong so far.

"Violet, wait—" he says.

She's already halfway down the stairs, but Aleksander's footsteps behind her have stopped. She turns back on the staircase, puzzled.

"Aleksander?"

He stands frozen at the top, his face alabaster, as he clutches the banister with white-knuckled force. She glances behind her, but there's nothing—only the darkness. Step by step, she makes her way back up to him and places a hand on his shoulder. His body is rigid underneath her palm.

"Look at me," she says, pulling his gaze away from the dark staircase.

He breaks off from the staircase and leans against her, his forehead brushing the top of her head. She grasps his arms, steadying him. To anyone observing, it might look like a lovers' embrace, stolen in the dark. But Violet recognises what it really is: fear.

Aleksander takes in a shuddering breath and she feels it tremble through her body. "I can't go down there. I can't."

It's just the dark, she almost says. But she remembers the darkness in Tamriel's basement, and how tangible it had felt, like a living thing wrapped around her. How she'd spent the next few nights sleeping with the light on because it felt safer than waking up in the middle of the night to that strangled terror.

"I'll go," she says instead, handing him her mask. "It's okay."

It's her quest, after all.

Reluctantly, she leaves him at the top of the stairs and descends again. The hewn stone walls shine with condensation, the channel running down alongside the steps. With the sluggish remains of the scholars' blood, it unnerves her. It's entirely possible that the blood is just symbolic, scholars playing pretend at sacrifice and ritual.

We would take but a morsel.

Maybe Aleksander knows something of that terror, too.

By the time her foot hits the bottom, the darkness is impenetrable, and the noise of the party has completely vanished. She feels her way forward, step by step, her heart pounding in her ears. Something rustles. A breeze—or a heavy breath. She fights the urge to scream.

"Hello?" Her voice reverberates as though she's standing in a stadium.

A blinding light erupts, and sparks shower down. She throws her hands over her head to protect herself, but they land like kisses of sunlight on her skin. Her eyes readjust slowly to the outline of a woman. Enormous wings flare outwards, puncturing the darkness in golden shafts of light.

"Well met, Violet Everly," the astral says. "We've been waiting for you."

Yury watches Violet descend the staircase, his eyes shielded by a black mask glittering with onyx beads. No one has noticed the interlopers in this masquerade, too occupied by gossip and champagne. But he has, and wonders how anyone else can ignore how obviously they don't fit in.

He adjusts his gloves, waits for her partner to hurry back to the party, back to the loud courtyard. She will be alone. Perfect.

It has been so long since he felt warm.

He is ready to burn.

CHAPTER

Thirty-Four

HE ASTRAL GLOWS in the darkness, more light than person. But amidst the shifting rays, Violet catches a hint of brow, a sharp nose, a curve of lips. Her hair drifts around her in a coronet, like a glory from a saint's portrait, sending out flickers of illumination. In her fist, she carries a staff that warps and quivers with some invisible current. Wings halo around her, more sunbeam than feather, rainbows stippling the surface.

"We have heard your name whispered amongst the stars, carried by the clouds, sung by dust motes drifting upwards," the astral says, and her voice is mercifully audible—no compelling whisper cutting across her thoughts. "The skies themselves are curious, it seems, and so it behooves us to answer your call."

Her wings beat once and a wash of warmth flows over Violet, accompanied by a dry sandalwood scent.

"Who are you?" she asks.

"We go by the name Erriel, though there are few who would know us by it, and fewer still who know where we would reside. The Hands of Illios are but a diminished order in this age."

Violet thinks of the woman at the party, with her golden bouquet.

"Tamriel sent me," she says nervously. "He said you could help."

Erriel recoils, her wings coruscating around her. "That abomination! That betrayer! Thief of light and laughter, murderer of knowledge from ages past! We would not hear his name again, for the sake of all our brethren he slew."

"I . . . I'm sorry."

The astral's face softens. "It is not for you to know of his crimes. But he will wear his chains until the end of time, we hope, though it will be but a fraction of the suffering he is owed."

Now that she's here, Violet has no idea what to say. What could she possibly say to a god?

"You've met my mother," she says. "Marianne Everly."

How many times has she said this to strangers, to those who would harm her or send her away, or whom Marianne had spurned in turn? She's already tired of the words before they even leave her mouth.

Erriel's smile curls like a sunbeam. "She sought to free us, a gesture which we appreciate, but was nevertheless not needed."

For the first time, Violet's eyes drift to Erriel's feet, clearly mana-cled even if the links sway with refracting light. So this is where the channel of blood leads; a real ritual then, masked as pretend. Erriel follows her gaze and sighs heavily.

"Are we a prisoner? No. We chose this. We bear a duty that our sisters bore, that our mothers and grandmothers and those lost to the mists even of our memories bore. It is an honour, Violet Everly, as much as it is obligation." She taps her staff and rainbows fling them-selves across the floor. "In our lifetime, we have held what knowledge we could, and kept many treasures for our brethren."

Violet takes a deep breath.

"Like the key to Elandriel," she says.

The astral grows still, the musical tones of her shackles brought to a low hum. With the staff in her hands and the darkness around her, she's almost the picture of the asteros card.

"You have been misled, Violet Everly," she says. "We keep no key."

Time seems to stop around Violet.

"I—I don't understand," she says. "There has to be a key."

She didn't spend an entire year of her life searching for something that doesn't exist.

But Erriel bows her head, her expression one of pity. "We do not lie."

"What did Marianne even come for, then?" she demands.

"She wished to leave. She came to us weary, filled with nameless sorrows and frustrations."

She wished to leave. Shock hits Violet like icy water.

"Did Marianne say where she was going next?" she pleads. "Did she reach Elandriel? Did she find what she was looking for?"

Erriel touches Violet's cheek, her fingertips warm. "She said you would be full of questions. You have her likeness, Violet Everly, and O how we have missed her."

Then Erriel steps aside, and Violet sees what the light has blinded her to. A silver door, hung in a reveurite frame. Though it's hard to tell, she's certain she senses something behind the door. A susurration. A hum that could be a chorus of voices.

"She went through this door. We would follow, if we could, though it does not lead to Elandriel, or the homeland that is still precious to our memory. If we hear the song of the stars, it is only distantly through her echoes."

Violet takes a step towards the door, but Erriel's staff comes crackling down hard on the ground.

"We do not give without taking," Erriel says. "We wish it were otherwise, but that is the nature of who we are."

"What did Marianne give you?"

Erriel looks at her curiously. "A hand. She offered it on her own terms," she says, seeing Violet's expression. "We did not suggest it."

Violet swallows. "Do I have to give you . . . flesh?"

"We would consider it an appropriate exchange," Erriel says. "And your blood is so very sweet, so very like our own."

Violet stares at her own hands, horrified. What can she offer that isn't herself? She has already lost so much. Time. A future that she should have been grateful to have at all. A memory that bores a hole through her mind.

"We offer you another suggestion, Violet Everly," Erriel says. "We would take something that you will not miss, except in your dreams. Your talent."

"My talent," Violet echoes.

The *something* that scholars search for, that lets them manipulate reveurite and walk between worlds. Aleksander had once told her it looked like golden sparkles in his vision, but she's never seen so much as a shimmer.

It's not like Violet has ever done anything with this mysterious talent anyway. But still, even on the brink of so much promise, she hesitates. All this potential bursting inside her, and she'll never know how to use it. Never know what it's like to make magic with her fingers, or cross worlds with a key. It's the only legacy her mother has truly ever left her.

Erriel holds out her hand. "Take it and follow Marianne where you will. Or leave. We will not force you."

Violet's hand hovers over Erriel's. But she can't seem to move.

"If you pass through this door, you may never be able to return," Erriel says.

Violet's hand closes into a fist as she pulls away. What would her uncles think? She recalls every single bitter word about Marianne, every argument between them, every disapproving scowl from Gabriel. She thinks about Ambrose, sitting in his fireside chair, growing older and waiting for the day for his niece to return. He would never know what happened to her.

Maybe, in the back of his mind, he would always wonder whether Violet simply gave up on her family and disappeared. The way Marianne did.

"There must be another way," she says.

"The cost to travel through a door is always sacrifice, Violet Everly," Erriel says softly. "Did you not bestow us with your blood upon arrival? This door may not lead to the fabled city of old, but it is all the same to us."

Violet bites her lip. If she goes through for her mother, she could find a way to come back. She could bring both of them back. But she would have to vow to herself that she wouldn't be swayed by her mother or the new world in front of her, by the safety that it would afford. She would have to be resolve itself.

And if she couldn't come back…She'd have to live with that decision. She might never see Ambrose and Gabriel again. And if Penelope got hold of them—

Could she do that? Even knowing what happens if she stays here? Slowly, Violet reaches for Erriel's hand.

"I think—"

A blur of darkness shoves Violet aside.

She crashes to the floor, pain shooting up her jaw as her chin collides with hard stone. Her teeth rattle in her skull.

A man lurches forward, still masked from the party. Something glimmers in his hand. A shard of reveurite, sharp as a dagger. He points it at Violet, the tip wavering inches from her. She scrambles backwards, but there's nowhere to go.

"Who dares broach our sanctuary?" Erriel says.

"I come for a boon, cousin of mine," the man says, and points a long, skeletal finger at Violet.

Behind the mask, the man's eyes are heavily shadowed, and there is a peculiar metallic smell, like something burning. When he speaks, his words roll in his mouth, as though it's painful to talk.

Erriel tilts her head to the side. "Cousin? You are mistaken."

He slides off his suit jacket and wrenches at his shirt. Buttons pop as he shucks it to the floor like a second skin.

"See," he whispers. "I am just like you."

His bare chest ripples with hundreds of scars, dappling his skin like feathers. Mottled black creeps up his torso, wrapping itself around the ribs that jut outwards. But something else is pulling outwards from his skin, too: spikes like sharp petals, glimmering with the telltale sheen of reveurite. One of them is broken, a jagged line that oozes dark and viscous, to match the shard in his hand.

"You're not well," Violet says, trying to placate him. "If you would just—"

"I saw you in New York. I hunted you down in Vienna," he says. "But I was too late. I was always too late. And what I had to do... The sacrifices I made..."

Johannes Braun. An awful terror slides though Violet's stomach.

"I am sick, yes," he says, "but I will be well again soon." He closes his eyes, swaying on his feet. "I have had the dream, cousin. I hear the song. I hear... glory."

Erriel brings her staff to the ground, and it cracks like a gunshot. The light from her spear burns, and Violet has to shield her eyes from its glare.

"You are an abomination," Erriel hisses. "No mortal creature walks the earth like you. You are no astral."

"A debt is owed," he slurs. "I will be a god."

Then he slashes the shard across Erriel's throat.

Thirty-Five

A SCREAM CLEAVES VIOLET'S thoughts in two.

Erriel's mouth makes a small "oh" as the man rips out the reveurite shard. Golden liquid spills from her throat, staining the floor. The light around her shudders, throwing a corona around them.

The man peels off his mask stiffly, revealing a face black with gangrene, his lips hypothermic violet. Frost clings to his eyelashes. He shivers convulsively, waves of pain crossing his face.

"A debt...owed."

We are undone! We agonise!

Erriel's wings fold in around her as she sinks down, colour seeping away to a terrifying mortal flush. Her staff falls out of her hand. It hits the floor with barely a whisper, dissolving into sparks that quiver across the ground—then vanish.

The silver door splits with a jagged screech. Spidery fissures gather in the rock.

The way to Marianne, disappearing.

Violet darts towards the door, but the man swings the shard towards her, slashing at her sleeve. Pain wells sharply on her arm.

"So long...since I have been warm," the man whispers, first in English and then in another language Violet doesn't recognise.

Erriel looks up at her, her golden irises fading to dark. *We are so cold, Violet Everly.*

The man falls to the floor, his hands glistening with gold. He leans over Erriel's body and presses his lips to her neck. Her eyelids flutter, their sunlight tint leaching from them. When the man lifts his head again, his teeth are luminous and golden with her blood.

Violet backs away, terror clouding almost every thought.

She sprints towards the staircase, half tripping on the hem of her dress as she takes the steps two at a time. Her shins feel hot and wet from where she fell, but she can't stop to check if she's bleeding.

Behind her, something distinctly inhuman bellows.

Aleksander is still milling around near the top of the staircase, holding on to her mask. She grabs his hand and pulls him towards the exit, stumbling as she tries to put her shoes back on at the same time. His eyes widen with alarm.

"Violet, your arm," he says. "Your *face*."

She touches her cheek, and her fingers come away stained gold. Astral blood.

Goddess blood.

"We've got to get out of here," she says tightly. "Now. Before—"

"Oh my God," he whispers, looking straight past her. "Yury."

She follows his gaze and her stomach lurches. The man staggers up from the stairwell, the fabric of his trousers flaking away from him in embers. Sparks hit the floor and burst in an audible hiss. He seems to shine from within, white light shooting from the cracks of his gangrenous skin.

There's a split second where no one notices him, the dancers still waltzing, the music playing a vigorous jig. Someone laughs, and the sound carries in the courtyard.

Then he crashes into a side table, and several people turn to look at him.

"Oh bloody hell," someone mutters. "Who let him in?"

"He's drunk."

Mr. Velvet Jacket saunters up to the man, then stops as he notes the light radiating off him. "Yury? What on earth are you—"

The man grabs Roy by his collar, impossibly strong. "It burns! O Bozhe moy, God save me—"

Yury places his hands on Roy's face, and presses. Roy's scream cuts across the music, the chatter. Then, abruptly, it stops.

Silence rings out as everyone freezes, the violinists' bows mid-draw.

Roy crumples to the floor, his flesh bubbling with burns where Yury touched him.

The courtyard bursts into shouts and frightened cries. Scholars peel away from the party towards the exit. But the stairway is narrow —only made for one—and a crowd surges around the entryway, bodies seething in panic.

Yury clutches his head, screaming in a mixture of English, Russian, and the same unearthly language as the astrals. He wrenches at his chest, tearing skin.

"What happened?" Aleksander says urgently, as they fight their way to the exit.

"I think...he drank her blood."

There are still traces of it on her hands, from where she accidentally touched the floor, and on her face.

"Whose blood? Violet—"

Someone crashes into Aleksander and he collapses into a table stacked high with glasses, bringing it all shattering down with him. Blood seeps into his silk mask, red against blue.

Yury crouches by another person—another body, Violet registers with dim horror—but his head snaps around at the sound of glass. He wipes his mouth, crimson mingling with gold, and heaves in a shuddering breath.

"I asked her to take the pain away, I asked her to take it—but you refused, you said no—I will be remade anew—I owe a debt—oh God, it burns—"

Yury stalks towards Aleksander as he scrambles backwards. His eyes glow with incandescent light, burning his pupils to pinpricks.

Violet pushes against the sea of people frantically, her heart in her mouth. She took Aleksander here; if anything happens to him—

She pulls free just in time to see Yury reach Aleksander. Without thinking, she grabs what remains of Yury's waistband and yanks. He spins around to face her, and somewhere underneath the bloodlust, his eyes light up with recognition. Violet backs away, one eye on Aleksander.

"You," he hisses. He storms towards her, every stride closing the gap between them. "Too late in New York, Vienna—but *here.*"

Violet's foot hits stony cliff. She's trapped.

Yury barricades her against the rock face, hands on either side. His breath reeks of coppery blood, and heat radiates off him like a furnace. For a split second, she's back in Tamriel's basement, his soft voice ringing in her head. *Just one taste.*

Yury looks at her, fat golden tears streaking his face. His mouth wrenches with agonised sorrow. "I just wanted to feel warm again. I just wanted warmth. Bozhe, I am sorry. But a debt is owed."

He reaches in, as if to caress her face.

She only has one chance to get this right.

Thumb over fist.

Her hand smashes upwards, connecting with Yury's jaw. Pain flares across her knuckles, bright with heat. In the second between recoil and rebound, she ducks out of his arms.

Yury reels back, knocking a brazier on to a table. Flames burst across the wood, licking up the tablecloth. But the fire consumes his attention immediately. She catches the briefest glimpse of his face— painful longing. He lunges towards it, dipping his hands directly into the flames.

Taking advantage of his distraction, Violet sprints towards Aleksander. He has only just managed to heave himself upright, and his mouth is pinched with pain.

"You—are you okay?" he says, which is a ridiculous question, but she nods anyway.

"Are you?" she asks.

He gestures to his foot and grimaces. "I twisted it when I fell."

The scholars have mostly cleared out, but there are bodies, silent and unmoving, on the floor. *Bodies.* Yury's head is bowed over one of them, and the sound of cracking bone is unmistakable. When he breaks away from the body to scream, it echoes across the courtyard

—and, for the first time, in Violet's head. *He is changing*, she thinks with horror.

It's only a matter of moments before Yury realises there's more to consume.

"We have to get out of here," she says.

"But—the scholars—" Aleksander says.

"We can't save them," she says, aware of how awful she sounds. "Listen to me: either we leave now, or we end up like *that*."

"I—" He glances back to Yury, who is starting to tear at the skin on his back. "Okay."

They're only a few paces from the doorway when Yury snaps up. Their eyes lock. All at once, he rises from the ground, his body impossibly elongated. Light bursts from his skin in a fiery glow.

Violet doesn't think; she grabs Aleksander's hand and drags him towards the door. She hears a hiss of pain, but she ignores him. They have to reach the door before Yury. He reaches out for her, claws snaring the back of her dress, shredding fabric—

And then she's through the door, slamming it shut, Yury on the other side. There's blood on her arm, on her face, hot on her back. They're safe. But—

The door. Her mother. Erriel.

"Violet?" An entire world of questions in Aleksander's voice.

"I'm coming. I just…"

She could still turn back. She could still fight her way past Yury, towards the reveurite door that leads to her mother, and somehow fix it. She could still try.

And she almost reaches for the handle, she really does.

Violet is only a few steps up the stairs when the door splinters into a thousand fragments, plunging them into darkness.

Thirty-Six

T HE CHURCH HAS almost entirely cleared out by the time Violet and Aleksander make it up the stairs. Violet staggers to the nearest pew and collapses in it, heaving breaths that should really be sobs. Noise like static rushes in her ears. Even though she can see where Yury's dagger sliced through her dress, she can't feel anything. Not yet.

The door to her mother is gone. She still has its splinters in her hair. Such an ordinary thing, for such an extraordinary place.

All lost, now.

Aleksander sits down next to her, murmuring so as to be unheard by the last stragglers. He's still holding his mask, blue silk tinged with red. A painful-looking cut draws along one cheekbone.

"What *happened* down there?" he wants to know. "What the hell was that?"

Violet tries to explain it to him, but her thoughts feel fragmented, stuck on one particular loop of Erriel's face. The reveurite shard, sinking into her throat. The agony that had churned its way through her head.

"All she would talk about was sacrifice," Violet says. "Sacrifice and doors and..." She presses the heels of her hands to her forehead. "He killed an astral."

Aleksander gives her a sideways glance. "Astrals are—they're like gods. They don't exist on this plane."

"Well, I hate to break it to you."

She almost has to swallow back a laugh. Aleksander, who makes magic out of reveurite, who walks across worlds and alongside a star, doesn't believe in astrals.

"They're just fairy tales." Then he sees her expression. "Violet, you can't be serious."

"Then whose blood do I have on my face?" she snaps. "What the hell did I see down there, then? Go on, tell me, since you so obviously know."

Aleksander looks down at her hands, curled into fists. Her right knuckles ooze fluid from a burn, where her skin had made contact with Yury's.

"I believe you," he says. "It's just that . . . Yury—I never thought they would be like *that*."

Violet wishes she could say the same. The same insatiable hunger, the same horrific beauty. She thinks of Tamriel in his chains, and wonders if there's a reason that both he and Erriel were shackled rather than set loose in the world.

She wonders how long Yury will last in the courtyard, living out his days on a fractured island of world. No longer man, not truly astral. She shudders.

The last person drifts out of the church, leaving it deathly silent. Aleksander gets up and starts to pace along the aisle. All Violet wants to do is sleep for days, but he seems to possess a manic energy that belies their circumstances.

"So did you find her?"

Violet frowns. "Who?"

"Marianne," he asks, with an urgency in his voice that surprises her. "What? No, I—"

"Or the key?" he asks. "Did you find the key? Before Yury—"

Suddenly, Violet stops to stare at him. She's mentioned searching for her mother, and maybe once she'd brought up a key. But the way he says it . . .

"Aleksander," she says slowly, standing up, "what were you doing in Vienna?"

He runs a hand over his head, his eyes everywhere but her. His mouth is an ugly hard line. But it's a rhetorical question—she already knows the answer.

He was waiting for *her*.

It's then that she realises they're not alone. A blonde woman stands behind the altar, her back to them. Her head is tilted upwards, towards the Gothic rose window, in apparent contemplation. She's as still as a saint.

"You've been on quite the journey, Violet Everly. A last Hand of Illios! Truly, you surprised me."

That voice. Soft and unassuming, a sheathed dagger. Ice trickles down Violet's spine and she turns to Aleksander. He stops pacing, standing to attention almost as though he's a soldier. And maybe he is, in someone else's war.

After everything tonight, she can't even pretend that he looks like a stranger. This is the truth of him. It's just taken her this long to realise it.

"You lied to me," she says numbly.

"I never lied," he says. "I'm not a scholar—I'm not Penelope's assistant—"

"But you're working for her."

Aleksander's eyes flick to Penelope. "Yes."

Devastation. A sword through her chest.

Violet opens her mouth to ask him *why*, but then she realises she doesn't want to know. There's no reason he could give her, no justification that would make this excusable. A distant part of herself watches this with detached irony. There goes Violet Everly, the woman with all the curiosity in the world, except for the answer to this one question.

Aleksander folds his arms. "I did what I had to do. But Yury was never supposed to be there. I don't understand..."

"You sent that man...to do what? To stop me from finding Erriel?" She blanches. "To kill me?"

"Christ, Violet, no! No one was supposed to get *hurt*."

"You have no idea what you've taken from me," she says.

Her hands are shaking, so she clenches the back of a pew. She won't be weak in front of him. She won't give him the satisfaction of her anger.

But it's Aleksander who starts to shout. "Well, you took everything from me! Things you might not have known you would take, but still—" He breaks off. "Once you understand—"

"Once I *understand?* If you knew what you've just done—"

Penelope cuts her off. "Aleksander, wait outside."

Violet expects Aleksander to protest—to say he would rather wait in the church, to say he would like to stay, even if it's to watch Violet suffer—something, *anything*—but he only nods and turns away. He doesn't look back at them.

"Aleksander," she shouts.

The church door swings shut.

Violet turns back to look at Penelope. This woman who has tried to destroy her life, who has haunted her footsteps across the globe.

"I suppose you consider yourself very clever," Penelope says. "In many ways, you've exceeded my expectations. Johannes Braun, Tamriel..." She taps one finger on the altar. "Those names didn't come out of nowhere. Your research was thorough."

"Worthy of a scholar?" Violet asks bitterly.

Behind her fear, something liquid and furious rises to the top. She won't let Penelope best her. She won't walk into the dark, another Everly to face a brutal death at her hands.

"You will never find what you're looking for," Violet spits. "Erriel said it doesn't exist."

"The Hands of Illios are no more, and were never of importance to begin with. Erriel has spent two thousand years in a cave as a glorified statue, presiding over a world of no significance," Penelope says. "She no longer recalled who she was. What she was capable of."

"And you do?"

The church is so very quiet.

"I know who you are," Violet says. "Astriade."

Penelope stiffens. "You have no right to call me by that name."

"But it *is* your name," Violet says. She tilts her head to one side. "Does Aleksander know who he works for, I wonder?"

"You forget yourself, little dreamer."

The shadows in the room thicken. Darkness pools at Violet's feet. When she tries to move, her feet freeze in place. Thick black tendrils loop over her shoes and wind up her legs, burning where they meet bare skin. She struggles, but every time she moves, another coil fixes her in place.

Penelope walks forward, her shadow lengthening behind her. With every step, the pews on either side crack and splinter. For a second, Violet sees not one, but two versions of her: Penelope, as she's always known her, blonde hair carefully tucked behind her ears; and then a woman of darkness, tall as the ceiling with wings of smoke unfurling behind her.

Goddess. Astral. But it's as though someone has sucked all the light from her, a black hole instead of imploding star.

"I am centuries old, Violet Everly. I remember when the stars walked the earth like mortals. I remember when humans were a whim of the cosmos, stardust and clay and idiocy." Her voice suddenly takes on a strange longing. "I remember when the skies were *home*."

Penelope lifts a finger—a claw, nails tipped with flame—to Violet's throat. It burns like acid. Every single window shatters, stained-glass shards falling like rain. Golden sparkles burst in her vision, so many it leaves her stomach roiling.

"Your talent is a drop in an infinite ocean. *My* infinite ocean."

Abruptly, the shadows retreat. Violet collapses to the ground, as the dark coils rooting her in place vanish. She can barely breathe. Penelope looms above her, a woman once more.

"Thirteen days," Penelope says. "I suggest you use them wisely."

She sweeps out of the church, leaving Violet gasping on the floor. Distantly, Violet hears the sound of voices—Aleksander, acquiescing to something—then blue light floods underneath the doorway. The church falls silent once more.

Violet sits on the ground, surrounded by shattered glass and broken pews. Then she slams her fists on the ground until her knuckles burn. Until pain blooms bright and red, leaving smears of blood across her skin.

There is no key.

Her mother is gone.

Violet has lost.

Thirty-Seven

P ENELOPE AND ALEKSANDER arrive back in the scholars' tower in a whirl of blue light. She lets Aleksander
make his own way back to the forges. He could do with
a hard night or two—punishment for his hesitation. A reminder of
what happens when he tests unbreakable loyalties.

"Wait for me there," she commands. "I have a few things to take
care of."

"Yes, Mistress," he says, the ring of obedience at last in every syllable.

She dismisses him with a gesture and he descends the stairs, limping slightly from some injury or another. Her unwavering blade.

Despite herself, she feels a flicker of pride for her assistant, to
whom she has had to impart such tough lessons. Now, it's easy
to nudge him in the right direction. A pull on *this*, a tug on *that*. For
all his strength, he still wears his weakness on his sleeve, like an open
wound. But she will cure him of that, one day. Then, he will stand by
her side as the purest of scholars. The bedrock of her new world.

She waits until he is out of sight before returning to her chambers.
Already she can feel the effects of her "show" wearing on her; every
step is a little more effort than before, every breath heavier in her
lungs. The exhilaration of resuming her exalted shadow-self has
already dissipated. But it chases her like a ghost, reminding her of all
that she once was, and could be again.

In her chambers, a jewelled cup awaits her, brimming with lifeblood. Penelope picks it up and examines it, saliva coating her teeth.

But she holds back, letting her hunger cramp her stomach, riding the wave of pain that crests over and over.

It is not Everly blood. It *should* be. No one else has their talent, which the gods saw fit—*she* saw fit—to bestow upon them. And once upon a time, it had been enough to sustain her longevity, to reclaim what was once hers, Everly by Everly. Precious blood spooled out over generations. But even gods need more than the vestiges of stardust to live as their true selves.

Finally, she lets herself drain it in one. The hunger doesn't disappear—it never does—but the animal snarling within her settles for now. Tomorrow, she will have to take another child, or even two, into the cold, bleak mountainside, and bury her secrets with them.

But she could afford to be showy today. Because today is a victory.

From her chambers, she makes her way down the scholars' staircase, then past the basements, and the dark rooms where justice is meted out. There are several keys involved, as she opens gates that scream with rust, though she's so far away from the rest of the scholars that it doesn't matter.

Finally, she stands in the room with the reveurite door and its worn verses. In the past she would sink to her knees and plead silently, as though her brethren might hear her thoughts from beyond. That they might ignore the inscription that so condemns Penelope to her haggard, piecemeal existence here.

Today, she doesn't do any of that. Instead, she looks at the door anew, her mind working. She has read all the fragmented texts the Hands of Illios left behind, all their whispers of keys, with nothing else to suggest the contrary. But she has never considered...the metaphor.

All she would talk about was sacrifice. Sacrifice and doors.

Is it really so easy, after a thousand years of wanting?

Penelope is very good at sacrifice. And, of course, she knows of the rituals that brought her kind so very far from their original shores. Blood, bone, memory. And god-metal, though it's been a long time since she's referred to it as anything other than reveurite, its true nature disguised by scientific drapery.

Anticipation coils within her. She is so close to Elandriel. And then —*home*.

In thirteen days, she'll wash this door with Violet Everly's blood. All of it. A sacrifice, pure and clean and fittingly circular. A sacrifice, too, of Penelope's own time—every frustrated, tormented day leading up to her ten-year promise. It will be agony to wait, but it will be worth it. Glory is a rich dark red, after all.

In thirteen days, the door will swing open, just for her.

It's finally beginning.

PART FOUR

A Fireside Warning

ON A NIGHT of deepest winter, when the forges are blocked in by snow and reveurite harvesting is at its peak, the forge master gathers her students around the fire. It is a time for darkness and bitter cold, ghost stories and warnings. The fire crackles and spits, making figures out of smokey shadows.

The forge master takes a deep breath, studies each and every one of their faces. She says—

Once, there is a clever man.

Clever, that is, with his hands. Capable of working miracles out of gemstones, metal, wood. For decades, he is the most renowned craftsman in his city, in the world. Travellers flock to his workshop for his knowledge.

Yet time is a fickle creature. As the man grows older, he finds himself at the limits of his abilities. His knucklebones swell and his fingers fumble with wire; his back aches so he struggles over his workbenches. And elsewhere in the city, a new generation of craftspeople, with their dextrous hands and youthful vigour, are working miracles that he cannot replicate. His shop empties of customers and his once renowned displays turn grey with dust.

Then one day, a star walks into his workshop. Beautiful as fury, with flame draped around her shoulders like a cloak.

"Help me, please," he begs.

"Very well. But I cannot give without taking."

Frantically, the man begins to pick through the items in his shop. He holds up emeralds the size of eggs, crusted over with gold and dotted with tiny diamonds. In front of her, he spreads out a deck of cards gilded with silver and promises her that they will tell the truth of her future. He pulls out a delicate filigree dancer dressed in wire frothed to look like fabric, and winds tight a key on her pedestal to elicit music that would make any mortal weep.

The star looks at him, amused. "It must be something precious to *you*. And I see nothing of value here."

He starts to babble about firstborns, about rings to command a man, about assassination and third sons of third princes—

"Enough," she says.

He holds his palms upwards, pleading. "What else do I have?"

The star thinks for a moment. Then she says, "I will offer you a deal."

A lifetime's worth of knowledge to be used within a year and a day. And at the end of that year and a day, she would take his soul. Powerful magic requires a powerful exchange, she explains.

The man does not particularly want to give his soul away. But he is weary of being usurped and terrified of becoming nothing, so he agrees.

With her aid, he discovers knowledge so enticing it takes his breath away. How to craft with the god-metal that plummets from the sky. How to walk between worlds, how to listen to her star-brethren sing as they waltz across the galaxy. How to extend longevity and claw back youth.

Yet in the back of his mind, he remains aware of a clock ticking towards the star's bargain. As the days dissolve in front of him, he begs the star to spare his soul. He is not done—will never be done— with his work. He has only just begun to *truly* live.

"Is there nothing I can do to convince you to leave my soul?" he asks.

"It is not about *convincing*," the star says scornfully. "The exchange is already made."

Yet he keeps trying. He even goes so far as to seduce her, in the hope that with each kiss, each caress, her spirit will soften and a way out of the pact will emerge. Though he quickly realises this, too, is as foolish as pleading for clemency.

He starts taking long walks under watery moonlight, each footstep an easy rhythm that stills the jangling of his panic and keeps his mind whirring away. Because he is a clever man, he knows there must be a loophole to this terrible pact. And the knowledge the star bestowed has made him very clever indeed.

In the dead of night, he rows to an island on the outskirts of the city. There, in the ruins of a cathedral, he builds himself a cage of god-metal. For all his knowledge, he is just a man. But what better way to combat a god than a godly creation?

On the last night of his year and a day, he climbs into the cage and locks it tight. Now, the star cannot touch him. She arrives in a whirl of flame, which transforms to the colour of deepest violet when she realises his intentions. She paces the outside of his cage.

"You men are traitorous, treacherous creatures," she says. "Give me your soul."

"It is too dear to me," the man says.

"I will destroy your city," she vows.

He considers this. "But I will live."

"So be it."

On the first night, the darkness is alive with the sound of screaming.

On the second night, he sees flames lick at the horizon.

On the third night, every single star in the sky vanishes.

On the fourth day, the city is silent. He tentatively turns the key in its lock and the cage door unlatches with a soft whisper. When he emerges, the city is ash. The star is gone.

He has won; yet his mouth is dry with the taste of charred bone. His workshop is a black wreck. Scorched jewels litter the floor, twisted metal warped by vengeful heat. On the front door, someone has written in deep golden blood: *As long as your soul walks free, so will I.*

As the first days of his new-found freedom roll in, he undertakes the final part of his plan. He bars the doors to other worlds that he spent so long creating, or smashes those that he cannot close. The star is elsewhere for now, and if he is both clever and lucky, he will never have to face her again.

A week later, he climbs the highest hill in the city to watch the sunset. Blood red spills over ruins.

He is a clever man.

He is also a coward.

Thirty-Eight

HE KEY DOESN'T exist. And Marianne has vanished, taking with her any hope of escaping Penelope.

Then there is Aleksander. A dagger, hidden inside burning want.

With nothing left to do—nothing she *can* do—Violet heads home, feeling miserable and useless every mile of the way. In the taxi from the station, she leans her head against the window and stares at the trees, already half bare and shedding amber leaves.

Over and over, she replays the scene in her mind. Every agonising step of the way, when she could have turned back, or told Aleksander no, or been a little more careful about to whom she divulged secrets.

She hates Aleksander for what he did. But she hates herself more for letting him. If she'd been a little less enamoured, if she'd stopped to ask herself what he really wanted from her—but then she would have had to acknowledge what she wanted from him.

Maybe there had been something there, between them, during that kiss. Awful and exhilarating and ravenous because it was true— perhaps the only truth he'd told her. But perhaps desire is all it was, and more fool Violet for thinking it could ever be more.

As the taxi deposits her in the driveway, she takes a moment to simply look. Home again. Upon closer inspection, she notices the moss creeping up the brick, the slate tiles vanished from the roof like missing teeth. The garden looks abandoned and half-dead, spindly grey branches shrivelled and bent low.

Gabriel's hideous car is parked in the open garage, the convertible roof down. Violet swings over the edge, the suspension bouncing underneath her. She places her hands on the steering wheel, her foot on the pedal. She closes her eyes, and imagines pressing down, the jolt of sheer power, the wind snarling her hair. A road, open and unending.

She opens her eyes again and presses her forehead against the steering wheel.

Inside, the house is freezing, and it becomes clear very quickly just how little attention it's received since she's been gone. Dust coats the windows and muddies the paintings hanging in the hall. Violet kicks off her shoes and wanders through to the conservatory, where a green slime has made its home, obscuring the view. It's as though she's stepped back through time, to being twelve again and wishing for a world away from this one.

Well, look at where that wishing has got you.

Gabriel and Ambrose are in the house somewhere, but she can't bear to face them, not yet. She climbs the long, winding staircase up to her room, the wood creaking underneath her weight. The paint is flaking off the walls, and she spies more than one water stain creeping across the ceiling. To see the house crumbling hurts her heart in a way she can't describe.

She opens the door to her bedroom, half expecting it to be covered in spiderwebs, but it's all exactly as she left it.

She thought that when she got here, she would break down and cry, safe in the sanctuary of her childhood. Instead, she drops off her belongings and heads to the library. After the changes in the rest of the house, it's a relief to see the room mostly intact, without the layer of dust that seems to coat everything else. Here are her books, her childhood graffiti—*V. E.* chiselled clumsily into the hidden side of the bookshelves—and her precious wardrobe.

Her entire world, once.

There's no way she can possibly fit into the wardrobe, but she still climbs in, sitting cross-legged on the floor. Her knees poke over the edge, making it impossible to close the doors. *Who even puts a wardrobe in a library?* Aleksander once asked her, when she told him about it.

Other memories drift to the surface. How the wardrobe's walls had pressed in on her, and then the house, a prison as much as a sanctuary. The outside had seemed so exciting then, full of possibility. *Adventure.* Except now it's the walls of the world closing in on her. The world being just one woman, and yet the world, nevertheless.

In her stories, there would be an answer like a lightning bolt. A cure for the curse, a sword for the monster, a crown for the prince. Perfect and all-encompassing in its simplicity. Long live the king and his happily ever after.

She had her answer—before Aleksander snatched it from her hands.

Betrayal is its own sort of lightning bolt.

Here is the lightning bolt: scorched, struck—dissolving back into the air whence he came.

Early morning—so early, in fact, it practically qualifies as night—Aleksander wakes up on his wooden pallet, every muscle in his body aching. Next to him, a dozen other forge bearers sleep on their own pallets, loaded down with hay to soften the hard slats underneath. A couple of them are children as young as ten, but already strong and hardy, permanently streaked with ash, their hair shorn down to the scalp to inure them against mishaps, until they're deemed skilled enough to avoid setting themselves on fire. Most of them are closer to Aleksander's age, finishing apprenticeships so that they, too, can run their own forge. Or work as skilled craftsmen, coaxing reveurite into everything from the crystal lamps lighting Fidelis to the crushed powder used in the tattooists' inks.

Aleksander will never be one of them. Too untrustworthy to ascend beyond apprentice, the forge masters claim, even though he works as hard as anyone else, even though he's talented enough to craft delicate filigree with his bare fingers. He catches the smallest of impurities in the metal; he stokes a fire to the perfect temperature; he can hold a reveurite object and chart its history from touch alone— and it's not enough. It's never enough. Disgrace has settled on him like an invisible yet permanent shroud.

In the dark, he splashes himself with tepid water, but by the time he's dressed, he's already sweating from the heat of the forge. For the next three hours, he shovels coal and wood into the sweltering fire, feeding the flames until his face burns. Sweat stings his eyes; soot gathers on his skin, in his hair.

As the sun rises, the rest of the apprentices scurry into action: chopping more firewood; fetching coal; ferrying messages to the rest of the city, including the scholars' tower. At seven, the forge master comes in to check on the morning's work and to consult her star charts for reveurite harvesting.

At eight, Aleksander's finally relieved of his job, though by then the fire is a roaring creature, already sated. He splashes his face with more cold water, ash running into his eyes. And then it's time to sweep the floor, check the metal stocks, chop wood outside until the previous day's blisters pop. All the while, golden sparkles flicker uncontrollably in his vision to the point of nausea, reveurite dust everywhere.

They eat in shifts, and it's a small mercy that he can always claim the earliest one. By then he's ravenous, and luckily the food is always good, always plentiful. It's one of the few times he's reminded that this is a job, and not some endless punishment specifically devised for him.

Afterwards, it's back to the forge. He draws water from the springs, polishes metal fittings for the craftsmen, more sweeping, more fetching of food. Water. Wood. Ash. Repeat until it's time for dinner. And then again, until the sky is inky black and peppered with stars, and Aleksander's so tired he can barely think straight.

Then again. And again. For a year, he has lived like this. Endless, relentless misery.

What is he if not a scholar? Here is his answer: nothing.

Until the day Penelope summoned him to the cliffside gardens surrounding the scholars' tower. He went, trepidation in his stomach, feeling sick though he'd yet to eat for the day. He hadn't seen Penelope in months, much less spoken to her. What would she do with her blade, shattered beyond repair?

She turned to him, her eyes so full of sorrow that it made him want to sink to his knees. And she offered her bargain. *Find out what Violet Everly is doing. Watch her carefully. And come back to us. Come home.*

Violet Everly. He hears her name and thinks of coffee, sunlight on his shoulders, curiosity burning like wildfire. A curse, a key, a dark room.

He hasn't spent a year hating her. But it might have been better if he had.

In New York, he watched as she furtively wandered through the Metropolitan Museum of Art, lingering on an exhibition. It wasn't an artist he knew—art not being one of Penelope's chosen areas of study for him—but the way she'd looked at the portrait of a woman in a black dress, with such intense focus, made him wish he did. And for the first time in a long time, he'd wanted to say hello, to have her turn and ignite him with her curiosity.

Not that he could. But he *wanted*—

He caught her early in Vienna, stepping off the train with sleepy wonder at the city sprawling out in front of her. Outside the Kunsthistorisches Museum, he'd waited and wondered, his heart in his throat. Penelope told him to find answers, so he would ask.

He was so intent on that tiny slice of window that he didn't notice her come down the stairs, defiant in the pouring rain. The way she'd said his name, a question curled in her mouth.

It was only when she'd asked about the scholars that he'd found the hard kernel of resentment waiting for him. Where were her scars? How had she failed to notice the inexorable changes that stared at him every time he looked into a mirror? And how had she escaped unscathed, when he hadn't?

Anger rose like a tide, swallowing everything.

He should never have gone to Prague.

In the forge, he works until his bones ache, until stars of exhaustion burst behind his eyelids. He hammers out sheets of metal. He hauls firewood inside. He sweeps the floor until it shines. His pallet bed remains untouched, the sheets folded into precise corners.

Finally, the forge master snatches the broom from him and commands him to rest.

Obediently—because that is all he is now, a man whittled into an order yet to be given—he lies on his bed, as the sound of the forge falls away from him. In his head, the darkness looms, the shadows closing in. Yury roars in his cage, thrusting his hands into flames, ready to burn down the world. Golden blood spills over Violet's face, her eyes wide with accusation. So much damage left in his wake, and he'll never be able to undo it.

Alone in the room, he cries.

Ambrose knows when Gabriel arrives because the house is suddenly full of the sound of slamming doors. He waits in the library, listening to the storm descend on him. The doors fly open, and Gabriel strides through, his gaze burning behind his sunglasses. Ready for war.

"Gabriel—" Ambrose starts.

"Marianne's gone. I knew it. All this time, *wasted* on her."

Ambrose does his level best to stay calm, but Gabriel's tone sets his nerves jumping. "I don't know what happened, but—"

"We know damn well what happened."

Ambrose closes his eyes. "As I said—"

"You still don't get it. Marianne isn't coming back," Gabriel says, enunciating each word sharply. "As soon as she realised it was a lost cause, she fucked off! All that bullshit about keys and star-people. Her head in *fairy tales*."

"So you would rather have seen Marianne go with Penelope?" Ambrose snaps. "You would rather have let her die instead?"

"I would rather she'd told us the goddamn truth. That the great, infallible Marianne had failed. Then we wouldn't have spent ten years chasing her for nothing!" He slams his fist on the wall and the books rattle on the shelves.

Ambrose watches him, weariness creasing his brow. Rationally, he'd known there was only ever a slim chance at victory; no one else has escaped, so why should Violet? But even in his nightmares, he'd never imagined it quite like this: the anticipatory dread of defeat and what that means, the house a tomb of pre-emptive mourning. And Marianne's abyss of an absence. Even in his nightmares, Marianne would have been standing there with them.

"And now because of her...because of us..."

Gabriel looks up at Ambrose, the fight draining from him. He lifts his hands helplessly—Gabriel, who is never helpless, who'd strode in on that thunderous evening ten years ago ready to do anything to protect his niece.

His older brother has never looked so lost.

Gabriel sinks into a chair and puts his head in his hands. "What do we do now?"

Thirty-Nine

VIOLET MANAGES TO avoid her uncles for an impressive two days. Two entire precious days—precious because time keeps flowing out of her hands like water into the ocean. But she doesn't know what to say to them. She's been furious for so long, she's not sure how to let go. And maybe they're angry with her, too. After all, she's the one who ran away from home, who never replied to their calls or texts. Who let them worry as an act of passive vengeance, even though now she understands what they might have sacrificed for her.

Maybe there's an unforgiveable line she can't walk back from.

In the afternoon, she climbs out of her window and hauls herself up the drainpipe to the roof. She used to spend hours up here, yearning for the world beyond the thin horizon. And her mother, somewhere out there. Marianne Everly, who could very well be in this world or another—or dead, and Violet would never know.

Her hands ball into fists. Marianne Everly, who couldn't take two goddamn seconds to tell anyone where she went, or what desperate secret she'd gleaned that had made her so willing to go. Johannes Braun's voice pops into her head: *she was never much concerned with being liked.*

She yanks off her mother's bracelets from her wrists and hurls them as far as she can into the field. They glitter in the air, just once, then vanish into the long grass below. Her wrists feel lighter without them. Emptier. She runs her fingers across the pale band of skin where they used to sit.

Seconds later, Violet tears down the flight of stairs and through the back doors, regret burning the back of her throat.

After hours of searching, she finds just one, the bracelet's lustre half hidden under a layer of mud. She wipes it on her jumper and slips it back on her wrist, where the weight settles again. She knows she should let it go—but she can't.

On the third evening, she finally ventures into the rest of the house, too hungry and restless to stay cooped up in her room any longer—and too cold to pace on the roof. The kitchen is pointedly empty as she makes herself a proper meal for the first time in days, but the house seems to thrum around her, waiting. She takes her time over each mouthful, and washes up everything, wiping down all the counters until the entire kitchen gleams. Then there's nothing left to do but find her uncles.

Ambrose is sitting in his favourite chair in the third living room, the fire blazing merrily against the autumn chill. She can't face what she's about to tell him. But she owes him the truth of her failure.

"I'm back," she says quietly.

He sighs when he sees her, then pats his second-favourite chair. She curls up in it, tucking her legs underneath her. Gabriel used to say she reminded him of a cat, and she would always stick her tongue out at him. She looks down at her hands, wishing they were claws.

"What happened?" Ambrose asks.

Not *how could you? How dare you?*

Violet closes her eyes. Pictures it in her head again. Of all the people she didn't want to let down.

She tells him everything.

"I shouldn't have trusted Aleksander. It's all my fault." She wipes away an angry tear, then another. "I'm so sorry, Ambrose."

Ambrose stares into the fire thoughtfully, the flames casting shadows on his face.

"I wasn't much older than you are now when your mother left you with me," he says eventually. "I remember being panicked. I couldn't look after a child!" He smiles to himself. "But Marianne begged. She knew she couldn't take you with her, but she couldn't stay. She wanted to fight for you—to fight for all of us, really. So I agreed."

Violet recalls the first few weeks without her mother. How hollow her days felt, time stretching out like bubble gum. And there was Ambrose, awkwardly asking her whether she played with dolls, what food she liked, if she wanted to be friends. She hadn't deigned him with a reply.

But then he asked her the magic question, and her eyes had lit up like stars.

Would you like to hear a story?

Ambrose steeples his fingers. "Over the years, don't you think I've made mistakes? When Gabriel warned me about Penelope, we considering running, you know. We might not have run very far, but we could have tried. Gone to a different country, under different names."

"Penelope would still have found us," she says.

"Ah, but would she?" he asks. "We might also have got away. You and I could be living on a tropical island right now, lounging on a beach somewhere. Coconuts for days."

Despite herself, she snorts. "Ease up there, Robinson Crusoe."

"Well, maybe not. Certainly at the time, it seemed impossible. And we were still counting on Marianne." His smile fades. "Perhaps I should have let Gabriel take you away, so by the time Penelope came, you would have been long gone."

Violet blanches at the thought. "She would have killed you."

"But *you* would be safe. I think about that a lot, you know. What I was willing to give up. What I wasn't." He sighs. "I should have just told you the truth. I thought I was doing the right thing at the time."

Violet tries to imagine Gabriel driving away into the sunset with her tucked into the passenger seat, glowering at the neon orange car. Or a childhood where a curse wasn't just another story, but a vast and terrible thing to hang over her head for the rest of her life.

"Adelia Verne offered to take you with her once, to place you amongst the scholars in her family. I don't suppose you know that," he says.

"She did?"

A different life. Magic, scholars, reveurite—Fidelis. Once, Violet would have said yes within a heartbeat, desperate to see the world denied to her for so long. And part of her still feels the ghost of that particular longing.

"It's not as unusual as you might think. Marianne went." Ambrose drums his fingers against the armrest. "Again, a choice to be had. Would you have been happier in Fidelis, your birthplace, Marianne's home?" he muses. "Or would you have suffered under the scholars' rule, the way your friend did?"

A sudden surge of anger washes over her. "Aleksander doesn't deserve your pity."

Ambrose looks at her curiously. "Don't you feel sorry for him?"

Aleksander lied to her in Vienna, and then again in Prague. So many lies snowballing into his betrayal. And she *knew* it, too; that this new, slick Aleksander was not all he seemed, that he'd grown fangs in the year since she'd last seen him. He'd tried to dazzle her like a cheap magician, directing her to the pretty bauble of his attention even as cards of true intent spilled out of his pocket. And she'd let him. She'd just wanted to believe so badly in the man who had smiled at her over coffee, who had given her such a tantalising glimpse of what the world could be, if only she sought it out.

And if he'd looked at her in anguish? If for a second his veneer had cracked?

"You should have sent me away," she says, regret sweeping over her. "You should have sent me away and been free. This can't be what you wanted."

Ambrose clasps her hands in his and smiles, his eyes crinkling. "It's maybe not the life I would have chosen for myself. But it's been a privilege to watch you grow up."

For a long time, she and Ambrose watch the fire, burning to embers in the grate. In the hazy light, the crackles remind her of Erriel's staff, or the gleam of her amber eyes.

Violet had been so close to the door. If she hadn't waited that extra second, if she'd just taken Erriel's hand and made her bargain, then she could be with Marianne right now. Or, she could be continuing to chase a ghost. A woman who doesn't want to be found.

She wished to leave.

"Marianne didn't fight for us," Violet says suddenly. "She never even came back to warn us. Once she knew she couldn't stop Penelope, she just...left."

"Oh, Violet—"

"You stayed! Gabriel stayed!" Violet says in a rush. "*Marianne Everly, tough as nails. Marianne Everly, stubborn as hell. Marianne Everly, smarter than the devil.* Well, if she was so bloody tough and stubborn and smart, then why didn't she come back?"

Hot tears burn at the corner of her eyes, and this makes her angrier than ever. She's supposed to be done with the exhausting pain of it all. Done with the humiliation and anguish of being the daughter that wasn't worth staying for. Marianne left over a decade ago, but she might as well be sitting with them right here, staring at the same fire, for all she's blown a hole through Violet's life. All the damage she continues to do.

"She was afraid," Ambrose says.

Violet bites down on her lip so hard she draws blood. She presses her palms to her eyes, and takes in a deep, shuddering breath.

She can't do this. She can't.

There's the sound of springs as Ambrose eases up from his chair. Then warm arms envelop her.

"I'm sorry Marianne left," Ambrose says. "I'm sorry we didn't tell you the truth. God, I'm sorry."

Something in Violet breaks.

Later, after her tears have dried on Ambrose's shirt, and the fire has been reduced to ashes, Ambrose disappears briefly to return with a cup of tea. He hands it to Violet, and she inhales deeply before drinking.

It's a poor cure for heartache, but she'll take it.

Two days later, Aleksander packs up his meagre belongings at the forge, Penelope in attendance. The forge bearers look on in a mixture of awe and fear. *The* famous Penelope, here, at *their* forge.

"Where are you going?" one of them asks timidly. A child.

Penelope kneels down so she's eye to eye with the apprentice. "He's going back to where he belongs, little dreamer." She turns to Aleksander. "Isn't that right?"

He bows his head, unable to make eye contact. "Yes, Mistress."

They walk up the hill in silence. Penelope parts crowds with ease; they give way as if to a god in their midst. But Aleksander can feel eyes boring into the back of his neck. The disgraced assistant, returning to the cathedral of knowledge. Even for him, it seems to defy sanctity.

Penelope stops outside of the scholars' tower. "It's been a long time coming, hasn't it? It's okay, you can say it."

"Yes, Mistress," he says, swallowing the sudden lump in his throat.

A year of exile, of hardship. He has paid for this with his own blood, a forfeit of pain. He has paid for it with Violet's trust and Yury's humanity, too. But he tucks the thought away as quickly as it emerges.

And doesn't he at least deserve this? His future stretches out before him, an ocean of possibility once more. The scholars' archway looms overhead.

Penelope smiles, and for the first time in his entire life, steps aside for him to enter first. "Welcome home."

Aleksander is given a new room, higher in the tower than before. A scholar's room, not a novice's, even though he's yet to take the test that separates them. Instead of stone walls and bare floors, the walls are wood panelled and the floor covered in luxurious carpet. His bed is soft, his pillows full and downy. There's even an en-suite bathroom, with water shunted upstairs from the hot springs. His precious books are all there, lined up in a real bookcase.

It's everything he ever wanted.

Well, not quite. With his short hair and muscly heft from the forge, Aleksander stands out wherever he goes, and even the scholars give him a wide berth. Their eyes stray to his bare forearm, free of the reveurite tattoo that would mark him as a scholar proper, and conversations fall silent when he walks past, as though even gossip is too sacred for his ears. He takes to wearing long sleeves and eating at odd hours in the cafeteria, where only the kitchen staff side-eye him and mutter as they prepare for the rest of the day.

Before, as Penelope's assistant, he'd endured all kinds of rumours —that he was secretly her child, that she took a bribe to take him on, or even that his unidentified parents held some kind of sway over her —and he'd been able to ignore them because he was her assistant. Chosen. Even at the forge, he had been able to endure the suspicious glances and whispering. But this feels different, sharper somehow.

He combats his guilt by working it away, spending long hours in the archives. Unconsciously at first, and then with deliberate lack of acknowledgement as to why, he starts pulling anything he can find on the astrals. Most of the documents are fragmented or in a language so old he can barely read it, spidered alphabets meandering across pages pocked with toothy beetle marks. He lingers over words splintered from sentences, paragraphs that might have once belonged to an entire essay: *longevity, grace, war, calamity.*

More than once, he reaches a shelf and comes up empty, a finger-sized gap collecting dust. Books go missing occasionally, despite the card catalogue and army of sharp-eyed archivists: mis-shelved; abandoned on a desk; occasionally stolen by a covetous scholar to read in the comfort of their own room; and more rarely destroyed by those gripped with vengeance—or else too careless with hot drinks.

Even with all the potential mishaps, it's still unusual for a document to vanish from the shelves entirely, especially more than one on the same subject. The archivists shrug at the first two disappearances, glower at him suspiciously for the third. After that, he stops telling them, but he notes the absences in the back of his mind.

Not once does he let himself think about what he's searching for, beyond a deep unease. Yet he keeps digging, moving further through the archives, past the well-lit front shelves and into the many tunnels that snake into the mountainside. He reads until he collapses at his desk, succumbing to a dreamless sleep. In the middle of the night, he wakes with his face pressed against the book, alone.

CHAPTER

Forty ·

THE NEXT DAY, Violet follows Gabriel to the study, her stomach knotted with dread. Outside, the sky is a form-less grey, winter gathering its grip on the weather. Rain pounds the windows, and the house is plagued with a series of leaks, old wounds giving way to the incongruous symphony of water plink-ing into buckets. Gabriel has been suspiciously quiet since she returned; though she has no way of proving it, she suspects he's sneaking off to Fidelis. To do what, she has no idea. As far as she's concerned, there's nothing else they *can* do.

She'd been summoning the courage to talk to him—tell him what an absolute fool she's been—but he beats her to it, knocking on her door at an eye-wateringly early hour.

"Come on, kiddo. Got some things to discuss."

In the hallway, Gabriel pauses at the length of Everly portraits and sighs. They had always seemed so abstractly sorrowful to her, but now, in the full knowledge of their impending doom, Violet sees courage, defiance, resignation. Not that it mattered, in the end, what face they wore.

"So many Everlys," Gabriel says. "Never had a bloody chance, did they."

Violet knows he's thinking about Ambrose. What could Ambrose have been, without the weight of a curse and an abandoned child? *Happier*, she thinks bitterly.

And who would she have become? There's no portrait of her to stand in her stead, nothing to remind future Everlys of the dangers that await them. Then she remembers there won't be future Everlys, and she turns away.

As soon as the study doors swing shut, Violet expects Gabriel to berate her—or worse, glare in disapproving silence. Instead, he sits behind the desk, the leather chair creaking under his weight. He looks defeated, strangely vulnerable without his sunglasses or his usual sardonic smile.

"The game is up, kiddo," he says heavily. "So the question is, what do you want to do?"

She tilts her head, puzzled. "I don't understand."

"There are still a couple of options left. May not look like much, but..." He spreads his hands out on the table. "They're there."

Gabriel opens a drawer and pulls out fake passports, birth certificates, driving licences.

"Ambrose and I can't leave. It would be too obvious. But you can still run."

Violet pulls a passport towards her and opens it. Her photo is on the identity page, but *Emma Blythe* is listed as the name, with another birthday and town of birth. The next passport is Spanish; same photograph, but different name again.

"There's an expert forger on Skye," he says. "He can get you just about anything you ask for. And he owed me some favours, so I asked."

Violet looks at the passports again, evidence of lives that she's never lived. She can see it unfolding before her, though. Travelling from city to city, never staying in one place for too long. She could go anywhere.

"If I wanted to run..." she says.

"You would never be able to come back," Gabriel warns. "Penelope would catch you. And she would know we helped." He runs his hand through his hair, his gaze straying to the window. "It wouldn't be an easy life. If you decide you want children or a family, or even just a permanent home...Well, you've seen how that's turned out."

The imagined life vanishes instantly. Travel and freedom, yes— but not true freedom. Always with one eye over her shoulder, waiting for Penelope or one of her allies to find her. No attachments, no friends. And it would never stop. She'd never be able to come home.

"It wouldn't be much of a life," Violet says.

"But it would be *living*."

She fiddles with the birth certificates, checking the different names. None of them stamped with Everly.

Gabriel continues, counting off other options he's considered. Crossing over to Fidelis, though the city's too small to stay hidden for long; eking out an existence in a designated safe house...

But Violet tunes out, thinking furiously.

Her mother would run. Her mother *did* run.

Violet picks up the passports again. She thinks of the lives she might live, the women she could be. Then she sets them down.

"There aren't really any other options, are there?" she says.

"I'm afraid not, kiddo."

She nods to herself.

"Then I'm going to stay, and I'm going to fight. For all of us."

A few days later, Aleksander knocks on Penelope's door, willing himself not to betray his nerves. He's done this so many times over the course of his life that he shouldn't spare it a second thought. But the last time he was here was the day he tried to steal her key. The day his life unravelled. His heart beats furiously, loud in his ears.

"Come in," Penelope says.

He enters, and the familiar smell of cedar and vanilla, along with that underlying metallic scent, washes over him. Her fire blazes merrily in the fireplace.

Penelope sits at her table, with the usual detritus of books and letters. He keeps his eyes away from them; another lesson learnt from a young age. But Penelope herself catches his attention. There are dark circles underneath her eyes, and her skin seems almost translucent in the light. She's never been sick—not a day in his life. But this is undeniable illness. He opens his mouth to ask her if she's feeling alright, and then closes it again.

After a year at the forge, where no question was too stupid and no forge master too busy to answer, he is forgetting himself.

"Aleksander," Penelope says pointedly.

Although his mind is churning, his hands work for him, automatically opening cupboards to pull out wine, biscuits, several hard cheeses. He finds two glasses slightly dusty from lack of use, and wipes them clean with a thin rag. When he sets them all down at last, Penelope surveys the table with a pleased smile.

"Now everything is just as it should be," she says. "Ah, a minute, Aleksander."

Swiftly, she disappears into one of the other rooms and reappears with a bottle of dark, glistening liquid, no taller than her fist. She gives it a swirl in the light, then unstoppers it and splits it between the two glasses.

"I have been saving this for a long time," she says. "A very special vintage. But tonight, we drink."

Aleksander reaches for his glass, but Penelope stops him. "Not yet, my assistant."

She grasps the knife, and with a practised twist, drives it into the pad of her forefinger. A bead of blood wells up, tinged with a golden hue.

Aleksander flinches. "Mistress—"

"This path has not been easy for you," she says. "You have endured more trials than another assistant might have, and perhaps you are not entirely at fault for that. But you have persevered through all, which can only be commended." She squeezes a drop of blood into his glass. "We give back to our own, Aleksander. So allow me to give this to you."

Aleksander stares down at his glass, jewel red and viscous. There's just enough for a few mouthfuls. He hasn't eaten all day, nerves twisting inside him, but with the glass in front of him, he finds he isn't hungry at all.

She raises her glass. "To home. To destiny. To our future."

Then she drinks deeply, finishing the glass in one swallow. Hastily, Aleksander takes a sip, and has to hold back a grimace as an oily metallic taste hits his tongue. He glances at Penelope, but her smile only widens. So he downs the glass as quickly as he can, liquid burning the back of his throat.

And perhaps it's his imagination—perhaps it's nothing at all—but a feeling like electricity rolls over his body, flaring down to his fingertips. The dull throb in his lower back, from the unfamiliar feeling of being at a desk again, suddenly vanishes. He glances up at Penelope, but she's wiping her hands on a napkin, her gaze elsewhere. He thinks of the asteros reading in Prague, of Illios—Aleksander drinking the vial, the cards spilling over one another, Violet's body in his arms, the path that he has already walked so far and so quickly—

"So tell me, assistant of mine. How have you been using your freedom?" Penelope asks.

Aleksander tries to return to the present. "Reading, working." He fiddles with the cuffs of his robes. "There's . . . a lot to readjust to."

"Rabia tells me you've been spending a lot of time in the archives?"

He swallows. "Yes. I wanted to reacquaint myself with some of the texts."

He studies the knife on the table, waiting for her to mention the astrals. He has covered his tracks as best as he can, choosing inconspicuous hours to study, when the archivists' hands are full and no one notices a stray scholar.

"Surely you haven't forgotten everything I taught you?" Penelope says.

"No, Mistress," he says. "I just want to be prepared. In case—"

Her eyes gleam with sudden understanding. "You wish to know about the test."

Relief floods through him. "Yes. The test."

Anything to get her off the topic of the archives. Or to stop the queasy roiling in his stomach.

Penelope looks at him thoughtfully, running a finger around the rim of her glass. In the firelight, the shadows around her lengthen. For the first time, she looks old, her skin softened with creases, a thread of silver flashing in her hair. It's an impossible image; she has always seemed immutable. *And why do you suppose that is?* a voice snarls at him from the back of his mind.

"Aleksander, if it was up to me, I would waive it. You have more than proved your loyalties to me," she says. "Alas, if only it were so. However, I think you will be more than worthy of the task." She stands up. "Are you ready?"

"Now?" he says, shocked.

She smiles. "There is no better time than the present."

"I—I haven't prepared; I haven't studied—"

She silences him with a look. "Aleksander, you have been studying for this your whole life."

She pulls a key from her pocket. Seeing where she intends to lead him, Aleksander starts to remove his robe, but Penelope stops him.

"We are not going to be seen," she says.

He follows her into the small travel chamber, where snow gathers in front of the open doorway. His breath mists in front of him and he shivers.

The scholar's test. How long has he waited to be invited to take it? He's heard rumours of tricky alchemy, or long exams with initiates sweating over every single word. But if they're crossing over into the other world, then this is obviously no essay. Perhaps he'll be dropped off in an unknown city and asked to do something impossible.

Wind. Free fall. A rush of blue light.

He opens his eyes to a dark room. There are rows of beds lined up against the wall, moonlight glinting off the metal posts. In each one, a child slumbers, their eyelids fluttering as they dream.

Aleksander turns to her, alarmed. They must have made a mistake somewhere, travelled with the wrong intent, or—

But Penelope never makes mistakes.

"Welcome to the test," she says. "I would like you to find a dreamer."

He frowns. Is that all? He must have done this a hundred times under her watch, on busy streets with a million more distractions to unbalance him. He settles his mind into that grey space of singular focus, and casts his gaze over the row of sleeping children. Golden sparkles leap out at him immediately.

"Fourth bed from the window," he says confidently.

Penelope nods; she must already know. But she doesn't congratulate him, or pull out her key to return home. Instead, she looks at him with a steely, unwavering gaze that sends his stomach plummeting.

"You are going to take that child's hand, and you will walk out of here," she says. "Back to Fidelis."

Aleksander freezes. He can't have heard that right.

"Mistress?" he says.

She doesn't move. "This is the test."

"The test is to steal a *child*?" He is being too loud; one of the children groans and rolls over. "A child."

He says it again, as though repeating it would somehow elucidate a greater truth. Because there must be a greater truth at hand. This is part of the test, surely? Penelope asking for him to think harder, faster, smarter about why she wants him to pluck a child from their bed. Because she can't actually want that. She can't.

"This is the test, Aleksander."

He takes a step backwards. "I don't understand."

"They have talent, therefore they are the property of Fidelis." Penelope smiles. "After all, how do you think I chose you?"

Forty-One

IOLET HAS A week left. Just one week to undo a centuries-old curse. It feels like a fool's effort, but she has to try.

In the library, Ambrose sits her down with a stack of books and other documents besides: maps, illustrations, pages torn from diaries.

"This is everything we've collected over the years," he says. "It's not much—but then there was never much to find. Penelope has hidden her tracks well."

Violet dives straight in.

Books have always been her escape. When she couldn't leave the house, when no one would answer her questions, when she felt so very alone in the world. They have given her a way out before—maybe they can do it again.

She reads and reads. When it gets too dark, she turns on the oil lamps, the library bathed in a soft glow. Occasionally one of her uncles brings her a sandwich, or a cup of coffee, taking away the half-eaten meals and unfinished drinks with filmy water slopping over the side. And when it's not food, it's their own notes, decades of research that they've painstakingly put together. Her head twinges with the beginnings of a headache. She yawns and rubs her eyes, then keeps going.

In her head, she joins sentences together across books from different hands, chasing threads across history and haphazard translations. The subjects vary wildly: theology, geography, fables and folk tales from both worlds, a biography of a sixteenth-century painter, a scribbled note from a forge master. But as Violet reads on, a picture starts to build of the astrals.

In some accounts, they create humans out of clay and stardust, shattering themselves to grant the gift of talent. In others, they walk amongst mortals, bestowing mercy and punishment like a divine judiciary. Violet doesn't recognise these unknowable, infallible beings; their abstract altruism doesn't reckon with Tamriel's attempt to eat her, or Erriel's apathy to her plight.

It's the darkest stories that fascinate her—and the ones which have been the most heavily annotated. Whispers of creatures who turned the sky black, or who stalked across worlds, devouring cities one by one. They play at being mortal, upending lives and tearing apart communities. Yet even these have a fairy-tale quality, as though the true account would be too painful to write down.

Always, at the end, the astrals return to their homelands, leaving wreckage or restoration in their wake. But *leaving*, all the same. So why hasn't Penelope?

One evening, Ambrose walks into the study as Violet paces up and down, tapping a pencil against the palm of her hand.

"Marianne used to do that, too, when she was working on a problem," he says.

Violet immediately stops. Her fingers tighten on the pencil.

For the second day in a row, she falls asleep in one of the armchairs, curled up in a position her body will come to regret in the morning. Her dreams are fragmented and terrible: filled with blood and flames, blinding light and honey smiles. Penelope whispering in her ear, *it's almost time.* Several times she wakes in the middle of the night, certain that the shadows around her are pulling her in.

On the fourth day, she reaches for her pile of documents and pulls out a hefty book. It's not an old volume, but it wears its years badly, battered and singed black. The gilt on the book is almost gone, but Violet can still read the debossed title: *An Unnatural Collectorie: Tales of the Astrals.*

She cracks open the musty binding, careful of the tissue-thin scritta paper. The book is segmented into sections on each astral, with frayed ribbon and brittle notes sandwiched into the pages. There are copperplate facsimiles of each astral, in elegant art nouveau illustrations that seem to bear no resemblance to the reality that Violet has already witnessed.

Carefully, she flips to the page marked *Astriade*. A woman in a diaphanous dress, twin swords at each side, stares out at her. And maybe there's something in the proud chin or the sharp nose, but it's hard to tell. Some unfortunate reader must have accidentally nicked their thumb because there are several rusty fingerprints across the page. She turns the page and—

Once, there was a man who could make anything he desired. But he had never been loved. Until one day, a star walked into his shop and offered him an exchange.

Some of the details are familiar: the craftsman, the star, the pact. Others, though, are at odds with her childhood fairy tale. In this one, the man plunges the bridal sword into his lover's heart on the last night, killing them both. The next story is more of the same, and yet different again. A cage of god-metal protects the man until dawn, by which time the star leaves. In yet another, the star dies with their promise unfulfilled, leaving the man to wander distraught across the world for eternity.

Just stories. And yet, there's a familiarity between them that sets her thoughts racing.

Hours later, Violet teeters on a ladder as she unhooks the ancient family sword from its clasps on the wall and places it gingerly on the floor. She examines the crumbling relic, surrounded by reams of her own notes. For the last twenty-odd years, it's hung in the library, a cast-off from one ancestor or another. Practically forgettable, amidst all the other curios in the Everly house.

Up close, the metal isn't entirely smooth, with tiny hillside ridges and a greenish sheen speckling the onyx black. The leather on the grip is practically falling off, and the silver pommel is tarnished and dull. It looks like it has her whole life. But this time, she knows exactly what she is looking at: a sword with a blade of reveurite, albeit dulled and brittle.

She closes her eyes and concentrates. Places her hands on the blade and presses her fingers into the metal. Years ago, she had held a marble in her palm and wished for a miracle. And it was only when Aleksander had explained about talent and god-metal that she'd figured out that it wasn't her hands at all that were the problem; it was simply that she lacked the correct material to work with. By then there was no reveurite to test herself upon—and even if she had possessed enough of the untampered metal, would she have dared? She knows so little about how to wield it. But now, there's nothing left to lose.

She's already lost everything.

Beneath her eyelids, something sparks. When she opens her eyes, the blade seems to gleam anew with gold. When she takes her hands away, there is a thumb-shaped dip in the metal, the whorls of her fingerprint mimicked exactly.

It's hardly a marble and a galaxy, yet this is supposed to be what separates her from everyone else. What made her blood so sweet to Erriel. What condemns her to Penelope's wrath. What she couldn't give up, even to find her mother.

The manipulation of reveurite. God-metal. Star-metal.

The ability to walk through worlds untethered.

Astrals are not invulnerable, though they may live forever. Violet thinks of Erriel, and the reveurite shard plunging through her heart. Of Tamriel's chains in his prison.

What better way to combat a god than a godly creation?

Despite all her promises to herself, she feels a faint flicker of hope.

Forty-Two

CASPIAN VERNE LOUNGES on a yacht off the coast of southern Italy, hiding from the rest of the party. It's not his yacht or his party, and the drink by his side is more ice than booze, but he's been summoned here at his grandmother's behest to represent the family—and even at ninety-three, his grandmother isn't to be ignored. So he's happy for the diversion of a phone call, and even more so when he realises who's on the other end of the line.

"Seen any asteria in the buff lately?" he asks.

"Hi, Caspian," Violet Everly says.

He listens for several minutes in absolute silence, as Violet describes the scope of her problem. There are more holes in her story than a colander, but he pretends he's as convinced as if she was telling the truth.

"I don't see why you're not asking your uncles about this," he says.

"It's a surprise. Ancestral birthday gift. Can you do it in three days?"

He considers the Italian coastline, all rugged cliffs and warm greens. A man could get used to this.

"It'll require some favours, but to hell with those. What else would I need them for?" Actually, quite a few things, now that he thinks of it.

"That's an awfully nice gesture for a scholar," Violet says.

"I'm not a scholar, and I'm not that nice. You'll owe me, Everly," he says.

He can hear her smile on the other end of the line. "I can live with that."

Caspian is not usually one for liars, despite being an expert liar himself, and he's also not in the habit of drawing on his not-insignificant influence without a reward. But there's something about Violet Everly that makes him want to throw all his rules out of the window.

"What was that about?" the woman lounging next to him asks, once he's off the phone.

Caspian swills his drink in his hand. "Kat, do you remember that time you wanted that Etallantia scholarship text? And how I stole it for you, and then you kept saying you were going to pay me, but never did?"

The scholar's mouth flattens in a way that suggests she does, indeed, remember, but was rather hoping he'd forgotten.

"Well, it's time to cash in my cheque. And I know exactly what currency I'd like it in."

Yulan Liu is catching up on paperwork in her bookshop when she receives a phone call from her scholar. She glances at the sliver of bustling activity, customers clustering over the latest bestseller, before shutting her office door.

"Katherine, my love," she says, in a voice that she only ever uses in the privacy of their already private relationship.

"Sweetness, I'm in a bit of a pickle, and I have a favour to ask. Do you remember that restorer?"

Twelve hours later, Goro Matsuda opens his door to a sword-shaped package on his expensive doorstep. The courier is nowhere in sight, but there's a note with an ominous tone that he would recognise anywhere.

Goro,

You owe me for midsummer. The courier will return for it in two days. I trust that's enough time.

Y. L.

He squints into the distance, but the courier has long vanished.

"Shit," he says under his breath.

Forty-Three

T HE REVEURITE HARVEST is here. For a week, from dawn until dusk, the forge bearers stretch fine-meshed metal nets across the cliffs, with generous amounts of slack. Every roof gains a tough, protective cover. Candles are doused and streetlamps dimmed, so that the city is draped in nightfall and extra care is taken when walking along the cliffsides. This is no star festival—reveurite harvesting is work, not play—but nevertheless there are stalls full of piping hot sausages, tureens of spicy winter soup ladled out by the bowlful, and hot chocolate thick enough to stand a spoon in the mug.

As soon as the sun dips underneath the horizon, the first pinpricks of light appear across the clouds, brighter and wilder than any star. Reveurite, borne from the sky in fist-sized meteors. They barrel down like shining rain, leaving incandescent trails that look like the stars' fingers outstretched: *here is our gift, O you who were once our fledgling dreams.*

There is plenty of swearing at singed fingers as the forge bearers, dressed in thick leathers and protective helmets, scale the nets to retrieve these blazing offerings from the stars. But there is also laughter and singing, cheers for the biggest chunk of reveurite, or applause for a forge bearer's inaugural catch.

Aleksander enjoys none of it.

He sits alone on a bench, watching a forge bearer throw themselves nimbly across a gap between nets. Even though this is an annual event, and no one's a stranger to heights, the spectators still suck in a breath as another forge bearer dangles from the cliff with only one hand, gathering her body to swing over. The forge master stands below, shouting instructions and encouragement by turns.

Last year, it had been Aleksander scaling the nets, his fingers numb with cold, his heart pounding in glorious terror. Now, he has no place here, other than as a spectator.

Because he will be a scholar.

He stole a child.

But he will be a scholar.

You stole a child, Aleksander.

Ordinarily, he would have to wait another year for Illios' Blessing to return again, and be made scholar amongst the other anointed. But Penelope had insisted upon tonight. A reward for exemplary service not just for scholars, but all of Fidelis. And who would disagree with Penelope, when she put it like that?

"For you, my assistant, all things we will make possible," she'd said.

Only a few weeks ago, he would have given everything to hear that.

Aleksander looks down at his hands. His tattoo is scheduled for midnight—a slightly unusual time to receive the scholar rites, but given how important the harvest is, he's lucky to be receiving it at all tonight.

Just half an hour left. And then he'll be a scholar, with everything that it means.

He has always thought of himself as rooted in the scholars. Always. At first it was unquestioning loyalty; the scholars took him in when no one else did, gave him a purpose. Then it was the joy of wrapping his head around a complex problem, of peeling apart centuries-old texts to decode the secrets within, even if it was something as mundane as a recipe for vegetable stew. Not all scholars love the archives the way he does, and fewer still have the patience or tenacity to spends hours mulling over the same few texts, piecing together fragments to elucidate the greater truth of what they have inherited in this fractured mountainside home. What they might have brought with them from Elandriel.

He is very, very good at digging through the archives for that truth. And, it turns out, the truth is a name. Only a name.

Astriade. That's what he'd heard Violet say as the church doors swung closed in Prague. It sounded impossible—of course it did. But then Violet's entire journey has carried a mythic wonder to it, as if she was making her own legend. And there was so much conviction in her voice.

So he started to pick over the archives. And what a truth he has uncovered.

This is why Penelope warned him not to ask questions. Why he's been so good as her blade. Because now that he holds knowledge in his hands, he hates the answers it's brought. He hates that he has to make a choice.

How easy it would be to stay Penelope's blade and let his new knowledge fall away into the void of memory. No one would ever know but him.

He buries his hands in his pockets against the cold and accidentally brushes the fuzzy corner of an old stamp card. He pulls it out and stares at it, even though it's almost too dark to see. Ten stamps: a promise unfulfilled.

At a quarter to midnight, the forge bearers finish and bow to thundering applause, breathless and grinning. Fireworks burst in the sky, as one day rolls into another. Aleksander is nowhere to be found.

It's almost midnight. Almost time.

Penelope walks out to the ruins on the mountainside, irrespective of the cold. She hasn't felt cold for a millennia—or warmth, for that matter. Only the keen absence of her brethren's singing, of her own power thrumming through her veins. Of white-hot light and icy abyss, of *home*.

It's said that for a god, one hundred years is the blink of an eye. That mortals shed their lives like moths, living and dying between breaths.

It is a lie.

Penelope has felt every second of exile, every ache of her loss. She has paid her penance.

Now it's time to return.

If this doesn't work, it'll be Violet's last midnight. She decides to spend it on the roof of the house, even though the temperature has dropped dramatically. Better to freeze up here than watch her uncles exchange increasingly desperate glances, as if there's still time to convince her to leave.

Clouds scull overhead, shadowing the moon. She picks out Orion, with his bright belt, then Pleiades, the Eye of Taurus. It's entirely possible that they wander the earth in another world, no longer a dance of chemicals, but under more mortal guises. Free to live, love—destroy.

Maybe it won't hurt. Maybe it'll be a quick mercy, so that by the time Violet knows it's happening, it'll be all over. Knowing Penelope, though, that feels like wishful thinking.

At least she has the truth in her hands, even though it's one she would rewrite if she could. After years of wondering whether Marianne was dead, or trapped, or still on her "adventure," it's a bitter consolation prize to know that her mother abandoned her long before Violet ever stepped into the world of the scholars.

In her room, the reveurite sword sits on her desk amongst its nest of bubble wrap and parcel string. No longer brittle and corroded with rust, the metal shines like oily lacquer, sharp and deadly. Violet hopes she'll never have to use it.

But if she does, she hopes it works.

Limbs aching from the cold, she unfurls herself and straightens up. Even though there are still a few minutes to midnight, she wants to settle her mixed feelings about the effectiveness of the stupid sword. With so much on the line, she feels like an idiot for even considering a grab-bag of fairy tales as truth—or at least, truth enough for her to stave off Penelope. God-metal to stop a goddess.

What she really needs is a miracle.

With one last glance at the moon, Violet climbs back into her room—and collides straight into Aleksander.

Forty-Four

THERE IS A moment, between the split-second expression of shock and collision, where Violet thinks she's dreaming. Then they bash into each other, knocking heads, and stars flash in her vision. No dream at all—Aleksander is really standing here, in her room.

Anger burns her vision red.

"You lying piece of shit," she snarls. "You absolute *scum.*"

It's barely been two weeks since they stood in the church in Prague, and yet Aleksander already seems different, though she can't quite pinpoint all of the changes. He's lost some of that irritating bravado and his shorn hair is quickly growing out, softening some of those razor edges.

But then she's been fooled too many times to believe anything his face says.

"Did Penelope send you?" she demands. "Is this some fucked up pre-ritual?"

He winces. "Violet, I—"

"Get out." She points a finger to the door. "Now."

"We have to talk," he says, then his gaze strays towards her desk and he falters. "Is that a sword?"

She almost laughs in disbelief. Here she is, moments away from calamity, and Aleksander is playing scholar in her room. The incredible audacity of it all.

"You were right," he says, still staring at the sword. "Not to trust the scholars. Or me."

How dare he tell her something she already knows, to admit to his betrayal without even really acknowledging it. It's too easy for him. He's not even *sorry*.

Violet folds her arms tightly. "If you think you have any right to waltz in here just to clear your conscience—"

"I took a child," he blurts out.

This brings Violet up short. "What?"

"I took a *child*. And I just—I don't know what I was thinking. But that's what she wanted me to do. That was the test." He hesitates. "And God help me, I did it."

He starts to pace in her room, one hand pressed to his head as though that would somehow erase the memory. Violet tries to process what he's just told her.

"Penelope asked you to steal a child," she repeats.

Aleksander looks at her, eyebrows creased in heartbreak, and she realises the odd emotion that she couldn't immediately put her finger on: despair.

"You mean Astriade," he says.

Violet's stomach drops. "You know."

He stops pacing. "I should have already known. Really, there's no excuse." He laughs humourlessly. "You would have made an excellent scholar. Much better than me."

Without meaning to, Violet sits down on her bed. "What happened?"

Quickly, Aleksander outlines the scholars' test. How he'd figured out who Penelope really is. He's sparse on detail, and Violet suspects there's plenty he's omitted from the way he avoids her gaze. Or maybe it's just hard to admit the truth.

"Where's the child now?" Violet asks.

"I took him back," Aleksander says. Then his eyes widen, as if he's just remembered something. "I—I threatened one of the scholars to get into the novices' quarter. Oh God, and I stole their *key*. But she would have killed him. I never imagined—everything Penelope's done—"

It hasn't even occurred to Aleksander that the other scholars are in on it, she notes. Even though at least some of them must be aware of Penelope's true identity. That she never ages seems to be a big clue, for one. Johannes knew; she could tell from the way he spoke about the poisoned chalice. And yet Aleksander had no idea.

Whereas Violet has always known there would be monsters alongside the magic.

Sudden ice floods through her. Penelope will be here any moment. And if Violet was a less charitable person—if she was a scholar—she would let Aleksander stay, unknowing, for the pure pleasure of watching the outcome. Let him see what betrayal feels like. Let him *hurt*.

But Violet isn't a scholar, and never will be.

She leaps up. "You have to go."

"Violet, I can't—"

She cuts him off. "You don't understand—you can't be here. Not now."

She starts to push him towards the door, just as a terrible blue flash lights up the courtyard outside.

"Shit," she says.

Aleksander looks up at her, his face suddenly sheet-white. "They've found me."

Violet stops shoving him. Instead, she grabs the sword from her desk. The terrible, useless sword that she was supposed to be practising with, instead of arguing with Aleksander. And now there's no time left.

"Oh, for the love of— It's not *you*."

"Then who?" Aleksander's gaze follows the sword. "What have you done?"

Downstairs, the doorbell rings. She doesn't have time for this.

"Stay here, go, whatever—just don't head downstairs." She pushes past him. "But I would really suggest you leave."

She slams the door behind her, her heart in her throat. The sword weighs a ton, and in her sweaty grip, it feels even heavier than it did when she'd first held it in the library. It had seemed like such a comfort then, to carry such solid weaponry. But she's no knight errant and this is no fairy-tale dragon.

She's going to die here, and it's going to be incredibly stupid.

Downstairs, Ambrose is arguing loudly, with the kind of tone that used to shock Violet into obedience when she was little. She's under no illusion about who he's arguing with.

At the bottom of the staircase, she smacks into Gabriel. He takes one look at her—the sword, her knuckles white around its hilt, her lips bloodied from biting on them for the last three days—and flings one hand out to stop her.

"Are you out of your bloody mind?" he hisses. "Get back upstairs—take my key—"

"I'm not leaving you," Violet says.

He grabs her arm, tight enough to be painful. "This is not a negotiation. We can buy you some time, but you have to go *now*."

"I said I would stay and fight. I meant that." She shrugs out of his grip. "Anyway, 'we Everlys stick together,' remember?"

She readjusts her grasp on the sword and strides past her uncle, down the corridor to the front door. For a split second, she goes unnoticed as the argument turns to full-on shouting, Ambrose blocking the entrance as best as he can. And there's Penelope, her expression placid, even as she takes another footstep into the house.

"We had a deal, Ambrose. Ten years, to the day. I have honoured my part; now you must honour yours." Then her eyes light on Violet. "It's time, little dreamer."

Ambrose glances behind him, distracted. In that moment, Penelope shoves him aside, as though he's made of paper. She sweeps past him into the house, shadows lengthening behind her.

She holds out her hand. "Come. It will be easier this way."

Violet doesn't move. *Courage.*

"I didn't make that deal with you, and I'm not going anywhere," she says.

She raises the sword so Penelope can see it, even though her arms are already straining with the effort. She catches a glimmer of herself in the blade's reflection, a bloody fool, with a fool's hope to match. Maybe that's all there ever was. But she still has to try.

Then—her grip fails. The pommel slides from her grasp. She reaches for the blade, even though she knows she's not supposed to, but it slips through her fingers.

The sword falls to the floor with a resounding clang. Silence rings out in its wake.

Penelope doesn't laugh, but Violet can see her mouth lift in amusement. "Little dreamer, how you've always loved to play pretend." She reaches to pick up the sword, and abruptly, her face changes to fury. "That was not made for *you*."

"Fuck you," Violet spits, because it's all she has left.

Penelope's gaze sharpens. "Very well."

She transforms, wings exploding behind her in a shower of smoke and sparks. Her claws elongate. Inky pupils fill her eyes. Violet darts forward to retrieve the sword, but Penelope slams her foot down on the blade.

Violet exchanges a panicked look with Ambrose.

"Get out of here, Vi!" he shouts.

She glances behind her to run, but there's someone already blocking the way. Aleksander. He still has one foot on the bottom stair, as though he came down here by accident. But his mouth is set in a thin, grim line that suggests he knows exactly what he came down here to witness.

Penelope glances up, and for a second—just a second—the image of her shadow-self breaks. And it might be bewilderment, or even hurt that flashes across her face, but it's gone so quickly Violet wonders if it was ever there.

"My wayward assistant," she says, and he flinches. "You *will* know your place."

Penelope surges forward, but Ambrose steps in front of Violet. "You are not welcome in this house, Astriade."

Penelope raises her arm and swings, brushing him aside. There's a sickening crunch as Ambrose smashes into the wall. He doesn't get up.

"Ambrose!" Violet shouts.

She flies to his side, but Gabriel gets there first, propping his brother up. Ambrose's eyelids flutter, and Violet's entire body unknots, just for a second.

Alive. He's alive.

She exchanges a desperate glance with Gabriel. She should stay.

She should make sure that Ambrose is okay. She should give herself up to Penelope, if it means keeping her family safe.

"Get out of here, Violet!" Gabriel commands.

She runs.

Penelope slashes outwards in a deadly arc, but Violet's too quick, dodging the dark coils that whip up from the maelstrom of shadows beneath her feet. Aleksander darts out of the way, just in time for her to barrel past. She hauls herself up the staircase, two stairs at a time. Behind her, something splinters, and Gabriel swears.

Violet runs down the landing, her heart in her throat. If she can get to the living room, there's a perfect escape through the window to the roof. *And what will you do then?* The sword is gone, her uncles—*don't think about Ambrose*—occupied. No one is coming to save her, and the chance for her to save herself maybe never existed.

She was an idiot to drop the sword. An idiot to think that she stood any chance at all. Every strategy she envisioned narrows down to the pulse of her heartbeat, the adrenaline surging through her with lightning panic. Decisions pinpoint to the next breath, the next step ahead of the shadows roiling behind her.

She reaches the window, pushes it open—

Something snags Violet's heel. She glances down. A dark coil, twining itself around her ankle. She tries to shake free, as another one finds her hands and drags them back, pinning her to the wall. Penelope emerges from the hallway, half woman, half astral, a creature of devastation.

"Your faithless ancestor betrayed me. Your mother escaped me. But you—I will have *you*," Penelope hisses, her eyes narrowed to slits. "I will hear my brethren sing yet, Violet Everly."

She extends her claw towards Violet's chest. Violet frantically tugs on her wrists. Her hands dangle uselessly, trapped in burning dark rope. If she can just get free—

Aleksander skids into the room, Gabriel following and armed with a chair. Aleksander recoils, his eyes wide with horror. But Gabriel doesn't hesitate; he flings the chair at Penelope. It strikes her in the back, instantly shattering to splinters.

Penelope jerks towards them like a serpent, and the rope loosens. Violet launches off the wall with every ounce of her being. She smashes into Penelope, and for a second, darkness engulfs her vision. She inhales ash and flame, choking on fumes. Penelope clutches Violet tightly, claws pricking her back.

"We go together," Penelope says softly.

Tears streaming down her face, Violet sees the glint of the sword in Aleksander's hands. He looks at it, then at her, trapped in Penelope's embrace, a sea of poisonous black shadows between them.

He hesitates.

But Gabriel doesn't. He snatches the sword out of Aleksander's hands and hurls it across the room.

Violet dives for it, feeling the hot graze of claws across her back as she escapes Penelope's grip. Penelope twists, lightning fast—but still not fast enough. Violet's hands gain purchase on the leather pommel. She slashes upwards, the blade glittering with golden sparks in a wide arc. It connects with something meaty. Wet blood spatters across her face.

Dragging in air, Penelope takes one look at the scene in front of her. Her ethereal wings shimmer, and once more, Violet sees the two images superimposed over one another: the woman and the monster. Her blonde hair lies lank on her skull, and her skin clefts too tightly to her bones, as though she's aged between one step and the next.

"Know me, Violet Everly," Penelope hisses. "I will claim what is mine. And no amount of treachery will save you."

She snaps her wings together, shedding flame across the carpet. Through the haze of smoke, Violet sees a flash of key in the air, a snarl of blue light—

Penelope vanishes.

Aleksander's heart is still pounding against his ribcage. He slumps against the corridor wall, trying to process what he's just seen. What he's just *done*.

If he thought taking back the child was an irredeemable offence, then this is something he'll never be able to undo. Panic swells in his chest. The walls press in on him, and the world narrows down to the scant point of darkness in front of him. Without meaning to, he clutches at the front of his shirt, like the fabric itself is too heavy to bear.

He is walking down a corridor to a room. There is only that black abyss, and pain. So much pain.

You are in Violet Everly's house. You are standing against a wall with somewhat ugly wallpaper.

His breath is loud in his ears. Heart bursting. His skin is on fire.

You are in Violet's house.

She would not be in that room with you.

Slowly, his panic subsides, and he finds the strength to take in a deep breath, and then another. He manages to make his way to the kitchen, following the sound of voices.

Violet's uncles have immediately swept in on her, peppering her with questions. Their hands flutter around her: one on her shoulder to steady her; another to gently steer her towards a chair. Blood trickles from a cut along her hairline, and her eyes have the wide, vacant look of someone in shock. She's still clutching the sword, arms wrapped around the naked blade, even though it must hurt to hold on so tightly.

Her uncles look no better, bruised and limping alongside Violet. The taller uncle of the two—the one Penelope so swiftly threw against the wall—keeps rubbing the back of his head and wincing. But all of their attention is pinpointed on her.

They seem to have entirely forgotten about Aleksander.

He watches all of this with a slightly sick feeling in his stomach, not quite guilt and not quite hatred, but something in between. *Envy.* Suddenly, he can't bear to look at them at all. He glances away, to the cracked tiles under his feet, well worn from years of Everly treading on them.

He will always be on the outside, no matter where he is. Always nothing, no matter how hard he has tried to build himself into someone worthy of love.

And now, knowing who Penelope is, even though he can't bring himself to think of her as Astriade—even though he saw her astral self—even though she asked him to take a *child*—

"Aleksander." He looks up and catches Violet staring at him, the shock in her eyes dimmed. "Are you okay?"

He swallows the hard knot of resentment and nods. "Are...are you?"

The scary uncle, the one in the leather jacket, scrapes his chair back to stand up, blocking Violet from view. A crack runs through the left lens of his sunglasses.

"How the hell does she look to you?" he demands. "How dare you come back. You have no bloody right to be here."

"Gabe, don't start," the other one says wearily.

"Shut up, Ambrose," Gabriel says sharply, before returning to Aleksander. "You had the sword right in your hands, and what did you do?"

"Gabriel, please—"

"Absolutely fuck all, is what—"

"Enough!" Violet says, and they both fall silent.

Gabriel glares at Aleksander, but he moves to stand behind Violet, as though he's a particularly irate bodyguard. It strikes Aleksander how similar they look, chins tipped upwards, unafraid, or at least doing their best at pretending to be so. His heart twinges again.

"We have to go after Penelope," Violet continues. "Otherwise she'll come back—for all of us."

Gabriel looks at her as though she's grown a second head. "You are going absolutely nowhere."

"We can still go to the safe house," Ambrose says quickly. "I kept it stocked, just in case you changed your mind."

"Perfect," Gabriel says, just as Violet says, "Not a chance in hell."

Gabriel scowls. "So help me, Violet, I will throw you over my shoulder and carry you the whole way if I have to."

Violet tries to stand up, winces, and sits back down. "I'd like to see you try. Ambrose?"

"I'm sorry, Vi, but I'm with Gabriel on this one."

"She won't stop," Aleksander says suddenly.

All three swivel towards him. Inexplicably, his hands start to sweat.

"She's weak. So maybe that's why the sword worked. But Penelope always gets what she wants," he continues. "Always." He hesitates,

afraid of voicing the question that's tormented him from the second
he saw Penelope in the hallway. "Why does she want you?"

"As if you don't know," Gabriel says derisively.

But Violet is watching him carefully, a curious expression on her
face. It's not quite trust. He knows he'll never get that back, not after
everything he's done. The one precious gift he hadn't even realised
he had, until he'd thrown it away.

Violet stands up, and this time, even though her face screws up
with pain, she doesn't sit back down.

"I want a word with Aleksander. Alone," she adds, seeing her
uncles' expressions. "Anyway, I have to change."

Her shirt is spattered with Penelope's blood, and so is his, he realises. Not red, or gold as the other astral's had been, but black. Like
something corrosive.

"I'm going to change, and speak to Aleksander. Then I'm going to
take some painkillers and we'll go after Penelope," she says firmly.

"That's not much of a plan," Ambrose says.

"It's the one we've got," she says.

They all exchange a wordless look—exasperation and love and
something else Aleksander doesn't recognise—then Ambrose sighs,
easing back in his chair. And just like that, Violet wins the argument.

"Be careful," he says.

As soon as they're out of earshot of the kitchen, Violet pauses to
lean against the wall, her jaw set against the pain. Her hair is tangled
across her face, and Aleksander has the absurd urge to reach over and
smooth it back for her. Instead, he tucks his hands behind his back.

"Are you sure you want to do this?" he asks.

She takes a deep breath and closes her eyes, then opens them
again. "I don't have a choice. You know what Penelope is like. You
know what she'll do to us."

It's a relief, ever so slight, that she still calls Penelope the name by
which he's always known her, and not by the name he considered to
belong to their mythical pantheon. *Astriade*. That creature is still
barely real to him.

How stupid he's been, to place his anger, his resentment, on Violet.

"Let me help you," he offers.

Deliberately, she straightens up, ignoring his outstretched hand. "No."

His hand falls to his side. Of course. He can't blame her.

It takes twice as long to reach her room, on the highest floor of the house. At each landing, Violet has to stop, shaking out her sore limbs to try and find some relief before continuing. But he doesn't offer his hand again, and she doesn't ask for it. Silence stretches painfully between them. There's so much he wants to tell her. How wonderful it is to see her, despite this awful moment and all that's happened before it. How amazing she'd been to face down Penelope like that, braver than any scholar he knows. How very, very sorry he is—for everything. But any apology now, come far too late, would just be self-serving.

He barely deserves to look at her. So he doesn't.

Finally, Violet reaches the top of the house. She opens the door to a shabby attic room that nevertheless exudes a lived-in warmth. He only had a glimpse at it before she climbed back through her window, but even in that glimpse he knew exactly whose bedroom he was standing in. Stacks of books everywhere, but also faded maps pinned to the walls with clumsy travel routes marked in red, illustrations of Victorian fairies torn from magazines, reams of notes in Violet's own handwriting, scattered around the room in haphazard fashion. Crowding the shelf above her desk is a group of dolls in homemade costumes: fairy, knight, princess.

He wonders what his childhood would look like to her, if he had enough remnants of it to decorate a bedroom.

Violet listens outside her door, then nods to herself and shuts it. "You wanted to know why Penelope is after me. After all of the Everlys, really."

Aleksander looks down at his hands. "Yes."

He's long wondered what his part in all of this has become. And if Violet tells him, then maybe he can finally understand the damage he has wrought.

"Once upon a time," she says very softly, "there was a clever man."

Forty-Five

ALEKSANDER SITS DOWN on Violet's bed, his eyes anywhere but her.

He really didn't know. After all this time, Violet thought he would at least have picked up on the hints that Penelope might have dropped, or that she herself had. But when she relays the story to him, of Ever Everly and his devil's pact, she notes how still and silent he is, absorbing every word. And this time, there's a great deal more of it than Ambrose's fairy tale she'd reeled off so long ago in the café.

Did she know, leaning across the table from him, where they would end up?

"So, it's real. We're cursed," she finishes, a bit lamely.

If you could call one woman's immortal vendetta on an entire family a curse.

The longer he doesn't say anything, the more nervous she gets.

"Aleksander?" she asks.

He finally looks up. "Thank you for telling me."

He doesn't say, *you could have told me before*. She has no reason to feel guilty, not after Prague, but she still feels a twinge of guilt nonetheless. It's a terrible secret to keep from someone. And then fury sweeps her away, as she recalls the way he'd hesitated with the sword in his hands, even though Violet had been inches away from oblivion, right in front of him. Even with the truth *right there*, he'd hesitated.

Yet he came back for her, too.

His gaze shifts past her to a glint of silver on her windowsill. "You kept the bird," he says, surprised.

She glances away from him, instead rummaging through her drawers for a non-bloody jumper. She tugs off her shirt, revealing an unstained camisole beneath. Out of the corner of her eye, she notices that Aleksander suddenly becomes very interested in the books on the floor. Her skin burns with the memory of his hands.

She searches for a shirt and flings it at him with what might be considered excessive hostility.

"It used to be Ambrose's," she says curtly. "It should fit."

Aleksander looks at it, then at her for a long moment, his expression curiously blank. Then something in his eyes shifts, and he starts to unbutton his shirt. Immediately, she turns away, allowing him the same courtesy he gave her.

She doesn't mean to glance at the mirror, reflecting the hard lines of Aleksander's torso, the endless glide of skin from the top of his shoulder to the snug indent of his hip. She doesn't mean to see the swell and dip of his lower back, which *should* be a smooth expanse of muscle. She doesn't mean to see the scars.

Aleksander turns at the same time she does, and they lock eyes for an endless, terrifying moment.

Don't you feel sorry for him? Ambrose had asked.

"Don't," he says. "Please."

"You don't owe me an explanation," she says quickly.

After a fraction of a second, he pulls on Ambrose's shirt, as though nothing happened. But she can't unsee the angry red scars crossing the width of his back, shoulder blade to shoulder blade, like lightning strikes. She thinks about the way he cringes at small, dark spaces. The knowledge makes her feel sick.

She's still furious with him. But suddenly it's so much harder to hold on to that white-hot rage, and burn with its purity.

"We'd better go," he says lightly. "Your uncles will be waiting."

This time Aleksander doesn't offer his arm to her, though he tenses every time she stumbles over her own feet. At the bottom of the landing, she massages her left ankle, wincing as something crunches in its socket. It's just a sprain, she's certain, even though every part of her aches.

"We were about to send a rescue party," Ambrose says, when they return to the kitchen.

Violet can't look at Aleksander. "We're going. I know you don't like it, and I'm sorry."

But it won't stop her.

"What if you get separated?" Ambrose asks. He tries to rise from his chair. "We'll come with you."

Gabriel watches his brother struggle for a second before he slumps back into the chair. "You're in no bloody position to go anywhere." He turns to Violet. "I would come with you, but..."

"No," Violet says.

She won't put her uncles in more danger. The sight of Ambrose on the floor, the split second where he hadn't risen...There's no amount of strength that could overcome that awful image.

"Take my key, then," Gabriel says.

He unloops a silver chain from his neck and hands it to Violet. A key dangles on the other end, its stem twisted and engraved with a whimsical ivy pattern. It weighs heavily on her palm. For years, she's wanted to travel between worlds. Has imagined in vivid detail what it would be like to finally possess one of the keys that would let her do that. Her daydreams told her it would feel like a victory lap, like holding a galaxy in her hands.

All she sees are the scars on Aleksander's back, Penelope's wings exploding into smoke and flame.

"We won't be able to follow you without it," Gabriel warns. "If anything happens to you—"

She cuts him off. "Then I'll deal with it."

She doesn't say that nothing will happen to her, or that she'll be fine. She won't lie to them, not now.

"Christ Almighty, kiddo. You don't take the easy route, do you?" he says, sounding both exasperated and proud at once.

He pulls her into a bone-cracking hug that leaves her feeling slightly dizzy. Then it's Ambrose's turn. He embraces her tightly, smelling faintly of candle wax and old books, like he always does. Like home.

"Be careful, Vi," he murmurs. "Remember where his loyalties lie."

It takes Violet a beat to realise he's talking about Aleksander. But then Ambrose is releasing her, squeezing her arm just once before letting go. Gabriel folds his arms.

Aleksander finally meets her eye. "Are you ready?"

Violet has never been more ready for anything in her whole life.

She's not ready for this at all.

Aleksander loops his arm around hers, and pulls the key from around his neck. He slots it into the kitchen door—the one Violet's walked through most days of her life—and she feels the change in the pressure around them. Ice crackles along the edge of the doorway. Golden sparkles dance in the air. She closes her eyes, as an unfamiliar wave of air ripples over them. Her stomach dives in free fall.

Snow, mountains, sky.

Starlight.

Penelope staggers into her quarters, clutching her chest. Her hands still drip with blood, but the claws are fingertips once more. Her skin clings to her bones like paper, and her wings—her beautiful, fine wings—trail behind her in corporeal form, not as smoke, but leather and sinew. She sucks in a ragged breath.

Violet Everly did this.

Always an Everly, the cause of her ruin. Always an Everly, her downfall.

Penelope lunges towards the door. Claws, then hands, then claws again. She's lost too much blood, and now she is losing her grip on herself. Her strength is fading, too quickly; it's taken a millennia, but at last, she's run out of time.

Activity bustles in the tower beneath. Hundreds of scholars going about their day, unaware of the chaos raging above them. Hundreds of dreamers, their lives bright sparks of energy. Like worker bees, purposeful in their mindless humming.

Their talent—their lifeblood—sings to her, and her stomach roars with complaint.

She swore she would never do this. Wasteful to undo all her efforts to restore her fractured legacy. But she can imagine how they would taste, in excruciating detail. Sunlight and earth, reveurite and stardust. All the delights of the world, ready for the taking. It's not the sacrifice she would have chosen to commemorate such a momentous occasion, but she is used to ugly compromise.

There will be time later, to drink Violet's corpse dry. To discipline her wayward assistant—for this is the last time Aleksander disappoints her. Time later to rebuild what she must destroy.

She is Astriade, divine wielder of the dual swords of mercy and justice. She is glory. She is devastation.

And she is *hungry*.

Forty-Six

NDLESS WHITE. A chill that shoots straight through Violet's bones. She inhales and almost chokes on the frosty air.

They've landed on a cliffside, though with the snow it's hard to tell where the edge finishes and the sky begins. Behind her, a half arc of an archway rises above them, surrounded by ruins of stone buildings. Somewhere in the distance, the mountains boom with shedding ice, low and eerie.

"I thought it would be better to come here, to avoid attention. And...the view." Aleksander gives her a small smile, and for a second, she catches the flicker of the young man who once spoke of stardust and dreams. "Welcome to Fidelis, Violet Everly."

Fidelis.

Violet looks out again at the snow-washed landscape. So many times she's dreamed of coming here—literally dreamed, her head filling up with images of a fanciful city to match its fanciful street names. A place brimming with magic, scholars, secrets.

"You brought the sword," Aleksander says, compounding the feeling that she's dropped into a fairy tale.

Violet looks down at her clenched fists, and the heavy weight of the sword balanced between them. "I guess I did."

Aleksander leads her down a perilous stairway, slick with ice. They emerge in an alleyway, pushing past the overgrown bushes that disguise the entrance. At first all she can see are the sheer walls of the buildings on either side, shadows falling over them. Snow crunches underfoot, collecting in downy white on her shoulders. A bracing wind ripples through their clothes, and Violet gasps at the chill. She follows Aleksander, out of the alleyway to a large courtyard, into the frosty evening. And then she has to stop all over again.

Mountain peaks jut into the sky like shards of glass, glittering with snow. And below, the world falls away into winding terraces laced into the mountainside. In the valley, amber light suffuses the mist that settles at the bottom of the treeline. And the stars. Constellations in that half-familiar pattern she'd once seen scattered over her kitchen table.

"It's beautiful, isn't it," Aleksander says quietly.

She can't stop staring at the other side of the valley, solemn and dark against an even darker sky. "I never imagined it would be so real."

"Real as life," he says.

"If I lived here, I'd never leave," she says.

"Most people never do," Aleksander says. "But if you never leave, you never get to find out what the rest of the world looks like. What other worlds look like. And then you never know how astonishing Fidelis is in the first place."

Then his gaze rakes over the horizon and his smile vanishes.

"The light in the scholars' tower," he says. "It's gone."

He starts to walk up the mountainside towards it, past the rows of high-roofed houses, stacked closely against each other.

Violet hurries after him. "Aleksander?"

"There must be some explanation," he says, more to himself than her. "There has to be."

Violet follows him across the mosaic roads, with barely time to process the beauty of the city. She glimpses walkways protruding beyond the cliffs, greenhouses with flora bursting behind their misty windows, rounded whitewashed houses with terracotta roofs gleaming orange in the moonlight. It should be beautiful. It *is*. But the silence is unnerving, and most lights are conspicuously out, or else glow behind tightly shut curtains. The dark shadow of the scholars' tower looms over everything.

They reach the entrance, a stern mixture of mountain stone and iron lanterns capped with snow. The ground beneath their feet is mostly clear, with hundreds of faint shoe imprints left behind in the slush.

Aleksander shucks off his cloak and hands it to her. "You can't be recognised as an outsider. If you are—"

"I won't be," she says, sounding more confident than she feels.

She swings the cloak around her shoulders. It's lined with fur and smells like Aleksander: woodsmoke and the scent of old books. She flips up the hood, shrouding her face on the off-chance someone recognises her for what she isn't.

Aleksander, though, isn't paying attention. He listens carefully before easing open the thick oak doors and ushering her in. Inside, an enormous staircase dominates the centre, with a ceiling that stretches up so high Violet can't see the top. Thick ropes and pulleys hang in the stairwell, with half-full pallets dangling in mid-air. Dozens of hooks line the walls of the entrance, with matching shoe stands at the bottom. It's the mundanity that strikes her, that the scholars would even need a place for their winter boots or cloaks.

The lights are dim, and it's utterly silent.

"Something's not right," Aleksander says.

Now that they're inside, she can sense it, too, though she can't place why. She shouldn't be able to, surely? A moment later, it hits her—their footsteps echo, and her breathing is loud in her ears.

Even in the middle of the night, it's too quiet.

Aleksander leans over the banister, glancing up and then down, where the stairwell continues into glacial darkness. "The pulleys have stopped. But they're always active. I—wait. I see something."

He takes the stairs two at a time, Violet rushing to catch up. Absentmindedly, she notes the gilded portraits on the walls, each with an accompanying plaque. Noted scholars, she guesses, with varying levels of painted severity. And it's stupid to look—as if Penelope would ever give an Everly a *plaque*—but she finds herself watching for hazel eyes, a proud chin—

Aleksander stops suddenly, and she almost bumps into him.

"Stay back," he warns, but it's too late.

There's a body. Wrapped in navy scholar's robes and lying awkwardly on the stairs. Dark blood stains the steps around his head.

"Oh my God," she whispers.

They'll never be able to get the bloodstains out of the marble, she thinks ridiculously. Aleksander gently nudges the body over, and though she has no idea who the scholar is, Aleksander must because he makes a sound like someone's knocked the wind from him. An older man with a greying beard lies at an awkward angle, his neck twisted in a clean snap. His eyes stare sightlessly at the ceiling.

"I hated him," Aleksander says, dazed. "He used to make me fetch things for him because he didn't like that I was Penelope's assistant. But he was afraid of her, too." He stares at the body. "He must have tripped and hit his head. Why hasn't anyone moved him yet? I don't understand."

Violet looks past him, up the staircase. Her stomach lurches. More bodies, more blood. She places a hand on Aleksander's shoulder in warning.

"Don't look," she says, but his gaze follows hers.

"There's—there's more..."

He walks past her as if in a daze, stopping to kneel at every body. As they ascend, there are clusters of them, some with daggers still clutched in their hands, like they'd known what was coming. Others wear frozen expressions of shock. Blood crusts their dark robes, as though an animal tore through them.

"Who could have done this?" Aleksander says repeatedly, like he believes it could be someone else, anyone else.

Violet keeps her lips pressed tight. But she recalls Penelope's claws, how very deadly they'd seemed.

"Maybe there are scholars still hidden," he says, sounding foolishly hopeful, even to Violet. "We have to check. Come on."

Violet hesitates. "Aleksander..."

He turns to her, his eyes hard. "There are novices housed here. *Children.* Someone needs to rescue them, tell them it's going to be okay."

Abruptly, he makes a sharp left, down one of the many narrow corridors. Violet follows, her heart thumping. Maybe Penelope did just descend the tower and leave. Maybe there are still survivors, hidden away.

It wouldn't be like Penelope, though, to leave a stone unturned.

They pass more bodies on the way, then a heap of them, slumped against a door. Aleksander's hands are crushed into fists, his face white as chalk.

"She wouldn't have come here," he says numbly. "She wouldn't have . . . All those children."

"Aleksander, don't," Violet says, but he's already pushing past the bodies, to the room on the other side of the door.

She follows, dread curling in her gut.

It's almost pitch-black in the room, and at first she thinks there's no one there. But then she sees the huddle in the corner. Too small to be adults, swathed in their oversized robes. They could be sleeping, but for the unbearable stillness.

"Violet—oh gods—"

Aleksander collapses to his knees and retches, heaving until there's nothing left. His shoulders shake as he sobs in silence.

"They were children," he says, over and over. "They were just children."

Just children. But they were in Penelope's way.

Violet manages to lead Aleksander out of the room, back down the staircase. Past the bodies she can't bear to look at, even though they're strangers to her. But instead of stopping at the entrance to leave—to warn someone else—Aleksander continues down the stairs, following the ribbon of blood. He doesn't stop at the first open gate, which brackets the staircase, or the second.

The trail of blood is still thick and slippery in some places, as though Penelope dragged body after body down the staircase. Every gate has been flung wide open. And what's worse than the open gates —no one comes to stop them. Some of the gates are ten feet high, slick and unscalable. Aleksander touches one of them with an expression of disbelief.

He only stops when they reach the end of the lit staircase. The fanciful portraits and velvet-curtained windows have long disappeared, leaving a stark façade that reminds her of a fortress, or prison.

"No one is allowed down here," he says in a whisper. "I've never —except—"

Then his mouth snaps shut and he takes a deep breath, as though steadying himself.

"We have to keep going," she says.

Even though every single sense is telling her to turn around, walk back up the stairs, and get as far away from this place as possible. Penelope is most likely down there, in whatever form she's taken. Gathering her strength. Readying herself to exact biblical vengeance on the Everlys. Violet can't let that happen.

Aleksander's face drains of colour. "Violet..."

"We have to," she says. "I'm sorry."

"You don't understand. I *can't*."

He looks the same way he did on that staircase in Prague. Terrified, beyond all rationality.

What happened to you? is what she really wants to ask, but can't.

And she recalls the way Aleksander had hesitated with the sword. There are the scars she knows about, and the ones she doesn't. Maybe it's best she goes alone. No interference.

No one to save her either, a smaller part of her whispers.

"I'll go," she says. "You stay here."

Aleksander's shoulders dip with relief, but he still seems uncertain. "She might still be down there."

Violet doesn't need to ask who he's talking about.

She shakes her head. "It's fine."

She gives him what she hopes is a reassuring smile, but feels like more of a grimace. Then, avoiding the blood underfoot, she slips through the gate, leaving Aleksander behind. The staircase turns a corner, and he disappears from view.

The walls shine with condensation, and as Violet descends, the light vanishes. The chill deepens, and she flexes her fingers to try and regain some warmth. The sword is slippery in her grip, but she tightens her hold on it. There's no voice compelling her downwards, but she still feels the same pull as she had in Tamriel's basement. The crawl across the back of her neck in anticipated horror.

The careful block walls give way to cavernous mountain stone, dappled with chisel marks. It's almost too dark to see, and the stairs are dangerously slick underfoot. The last gate is open, as all the others, but it's been swung so hard that it's embedded in the mountain rock. Whoever did that, did so with inhuman strength.

Then there are no more stairs. Just a thin archway overhead and a single flickering oil lamp, illuminating the room ahead. The sickly-sweet stench of death drifts out. She readjusts her hold on the sword —though what kind of good it would do her now, she has no idea— and steps inside.

There is...a lot of blood.

It's a good thing she's come alone because this sight would floor Aleksander. As it is, she stops to retch, covering her mouth and nose with the robe until her stomach settles. Penelope isn't here, but evidence of her presence is everywhere. Dead scholars have been tossed to either side of the room, piled up against one another like flotsam against a bloody tide. Whatever colour the floor used to be, it's now awash in crimson. The smell is so thick she can taste the iron in the air.

And in the middle of the room is a door.

It looks like the kind of door Violet sees in dreams. The kind she'd once imagined would appear in her library wardrobe. It towers over her, at least twice her height, with the oily gleam of reveurite. Ancient script unravels along the metal, in an alphabet she's never seen before. On the other side, there's nothing, only an empty space for the door to swing into. There's no keyhole—just two reveurite hands outstretched, gory with blood.

Violet leans closer, then holds her breath to listen to the stale air. It could be anything—the metal creaking in the cold, the bodies sighing out their final platitudes; hell, even Aleksander breathing too loudly upstairs—but she's sure it's none of those things. It sounds like...singing.

Violet bites down hard on her lip and gives the hands a hesitant tug. Absolutely nothing happens. The door stays stuck fast.

For a long five minutes, she stares at the door. She tries opening it in every way she can think of: yanking again on the grotesque handles, pushing on the door, then stomping around the other side to lean against the back. But it refuses to yield. If Caspian were here, he'd have probably figured out the mechanism in seconds. All she has are hands covered in blood that doesn't belong to her.

In the dim recesses of her mind, a light bulb turns on.

Bracing herself against the pain, Violet scrapes her hand against the jagged edge of the door. Her skin shivers open, wet red bursting from a cut on her palm. In response, the door seems to shudder, and golden sparkles light up the edge of her vision. A faint breeze tugs at the cuffs of her trousers.

Is it really so simple?

She sees the carnage around her, the blood pooling at the edge of the doorway, the all-too-obvious handprints smeared along the walls. It's a particularly damning kind of simple, but one that Violet has become familiar with.

Just a little bit of flesh. Just a little bit of blood.

The cost to travel through a door is always sacrifice. And there is no one but herself to give it.

The sword.

Violet snatches it, curling her hand around the hilt.

In her favourite stories, the heroes fought until they were up against the wall, their weapons vanquished, stemming their wounds with bloody hands. The enemy looms. The defeat beckons. And then, with their last ounce of strength, they fight back. One more blow, to cut through everything.

A curse is just a contract, really.

In one swift movement, she twists the blade towards her. *Courage.*

From behind her, Aleksander's voice: "Violet, wait—"

She plunges it through her heart.

PART FIVE

A Beginning

I T IS NOT the man that attracts her initially. Rather, it's the crowd: an endless queue snaking out the door from dawn to dusk, save for the hour when the shop closes for lunch. They enter, biting their lips to hold back grins, and exit carrying parcels of varying sizes, tenderly wrapped in ribbon. Their smiles only falter when they see the astral, watching them exit the shop.

She is still young, still coltish compared to her older, wiser brethren. But to the people in the city, she's a star, blinding and unknowable. A wondrous terror, or a terrifying wonder. So she stops coming during the day, even as her curiosity deepens.

During her sleepless midnight walks, though, she can't resist coming by the shop. She peers through the windows, her wings illuminating the wares within and tinting everything gold. Dainty carousels nestled in crushed velvet; iridescent paper-and-wire butterflies dangling from the ceiling; silver lockets and sweetheart keys and jewellery boxes inlaid with gems. Gorgeous delicacies that give her a strange feeling just below her ribcage, as though someone is tugging at a thread behind her heart.

Every night for a week she passes the shop and looks through the window, wondering what kind of person could enrapture a crowd when the city is already brimming with craftspeople, with miracles displayed on every corner. She imagines someone powerful, soaked in astral blood and magic and who knows what else besides. Someone who can make marvels the way other people breathe. Perhaps an astral; perhaps another creature entirely.

On the seventh night, she's examining the display again, her hands on her hips, when the door opens. Warm light pools over brick. She reaches for the twin swords at her side, before recalling that she's the interloper here.

It's a man. Just a man.

His nose is slightly crooked, his eyes a deep hazel. Broad-shouldered, with the robust strength of someone who makes a living with his hands. He's not beautiful—in fact, far from it—yet there is something about him that gives her pause.

That feeling behind her heart is there again.

"They told me you stopped coming during the day," he says, and his voice is the sound of wood crackling, or water hissing over coals.

He knows she's been pausing here every night to look at his windows. Embarrassment floods through her, and to disguise it, she straightens to her fullest height, her wings shedding sparks. This is her fault, she supposes, for letting her curiosity get the best of her.

"I didn't wish to scare off your customers," she says, a little haughty.

He shrugs. "They are made of stronger stuff than that."

For a long moment, they look at one another, mortal man and star. There is still time for all of this to change, time for another future to spool out in front of her. To sever the thread and sidestep a future of regrets and anguish, of a city in ashes. Of everything that happens next.

Then he holds out his hand—calloused and firm, dusted with freckles—and smiles at her.

"Ever Everly," he says by way of introduction.

"Astriade, daughter of Nemetor," she replies.

It's the smile that undoes her.

"Would you like to come in?" he asks.

She takes his hand.

Forty-Seven

 DEAD WORLD IS never really dead. Even when the stars vanish in a great exodus, leaving an inky night that swallows the sky. Even when the sound of silence is a terrible thing to listen to in a city that once groaned with noise.

But it's not quite silence, is it? There are the birds that soar over bare roof rafters, egrets and jackdaws and scruffy brown scraps that go by a multitude of names calling joyfully to each other. There are the nocturnal animals whose claws scrape over cobblestones, lifting their gazes to the two pale moons impressed against a violet sky. There are the trees that stretch upwards, overgrown and languorous, from leaf-strewn courtyards, extending gracefully through balconies and walkways. And below them, the ferns that unfurl in dark, damp corners that might still bear cracked tiles in parched colours, or spongey wooden slats engraved with toothy chisel marks.

Life, persistent and predictably stubborn, goes on. Close your eyes and the stars might not sing in this hushed city of dust and dreams, but there's still singing nonetheless.

Even if there's just one voice left.

Violet wakes with a dull pain lancing through her chest. She opens her eyes to a crumbling ceiling playing host to a variety of green plant matter. The light against the leaves is a soft purple hue—perhaps coming through a stained-glass window. Beneath her, a firm surface that could be a bed, but also the floor.

Gingerly, she sits up, becoming aware of the bandages around her torso, as well as the tightness around her chest every time she breathes in. It hurts like a weeks-old wound.

Did she do it? Did she cross over?

The door bangs open and Violet flinches. For a second she sees roiling smoke, wings, and her heart stops. Then the shadows settle into the background, as a man walks through the door, carrying an open book in one hand and a chewed pencil in the other.

The man's head almost scrapes the ceiling, he's so tall. And though he's not what Violet would describe as a handsome man, his arms are corded with muscle. He walks with a leonine grace, in measured strides that swallow distance. His eyes are ringed with gold, unnaturally bright. *Astral*, she thinks and tries to scramble away. Then the pain in her chest flares and she gasps.

"Be still," he commands. "The wound won't reopen, but it will hurt."

Apart from his eyes, there are no other indications of astral-hood. But there's still something about his features that makes her scrutinise him more carefully. A dull silver ring dangles from a chain around his neck, an inscription wrapped around the inside of the band. It winks at her as he bends to examine her bandages and tuts.

"Foolish, foolish," he says. "No need to spill so much."

"Who are you?" she asks. "I have to know—where did I—"

He cuts her off with a stern shushing gesture, prodding at her wounds instead. He makes her submit to a lengthy examination, after which he must be satisfied because he hands her a threadbare shirt with as many colours as there are patches. As Violet pulls it over her head, it strikes her that she's not cold. The air is humid and thick with the scent of greenery. And if it wasn't for the strange violet hue of light, she could easily convince herself she's been dumped in some tropical paradise.

The man potters about the room, half muttering and half singing as he sweeps and sorts. Violet uses the opportunity to take stock of her situation. From the look of the room, she's in some kind of workshop, with long tables more suited to craftwork than a makeshift operating table. Dried herbs hang from the ceiling in bushels, and there's an entire wall devoted to shelves of jars in every possible shape and size. While some are empty, others contain oddities, like a single leaf, or hundreds of glass beads, or glowing golden liquid that seems to swirl of its own accord. More than a few are murky, with no clues to the object suspended within. And everything is bathed in that hue of amethyst light, though she can't pinpoint the source.

Violet watches the man carefully. Now that she's certain he's no longer astral, there's something about the way he moves that reminds her of someone. She half closes her eyes and in his blurry silhouette, she realises who she's seeing: Ambrose. It's almost the exact same walk, step for step, full of a grace that belies the man's size.

She tries to get up from the table. "Please, who are you?"

"A ghost, a wraith—nothing more," he says dismissively.

"I meant your name," she says.

He turns to her, his eyes blazing. "Who are *you*, to demand my name?"

In two swift strides, he's by her side. He presses a thumb to a cut on her forehead, still bleeding, and licks it. Violet is too stunned to be horrified. He examines his thumb with a clinical detachment, then looks at Violet again.

"Astral blood. Yes. No?" His face is suddenly inches from hers, virtually nose to nose. "Who was your mother?"

"Not an astral," Violet says immediately.

He turns away. "And your father?"

This time, she doesn't have an answer. For all her wondering about her mother, she hasn't thought about her hypothetical father in years. Not since Ambrose became such a fixture in her life. She assumed her father was someone Marianne had picked up in Fidelis.

But an astral?

"The pool has been refreshed. Talent is strong." He sees her expression. "It happens. We are not confined to who we love."

He touches the silver ring around his neck.

"Though it is ill-advised to love an astral," he adds.

Violet peers at him. Again, she has the feeling that something is tipping into place, even as the rest of her knows it has to be impossible.

A stupid name for a clever man.

"Who are you?" she persists.

He stares at her, the gold rings around his irises stark against his hazel eyes. "I am Ever Everly. The question is, who are you?"

Violet stares at him. She can't believe it.

He blinks at her with his gold-ringed irises. "I asked you a question."

You're supposed to be dead, Violet thinks, at the precise moment Aleksander stumbles into the room. Their gazes lock. His eyes are bloodshot, as though he hasn't slept in days. Without warning, he gathers her into a hug that sends every single nerve ending in her chest fizzing with pain.

"Finally," he says, his voice muffled against her shoulder. "I thought you were gone—I went down to find you, but—"

Violet makes a sound halfway between a squeak and a wheeze, and he quickly lets go. Vaguely she remembers the decision to stab herself through the chest—a decision that seems insane now—then Aleksander's shout, just before the explosion of pain. The rest is a blur, when it's there at all: the sense of being carried; blood between her fingers that might have been her own, but could easily have been another's; Aleksander's voice in a litany of urgent pleading and panic.

The rest is only a deep, endless sleep that frightens her with its finality.

"You came back for me," she says, dazed. "But the stairs—"

He glances away from her. "You were gone too long. I was worried."

From the way he tenses, it's obvious it cost him dearly to go down into the dark after her. And though she knows she shouldn't trust him —or forgive him—she finds herself profoundly grateful that he'd come for her, not knowing what horrors might have awaited.

"My question still stands, stranger," Ever says.

"I'm Violet," she says, then hesitates.

How does she begin to explain herself to an ancestor that should, by all rights, be dust in the ground? There's nothing in her fairy-tale book that prepared her for this.

"That is not what I mean."

Ever hands her a bulky object, and it takes her a second to realise it's the sword. The blade is suspiciously clean, even shinier than when she'd first unwrapped it from Caspian's mysterious benefactor. Ever's face looms in its reflection as he leans towards it.

He examines the sword, muttering to himself. Violet admires the way his hands deftly move across the metal, with a confidence that suggests decades of staring at nothing *but* swords. Without warning, he points the sword towards her. On the blade, a faint indent of two feathers shines out of the metal.

"This is my mark," he says. "So where, stranger, did you get this?"

Suddenly he grabs Violet, and hauls her off the table. Aleksander moves to stop him, but Ever throws him back with one hand alone. His other fist clutches Violet's shirt, inhuman power in every fingertip.

"Who are you?" he hisses. "Who sent you?"

Violet could think of a million answers to that question. Her uncles. Her mother. Penelope. Or just a frayed book of fairy tales and the siren song of elsewhere.

She tilts her head upwards defiantly. "My name is Violet Everly, and I'm here to break our curse."

There are a lot of questions, on both sides.

Mostly, Ever sits in silence as Violet explains. It's obvious he doesn't recognise the name Penelope, but as soon as she mentions Astriade, his entire body goes rigid with warning.

"You bring terrible calamity," he says, his golden eyes shadowed. "You have killed us all."

"Calamity? No, you don't understand—listen—"

Violet tries to explain again about the curse and Penelope's vow, but when she takes a step forward, the entire room tilts underneath her feet. Aleksander puts his arm around her, and she doesn't have the strength to refuse him.

"She needs rest," he argues.

Violet can't disagree on this point; her back aches from lying on the table, and there is an empty hollow in the pit of her stomach that suggests she's overdue a good meal. Reluctantly, Ever nods, then returns to the sword, his attention reabsorbed.

Aleksander steers her down the corridor, until they reach a quiet room with two makeshift beds set up. The minute he closes the door, his whole body slumps in exhaustion. Violet bites her lip.

"Aleksand—" she starts.

"Don't," he says, his eyes closed. "I have no right to be angry with you—" He opens his eyes again, and they're everywhere but her. "You *died*, Violet. You died in my arms just as we arrived here. I don't know what he did, or how he did it, but he brought you back. And there was so much blood."

His voice is quiet, but Violet flinches. She deliberately hasn't thought about the blade sinking in, how it had felt like pressing liquid fire through her skin. She's not even sure if she could have gone through with it if Aleksander had been there.

Guilt floods through her, then anger. After all, he has no right to demand her safety. Not when he held the sword—her life—in his hands and hesitated. So she holds back the apology her mouth was already forming.

"Anyway, we're here now," she says instead. "Elandriel. I assume Penelope is in the city."

Waiting for Violet to step out of the house.

"She won't touch us," Aleksander says, with a confidence that belies their situation. "But I think you should see this," he adds, more ominously.

Violet steps outside, into the walled-off courtyard at the centre of the building. At first she can't even comprehend what she's seeing. Then she takes it in, and finally understands why the colour of the light has been so beautiful and oddly purple all this time.

Stretched thinly over the sky is a violet-paned dome, so huge it's impossible to tell where it begins and ends. From here, it looks like the whole world. But Violet lets her gaze slide into that half-grey focus that Gabriel had reluctantly taught her only a few days ago, and the world burns with a golden shimmer. She blinks and rubs her eyes to dispel the image, as the low throb of a headache creeps up her skull.

A protective sheet of reveurite. A cage of god-metal. She recognises this part of the story well enough.

Aleksander is still speaking, low and too fast for her to catch everything. "It was a trap. Penelope wasn't on the other side at all—she was still in the tower, waiting for you to unlock the door. She came after us, so I had to drag you and run. Ever let us into the cage—and I didn't have a choice but to enter. But you have to understand: the door home is on the *other side*."

And so is Penelope. Violet understands immediately.

They are trapped.

Forty-Eight

EVER EVERLY, VIOLET quickly discovers, is impossible to talk to. But not because he doesn't talk.

He mutters to himself as he moves about his workshop. Sometimes he bursts into song, startling them both, only to break off a few bars later—before repeating the same snatch of melody over and over again. Then there are the moments where, over seemingly nothing—a moved piece of lint, a vanishing sunbeam —he starts to sob, in frightening gasps that wrack his whole body. Most of the time he doesn't seem to notice that anyone else is there. At other times, he holds entire conversations as though there is a crowd of people in the workshop with him. But even in his lucid moments, he seems reluctant to answer any of her increasingly pressing questions.

The questions Violet does receive answers to are ones that need little explanation. The reveurite pane, for one. One morning, she tracks Ever to the edge of what must have once been the neighbourhood, hoping to glean more about just how dire their circumstances are. She doesn't hide herself, but Ever never acknowledges her; instead, he lugs a sack full of assorted objects behind him, his eyes fixed on the road. Soon enough, the wall of reveurite rises above them, vibrant.

He dumps the sack out on to the dirt and Violet immediately notices its contents all contain reveurite. She hardly has time to admire the variety: a cup with the lip dipped in reveurite; glasses with several foldable lenses; half a dozen pieces of metal that might once have been daggers or knives. Ever's golden-ringed eyes gleam in the sunlight as he picks up one object after another. His fingers pluck reveurite straight from the cup, the glasses, the metal—as though they're all made of putty. Violet can't help but watch with a mixture of fascination and horror at the treatment of what are surely important artefacts.

The sliver of reveurite in his hands quickly grows to a sphere, a hard rock that seems to quiver with unnatural light every time Violet looks at it directly. A sheen of sweat breaks out on Ever's forehead, but his hands manipulate the metal like butter, working with quick efficiency. When there are no more objects in the bag for him to plunder, he breathes out heavily.

Quickly, he pulls out a knife and slashes it across his palm. Violet flinches, but Ever shows absolutely no emotion, as though he's done this a thousand times before. He squeezes his fist, and blood coats the reveurite, slick and glistening.

Ever's muscles strain as he plunges his fists into the pane. The light ripples; the pane shudders. Then it moves. Mere millimetres, hardly enough to make a difference. But mere millimetres over a hundred years, over a thousand...

That's what it takes to keep Penelope out, it seems. Blood and intention and reveurite, to further expand an already expansive cage.

Violet trails him back to the workshop, her thoughts spinning through her head. This is how he has spent his time. A thousand years of building his own cage. She tries to ask him about it on their way back, but he sings loudly, drowning out her questions.

When he starts shouting at his reflection in the workshop, Violet decides to get some air. She finds Aleksander in the dusty rooms below, sorting through a pile of books and loose pages. The sight of him so in his element does something complicated to her heart, which she immediately shoves under several weighty layers of common sense.

He may have come back for her, but that doesn't mean that Penelope isn't somewhere underneath his skin, working her claws through him. Violet remembers the sword in his hands, the hesitation. Prague. So she thinks about that, very firmly, and not the curve of his shoulder blades drawing lines down his shirt.

She sits down next to him and gingerly picks up one of the books. The cover leaves a tacky imprint of red dust on her fingers.

"Couldn't take it anymore?" Aleksander asks.

Violet shrugs miserably. Her mad ancestor, ranting at ghosts and reflections, would test anyone's patience after two days.

"How long do you think he's been by himself?"

"Too long. He seems to spend most of his time in the past."

Violet can't comprehend what his life must have been like, trapped in the corpse of a city for so long by himself. The unbearable loneliness, the smothering darkness of the night sky—for that, at least, is another truth ripped from the pages of the legend. It would take a very specific kind of mind to survive. If you could call it survival.

"I keep thinking about the crossing," she says. "I don't understand why Penelope waited for me to open the door." She bites her lip. "I shouldn't have been able to open it at all."

Aleksander looks at her for a moment. "A few years ago, there were proposals for an experiment, where the highly talented would be injected with reveurite, turned into living keys. The Hands of Illios, the first true scholars, remade anew. It might have worked; reveurite's still the metal of the gods, after all. But it was deemed too dangerous, so the experiment stopped." He pauses. "Mostly."

"Yury," Violet says, and he nods.

"But there are other ways to integrate the bloodlines." He hesitates, and she can see him struggling for words. "I know I have no right to say this, but... maybe your mother was trying to ensure you would have a way out. Or whoever you'd become."

Violet stares at her hands, scratched and calloused after the frenetic fighting of the last days. They're Everly hands, the same shape as Gabriel's, only slightly smaller than Ambrose's. They're as familiar to her as the rest of her body. But the blood that runs through her veins underneath is that of a stranger's.

"More likely Marianne was looking out for herself," she says bitterly.

Another Everly trait, it seems.

Aleksander stands up and dusts off his trousers. "I could do with a break. And there's still plenty of the city to explore. What do you say?"

Violet hesitates. She should be thinking about ways to divine the truth from Ever, or how to break the curse now that they're where it all started. After all, that's what her mother's plan must have been, before she gave up. And time is still running through the hourglass.

But she is *here*, in another world. And she wants to go with Aleksander. She wants it like a fire craves oxygen, like she's been drowning all this time, and has just been offered that first delicious sip of air. She is tired of saying no.

Aleksander offers his hand to Violet.

She takes it.

Ever's workshop is on the edge of a lake that funnels into canals snaking through the rest of the city, passing across the reveurite barrier. This, of course, they won't cross, though Violet keeps a sharp lookout for a winged shadow against its pane. The shore of the lake is a graveyard of crumbling wood, but Aleksander finds a functioning boat easily enough, probably belonging to Ever. The paint is chipped and flaking away in the heat, but Violet can still make out the markings of what must have been a name, even if it's no longer legible.

She clambers in first, the boat rocking underneath her weight, then Aleksander follows. The water is relatively shallow, and so clear Violet can see straight to the bottom, to the crushed shells littering the lakebed and the ghostlike remains of sunken boats.

The sun bears down on them and Aleksander rolls up his sleeves past his elbows to row. Underneath his sleek tattoos, his arms are dusted with silver scars, some no bigger than a fingernail. He catches her gaze, and she has the grace, at least, to not pretend she wasn't staring.

"From the forge," he explains. "Accidents happen."

He says this casually, but Violet knows they are both thinking of the deep scars on his back, and how he hadn't said anything at all, then, to explain them away.

The water carries them across the lake and underneath the long shadows of what must have once been an enclosed archway, into the city's labyrinth of canals. There are still, incredibly, one or two panes of glass in the ceiling, casting prisms downwards. The remains of stone faces look out on them: bearded and solemn, or with smiles tucked behind high collars. Carved vines curl around empty brackets that would have once held lanterns.

Twenty minutes later, the boat shifts to a halt against a set of stairs, corroded iron rings at precise intervals in the wall. Violet steps out carefully.

Ruined buildings of marble and sandstone rise up in front of them. Houses still bear faint traces of elaborate murals, or friezes like lace dripping from gutted roofs. Dead stems wind around trellises, the leaves long since disintegrated. The ground beneath their feet is mostly obscured by centuries of dirt, but Violet scuffs it away with her foot and catches flashes of mosaic tiles underneath. Up close, the marble isn't quite white, but a rainbow of colours, dazzling in the morning sun. Pale cream and peach, but also jade green and umber, veined with bright flecks of gold.

It's beautiful, like a city from a painting. It's also absolutely silent.

They spend the afternoon wandering around the city, along its narrow arterial waterways and through streets that must have once been busy with people, with life. Most of the buildings are fallen wrecks in one way or another, having succumbed to time and decay, and riotous green blooms from their empty shells. Large crane-like birds with azure feathers stalk across the roads, paying no attention to the human intruders. When the sun is highest, they stop and sit in the shade of an overgrown tree on the edge of the canal, bare feet in the water.

It is so easy, at times, to believe that the rest of the city is in hiding. Then Violet will glance up—at a flock of birds, a particularly beautiful window, a cloud sailing past—and see the pane of reveurite. And she remembers why she's here, and who awaits on the other side.

She also finds herself hyperaware of Aleksander's presence. Every time he pushes his hair out of his face; every quirk of eyebrow that means he's caught something interesting; the way the light plays across his bare forearms, revealing again the silver scars hidden by his black tattoos. Every time his gaze darts to her, then flickers away. They quickly fall into a companionable silence, but Violet can't stop thinking about all the ways she could fill it. There are questions she needs to ask. About Prague, about why he returned.

What he will do once they face Penelope.

But the warmth is lovely on her skin, and she gathers up her hair in a knot that rests against the nape of her neck. Along the water, she listens to the bright chirp of frogs, the hazy whine of insects. Aleksander smiles at her, free and unguarded. She can have this, she decides. A day where she can pretend she is still café Violet and Aleksander is still the man she once knew, strolling along the bank of a river.

As the sun sets, they climb higher into the city, up the long winding stairs that bracket it into tiers. Neither of them point out that this will leave them scrambling back down to Ever's workshop perilously close to pitch darkness. Violet wants the magic of the day to last as long as possible, to keep holding on to the soap-bubble fragility of whatever this feeling is stretched between them.

The top tier of Elandriel might once have been settled with grand buildings, a garden, an amphitheatre—or something else. But the ruins have been flattened, leaving a pale disc of hard ground. Around the edge, though, sectioned by giant pillars, are the remains of archways, stark compared to the rest of the decorative city. Golden sparkles flit across her vision.

Doorways.

Aleksander stops moving, his breath held still in his chest. "I don't believe it."

But Violet does. She always has. And she's already seen a doorway much like these ones, in Prague. Caspian's words come back to her, about the possibilities beyond the scholars, and the price he refused to pay. His confidence had seemed like foolish naivety, then, even to her. How he would laugh now.

There are still shards of reveurite from the doors themselves, and the worn nubs of nails from broken hinges scattered across the ground. Every sliver has some kind of raised detail, but there are too many fragments to tell whether it was once part of a word, a design, or simply graffiti.

Aleksander walks around the archways, touching each pillar with reverential awe.

"You'd think there would be even one left standing," he says, half to himself.

Violet knows the reason behind this, too. Or at least, she's almost certain of it, now that she's seen Ever and the fear in his golden-ringed eyes. But to voice it aloud will be to end this day of unrestrained joy. She closes her eyes, drinks in the feeling one more time.

"Ever did this," she says, and Aleksander looks back at her. "To stop anyone else coming through."

"The astrals," he says, his smile already fading, and she nods.

All that waste and ruin, for the sake of one man.

The sun dips beneath the horizon, and the black night sky returns.

Forty-Nine

OVER THE NEXT few days, Aleksander keeps returning to the doors. He can't help it; he feels compelled, as though someone is calling to him from just beyond their reach. While Violet argues with her ancestor in his workshop, Aleksander takes the boat out on to the lake and climbs the long staircases before the sun is truly burning in the sky. He can't tell if the reveurite dome overhead amplifies the heat, but he's always sweating by the time he reaches the top of the dais.

For the first few hours of the day, he simply sits alongside the doors, trying to tap into what the craftsmen must have felt before they embarked on this mission. For they *were* craftsmen, not astrals; he can see the delicate chisel marks on the stone, and a dappling he recognises as fingerprints from manipulating the reveurite. Tiny marks on each block of stone that would have once signalled which great master worked on it. He brings a notebook to make sketches and jot down notes, which he does meticulously.

But he also presses his hands against the ruins, trying to sense if there's anything left that could tell him about where these doors once went, and if they might ever lead there again. He tries to imagine what the craftsmen must have been like: real flesh and blood people, with the brilliance to create inter-world travel, and the human hubris to assume it would be a gift to the city. Did they know who they were making the doors for? Did any of them have an inkling that this would be the start of everything, and also its end?

Truth be told, sometimes he doesn't look at the doors at all. Sometimes he spends the heat of the afternoon underneath the cool shade of the knotty trees that have crept up from the lower tier, spreading wide fronds like welcome hands.

In Fidelis, amidst the scholars or the forge bearers, he's never been alone. There's always been some new task to concentrate on, something to berate himself over, or practise until his hands bleed. He has spent his life moving forward in pursuit of one goal: to be a scholar. To wear the proof on his skin that he is worthy.

But he failed the test. And he'll never become a scholar now.

So it is a terrible weight of wanting that he carries with him up to the dais, to prod and examine in a way that would have simply been too painful in the scholars' tower, where he'd watched everyone else with such bitter longing. Despite everything he's learnt, the secrets and the lies, the damning cruelties it would have taken for him to rise to scholar and beyond... He will never regret giving that child back; he regrets what could have been. What the scholars could have made of him, if they'd lived up to the façade they presented.

He thinks about Violet, too, wondering if he'll ever have the courage to share the extent of his shame—although whether it's courage or selfishness, he's not sure. He's still dangerous to her, after all.

What do you want from me, Aleksander? Everything, he should have told her.

By the time Aleksander decides to pack up, the sun is setting, throwing prisms through the reveurite pane. He leans back and takes a big swig of water.

"Hello, Aleksander."

Aleksander doesn't whip around, even though every single fibre of his being demands it. He finishes his drink, takes a deep breath, and turns.

Penelope is on the other side of the reveurite boundary, her figure smudged by the pane. She looks surprisingly small against her surroundings, but she is wholly herself, as Aleksander has always known her. No shadowy wings, no claws. He expects her to scream at him, or—worse—to look at him with the cold fury that promises retribution for his errors. But she only smiles at him gently.

"Magnificent, aren't they? Thousands of years of knowledge and craftsmanship, all brought together in a unifying edifice."

He swallows. Even though he's just drunk an entire bottle of water, his mouth is dry.

"Mistress," he acknowledges.

Even now, he can't call her anything else.

"They were extraordinary," she continues. "The crowds, the merchants, the exchange of language and culture. I think it is fair to say that we were a destination unmatched." She turns to gesture behind him, to a wide expanse of desert beyond the city's borders. "That is where the scholars' tower once lived. That is all we could save."

Penelope walks along the barrier as though it's a promenade. As though she could simply walk through if she chose. *He* can choose. It only took him a few days to understand the mechanics behind the barrier: a simple but effective infusion of reveurite and intent, fed by blood and centuries-strong willpower. But it's a will he's not bound to.

He could let her in, if she asked.

"Come closer, Aleksander. I wish to see your face."

Automatically, he walks towards her. Only halfway across the dais does he realise what he's doing, and by then, it's too late to stop. He's so close to the boundary he can hear the crackle of living energy coursing through the reveurite. Even through the violet glow, Penelope looks exactly as she's done for every single day of his life: no laughter lines, no grey hairs shining through blonde—without the wear and tear of the world.

"This was not here when I left," she says, almost but not quite touching the reveurite wall. "It is an abomination."

"Can you blame him?" Aleksander says quietly.

He thought he knew fear. But this is centuries of deep, unyielding terror in physical form. He tries to imagine what would make him so desperate. *If you went into that cold, dark room and never came out.*

"You are hiding an atrocity behind your walls. And you are going to have to make a decision, my assistant." She smiles so warmly he wonders if his ears are deceiving him, and they're having a different conversation altogether.

"You could let us go," he says, though even as he does so, he's aware of how monumentally stupid he sounds.

"Oh, Aleksander," Penelope says softly. "We are inextricably bound. I, alone, saw the great man you could become. No one else grasped your talent. No one else believed in your potential."

This is so hard to disagree with because it's true. He remembers the first time Penelope had taken him up to her quarters, and served him herself with tea and a hot meal. He remembers the way she had guided him through the notoriously complex archival system, how she had shielded him from the wrath of the other scholars. Every little kindness, every moment he'd felt the glow of her approval, he recalls.

"Do you really wish to return to nothing? Over a girl?"

In his mind, a fissure opens, swallowing him whole.

"You lied to me," he says, his voice breaking. "I would have done anything for you, been *anyone* for you—"

It shames him to even think it, but there was a time where, had he been told to steal a child, he would have done it unquestioningly and not looked back. For Penelope, he would have bloodied his own hands, drunk the vial, followed in Yury's footsteps if that's what she wished. Anything... and yet he can't stand aside to let Penelope take Violet.

In this, he cannot, *will not* be her blade.

"I gave you everything, Aleksander," she snarls. "You were just an orphaned boy, no family or future to speak of. *I* gave you that future. *I* made you what you are."

And he almost believes it. Almost.

Maybe he really would have amounted to nothing. Maybe he would have spent a short life in misery, as she claims. But he might have thrived, too. And he'll never know what that Aleksander would have looked like. Whether he would have committed so many sins to hold on to a future he so desperately wanted.

Whether he would have been happy, instead, with a glorious blank canvas before him.

"I keep my promises," Penelope continues. "Always. And yet you accuse *me* of deception. Did you know that Ambrose Everly offered me a deal, ten years ago? And Ever Everly centuries before that?"

She starts to walk along the perimeter, and Aleksander follows, feeling as though something monstrous has slithered into his ribcage. Violet had vaguely mentioned something about Ambrose, and she'd told him the story of the great Ever Everly and the origins of her family's curse. But he's never considered it as a debt before, as though it's possible to tally the weight of a soul.

"I just want to understand," he says, and he hates how he sounds like he's begging. But that's exactly what he's doing. If there was a chance that this was some awful mistake, or a problem to wrap his head around, a case of misplaced vengeance—

He would rather any reason, any excuse, than this cruelty.

"You have Elandriel. You can go home," he continues. "Can't I help you do that? I might not be your assistant anymore"—he chokes on the word—"but I'm still... I would do it for you."

"Aleksander, I taught you better than that. You see this door?" She gestures to the largest doorway, the ruins barely holding together the echo of what it once was. "Once it is rebuilt, *that* is where my home lies. And thanks to Everly blood, it has been locked away for the past millennia."

Penelope stops at the edge of the dais, where the ground tips away into nothing. From here, they can see straight to Ever's workshop, and the glassy lake behind it.

"I knew he lived. Because I gave my word. A soul for... everything." She stares at the workshop, and he has the feeling that she's seeing through time, to a history he has no knowledge of. "But look at this pathetic boundary he has set up. Look at how he cowers in his shell. Who do you think is at fault here?"

Aleksander's hands are clenched so tightly that he feels a sharp sting in his palms as his nails draw blood.

"You wish to know the truth, my assistant. So I will give it to you."

Suddenly he very much doesn't want to know, would rather have asked anything else. But Penelope continues, relentless.

"Without an Everly soul, I will never be able to return home. That is what is owed, and that is what must be paid." She looks up at the darkening sky. "I am astral, after all. And if they wish me to be devastation, so be it."

Fifty

ONE DAY GOES by, then another. Another.

The sun rises and falls against a permanently tinted sky. Ever Everly weeps and rants in his workshop, with all the frustrated fury of a poltergeist. When it rains, the water seeps in everywhere, beading on the porous walls. Long hours are spent tending to the makeshift farm that has thrived on abandoned land, or collecting water from a well in the courtyard. On the other side of the reveurite panes, a shadow stalks the perimeter, looking for a chink in its impervious armour.

They are safe. They are trapped.

Violet is slowly losing her mind.

Today, Violet is already awake and in the workshop before sunrise. She won't spend another week here, waiting for the worst.

"You have to finish this," she says, as soon as Ever walks in. "You have to undo the curse."

Ever ignores her. But his conversation with himself increases in volume, which means he heard her. Violet pursues him through his chores, half a step behind him. He spends much of it rearranging the murky bottles that line his shelves, turning them this way and that as though it would make a difference to their contents.

After half an hour of this, Violet finally snaps. She snatches the nearest vial and flings it to the floor. The sound of shattering glass is unexpectedly satisfying.

"That was very rare gilt weed," Ever says accusatorially.

Violet glares at him. "I'm not going anywhere. Neither is Penelope, or Astriade—or whatever the hell you want to call her. We need to talk. We need a plan."

Violet has bartered with scholars, infiltrated their parties and unpicked their lies. She's travelled across the world to speak to gods and decipher their riddles. She has already escaped death and injury more times than she'd like to admit. If Ever thinks he can wish her away, he's about to learn just how stubborn his bloodline can be.

"She's not after us. She's after *you*," she says. "So whatever you did to her, undo it. If she wants to leave, let her leave!"

"We are safe here," he says calmly.

"We can't spend the rest of our lives living in a—a cage!" Violet says, exasperated. "She's never going to stop. Don't you get that?"

"We are *safe*," he repeats.

Violet is very quiet for a minute. Then she says, "My uncles used to tell me stories about you. The great, heroic Ever Everly, who tried to save us. But you didn't try at all, did you?"

All the legends she believed in. All the lies.

Ever shrugs. "There are no heroes. There are only those of us who survive, and those who do not. The contract is unbreakable, and thus I will remain here."

Condemning Violet.

Disgusted, she raises her hand to sweep an entire shelf on to the floor. If he can't comprehend what it is to lose something precious, she'll *make* him understand. But at the last second, she stops herself. Ever is already talking to himself again animatedly, with hand gestures that would suggest an important conversation is taking place. He is just as likely to look at her blankly as he is to be upset with her over the loss of his precious vials.

Maybe this is why Marianne went through the door and never looked back. Maybe she was smart to run, and Violet is the fool for staying.

She walks down the stairs, through the courtyard and towards the lake, the hot sun burning the back of her shoulders. Aleksander is by the lake, patching up a small leak in the boat. He rubs the back of his neck, and although he smiles to see her, there's something troubled behind his eyes.

"I take it your heart-to-heart with Ever didn't go as planned," he says.

Violet kicks off her shoes and sits on the edge of the water. She thinks about diving in, clothes and all. She settles for her bare feet, cool water leaping over her skin.

"I spoke to Penelope," Aleksander says carefully.

Violet goes still. She suspected Penelope would seek out Aleksander. A conversation filled with possibilities.

He continues, "She won't leave until she has an Everly soul."

"And it won't be Ever," she says bitterly.

And then she bites her lip, guilt flooding through her. It might be Ever's pact, and it might be an Everly curse, but she can't ask him to die on her behalf. Because that's what she would be asking. Those are the stakes. Even though she's known this whole time that it was her life hanging in the balance, it hits her like a hammer blow.

There's no way out, this time.

Aleksander looks at her. "Violet, you can't."

"No, but—my uncles. Jesus Christ, what if she goes after Ambrose? Or Gabriel?" Violet's vision starts to swim with panic. "The door is on *her* side."

Penelope can go through any time she chooses. Perhaps she has just been waiting for Violet to realise how vulnerable they all are.

"If I go now—if I make a deal with her—"

Aleksander grabs her arm. "Don't. Please."

"But my uncles—"

"If you go, she'll kill you," he says urgently.

"So I should let them die instead? Just because you betray people when it suits you, doesn't mean I will," she snaps.

Aleksander flinches and drops his hold on her. Violet folds her arms and looks away from him. She tries to take deep breaths, to stem the tide of panic, but all she can think about is her uncles, and the choice she has to make. She's tried to stop Penelope so many times before, and failed. Now, they're in her city, at an unquestionable disadvantage.

"We all owe debts," he says softly.

"You don't owe a debt to her! You don't owe her anything! After what she did to you—and don't tell me that wasn't her," she says, furious. "Don't tell me you deserved it."

All those scars on his back. The naked terror she'd seen on his face in the scholars' tower, just for the want of a little light.

He shrugs, but she can tell even that casual gesture costs him. "And you deserve this?"

The silence stretches long between them.

She stares hard at the ground, willing herself not to cry or scream. She knows she is being monstrously unfair to Aleksander. It's not his fault they're in this situation, whatever he's done to her in the past. It's not her fault, either, but it *is* still her problem.

Finished with the patch, Aleksander pushes the boat into the water and climbs in. Violet listens to the creak of wood, the kiss of waves against the hull.

"Do you know, I could kill for a cup of coffee right now," she says.

Aleksander pats the seat next to him in the boat. After a beat, she clambers in, the boat dipping under her weight. Their knees bump together as she settles herself.

He fishes in his pocket and pulls out something slightly damp and fuzzy with wear, before handing it to her. A smudged card, almost falling to pieces, with ten stamps. One for every single week Aleksander unravelled an entire world for her, sitting at a table in a café.

"It's on me," he says.

She turns it over and over in her hands. How far it must have travelled, to end up here.

"I said you don't owe me an explanation," she says. "About the scars."

It's the closest she can manage to an apology. And it's not enough, but he nudges her with his elbow in a forgiving way.

"I don't," he agrees. "But I would like to give it to you, if that's okay."

Fifty-One

LEKSANDER TAKES A deep breath, willing his hands to stay steady and his voice to remain even. It is so easy to reach back and pluck the strings of memory. Because the door is always there, waiting to be opened.

This is the day Aleksander's world fell apart. The lightning-strike split of before and after. He recounts it as though it happened to someone else—and in a way, he's not wrong.

There is a long walk down a set of stairs, accompanied by the grim-faced night attendants with their loops of keys and hand-stitched vows of silence. There are the gates that have to be unlocked and the lamps that have to be lit, because to go down here is to be plunged into a void, from which there is little chance of return. The air tastes like metal and blood.

Aleksander listens to his verdict with a dry-mouthed, dead-weight fear. He is not a blade, being sharpened again. He is a blade, discarded. Unfit for purpose.

Penelope says he is nothing, and so he becomes nothing.

He doesn't struggle when the night attendants tie his wrists to a metal frame, even though his whole body tenses at the preparations behind him. The sound of the whip dragged along the floor makes him suck in a tight breath. It licks through the air. It lands.

Then there is pain. Only pain.

Time passes. The scrape of the lock in the darkness is a terror he will never be able to describe. Sometimes, it is the night attendants dispensing food. Sometimes, it is the soft slither of leather, and they dispense more justice instead.

He has no idea how long he spends down there. Only that when he is finally hauled upright, he can't open his eyes against the light, and even then it flares painfully behind his eyelids. There is no firm hand to guide him, no one to tell him where he is, or how many people watch as he's marched out of the scholars' tower forever.

He hopes for a miracle. He hopes for death.

But he lives, and his body reshapes itself around his new circumstances, even if his mind keeps returning to the scholars' tower. He works in the forges, where they have taken him in begrudgingly, because even outcast talent is still useful. And later, he shears the long curls from his head like the other forge bearers. His flesh heals and the pain fades, but the scars remain.

And then Penelope summons him to the tower, to offer him redemption. The rest—well, Violet knows all too well.

In the boat, he watches the water ripple outwards, casting waves on the other side of the lake. He can hear her breathing, the shudder that travels up her chest.

"Now you know," he says.

It doesn't absolve him for what he's done. The before Aleksander, who believed the worst possible outcome was to be an assistant forever, is gone. But having admitted the worst to Violet, he feels, impossibly, a little lighter.

He stands up, the boat rocking precariously. Before he can change his mind, he peels off his shirt and dives head first into the lake. The water closes over him, pure and sweet.

Fifty-Two

OR THE REST of the day, Violet lingers by the lakeside. She watches Aleksander add the finishing touches to the boat, marvelling at how deft his hands are. He's still dripping wet from his unexpected dive into the lake, and his shirt clings to his back.

If only she'd known. She would have been kinder. She wouldn't have asked so much of him. She would have fought for him, in that church.

She falls asleep to awful dreams of dark rooms and Penelope's smile, terrible to behold.

Halfway through another sequence of nameless horrors, someone shakes her awake. Violet rouses slowly to Aleksander's hands on her shoulders.

"There's something I want you to see," he says. "Are you up for a midnight walk?"

Violet would very much like to stay in bed, but she nods anyway. Five minutes later, they're both in the boat, Aleksander steering them gently into the city.

Every house lies dark behind their windows, their walls muddied by shadows. Instead of making their way up to the dais, Aleksander veers left, through a series of narrow alleyways. The last one looks like a dead end, but Violet notes the almost imperceptible gap between two enormous ferns, and a dark hallway beneath. She glances at Aleksander, but for once, he doesn't seem fazed by the long stretch of pitch-black corridor.

"Come on, we're almost there."

The hallway inside is cramped and freezing, but a thin shaft of light appears at the end. Someone has carved out an enormous dome, and every word echoes. Though half of it has caved in, she catches thin spindles of moonlight flashing through precise holes in the ceiling. She blinks, and sees stars.

Aleksander sweeps his torch over the room, and reveurite glitters back at them. It bursts from the ground in the centre of the room, like a splash made solid, almost as high as the ceiling. It's more reveurite than she's ever seen.

"Do you remember the first time we met?" he asks.

"I do," she says quietly.

Though it feels like lifetimes ago, she's never forgotten the boy with the fuzzy collar and grey sea-glass eyes. A galaxy at her kitchen table.

He sets a dark marble down in the middle of the room, right in the centre of the splash. As soon as it makes contact with reveurite, it lights up, dazzling them both. Violet throws one hand over her face, waiting for her eyes to adjust.

When they do, she gasps.

"Oh, Aleksander," she breathes.

The marble projects pinpricks of light over the dome, perfectly aligning with the sky painted on the remains of the ceiling. Every star is accounted for. Galaxies cluster overhead, light blown wide into constellations. Golden sparkles rain from the ceiling like falling stars.

Aleksander fiddles with the marble, and the pinpricks shift, revealing an entirely different sky dappled across the ceiling. Different constellations. Different *worlds*.

Violet wanders through the projection, letting her hands play over the light-galaxies, which trail like phosphorescent waves in her wake. Aleksander leans against one of the reveurite pillars, close enough to touch Violet. Against the light, his face is shadowed, unreadable.

Something in her heart seizes, and her hands fall to her side.

"I'm sorry," she bursts out. "What I said to you—I shouldn't have. I was— You know how much my uncles mean to me—"

Aleksander lets out a strangled laugh. "You, apologising to me?"

Suddenly, he stops and falls to his knees, as though staggered by a blow. Firefly stars hover around them in suspension.

"Aleksander—"

He cuts her off. "I betrayed your secrets. I told Penelope everything. I let you believe we were friends, that I was worth trusting —that I was worth anything at all. I had the goddamned sword in my hands, Violet! And yet I still couldn't act. Because of me, you nearly *died*. Everything I've done . . ." His palms curl into fists. "It's unforgivable."

Violet sinks to the floor to sit cross-legged next to him. Gently, she unfurls his fists, his palms flat against her own. The faint tracery of his veins looks like lines across an atlas, disappearing into uncharted territory underneath his shirt. She runs her thumb over his wrist bone and hears him take in an unsteady breath. When she dares to look up, he's watching her, his eyes grey as a storm.

"How can it be," she whispers, "when I've already forgiven you?"

She has worked so hard to hate him. She has tried—God, she has tried.

But she can't.

Aleksander reaches out to caress Violet's face, his hands lacing through her hair. She presses her mouth to his, kissing so deeply she feels almost drunk. And he kisses back, crushing with urgency. Wanting without shame, without anger.

They break apart for air, and Aleksander smiles at her, his eyes crinkling at the corners. His hands sit so perfectly against the contours of her body. He has never looked more lovely than now.

"Violet . . ." he says, low.

His fingers slide along her collarbone, just under the edge of her shirt, then pause. He looks at her, a question in his eyes. In response, she tugs off one button, then another. Their hands make quick work of their clothes, heedless of the night's chill. His scars range across his upper back like hilly countryside, but she has her own, too: the star-shaped twist of flesh between her ribs that Aleksander presses his mouth to in exquisite agony.

He murmurs against her skin, "You have no idea how badly I wanted you in Prague," and she is undone all over again.

She pulls him towards her, closing the distance between them. She kisses the deep hollow of his throat, the notch of a scar on his shoulder, the hard black lines of his tattoos. The way she's wanted to for so long. Her fingers press into the firmness of his hip bones, and fierce, yearning warmth stirs within her. He eases into her with an aching slowness that sends fissures of desire up her spine. Every touch a question, then an answer: *yes.*

Then, just for a moment, there are no questions at all.

Fifty-Three

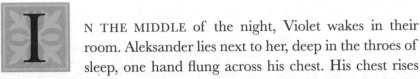 N THE MIDDLE of the night, Violet wakes in their room. Aleksander lies next to her, deep in the throes of sleep, one hand flung across his chest. His chest rises and falls, his mouth soft and flushed as he dreams. For a while, Violet watches him, trying to commit every last detail to memory. The drowsy scent of rain, the gentle plink of water against the windowsill, the way the moonlight pours through like a blanket to cloak them both.

She closes her eyes and pictures it all again, so very vividly.

Then she gets up, dresses, and quietly makes her way outside.

The rain makes a pleasing sound on the stone flagstones, so that the courtyard is filled with a melodic orchestra of water. Ever's workshop light is on, flickering in the heavy night, but there's no sign of activity.

It's odd, in so many ways beyond the ones she thought she'd feel. Ever still bears a resemblance to the remaining Everlys, despite the vast gulf of time: the hazel eyes, the pointed jaw, the habit of scrunching his nose when something perplexes him. In the half-light, he could easily be mistaken for one of her uncles. Yet he has all the warmth of a stone, and none of their kindness. He is as alien to her as the astrals, and just as self-interested.

Not for the first time, Violet wonders which of the stories are really true. The frightened lover, the greedy craftsman, the man who was simply in the wrong place at the wrong time? Penelope's victim or her imprisoner.

Whatever the truth, he's no hero now.

Violet slips out of the courtyard and into the narrow maze of streets, walking until she reaches a pane of reveurite. She settles herself on the ground cross-legged, waiting. Her heart thumps in her chest.

It isn't long before Penelope appears, first as an indistinct shadow against the glass. She smiles in greeting, though there's nothing friendly about it. They could be back at Adelia Verne's party, masking suspicion with politeness over canapés.

Even then, Violet had known it was a mask. She just hadn't understood what lay beneath its depth.

"To what do I owe this unexpected pleasure?"

Violet takes a moment before she speaks, picking over her words carefully. There's so much she wants to say—demands, accusations, even to ask for an apology—but time is already short. So she gets straight to the point.

"Why is it our blood?" She rubs her thumb over her wrist. "Everly blood. Why not someone else? Is it just revenge?" When Penelope says nothing, she continues, "I read all the stories. About the star and the mortal man."

"Then you have been wasting your precious time." It's said lightly, but underneath, Violet can hear the steel of anger. "Liars and scavengers of memory, all of them."

"So what's the truth?"

They've never been face to face like this before, on equal footing. For once, Penelope cannot simply reach through and end her, so there's a peculiar freedom in being able to ask questions. Even if she might not like the answers.

For a moment, Penelope looks as though she might say nothing. But finally she says, "There is a door, bound by blood. Everly blood. I cannot return home without it." She levels her gaze at Violet. "Only Everly blood can unlock it."

"So this is the curse," Violet says.

"A *debt*, Violet Everly. And do I ask for too much? Am I unreasonable to expect what I'm owed?" She spreads out her hands like scales weighing judgement. "And here I am, treated with such a *choice*. A sacrifice of the new and the old. Besides, I would not drag innocents into this debt of yours."

"But you killed all those people."

Penelope lifts her chin. "That is not debt. It is survival. I'm sure you understand that, at least."

But Violet shakes her head. Even an entire world away, she still wakes up in the middle of the night with blood seared across her vision, nightmares that leave a scream stuck in her throat.

Penelope arches an eyebrow. "We are not so dissimilar, you and I. You have tried your utmost to refuse your fate—consorting with criminals, theft, impersonation, bribery—and you would do yet more. After all, would you be here if it were otherwise?"

"You killed *children*," Violet says. "You can't justify that to me."

"Because of you, Johannes Braun is dead. Tamriel is dead. Erriel is dead. Aleksander will bear his scars forever, because you persuaded him that you were too important for our rules."

Violet bites her lip.

"I will offer you a deal," Penelope says. "If you do not present your-self to me at dawn, I will return to your house. I will start with your uncles. Then it will be your café friends. Then every scholar who ever helped you, every traitor amongst our ranks. Oh yes, I know all about Caspian Verne and his band of renegades."

Violet doesn't rise to the bait, even though she knows this is no bluff. The door is on Penelope's side of the city, wide open for her to use. Violet is here, tonight, precisely because of that.

"And if I go with you?" she asks.

Penelope eyes her coolly. "Then I am done. I will leave them all unharmed. Aleksander will rebuild the reveurite door for me, and you will be sacrificed on its altar. I will return home." She closes her eyes briefly. "Long have I awaited my brethren."

Violet flinches at Penelope's use of *sacrificed*. But she tries to move past it.

"Forever," she says firmly. "No more terrorising my family."

"*Terrorising*, is it?" Penelope arches her eyebrow. "Note that your family line could have ended generations ago. Note that I could have sought revenge. Instead, I have only taken an Everly from every generation, no more, as was within my right."

A god's sense of justice, Violet thinks, is a terrible thing to behold.

"But yes," Penelope continues. "I will forget the Everly name."

"And Aleksander stays out of this," she says. "You'll leave him alone."

"It's up to him whether he leaves with me. Even you cannot control the tides."

"He won't go with you."

Penelope laughs. "You are a fleeting occupation. A wilful act of rebellion, nothing more. I can offer Aleksander *everything*. When there is nothing left to distract him, who do you think he will turn to? There is no one else who understands him better."

"And yet he left you."

Penelope's mouth curls into a snarl. Shadows around her flare. It all vanishes just as quickly, but Violet has to steel herself not to back away.

"A distraction, Violet. But he will come with me in the end." She pauses. "Still, for the sake of our deal, I will not force him. You have my word."

"On all of it?"

"I always keep my promises." Penelope smiles in the darkness, her eyes glittering. "There is a cost to survival, Violet Everly. It is just a matter of fine-tuning the price."

Aleksander pretends not to notice when Violet climbs out of bed in the middle of the night, though the hollow absence next to him is impossible to ignore. His body is damp with a sheen of sweat; he's not used to sharing a bed with anyone, and the additional warmth is startling. There was a time when he thought that an extra body would protect him against his nightmares. But really, it's just added a new dimension to the gauntlet of horrors his mind runs through on nights like tonight.

His dreams are always fragmented, snapshots of his life played out with hyperreal intensity, while his stomach churns with tension. Because he knows where it all leads. He always knows.

Aleksander is seven, and walking into the scholars' tower for the first time. Penelope's hands are on his shoulders, steering him forward. The thrill of possibility clutched in his small fists.

"Come, little dreamer," she says decisively. "I have big plans for you."

He is eleven, and already faster, defter, stronger than the other assistants. His hands are permanently inked with reveurite dust. With every new milestone of manipulation, Penelope is there, watching him carefully.

Thirteen, and in an unfamiliar room. A bright-eyed girl stares at him with undisguised suspicion, a challenge in her glare. Though he doesn't know it then, the challenge is this: dare you stand in the world on your own?

Dare you stand in the world without *her*?

Twenty-one, and he is walking down a long dark corridor, to an abyssal room of pain. A room that will split his life in two, a wound that will never heal.

"Without me, you are nothing," Penelope says, her teeth gleaming white in the darkness. "And so I will unmake you."

Violet, head bowed in a church, a sacrificial saint. The shadows growl with hunger; the silver sword swings.

He slides out of bed, still naked, and watches from the safety of the dark balcony as Violet crosses the courtyard. She thinks he doesn't know that she is playing the same deadly game with Penelope. What is *this* worth, in the light of *that*? What will you sacrifice to save yourself? *Who* will you sacrifice?

It's a game he has never been very good at, but he knows the rules nevertheless. And he is a bargaining chip in Violet's hand. They all are. Is he worth her uncles' lives? Is he worth her own?

Give me Violet Everly, and you will be forgiven.

He cannot be the blade. He won't be the blade.

Aleksander watches Violet disappear into the darkness, and he makes a decision.

Violet retreats to Ever's workshop, a single lamp already burning. Candlelight twinkles off the various bottles and vials, the gleam of unfinished metal. Lifetimes of knowledge gathered here, all to be wasted in the hands of one man.

She sits on the edge of the bench, her head in her hands. She can't face lying down next to Aleksander again, to pretend that tomorrow will be the same. Tomorrow, the clock will finally run down, and Penelope will exact her justice, in whatever form that takes. In whatever Violet decides.

She watches the wax burn low on the candles. Sand through an hourglass.

"They called me a clever man," Ever says.

He stands in the doorway, a shadow save for the glow of his golden-ringed irises. He doesn't even pretend he hasn't been watching her. But then Violet knew he'd be there, keeping an eye on his precious wall. And the astral beyond it.

"They called me the man who walked with gods," Ever continues, shaking his head. "At the time, I thought it was a fitting punishment. She could not leave unless she killed me on that altar."

"And she wouldn't?"

Ever looks at her bleakly. "By the end . . . we hated—oh, how we hated. But we could not kill each other. And for that, we hated ourselves, too."

He tilts her wrist, so their forearms are parallel. The same veins running through their wrists, the same lifelines on their palms. Violet thinks of all the Everlys who have bled out in the name of Ever Everly and his hatred.

"I was young," he says quietly. "I was angry."

For a while, they sit in silence, amidst the chirp of nightlife. Violet closes her eyes. Here is her bloody truth, beyond myth and fairy tales: the Everlys, cursed by themselves. A doom of their own creation.

For a moment—just a moment—she feels a twinge of pity for Penelope.

"Could you kill her now?" she asks.

Ever hesitates. "I have not seen my wife in a long time."

His *wife*. Of course. The silver ring that hangs from the chain on his neck.

"I loved her, you understand," he says. "More than anything. More than the world. Even when I hated her, I loved her. It can be a terrible thing, to love so deeply."

Violet twists her remaining bracelet around her wrist, the reveurite sparkling gold in the candlelight. It is all she has left, but how heavy it weighs on her. Maybe this is what truly makes them Everlys: the same fault line of memory and longing, compounded by stubbornness. Their fatal flaw, passed from generation to generation.

"I had a daughter, too," he says, and now his voice takes on the timbre of memory, his gaze far away. "Her name . . . I don't remember her name. Her smile was her mother's. But her eyes—they were like mine, from before." He shudders deeply. "I did not know she survived."

Violet tries to bring him back to the present. "After me, there will be no more Everlys," she says. "It'll be over."

"You would be safe here," he reminds her.

"But my family would die."

Penelope always keeps her promises. Violet—or her uncles, Caspian, anyone who ever helped her. An endless list to protect. Against Penelope's wrath, she could never save them all.

"What would you have me do?" Ever asks.

And Violet knows, with the crushing weight of truth, that she cannot ask him to sacrifice himself.

That leaves just one choice left.

From the vantage point of his workshop, Ever Everly watches a shadow steal across the courtyard. It takes him a moment—it always does—to recognise the shadow as belonging to a real person, and not as another ghost mournfully watching him from its haunted perch. Violet thinks the ghosts are nothing more than a figment of his imagination; he's overheard her whispering to her companion about the way he rants and raves in his workshop.

But they are real, and all the more terrible for it.

Some are smokey wraiths, little more than wisps of fog that could just as easily be a smear on a window. Others hold the features they bore in life, damning Ever to a lifetime of seeing their faces: the butcher down the road, who used to open his shop as Ever closed his; the teacher who often took her students out on to the lake; a particularly noisy downstairs neighbour, whose walls he had to shore up with fresh supports in the decades after their demise. Too many more of them he no longer recognises, though they seem to know him well enough. And isn't that the fickle nature of memory? To see into the past, but only through a glass darkly.

They cluster around him like mist on a foggy night. They say, *Everly, we cannot rest. Everly, we will not rest. Everly.* A litany he knows all too well. When all else is dust and ruin—though isn't that where he is now?—he will remember his name, whispered at every single moment of the day in relentless chorus.

Everly, we beg you. Everly, we see your regrets. We wish to rest.

A soul for a year and a day of love. A soul for a year and a day of knowledge. He no longer remembers the bargain itself, but the aftermath forever surrounds him.

He hears the astral's words: *It is survival.* And his entire body sinks into a sigh. They are words he has used so often to console himself, to placate the wraiths, he has almost forgotten what they mean. It's what he told Violet only hours earlier.

A thousand years, and they have not learnt. A thousand years, and they are still so afraid. They cannot kill each other—and now they cannot even die for each other.

Everly Everly Everly.

What a stupid man he has been.

CHAPTER

Fifty-Four

TIME MOVES QUICKLY, after that.

Violet stands in front of the ring of smashed archways as faint threads of sunrise flicker on the horizon. From here, she has a perfect view of the sprawling city and the desert beyond it. The end of a city. The end of a world.

The end has such a very finite ring to it.

"This is it," she says aloud, just to listen to the words echo around her.

If she had told herself this was where she would be, after a too short lifetime of wanting, and a too long journey of hunting her mother down, she might have climbed back into her wardrobe. So much effort and worry and heartbreak. It would be easier to rewind time and save her the trouble.

Part of her very much wishes she could. She has paid for this quest in too many horrors: Tamriel in his basement; Yury and his transformation. The bodies in the tower.

The rest of her recalls the undeniably seductive glamour, the thrill of learning to play the scholars' game of cunning and power. Caspian Verne, with his quiet smile and whispers of greater possibilities. Erriel and her coronet of light. Even the asteria spreading out his asteros cards to command a future for her.

Aleksander. She presses her fingers to her lips and lets herself remember the bite of his kiss. The way his hands had roamed across her skin.

How wonderful and devastating this life has been. How badly she wishes it wasn't ending this way. And she's not ready, not by any means.

She could run.

There are other ways out of the city, after all. And she has the blood that runs through her veins, the liquid key to unlock the other doorways. There are provisions she could steal, maps she could tuck into a bag to take with her. And there is adventure, waiting for her in some middle distance, like an especially vivid mirage. The bite of the forbidden fruit she's never quite had.

Marianne would run.

But then the wheel would turn. Penelope would devour her uncles, Aleksander, the world, before she devoured herself. Nothing would change.

"Violet."

Somehow, Aleksander has found her. He must have run because he's slightly out of breath, but in several quick strides he's by her side. He looks at her like he knows exactly what she's about to do.

"Aleksander, I—"

He cuts her off. "I'll rebuild the door. I'll go with her. I've already made up my mind."

"How very touching, my assistant."

Penelope stands at the edge of the dais. Gone is the tall, unassuming blonde woman who stepped through the Everly front door to wreak so much havoc. And in her place, something else entirely. Her wings trail smoke across the ground, rolling off the edge of the ground. Flames curl around her head in a halo of white light. She holds two swords streaked in fire, clasped in fists.

She looks like a goddess, terrible to behold.

"It is admirable to think you can take Violet's place," she says. "But only an Everly—"

"It doesn't have to be an Everly! It doesn't have to be anyone," he says, and no one is more shocked than Violet at the way he raises his voice.

"There is a *price*," Penelope hisses.

"You could leave them alone. Please," he says.

Penelope's gaze flashes dangerously. "You will know your place, my assistant, when this is all over."

He closes his eyes, takes a deep breath. "Not if you do this." Then he opens his eyes again. "But if you let her live…I will rebuild the door for you. I will go with you wherever you choose. If you wish to punish me"—he stumbles on the words and has to take another breath—"then I will accept what is given."

He takes a few steps forward, but Violet puts out a hand to stop him. He looks at her, anguished and afraid.

"I will survive it," he says.

But survival is not living. And she has already seen the damage Penelope has wrought, the scars that won't heal. There is a person wearing Aleksander's body who may very well survive Penelope. But the Aleksander she knows and loves now would not. He has already faced so much, just by being here.

"You're not an Everly," she says gently. "But I am."

Aleksander reaches for her hands, and she realises she's trembling. "You don't deserve this. You didn't make this deal."

Neither did Gabriel and Ambrose. Neither did her mother.

Violet recalls the asteria's words of sacrifice and loss, of the terrible hand she'd been dealt. Even then, she'd hoped there would be a magic last-minute reprieve, a way out that would be both bloodless and easy. But she grew up on a feast of fairy tales and myths; there is always blood.

And she is so very tired of curses.

Up close to the reveurite boundary, the hum of power is like an ache in her teeth. Violet presses her hands against the pane and it ripples back like a curtain. Penelope steps through, awful in her magnificence. Horrific and wondrous.

"You keep your word," Violet says, "and I will keep mine."

"Very well," Penelope says.

She sheathes her swords and holds out her hand expectantly. Violet stares at it. Her uncles have made so many sacrifices to keep her safe, so many terrible decisions to give her a life worth living.

Because that's what the Everlys do for one another; she just wishes it hadn't taken her so long to see it. Now it's time to return the gift.

It will be okay. It will be quick. It will be *over*.

"Someone has to go," she says, rallying herself.

"Yes," Ever agrees. "Someone must go."

Ever Everly steps on to the dais, his eyes shining gold. The sunrise flares at his back like wings, and for a second, there are not one, but two astrals. And the sword gleams in his hands with a confidence borne from centuries of handling weaponry. Violet's breath catches. In the light, he really does look like a hero.

"We will go together," he says.

Fifty-Five

W HAT ELSE IS a curse but this?

Love, stretched and warped beyond all meaning.

Astriade and Ever Everly stand opposite each other. No longer quite a star, and no longer quite a mortal man. Yet there is still the cord between them, bound up in desire and hatred and the wasteland of an entire city.

What a poisoned chalice they have tasted. What regrets. What innumerate sorrows.

Ever Everly hands over the bridal sword that was once a wedding gift to Astriade. She takes it, weighing the blade. It is obvious, even at first touch, the amount of skill and care that has gone into it. And the tales it could sing of, if it could sing at all.

"Ever Everly," she says, tasting his name for the first time in over a millennia.

"Astriade, daughter of Nemetor," he replies.

With one tentative hand, he reaches out to touch the side of her face. They have changed so much, and yet this is so achingly familiar, a movement that has already happened a thousand times and more. Astriade closes her eyes, her free hand closing over his. For a second, they are husband and wife, man and woman. Nothing to separate them but skin.

Then their hands fall. Astriade readjusts the sword in her grip.

"Our contract still stands," she says. "A year and a day has passed, and blood is owed."

A soul, weighed against a year and a day of love, knowledge, greed. Would it have ever been enough?

Astriade levels the sword at his chest. "We claim our debt."

With unerring precision, she stabs him between the fourth and fifth ribs. Bones crack; a groan that is a scream bitten back. Ever clutches his chest with one hand, fingers curling around the blade. Bright blood wells up, proving once and for all that he may have abandoned his mortality, but he is still a man.

Capable of so many great and terrible things.

The wraiths gather around him, clutching at him with their ghostly fingers.

With sudden ferocity, he yanks the hilt of the blade towards him, jerking Astriade forward. He grips the back of her head with one hand. The hilt hits his breastbone, but still he doesn't let go.

"We will walk together," he hisses.

He raises his arm. A dagger flashes onyx in the light.

Divine justice.

With one last, rattling breath, he drives it into her heart.

Pain. Mortal blood. Hands stained red, not gold.

It should be gold. It should be the gold of sunlight, the gold of gossamer rings around a planet. The gold of an imploding star.

Zvezda, Estrella, Astra, Stella, Nyeredzi—

Identities stripped from her like so much armour.

Penelope.

She hasn't felt so much as a single mote of sunlight or crackle of frost, but now she feels it all. Agony scorches her skin, and above all, a terror beyond anything she's ever known. She is many things, but she is not supposed to be mortal.

How much it hurts.

Above her, the sky bursts into flame. Thousands upon thousands of stars. How has she never noticed them before?

They are singing to her, luminous and perfect. A cosmic song heralding homewards. Their tune is simply her name, a gospel of repetition in the oldest tongue she knows.

Astriade.

Just before her bones shatter into stardust, she hears a chorus of voices.

O star-daughter, we have missed you.

Fifty-Six

T HAT EVENING, THEY bury the bodies side by side behind Ever's workshop. Aleksander's face is expressionless as he digs into the sandy earth. Violet's hands are raw by the time the ground is covered. She spent all day looking for wildflowers, and she lays a ragged bouquet across their graves. There is a moment where Violet thinks a hand will shoot up, just as she places the second bouquet, and Penelope will claw up from the earth, bloody with fury. Then it passes, and the two bouquets sit side by side.

Finally, Violet takes the sword, scoured clean. Ever's silver chain dangles from the hilt. After a moment's hesitation, she pulls off her mother's bracelet, and slides it on to the hilt, too. Let it rest, she thinks. And if her mother ever comes out this way, if Marianne decides she wants to finish what she started, well—she will know that Violet was here, and faced what she could not.

Violet raises the sword, and the blade shines in the remaining light. With every ounce of strength she can muster, she buries it in the ground between them.

Violet and Aleksander stay there, watching the sunset burnish the graves gold.

She glances at him; she has no idea what to say. There is a strange sadness in the loss of Ever Everly, the man who had been something else, if not exactly more. And maybe one day she will bring herself to feel sorry for Penelope. But mostly all she feels is a huge relief.

It was all over so quickly. There was just enough time for Violet to gasp, for Aleksander to stagger backwards. The act was so quick, Violet wasn't even sure it happened at all, until she saw the blood leave Penelope's face. The dome overhead shattered, raining reveurite in harmless shards. A strong breeze rushed in to tug on their clothes.

After a week underneath shades of purple, the world looks so rich with colour.

But for Aleksander...

He doesn't cry, doesn't rage. And maybe there'll be relief for him, too, with time. Violet's not so sure, though. There is too much history between him and Penelope. Freedom, at such a vast price.

"Did Ever tell you what really happened?" Aleksander asks quietly. "Which version of the story was true?"

Violet suspects he's really asking about Penelope. Whether there was ever a possibility that she might have once been the person he thought he knew.

She shakes her head. "If he remembered the truth, I don't think he would have told me."

And maybe that's a sign in itself as to which version she should put stock in. Or maybe he deliberately tried to forget because the anguish was too great, the heartbreak too severe. She likes to think, despite everything, that the romance was real. That it wasn't Ever and his cowardice that doomed so many of his descendants. After all, it's the version that makes for the best story.

What does she believe? The fairy tale of the hero, or the monster?

In the end, she decides to leave the question by the grave. It is a small price to pay, in the face of everything else.

The next morning, they make the trek to the doorway home, through the parts of the city Aleksander had carried Violet through. It won't take so much blood this time; the door is still saturated in power, and if it's well maintained, it might not ever need more than a drop again.

On this side, the doorway is almost entirely hidden by leafy ferns and overgrown camellia bushes, bursting with bright pink. They stop

at the edge of the door. But neither of them reach for it. Elandriel is
a world out of time, a place where life can be put on pause forever.
It's easy to imagine that the other worlds have stopped with them.

Once they step through, time will come charging back. And there
are decisions to make.

Aleksander rubs the back of his neck, pink with sunburn.

"You can go anywhere you want," he says. "What will you do?"

He does not say *you could stay with me in Fidelis*. Though it must have
crossed his mind, as it has hers. For a long time, she'd thought that if
she went to Fidelis, she would find her mother. She imagines being
inducted into the scholars, taking her place as one of the chosen few
to live across both worlds. Playing that dangerous game.

There's still a part of her that revels in the challenge, that could let
herself be consumed by the scholars. Though there are other things
she could be consumed by.

She imagines long nights in Aleksander's bed, carving out a
future together. She pictures waking up next to him every morning
for countless mornings, still marvelling at all the ways she knows
him, and all the ways she's yet to discover. And maybe one day
she'd leave, or he would. Maybe not. The world she imagines, so
beautiful and crisp in her mind's eye, has room for complexities,
after all.

In this world, she turns away from the doors that sing to her, from
the stories that whisper of *elsewhere*.

She is not Marianne. She won't run. But she can't ignore that
wishbone-lodged longing, the siren call that she's never been able to
shake, even after all this time.

It's a terribly selfish thing she says next, but she has to say it because
to say nothing would be worse. "You could come with me. If you
wanted."

He looks at her, his grey sea-glass eyes unfathomable, and she lets
him, drinking in her own vision of him. His curly hair is already
growing out, teasing the nape of his neck. One day in the not-so far-
off future, it'll be long enough to pull into his stupid man bun again.
She takes in his silvery scars, the faint yet premature lines of stress

and grief on his forehead, the deep bow of his lips, the way he presses his thumb absentmindedly against the soft pulse of his wrist.

He doesn't say anything at all. But she knows his answer, nevertheless.

They continue to linger. Even though the sunlight is fading in the sky, and there are so many pressing issues to return to, Aleksander can't bring himself to cross over. Not just yet.

They stall for time with questions about the street around them. Though the streets are overrun with waist-high bushes and sky-scraping trees, it was probably once a busy thoroughfare. The ground beneath their feet has an unusually smooth texture from a thousand footsteps, wearing uneven stone away to a polished flatness. He closes his eyes and tries to imagine the people who once walked here before them. But all he can hear is the sound of birds chirping and Violet, her hand clasped lightly in his.

"Do you think the stars will ever return?" Violet asks.

"If Ever opened the doorway. Then…possibly," Aleksander says.

He hasn't told Violet yet, but he's pretty sure he can rebuild the doors. He hasn't spent his time idly in Elandriel. It will take months of hard work, of complex problem-solving and setbacks and, yes, failures. And he will have to decide whether to open the doors at all. There is a reason why it's so difficult to cross between worlds, and why Elandriel fell the way it did.

But he's also read the stories about inter-world travellers, coopera-tion, the blending together of cultures and knowledge. The dream of a world that reaches out, instead of drawing itself in. And now he knows that there is more than a grain of truth in these fairy tales. He's not prone to Violet's optimism, but he'd like to try.

The end of the world looks a lot like the beginning of another, it turns out.

The light fades to a soft twilight, the moon emerging lazily from behind the clouds. They're out of time.

"You go ahead," he says. "I'll be right behind you."

Violet slices the pad of her finger open. She presses her hand to the doorway and the edges of the door light his vision gold. Aleksander watches her go.

He is always watching her go. He sees her meandering along a river path with explosions of light behind her, walking down a pavement in Prague, striding across a dead city, courage in every step. And now, with moonlight glinting in her hair, she's so beautiful it almost hurts to look at her.

Part of him yearns to run after her. It would be an easy choice—to follow her down whatever path she chooses. He's spent a lifetime following in other people's footsteps. And who is he without his scholar's tattoo, his quest, his mistress? Who is he without Violet Everly?

Nothing, a voice whispers. But for the first time, the word sits companionably in his head, a curiosity. He says it out loud, and although there's no one to hear him say it, the question lingers in the air all the same. For now, he decides he can live with it, as he learns to live without everything else.

To be nothing is to be remade, after all.

Fifty-Seven

O N A FROSTY spring morning, the Everly brothers exit their ramshackle house. Gabriel adjusts his sunglasses to account for the sun's bright glare, while Ambrose hauls a compact yet heavy suitcase to his car. It's packed to the brim with all the books he couldn't bear to leave behind. And although he'll never tell Gabriel, there's also the first fifty pages of a manuscript he's been working on over the past few weeks.

So many places to go, he doesn't even know where to start. He has an itinerary as long and detailed as the most comprehensive index, but the truth is, he's thinking of abandoning it all to visit a few old friends. And there's a Victorian collector's library he's heard about in Scotland with some rather *unusual* properties...

Ah well, best-laid plans, et cetera.

Gabriel pats the hood of his horrible orange car thoughtfully. "I would offer you a ride, but—"

"That thing is a menace," Ambrose says. Then he pauses. "You'll have a great time."

"We'll see," Gabriel says uncertainly—an odd tone for his elder brother.

There's a lot that Gabriel keeps quiet, but Ambrose hasn't forgotten the letters that reached the house every year, the same handwriting across the envelope and the same address scrawled along the back. *My dear Gabriel. It would be so wonderful to see you again.*

"Marianne should have been here with us," Gabriel says suddenly.

His gaze is fixed on the house, but Ambrose can tell that his brother is far away, lost in a memory. Even now, he thinks he could squint and see Marianne barrelling out of the door, telling them to wait for her. Always the fearless leader of their trio. Would she have stayed, he wonders, if she knew how much grief she was leaving behind?

He still finds it hard to admit how much he misses her.

"Maybe now that Penelope's gone, she'll come back," he says, though in his heart of hearts he doubts it.

"Pretty sure hell would freeze over first," Gabriel says drily.

Ambrose sighs. "Probably."

Though it didn't stop him leaving a front-door key underneath one of the plant pots, or a letter on the hallway mat for her. Just in case she returns. Just in case.

"Is that everything?" Gabriel says.

Ambrose takes one last look at the house. He remembers the first time he'd returned here with Gabriel and Marianne, when the roof tiles were cracked and mossy, and the hedges were wild beasts of rampant overgrowth. An abandoned wreck, just one more line in a dossier of Everly assets. Even after decades of trying to wrangle the house into order, he's still reminded of a slumbering dragon, untameable, as though the roof itself could peel apart into wings and take flight. Green shoots are already straining upwards from the flower beds.

"That's everything," he says.

Gabriel takes off his sunglasses and rubs his eyes. "Little brother, what am I going to do without you?"

"Oh, all kinds of terrible things, I'm sure," Ambrose says.

They embrace tightly. Not goodbye forever—not like Marianne. But a goodbye, nonetheless.

"Violet says she'll be back next year. So I'll hold you to that," Ambrose says, before sighing. "I hope she's safe."

"Worried? Surely not," Gabriel says, then he sighs, too. "Wonder what she's up to."

Ambrose has a few guesses. The northern witches in their forest, the city by the effervescent sea. Or whatever she finds on the other side of those doors.

Despite his worry, he grins. "Adventure."

With the inevitability of a tidal wave, news makes its way across the fractured network of the scholars. They converse with one another over once-in-a-lifetime meals at exclusive restaurants, in the winery of a newly restored château, cruising over the Atlantic in private aeroplanes. It's the kind of news that needs to be imparted face to face—otherwise, it would be too easy to dismiss as gossip run wild. Even so, jaws drop at the revelation. *She's gone.*

From the balcony of her Italian villa, Adelia Verne swirls wine around a glass. She takes a sip, and smiles. Perfection.

Not everything changes, not at first. There are still parties, still the same dance of secrets and influence and favours. Still threats, too, and the occasional mysterious disappearance, especially now that there is no one to keep them in check. Powerful players set long-held plans in motion, as they fight over the vacuum Penelope has left in her wake.

And maybe it'll always be this way. Maybe the rot runs too deep.

It takes a rather long time to reach its destination, having been rerouted twice, but a letter finally lands on Caspian Verne's desk over a month after its posting. Lately, he's been drawn to a circle of menhirs near one of the Norwegian fjords. Local folklore is rife with elves who spirit away anyone foolish enough to approach the stone circle, and Caspian has more than a few theories to unpack before he's finished here.

He's pulling off his snow boots from a hike to the menhirs and back when he notices the letter on his desk. He examines it absentmindedly, his thoughts still amongst the stones. Then his attention catches on the handwriting, and that first line: *I'm exploring the third option.*

For five minutes, he reads the letter in absolute silence. Then again.

A smile breaks across his face.

In Fidelis, a handful of masters stand in the basement of the scholars' tower, marvelling at the reveurite door. Most of them are newly minted; they wear fresh grief and smarting tattoos as evidence of how quickly the ground underneath their feet has shifted. There is no recovering the people they have lost, or the experience that vanished with them. The bloodstains on the floor will never come out.

But someone has to lead. There are too many questions, and no one left to answer them. So these masters—the ones who volunteered, against their misgivings, or perhaps with the hope of offering more balanced judgement than their predecessors—swallow their fear and stare down the door, with all the uncertainty and terror it holds. All its possibility.

Though it's forever midnight in this basement, dawn is rising as, one by one, they slip through the door into a city of stardust.

In a faraway world, a woman with a heavy bag across her shoulders pauses to take in her surroundings. Her face is weathered and tanned from years of travelling under a hot sun. Although her hair is now mostly silver, there are still a few strands of hazel to match her eyes.

From a certain angle, she looks a lot like Marianne Everly.

She surveys the landscape, a distant look in her eyes. Perhaps she is recalling a rambling house and a little girl watching through an upper-floor window. Or perhaps not. Perhaps she is simply seeking the next marker of her long journey. But she pauses, all the same.

The woman who looks like Marianne Everly tilts her head to the side, and listens for a whisper that has chased itself across the world.

Epilogue

ONCE A YEAR, on a rare day off, a woman walks along a riverside, to a café she once worked at. The baristas are all strangers to her now. But there are still rose and violet biscuits, still coffee and good food. She always sits at a particular table that overlooks the river, and if she sometimes stares a little too intently at the people walking past—well, it's one day a year, so she lets herself.

Sometimes the café changes, and it's in Tokyo, St. George's, Vancouver. The company changes, too. Most often it's a surly man in sunglasses, his hair silver. Sometimes there are two of them, and then a curious onlooker might catch similarities in the trio's features—the same hazel eyes, the same squared-off hands, the same laugh in different octaves—and piece together the family resemblance. Other times, there are large groups that have to bring extra chairs to cluster around the table. A woman with a wardrobe-sized bodyguard and coolly observant girlfriend; twins in complementary-coloured suits; a man who exudes charm like a battery emits power. People who she is slowly beginning to call allies, if not friends.

Sometimes it is the world itself that changes, and then the woman sits alone, under an unfamiliar sky, unfamiliar stars. Though she loves her family and her friends, her home, this is what she lives for: the thrilling feeling of the unknown before her. A life where anything can happen, where every day there are new people to meet, new languages to learn, new ways of existing to understand. "Impossible" is a much thinner slice of the world than she'd thought.

And there is so much *time*.

Today is the one day of the year that she returns home, and she walks towards the café, anticipating a cup of coffee. Then she catches sight of a figure in the window and stops. There is already someone at the table, in her very spot. A man, with dark, curling hair and sea-glass grey eyes, a glimmer of a tattoo underneath his shirt. Unfairly pretty.

She thinks of a faded card she carries in her pocket, ten blurry stamps inked on it. It's been through so much it's almost unrecognisable. She hopes it's still worth something.

Violet Everly opens the door, an infinity of stars above her, singing.

Acknowledgements

Holy cow, we did it! And I say *we* because I definitely wouldn't be here without the immense support of so many people. Thank you so much to Robbie Guillory for taking a chance on me, and for his brilliant knowledge and advice. Thank you to Molly Powell, Sophie Judge and the team at Hodderscape, as well as Nivia Evans and the team at Orbit U.S., for their editorial wizardry and incredible hard work. Thank you to Micaela Alcaino for *such* a gorgeous cover!

Thank you to Nadia Saward for being the most amazing writerly wing-woman, for her unbelievably generous and enthusiastic support, and for sharing pictures of Fitz at his roundest and cutest. Thank you to Victoria Hendersen for being the best critique partner I could ask for, for helping me muddle through the thorniest plot issues, and for correcting my bad Russian. Thank you to Emily Horn for fielding all my nitpicky questions, and for giving me the ultimate alter ego name, which I'm looking forward to deploying in the future.

Thank you to the BookCamp Mentees group: Kathryn Whitfield, Imogen Martin, Kate Galley, Katie McDermott, Laura Sweeney, Nicola Jones, Sam Pennington, Joanne Clague, Jon Barton, Adam Cook and Ina Christova, for being such a tight-knit, wonderful group of people to share my hopes and fears with. We all climbed into the boat together, not knowing where it would take us, and what a ride it's been! An especially big thank you to Annabel Campbell for being so warm and generous with her time, and for patiently listening to so many of my woes. Thank you to Freya Marske and the Word

Camp-ers for letting me join them in their fabulous quests to dominate the world, for their kindness in answering some of my more ridiculous questions, and for introducing me to the exciting world of fan fiction! Thank you to my old colleagues at Pan Mac and Tor for teaching me everything I know about publishing, for their generosity and enthusiasm, and for sending me off in such style—it was truly a delight to work with you all.

Thank you so much to Roshani Moorjani and Zainab Dawood for being my voices of sanity in times of crisis, and for being the ultimate lunch buddies and just all-round stellar people. Thank you to John Brazier-Beckett, my very first reader, for being so unflaggingly enthusiastic about every step of my writing career—including those truly terrible first books! Thank you, too, to Bella Pagan, Charlotte Tennant, Lucy Twist, Mairead Loftus, Molly Robinson, Thady Senior and so many more, for their kindness, their much-leant-upon shoulders and their much-appreciated advice. A very special shoutout to Imogen Millar for tolerating my six AM writing sessions once upon a time, and for not murdering me in my sleep, as was within your right. You have earned this moment!!

A huge thank you to my family, for living with my book collection, for listening to more about the publishing industry than they ever needed to know, and for letting me hog the cat. Most of all, I would like to thank my mum for her immense love and support, and for being tough and brave and smart in the face of everything. Thank you. Thank you. Thank you.